A WILDER NIGHT

Matthew shifted Fanny and pressed her back into the shallow cave he had carved out. Then he turned, with his back to her, and wedged himself in against her. He relaxed as her arm came around his waist to hold him close.

Fanny awakened with the sensation of warmth pervading every fiber of her being. She splayed her fingers across the flat expanse of his stomach covered by his buckskin shirt. Reaching down with her hand she found the edge of his shirt and gently tugged it upward until she could run her hand underneath it. At last she found the smooth hot skin of his stomach.

He was turning to her, shifting around until he faced her in the shallow space. She could see his face now. It was solemn, but there was a hot need in his eyes that she knew was echoed in her own.

She could feel him trembling. She was trembling, too. And then his mouth was on hers...

A WILDER LOVE

Also by Laura Parker

REBELLIOUS ANGELS
A ROSE IN SPLENDOR
ROSE OF THE MISTS
THE SECRET ROSE

Published by
WARNER BOOKS

LAURA PARKER

A WILDER LOVE

WARNER BOOKS

A Warner Communications Company

WARNER BOOKS EDITION

Cover illustration by Pino
Hand lettering by Dave Gatti

Warner Books, Inc.
666 Fifth Avenue
New York, N.Y. 10103

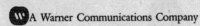 A Warner Communications Company

Printed in the United States of America

First Printing: March, 1990

10 9 8 7 6 5 4 3 2 1

For all my friends and fellow writers in the Greater Dallas Writers' Association, especially in memory of Anita Cole, who loved the American West.

CHAPTER
1

New York City, July 1886.

"But why would anyone be after following us?" Fanny Sweets demanded of her companion as she was handed up into a hansom cab parked at a Fifth Avenue exit of Central Park.

"I didn't say we *were* being followed," Phineas Todd answered as he climbed in behind her. "Only, perhaps we were." He shouted directions to the cabbie and then settled back on the seat with a slight frown. "I'm certain we lost the fellow when we left the train and crossed the park. In any case, it mustn't affect business. You'd best keep your mind on that, Fanny, me girl."

"I am, I am," Fanny answered, but she wasn't convinced by Phineas's tone to dismiss the matter. In fact, she was more certain than ever that something was amiss. If there were danger in the offing, she didn't like the idea of being left in doubt of its origin and cause.

1

Even so, she knew there was nothing to be gained by pressing the matter. Phineas was as close-mouthed as a clam when he chose.

As he reached up to adjust his collar, Fanny glanced sidelong at him. He was slight of stature but with a bantam-weight cockiness which he accentuated by wearing a high wing collar, silk polka-dot tie, and button cloth-top shoes. His thinning brown hair was parted precisely in the middle and pomaded to lie like bird wings along either side of his head. His features and manner were familiar, but there was something held back from her, as always.

He was a private man, a mysterious man. During the five years of their "business arrangement," she had learned very little about him. Why, she didn't even know precisely where he lived. He simply appeared at her door from time to time, as he had this morning, and then they would set out to work. Yet, lately he had been acting even more peculiarly.

For instance, he'd insisted that today they move their business uptown, though they had never before ventured far from the Bowery. Usually they picked their quarry from among the middle-class shoppers on Fourth Avenue. Its narrow sidewalks were crowded with the cheap displays of store merchants who hoped to catch the eye and slow the step of a prospective buyer. Peanut and fruit stands, candy stalls, and vendors with pushcarts of every description further impeded the progress of the passersby. The natural crush and jostle of humanity was an invaluable aid to people in their profession. So then, why were they riding down Fifth Avenue in a cab?

Phineas turned his head and winked at her. He

seemed calm enough for the moment. Perhaps she was just nervous because they were going into new territory.

Fanny's thoughts drifted as she turned her head to look out the window. Fifth Avenue had always seemed as far away from Five Points as the moon from earth.

The broad avenue was lined with many fine coaches looking like so many black beetles on parade. The merry tinkling of harness bells and the clip-clop of hooves on stone gave a cheerfulness to the sunny day. Likewise, the sidewalks were filled with strolling couples dressed in finery the likes of which she had never before seen. And the houses! Stone mansions every one of them. She wondered fleetingly just how many pockets one would need to pick in order to afford such a place.

"Faith!" she called and leaned out of the cab to wave at one smartly dressed couple. "Ain't we uptown today!"

"Enough of that!" Phineas said as he pulled her back inside.

"Oh, now what's the matter?" she demanded testily. "I was only being friendly."

"By cutting a caper for the society crowd? You're no more than a speck of Irish flotsam to that sort. Remember that. It'll help keep your mind on business."

"So you've said before," she answered sourly.

"And so I say again. Now turn round so that I can see you properly." When Fanny turned to face him, Phineas righted her straw boater, which the wind had tilted. Then, as patiently as any mother, he untangled the ribbon streamers and smoothed the escaped wisps of red curls from her brow. When he was done, he paused to admire his handiwork. There was a dusting of gold freckles on her small nose and her blue eyes were as wide and clear as a spring sky. Dressed in a dropped-waist dress that exposed a youthful length of black-stockinged leg, she looked not a day over twelve years of age when, in fact, she was seventeen.

Suddenly he squinted and plucked at her bodice, which gaped a bit at her bosom. "What's this? Have you been growing again?"

"Of course I have!" Fanny knocked his hand away and twisted around as she adjusted her buttons. "I strapped meself down, but it ain't the same as last year. It's time I gave up this disguise. I'm nearly eighteen!"

"So much the worse for-you," he answered severely, but as he again caught sight of her black-stockinged legs his expression became bemused. Those shapely calves weren't the limbs of a child. Perhaps it was time she let down her hems and put up her hair. For both their sakes, it was time she was on her own.

He touched his right breast pocket, feeling the slight bulge beneath his coat. He seldom carried a weapon. It was an uncomfortable reminder of his past, a past that had too quickly caught up with him just when he had thought himself clear of old debts and ties. Damn Rory MacAvoy to hell!

He wished he could take Fanny with him. He'd grown unexpectedly fond of the orphan he'd been forced by circumstance to take under his wing. She'd become like a daughter, really. He'd never married, so there'd been no colleen of his own. Still, the thought that she was growing irritated him, for that fact, in part, was the cause of his present troubles.

He glanced quickly at her and then away. "When I took you on you were a wee bairn, but look at you now. You're nearly five feet two."

"One," Fanny amended. "I measured this morning like you said to."

"Well, what's an inch but the proof of what I say? You'll soon be as tall as an Amazon. If a gent loses his wallet as a child and her father are strolling past, does he suspect them? Not likely. But if you come swelling up out of your bodice like some tart, there'll be no mercy for us if you're caught."

"Then I won't get caught," she answered saucily. "I'm the best pickpocket you ever worked; you said so yourself!"

"So I did," Phineas answered with the beginnings of a smile. "We've only been nabbed once, and *I* talked the coppers out of locking you up. So don't forget who taught you all you know. Before my accident I was the best, and none other!"

Fanny glanced at the crippled right hand that lay in his lap. It was a mute reminder that even the best could lose the game of chance they played. The story of the accident was one of the few things she did know about him. Not long before they met, Phineas had been caught lifting shore-leave purses from Greek sailors. They hadn't called the police but meted out their own brand of justice by smashing his right hand with a billy before beating him senseless. When it healed, the hand was completely useless.

Phineas frowned when he saw her staring. "Don't you go pitying the likes of me!" He raised the crippled fist. "I serve myself well enough, and you besides, don't I?"

She reached out and touched the fist in a rare gesture of tenderness. "Don't think I ain't grateful to you."

He nodded curtly and looked away.

Determined to match his mood, Fanny slumped down in her seat, offering sulk for sulk. Besides, the most interesting section of Fifth Avenue had given way to stores, churches, and red-brick or brownstone dwellings of more modest means.

Despite her pique, she soon noticed that Phineas was fidgeting. Every few minutes he adjusted his collar, checked his cuffs, and then readjusted his collar, the lines of tension about his mouth and eyes never easing. He was afraid! Even as the thought formed, she saw him glance back over his shoulder through the cab's rear porthole.

"What's the matter?" She sat up to look out of the window herself. "And don't say 'nothing,' " she added, though she saw nothing unusual in the line of identical cabs following them. She gave him a sharp look as she turned around. "Is it Harry Westin? He's threatening again to run us out of business, ain't he?"

Phineas shook his head. "I've never given Harry's threats so much thought as that!" and he snapped his fingers.

"Then who's following us?"

A rare frown pleated Phineas's brow. If only he had bought police protection, as many thieves and harlots did, he might not be in this predicament. "I tell you, Fanny, I should've run for alderman. Politics, now that's a profession in which thievery knows no bounds.

Ah, not much farther now," he added, as the hansom turned into Twenty-third Street.

Defeated again, Fanny sat back with a huff of protest.

For the next fifteen minutes the cab crawled along with the traffic toward the pier while Phineas nervously drummed his fingers on his trouser leg and Fanny gnawed the ragged edge of a fingernail. Finally they were forced to a standstill. "That's it, then. We'll walk!" he announced and swung open the cab. "Hurry, Fanny!"

He paid the cabbie quickly, then took her hand and pulled her into the crowd of men, women, and children streaming down the street.

"Where are they all going?" she asked in astonishment as the boisterous throng closed in about them. "It looks like a parade."

"It is, in a manner of speaking," he answered as he slowed his step and tipped his hat to the pretty lady who purposely caught his eye. She was a tart, of course, but a pretty tart deserved her due. "They're going to catch the Twenty-third Street Ferry for Staten Island to see Buffalo Bill's Wild West Show."

"The Wild West Show? Faith, but wouldn't I love that!" Fanny declared with heartfelt longing.

"Would you now? You've never said so before," Phineas observed, his thoughts divided between conversation and the masculine shadow at the corner of his right eye.

"Well, I would," she answered. "I ain't never seen a real wild Indian before."

He nodded absently. Had he recognized the man following them or was it only his imagination? "You promised to keep your mind—"

"On business," Fanny finished for him. "I swear I will!"

Phineas didn't answer, but she noticed that he increased his pace again to match the crowd's.

As they neared the pier, she saw billboards for the famous show plastered on every warehouse and fence. She couldn't read them, of course, but there were colorful pictures on each, depicting scenes from the show. One showed Indians attacking a stagecoach, another an Indian village. A third was a demonstration of marksmanship by "Little Missy" Annie Oakley.

As they paused on the curb, she saw that the sidewalk across the street was filled with street vendors hawking their wares of peanuts and fruit and souvenirs and Cracker Jack. The smell of caramel corn made her stomach rumble, a reminder that she hadn't eaten in order to squeeze into her dress. Now the sugary and toasty aromas made her strain against Phineas's arm. "Can't I at least have a box of Cracker Jack?"

"Very well." Phineas paused near the long line of people waiting to take the ferry across, pulled a coin from his pocket, and handed it to her. "I'll meet you at the ferry in two minutes. Exactly!"

"You mean to buy tickets for the show?" Fanny asked in amazement.

He smiled. "I mean to obtain them in my own fashion."

"Lift them, do you mean?" Concern replaced Fanny's elation. "Better let me do it."

He frowned at her. "Certainly not! This is my treat. Besides, I like to keep my hand in now and again, regardless of your opinion of my skill." He looked up suddenly, his voice growing distracted. "Hurry and get your Cracker Jack. I don't mean to miss the boat on your account.''

Fanny stepped into the street crowded with pedestrians eager to reach the ferry, and Phineas was lost from sight. The dock side of the street was even more jammed, and Fanny winced as her toes were trod upon. Ducking her head and hunching her shoulders, she attempted to plow a path through the crush of people who were vying to buy refreshments, but the struggle was useless. The wall of people seemed impenetrable. Just as she was about to give up, a space in the crowd miraculously appeared before her.

At first she saw only a pair of buckskin leggings where a sea of women's skirts and stove-pipe trousers had been. Lifting her head she glimpsed in rapid succession a bright red shirt, wide silver bracelets worn on thick wrists and upper arms, a chest plate of long ivory beads, a bead choker, and a long switch of glossy black hair pulled forward over one shoulder. Finally she was gazing up into the most unusual face she had ever seen.

Copper-colored skin sheathed the high, wide cheekbones and a broad-bladed nose. The wide mouth was straightened by tension that accented the squareness of his jaw. The forehead was wide and high. But it was the eyes, uncannily dark and staring impassively down at her, that caused goose bumps to rise on her arms.

"Golly, it's a Injun!" cried a small boy beside her.

"That's right, son," a man in the crowd answered. "And ain't he a savage-looking one?"

"Best keep back, else he might take your scalp!" offered another of the onlookers with a laugh.

Another man leaned near Fanny to say, "If you're scared of Injuns, girlie, then I wouldn't go over to the island. Buffalo Bill's got a whole tribe of Sioux camped on the other side just itching to scalp little ladies like you!''

She took an instinctive step back from the grinning man, her scalp tingling in spite of common sense, which told her that she was perfectly safe. Then, glancing at the Indian, she saw his gaze narrow with the crinkling of his eyes. Though nothing else moved in his boldly sculptured face, she had the distinct impression that he was amused. The realization surprised her. Everything she had heard about Indians led her to believe that they were wild, vicious, uncivilized creatures incapable of human feelings.

Yet, when he took a step toward her, she didn't move. She didn't even cringe when he reached out, the silver bracelet on his brown wrist gleaming in the sunlight, and lifted one of her long sausage curls from her shoulder. He weighed it in his palm and nodded his head. ''Very fine,'' he said in a deep, flat voice. ''Make good trophy!''

Thinking fast, she grabbed his broad wrist in both hands and sank her teeth into his flesh. When he released her with a yelp, she didn't wait to see what he would do next. She ducked back into the crowd and ran for her life.

She didn't quite believe she'd stood in any danger from the Indian, yet, now that she thought about it, she clearly remembered seeing a tomahawk hanging from his belt.

''Real savages!'' Mrs. Weaver had proclaimed. She was a neighbor who read the newspapers and was a fount of information. ''The *Herald* says some of them Indians are the very heathens who killed General Custer,

God rest his soul! Imagine bringing murdering, thieving cutthroats to a civilized city like New York!''

Fanny hadn't imagined it, not really, until this moment. If she had, she might not have been tempted to steal one of the Indian's silver bracelets.

Slowing to a stroll, she glanced down at the wide, shiny crescent of silver in her hand. It seemed almost alive, for it was still warm from contact with its owner's wrist. It had been a very chancy thing, biting him as a ruse to steal the bracelet, but the temptation had been too beautiful to resist. The metal band had fit his wrist more tightly than she had expected, making her anxious that he might feel it leave his arm. Of course, if he had . . .

She glanced back over her shoulder, but there was no howling savage in pursuit, and so, with a smile, she pocketed her prize. She hadn't lost her touch. Just wait until she told Phineas of her adventure!

But Phineas wasn't interested in her adventure. When she reached him, he caught her by the arm and pulled her into the line. ''Where have you been? I was about to go on without you!'' As he tried to hand a pair of tickets to a gate attendant dressed in cowboy garb, Fanny tugged on his arm. ''What's wrong now?'' he demanded testily.

She gave him a sly look. ''I don't know that we should be going to the show, after all.''

He stared at her. ''Why not?''

''We-l-l,'' she dragged out reluctantly. She couldn't tell him in front of everyone else that she'd just stolen a bracelet from an Indian. ''I forgot something. Aye, I forgot something!''

"Move along, folks! You're holdin' up the line," the attendant said gruffly.

"Whatever it is, it can wait," Phineas answered and pushed her through the turnstile.

Once on board the ferry, Fanny shrugged off her reluctance. After all, it was unlikely she would be singled out from the crowd. "There must be thousands of showgoers," she said with awe as she looked back toward the shore.

"Each performance attracts more than ten thousand, the ticket man informed me," Phineas answered, his thoughts about anonymity running parallel with Fanny's, though for a different reason. He looked down at her. "Where's your Cracker Jack?"

Her grin became smug. "I got something else instead. Something better! Maybe I'll be showing it to you later."

"You are keeping an eye out for business?" he asked and gave the well-dressed couple strolling past them a speculative glance. "I see two or three possibilities."

Fanny shrugged, sullen once more. Phineas hadn't even asked her about her secret. He didn't care. Perhaps she wouldn't tell him about the bracelet. Besides, he would expect her to fence it, and she rather liked the idea of wearing it herself. She was, after all, a grown woman, and a woman deserved a piece or two of jewelry.

"Did you hear me, Fanny?" Phineas demanded when he realized that her thoughts were far away.

"Aye. That I did," she murmured and squared her shoulders and took his hand. "Walk me about a bit, Father, dear. I've cocked my eye to a couple of likely pigeons. I was only waiting for you to give the word."

But Phineas gave a slight shake of his head as they moved across the deck of the ferry. "In due time, my girl. Be patient. We need space to operate in. Here, one mistake and we're trapped. Once we're on the island, I'll give the word."

Fanny nodded absently as her free hand stole into her pocket and closed over the bracelet. No, she definitely wouldn't tell Phineas about it—not because she wanted to keep him from having his share, but because it was hers, a souvenir of her holiday, so to speak.

CHAPTER
2

"You don't want to see the Indian village?" Phineas said in surprise as he and Fanny walked through the back lot of the showgrounds with the other visitors. "But it's one of the fairgrounds' main attractions."

"I don't care," she answered sulkily and dug her heels in to bring them to a stop.

"Fanny, really—"

"I won't! I won't!" She stamped her foot, one of the childish mannerisms she employed when they were in public together. "I won't go! And you can't be making me!"

"Very well," Phineas replied in an unflappable paternal tone. Though he didn't understand what had prompted her tantrum, he knew well enough not to cross her in public. "Choose something else."

Fanny pretended to look about, but her mind was on other things. For more than two hours they had strolled the verdant parklands of the island while practicing their trade. Occasionally they had paused to watch the show performers practice. They had seen cowboys do fantastic tricks with ropes, then watched in horrified wonder as fantastically dressed Arabs swallowed fire without apparent harm. Some of the hardier men in the crowd had been persuaded by the show's riders to try the bucking broncos. All had failed to remain astride more than a second or two. It had all been very interesting, but the thought of encountering one particular bloodthirsty Indian kept her tensely alert. Each time she spotted buckskin or feathers in the crowd, her heart skipped a beat. Indians, she had discovered, looked so much alike she doubted she would recognize him before he spotted her. Walking through the Indian village was a risk she wasn't about to take.

Finally she noticed that Phineas was frowning at her, and she looked up with a matching scowl. "I want to go home. Me feet ache something fierce. Feels like me toes been pinched by crabs."

"Well, why didn't you say so before?" he answered.

"Didn't notice," she answered and lowered her eyes before he spotted the gleam of a lie in them. Under her breath she added, "Besides, business comes first. I did me part well enough, didn't I?"

Phineas nodded. His secret pockets were bursting with the baubles she had slipped from wrists and pockets as they moved among the crowds of visitors. "For that you've earned your reward. If your feet ache, then I suggest we go along to the grandstands. The show begins soon." He took her hand and said in a grand voice, "This way, child. We've box seats."

Reluctantly, Fanny allowed herself to be drawn along. She really did want to see the show. At least, in the thick of the crowd she wouldn't be easily spotted.

The grandstands vibrated with the crowd's excitement as people jockeyed for the best positions in the bleachers. Yet, despite the heat of the late afternoon sun, spirits were high and scuffling was kept to a minimum. As Fanny and Phineas found their seats in the front row of an enclosed box, an unseen band struck up the first notes of a western tune, hushing the crowd.

At one end of the outdoor arena hung a vast painted canvas backdrop depicting the prairies and mountains of the American West. No sooner had the band finished its tune than an Indian war whoop was heard. All at once the air was filled with savage war cries as dozens of Indian braves came galloping out from behind the backdrop. Dressed in war paint, buckskins, and feathers, they waved rifles or bows overhead as they rode straight for the bleachers. The crowd gasped in nervous excitement as the howling warriors approached.

Suddenly new cries were heard and a pack of hard-riding cowboys broke into the arena. They galloped through the Indian lines at full speed, their own peculiar howls vying with the Indian whoops for dominance, as the crowd cheered its approval.

Quick on the cowboys' heels came Mexican *vaqueros,* riding beautiful horses whose silver bridle and saddle decorations winked in brilliant display. Then came the unmistakable blue of the U.S. Cavalry.

After the riders came the animals Fanny recognized from the advertisements. They were big, wooly-hided, brownish-black creatures with shiny horns, small feet, and huge hulking bodies. Following them were elk, strung together to keep them from bolting. The procession then continued with Indian women and children on ponies, then teams of burros, dogsleds, even goats. The Salisbury Stagecoach rolled into view. Marching along behind, in time to "Oh, Susannah," came the Cowboy Band.

Finally, when the arena was full to bursting, the moment arrived that everybody had been waiting for. Buffalo Bill Cody himself came riding forth. Her fears of exposure momentarily forgotten in the excitement of the moment, Fanny stood up and leaned across the railing of her front-row seat in hopes of getting a better view.

He rode in proudly on a gray horse as the other riders made an aisle for him between them. He wore buckskins trimmed with brightly colored beadwork, fringes, beaded gauntlets, and a Mexican sombrero. When he reached the head of his cast, he paused, sitting his horse with authoritative ease. Then he swept off his sombrero with a flourish to reveal his legendary shoulder-length reddish-brown hair, and said in his theatrically ringing voice, "Ladies and gentlemen, permit me to introduce to you a Congress of the Rough Riders of the world!"

The audience clapped and shouted its approval as the riders and other show people made one sweeping turn about the arena with their leader at the head, then one by one disappeared once again behind the canvas.

Fanny settled impatiently back into her seat, eager now for the main part of the show to begin. Finally there was movement at one corner of the canvas and then a live elk appeared. With tentative steps it crossed half the distance between the background and stands before it paused, lifted its nose, and sniffed the air. Suddenly a woman in the bleachers gave a frightened cry. A moment later an Indian raced through the surprised crowd and cleared the railing to land in the arena in one graceful leap. He carried a bow. There were feathers in his long black hair and moccasins on his feet. But, for all intents and purposes, he was naked.

Well, nearly, Fanny decided with a raised brow. He wore a length of rawhide pulled between his legs and secured by a cord about his waist. As he moved, the long, rippling muscles of his brown thighs and calves were clearly visible. When he had leapt the railing, Fanny had glimpsed the tight curve of a bare buttock. It was positively indecent. She darted a glance at Phineas, but he wasn't interested in the show. In fact, he was looking back over his shoulder, as though searching for someone in the seats behind them.

When she glanced back at the arena, she saw that the elk was picking its way on dainty hooves straight toward the box in which she sat. The Indian was coming toward her, too. In belated realization that this might be the Indian from whom she'd stolen the bracelet, Fanny slumped down in her seat and pulled her straw boater low on her brow. But as he came closer, she saw his face clearly and a sigh of relief eased out of her. He had the same broad face, but his nose was wider, his features more weathered, and his mouth drooped in one corner, where a horrid scar distorted it.

The elk paused within an arm's length of Fanny's box, struck a pose, and then made a startled leap away, straight toward the Indian. The Indian gave a yelp of surprise, turned, and ran. The crowd roared in amusement as he disappeared behind the canvas with the elk in pursuit.

The next event was a display of shooting. Fanny fidgeted impatiently in her seat during the firing and banging of rifles and pistols, unimpressed even by the prowess of a young woman in short skirts named Annie Oakley who had been introduced as "Little Sure Shot, the greatest female shot in all the world."

"It's all noise and smoke and gunpowder," she murmured in disappointment midway through the demonstrations. A vendor in the crowd caught her eye and she perked up. "Buy me Cracker Jack, Father. I didn't get the first."

She was nearly finished with her treat when the third event was announced as "The dash of the Indian ponies."

There were ten starters, all dressed in buckskin shirts and painted brilliant shades of red, blue, and yellow. Even so, Fanny sat up straight in her seat when the last man in the race entered the grounds on an iron-gray pony. She didn't need a second look to know who it was. In fact, she wondered why she'd doubted she would recognize him again.

He was a head taller than most of the others, but that wasn't what made him stand out in her mind. He sat his bareback pony much as Buffalo Bill had sat in his saddle: proudly, a little aloof, and supremely self-confident of his position.

From the moment the shot was fired to begin the race, Fanny was in no doubt as to who the winner would be. He leaned low across his pony's neck while the others gave piercing cries and shook their tomahawks in the air as they urged their ponies into a gallop.

Even at a distance, she could see tension in every line of his muscular body, and a curious thought came to mind: He isn't acting. He desperately wanted to win. And he did. Yet, even as the crowd applauded and cheered him with the spontaneous title of "Indian Gray Pony!" he rejected their approval. He didn't turn to his admiring audience or even show by a raised hand or look that he even noticed them. He turned and rode away, every line of his back proudly defiant.

Her curiosity piqued anew by the man, Fanny scarcely heeded the demonstration by the pony-express riders which followed next. Instead, she constantly watched the sidelines for his reappearance. Finally, after what seemed to her another interminable exhibition of shooting, which again left the air blue with smoke and stinking of burned powder, she caught sight of feathers as the Indian riders formed up to one side of the backdrop. A few moments later the Salisbury Stagecoach rolled out and came to a halt before the painted mountain scenery. Several men followed and began enacting a little scene for the crowd.

The man who identified himself as a stage agent warned the driver against the dangers of his journey, citing the likelihood of Indian attack. But the driver brandished his rifle and proclaimed himself a crack shot. When the passengers were all inside, the driver cracked the whip and the six-mule team sent the coach rolling across the imaginary plains.

As the coach reached the middle of the arena, a band of forty Indians emerged from hiding and set out after the coach, screaming at the top of their lungs. Her heart pounding in excitement, Fanny searched the approaching riders for "her Indian," but the dust kicked up by dozens of hooves partially obscured her vision and made identification impossible. The driver whipped the mules, but the Indian ponies were faster and the coach was quickly overtaken by the first rider.

Shots were fired by the Indians and returned by the stagecoach passengers. As Fanny watched an Indian fall with his pony, the woman seated behind her screamed and promptly fainted. More Indians caught up with the coach. One of them leaped from his mount onto the back of the coach. Fanny knew instantly who it was, though he wore only a breechcloth and war paint.

After that, everything seemed to happen at once. The harsh notes of a cavalry's bugle sounded. A new cry went up from the crowd as Buffalo Bill Cody himself came galloping onto the scene leading a party of scouts to the coach's rescue. More shots were fired, the pursuers becoming the pursued. The Indians slowed, wheeling their horses to face the riders in hand-to-hand combat, while the audience rose to its feet to cheer the soldiers. Some riders on both sides were felled by the fake gunfire while others chased one another through the arena exit.

The mock battle was so intense that Fanny dug her nails into her palms to keep from crying out a warning to the Indian who now stood atop the coach. As she watched dry-mouthed, Buffalo Bill approached the stagecoach at a full gallop and fired. The Indian jerked as though he'd received the shot, teetered a moment, and then crumpled and fell from the coach into the dust.

A jubilant cry exploded from the standing crowd, but Fanny felt as though it had been she who had been struck by Cody's shot. As she stared in disbelief at the motionless body of the Indian, Cody dismounted and drew a skinning knife from his waistband. Before she could even guess what would happen, he bent over the prone man and then rose up, waving the trophy of a scalp in one hand.

Fanny sprang to her feet with a cry of horror. Flinging her leg over the railing, she was halfway over the top when she was caught from behind.

"Really, Fanny!" Phineas cried in exasperation as he summarily hauled her backward. "What's the matter with you? It's only make-believe."

"Make-believe?" Fanny turned an uncomprehending gaze to him. "But the scalp!"

"A theatrical trick," Phineas answered. "Just look!"

Fanny spun back toward the arena. Sure enough, when the acrid pall of smoke had drifted away from the center of the arena, she saw that the Indian had risen to his feet, refusing to be carried on a stretcher like the other "dead," his long black hair still very much intact. He bowed to the audience along with the other players, but she noticed that he didn't smile or lift a hand in salute. All the tension drained out of her body, and she sank back weakly onto her chair, feeling in equal parts relief and chagrin. "I knew it wasn't real, only..." What was the use? She'd made a fine and thorough fool of herself.

"Fanny, lass," Phineas said with a shake of his head, "you're after being more gullible than—"

Too caught up in her own emotions, she didn't notice that Phineas halted his chiding in midsentence. It was only when he grabbed her roughly by the shoulder that she knew that something was wrong.

"Don't turn round," he said sharply.

Fanny looked up at him just the same. "Why?"

He released her slowly. "Remain in your seat," he said very softly. "No matter what, don't move from this spot. I'll come back. You've my word."

He didn't wait for the argument that he knew would be forthcoming from her. He pressed her shoulder hard and then turned and walked rapidly away.

In spite of his warning to the contrary, Fanny turned around as he retreated. Though she scanned the faces of the spectators, she couldn't discover anyone who seemed to be paying particular attention to him. A worried frown creased her brow as she debated what to do. If he was in danger, he would need her help. Yet she couldn't quite believe that they'd been tracked all the way to Staten Island. Not even Harry Westin would do that. When Phineas returned, she'd force him to tell her who it was he feared. Until then, she might as well enjoy the "Cowboy's Frolic," which was getting under way.

She looked down at the three pennies he'd given her and then promptly traded them to a passing vendor for another box of Cracker Jack. She forgot all about Phineas as cowboy after cowboy climbed atop the most ferocious horses she'd ever seen. "Bronco busters," the announcer called the fearless riders, but to Fanny's way of thinking, the horses were doing more than their share of cowboy "busting." This act was followed quickly by more shooting exhibitions, where men and women riding at full gallop broke glass balls and clay pigeons which were launched into the air. After them came a set of races in which an Indian runner tested himself against a mounted Indian in a fifty-yard dash. To everyone's amazement the runner won more often than the rider.

As the afternoon wore on, she continued to look for

"her Indian" in every act. To her surprise, she discovered that she wasn't the only one to notice his appearances. Whenever he entered the arena, a new level of excitement rippled through the spectators, for they sensed, as she did, that there was something more in his performances than mere acting. He was in control of his actions but not, it seemed, of the emotions which drove him to wilder exploits than his fellow showmen.

It was he who fired the fatal shot that killed General Custer in the reenactment of "Custer's Massacre." He stood proudly over Custer's body, undaunted by the crowd's hisses and boos, the American standard clutched in his left hand. Even when, "Too late!", Buffalo Bill himself came upon the scene in quiet dignity and swept his hat from his head in mute respect for the fallen soldiers, the Indian held his ground. Fanny felt again a shock of amazement that she had dared rob this warrior.

Finally, as the sun swung low over the New Jersey coast to the West, the last event got under way. It was the "Buffalo Chase." Without warning, buffalo came galloping onto the grounds. Those people who had come late and bought standing-room-only tickets were lined up on either side of the grandstands. As the huge animals came thundering toward them, many fled in fear of their lives. But mounted cowboys appeared and expertly turned the buffalo away with plenty of room to spare.

Then once again the crowd was treated to the spectacle of galloping Indians in full regalia, circling and dashing across the grounds, while the cowboy band played, "Oh, Susannah!" And then it was over.

Exhausted and exhilarated beyond anything she had ever experienced, Fanny slumped in her chair to await

Phineas's return. The crowd thinned out quickly, eager to find passage back to the city before dark set in. While she waited, she pulled the bracelet from her pocket and slipped it on her arm. It hung loosely from her wrist, its size a reminder of the large, muscular wrist of its owner.

"Hey! Ye there!"

At the sound of the angry voice, Fanny whipped her hand behind her back and sat upright in her chair.

"Ye!" A skinny, ill-dressed young man strode up to her and grabbed one of her curls. "Where's Phineas?" he demanded in an angry Irish brogue.

"Ow!" Fanny cried, more for effect than from pain. "You're hurting me, you are!"

"I'll be doing more than pullin' yer curls if ye're not after telling me where that spalpeen, Phineas Todd, is hidin'." He jerked her curl again. "Where is he, I say?"

Fanny winced from the torment, but her thoughts came thick and fast. Phineas had been right about someone following them. He must have noticed the man earlier and gone to search for him. "Ouch!" she cried as he pulled her hair a third time. "I don't know who you mean!"

"Don't ye?" The man thrust his face toward hers.

It was the face of a bully: small-eyed with pushed-in features and skin the texture and color of bread dough. Yet she wasn't frightened. She had handled too many Bowery toughs to be cowed by one rough-handed ruffian. Still, she wished the grandstand weren't so deserted.

"Leave go!" she shouted and twisted away to cover the act of pulling a small knife from its hiding place up her sleeve. "Leave go of me, I say, or I'll call the cops!"

"No, ye won't," he answered as he tightened his grip on her hair.

Fanny lunged at him with her knife, but he, too, was accustomed to the unexpected and sidestepped her jab.

"What's this?" he said with a chuckle of disdain as he spied her puny weapon. "Give me that!"

He grabbed her wrist in his free hand and forced her arm up behind her back until the pain made her release the knife. "Ye'll be comin' along with me, nice and quiet. If ye don't, ye won't be after likin' what'll happen next."

"Fanny!"

At the sound of Phineas's voice, the man whipped about with a cry of satisfaction. "So there ye are, Todd. Didn't think to get away, did ye? There's folks wanting a word with ye!"

"Phineas! Help!" Fanny cried, twisting and kicking at the man holding her.

Phineas paused several yards away from them. "Leave the lass alone. She's nothing to do with it."

"That's not how I heard it." The tough freed her arm to cuff Fanny on the side of her head, adding a threatening curse under his breath to Phineas as she continued to struggle. "If ye dinna want her to be hurt, tell her to behave like a lady."

Fanny saw Phineas hesitate, as though about to say something, but then suddenly he pulled a revolver from his pocket and fired a shot in their general direction before he turned and ran.

"Phineas, ye coward!" the young man shouted in angry astonishment. "Where do ye think ye're going?"

The distraction gave Fanny the advantage she needed. She twisted about in his grasp, then struck, biting him in the forearm with all her strength. As he screamed in pain, she pulled free and gave him a hard kick behind one knee which sent him sprawling among the seats.

Immediately she threw a leg up over the railing and hurdled it. A curse escaped her as she felt her stockings snag on the splinters. Phineas was always scolding her about the cost of stockings. But as soon as her feet hit the hard-packed earth of the arena, she forgot all about stockings, for her attacker was cursing roundly as he regained his feet.

She sprinted across the huge empty space as if pursued by the band of howling Indians who had filled the arena half an hour earlier. Only when she reached the painted canvas backdrop did she pause to look back. To her dismay, her pursuer was only a few yards behind her, shouting in very graphic terms what he meant to do when he caught her. Desperate to find a place to hide, she ducked behind the canvas.

The grounds behind the set were filled with lingering visitors who'd stopped to watch the cowboys herding cattle back into their pens. The throng slowed her progress, and a moment later she heard a shout and saw her assailant running toward her.

"Stop her!" he shouted. "That lass stole me money! Stop her!"

Anger replaced fear as a man caught her by the arm and cried, "Got her!" She struck him in the belly with a hard little fist and wrenched her arm away as he doubled in pain. Desperately, she spun about to face the crowd gathering about her. "Stay away! Stay away from me!" she warned as she advanced on them.

Shocked by this display of ferocity from a young girl, the crowd instinctively fell back. Fanny ran straight through a break in their ranks and into the cloaking shadows of the nearby woods.

Her heart thumping like a piston, she crouched down behind the first sturdy clump of shrubbery she came across and waited. She heard the pounding footsteps and angry shouts of the men who gave chase. She blinked back a trickle of sweat that ran into her eyes. Though every instinct urged her to run, she resisted. If she made any sound, the men would be sure to hear it and come after her. As she huddled behind the bush, straining for every sound that would tell her where they were, a hot, dizzying sickness swept over her.

Phineas had deserted her! He'd never done that before. Even the time she'd been caught red-handed with a man's wallet, he'd come to her aid against the arresting officer. Phineas was good with words. He'd talked the officer out of the arrest, promising to give his errant "daughter" a sound beating himself. But now he'd run away, leaving her in the grip of a man who meant her harm. Tears sprang into her eyes.

The snap of a twig nearly startled her into action, but she clapped an iron will on her nerve, tensing her muscles until she trembled like a person with palsy. Finally the voices and footsteps retreated. Still she waited, crouched in the cool dampness. Minutes passed, then a dozen more. Still, she waited. An hour passed as the purple haze of twilight dwindled into the inky black of night.

As she waited, fear and uncertainty turned to anger. Damn Phineas's cowardly soul! Wasn't she always the one who took the most risks? She should have protested their fifty-fifty split long ago. For all the protection he'd offered her today, she might as well have worked alone. Yes, that was it. When she got back to the city, she'd tell Phineas that they were finished. She didn't need a coward for a partner. Damn him! Damn him to hell and back!

The anger revived her courage. When she got back into the city, she would...

Her thoughts were brought up short. How would she get back into town? Phineas had their tickets for the ferry. She had no money to buy passage back. She could sneak aboard a ferry—but no, too many people had seen her, heard her accused of stealing a purse. Certainly the police would be on the lookout for a girl of her description.

She stood up resolutely and brushed away the leaves that clung to her skirt. There was only one thing to do. She'd have to spend the night on the island. In the morning everyone would have forgotten about her, and she would walk bold as brass onto a ferry. But now what?

She walked slowly to the edge of the woods, halting just inside the shadow of a tree. From her vantage point she could see the performers' settlement. A host of militarylike tents had been set up along a grassy lane. Many of them were aglow like lampshades, the silhouettes of their inhabitants thrown in sharp relief against the canvas walls. Laughter drifted toward her in the breeze, as did the aromas of their suppers. Someone was strumming a tune on a banjo. The village looked cozy and inviting—but not for her.

Instead, she turned her gaze to the other settlement, the one which hours earlier she had refused to go near.

In the distance the black triangular silhouettes of Indian tepees were clearly visible. Finally she spied one tepee set a little apart from the others. No fire blazed before it. It seemed empty. She hurried toward it, her heart settling down once more. No one would think to look for her there.

CHAPTER
3

Matthew Morning Star stood with his arms folded in silent protest against the words directed at him. This was not the first time he had been summoned to the chief's tepee for a council after a performance.

"... that anger frightens the white man's child," said Chief Red Shirt, leader of the Sioux performers in the Wild West Show, though he was no older than the brave he chastised. "If you offend customers, what will happen? I will tell you. You will be sent away in disgrace."

"What disgrace is there in presenting ourselves as warriors?" Matthew challenged. "Are we only to ride prettily for the crowd and then die as easily as flies under the flick of a horse's tail? Where is our pride, then?"

Red Shirt looked up from his cross-legged position on the floor. "This is not war. In war there are no blanks in the guns. In battle a warrior does not regain his scalp as easily as he loses it. If it is war you seek, go home to the Black Hills of our people. Listen there

31

to the music of the forbidden Ghost Dance. Fill your heart to bursting with hate and rage. Then ride against the white soldiers. But remember the past. For every white man you kill, the bluecoats will murder five of our women and children.''

Pausing, Red Shirt folded his arms across his chest. ''As a chief of the Sioux, I have said what I must. We will speak of it no more.'' To Matthew's surprise, Red Shirt did not dismiss him but indicated that he should sit down. When he did, Red Shirt said, ''We will smoke together and ask the Great Spirit for guidance for you, brave warrior.''

This was the final word spoken on the matter. The sacred calumet, lying by the chief's knee, was unwrapped from its exquisite beadwork bag, filled with tobacco, and lit with the appropriate ritual. For the next half hour, it passed silently back and forth between the two young men.

Matthew found himself relaxing under the soothing influence of the smoke. The stem of the ceremonial pipe had been smoothed and oiled to shiny perfection in its passage through many different hands over the years. The smoking of the pipe represented strength, continuity, peace, and longevity, and Matthew drew contentment from the rite as he savored the moments.

Finally the tobacco was gone, and in silence he watched Red Shirt clean the pipe with loving care and put it back into its pouch. Only then did he speak.

''I spoke in anger before, Red Shirt. Many things disturb me this day.''

Red Shirt nodded. ''Days are like the wind. Some are gentle, while others breed storm and strife. But even the storm brings rain to nourish the earth.''

''All things work ultimately for good,'' Matthew

grumbled, switching from his native language into English. "It's a philosophy that promises much but changes nothing. Today one of those white children, whom you would not offend, stole a silver wristband from my arm."

Red Shirt smiled and answered in good English. "The foolishness of a child should not disturb a warrior."

Matthew didn't smile in return. "I've learned many things while living in the great eastern city of Boston. One of them is that many white men do not believe that it is dishonorable to steal what they cannot get by buying or trading. They prefer stealing. It makes them feel strong and therefore deserving of that which they take from the weak."

"Harsh words for a people among whom you freely chose to live." Red Shirt's expression softened. "I know the pain you carry, my friend. Yet you left us to go among those whom you once called enemy in order that you might understand and forgive. Have you not gained that understanding? Have you found no peace?"

The gentle rebuke left Matthew with nothing to say. An apology would only embarrass them both.

"We have long been friends," Red Shirt said after a moment's silence.

"Since we were carried in cradleboards upon our mothers' backs, twenty-two years have passed."

Red Shirt nodded. "We were born under the same moon, yet I speak to you now as an elder to the young. You are not in harmony with your world, Matthew Morning Star. You must bring the elements of your destiny into an alliance before you can know an hour of greatness."

Matthew nodded. "Wise words but of little use to me."

"You are a loner. That is your destiny, perhaps, but

even a solitary man should not be without comforts in his lodge.'' His dark eyes sparkled. ''Why do you not alter your scalp-lock decoration and bring pleasure under your roof?''

Matthew blushed, for he knew to what his friend referred. Among the feathers and fur decoration attached to a lock of hair at his crown was the beadwork symbol of an unmarried man. ''You have no wife. Why should I disturb my peace with a squaw?''

Red Shirt laughed, a wide grin splitting his handsome face. ''The disturbance need not be permanent. A man may find pleasant company among the Arapaho women of this very camp.''

''They are whores,'' Matthew answered censoriously.

Red Shirt shook his head in bemusement. Matthew had always been both the more unconventional and yet the more idealistic of the two. ''They are not Sioux women, and so it is not for us to judge. They show pleasant enthusiasm when mounted. When freely offered, may a man not ride for an hour a horse that is not his own?''

Matthew refused to meet his friend's eyes. He, too, had known for weeks the source, at least in part, of his restlessness. He wanted a woman. Yet he had sworn a secret oath before he left his people ten years earlier to refrain from even a casual alliance with a woman. Then he had been a stripling of thirteen. Now he understood the enormity of his oath. Still, he wouldn't dishonor the oath nor would he speak of it with his childhood friend.

Even so, during these last weeks he had watched in masculine appreciation the Indian women in the cast and felt a warm return of his interest as he passed them. He felt pride in those shy gazes, for it was no disgrace to be found worthy of a woman's regard. But lately he had felt himself responding to the bolder stares of the white women who came as visitors to the show. Their speaking glances seemed to reach out to stroke his bare chest and naked thighs. He never looked at their faces. It was not proper even to address women of his tribe. Nor was it right for a Sioux warrior to be so humbled by a weakness of the flesh. His lustful nature had become a burden, and so he denied himself over and over again in order to master the hunger that raged like a banked fire in his loins and heart. It was the way of a Dreamer, a man visited by visions.

"Do not neglect that fire too long lest you scorch your soul as well," Red Shirt said softly.

Matthew's head jerked up. There was no reason to ask how his friend guessed his thoughts. Red Shirt was one of the revered Shirt Wearers. That he could sometimes read the thoughts of another was accepted; yet it was disconcerting all the same.

Matthew rose to his feet in a single limber move. "I must go. I neglect my fire." A trace of a smile entered his black eyes. "My campfire."

Red Shirt rose and extended his hand, American fashion. "Patience, Matthew. Save your bravery for a time when you will face the most fierce enemy of all: yourself."

Once outside in the cool air, Matthew released a very unwarriorlike sigh. This wasn't the first time he'd been cautioned against taking his part in the show too seriously. He hadn't meant to repeat the mistake. It was the theft of his wristband, a gift from his father just before his death, that had caused him to take his anger and frustration out in his performance. Recalling the incident, he flexed his hands into fists. He had once ridden in a real battle with the bluecoats. He knew their deadly power and his own rage at his people's helplessness. He had fought well for a boy of twelve, counted coup on his mortal enemy and made his father proud. His father would be shamed by his loss of the armband to one of the least of the white man's tribe.

The bite had surprised him. Possessed of a sense of humor, he enjoyed giving white children the scare they expected when confronted with an Indian warrior. He had only touched the girl's hair because the color was so unusual, as flame red as a sunset on the dry summer prairie. Besides, he knew she wasn't afraid of him. There had been defiance in her light eyes, something bold and brave . . . and cunning.

"Outfoxed by a little girl," he muttered under his breath as he walked away from Red Shirt's lodge. Was all that was Sioux, and therefore good in him, being lost by his living too long and too far away from his people? It had been many long years since he'd ridden the land of his ancestors, the Dakota Sioux. "Time to go home, Matthew," he murmured to himself.

He smiled as he passed a family sitting before their campfire and refused with a wave of his hand their offer to share their meal. More than nourishment, he needed peace.

As he entered the edge of the oak grove near the camp, he paused to breathe deeply. With his eyes closed he could almost imagine that he was home. The odors of wood and smoke, boiled meat, horses and manure were comforting and familiar. Even the cool thread of the night breeze reminded him of home. There was the toad's croak, the rusty saw of the grasshopper, and the low call of the owl in the sigh of the wind. Opening his eyes, he saw the last glimmer of the setting sun that rouged the sky like a distant prairie fire.

But this wasn't the Dakotas. This was one of the largest encampments of white men on the earth. He grumbled as he imagined his Harvard history professor's reaction to such a statement.

Mr. Morning Star, you will kindly refrain from expressing yourself in that most bucolic of phrasings. You are a university man now and expected to conform, however tenuously, to civilized speech and thought.

He had conformed well enough to earn an education at the finest university in the United States. He had learned how the white man thought and much of his motives. The task was accomplished. He should be content. Why wasn't he?

He sighed again and set off in the direction of his lodge, which stood alone on the far side of the camp. Tonight especially, he needed the peace and privacy of his thoughts.

Fanny lay in the dark wondering how it was possible to feel both relief and trepidation at the same time. Perhaps her mixed feelings had something to do with her surroundings—not that she knew exactly what they were. This tepee was as dark as the inside of an egg.

When she'd first reached it, she'd stood a long time in its shadow, listening for any signs of life within. There hadn't been a single sound, not a snore or snort or even a sigh. It was a safe place, perfect for hiding. Not knowing how to enter it, she'd simply rolled up one edge of the leather hide covering and scooted underneath. She'd been surprised to find that she'd rolled onto a scratchy blanket. At least it had felt like a blanket. It smelled rankly of horse sweat.

After a moment of indecision, she'd felt about tentatively with a hand, encountered packed earth beyond the blanket's edge and then another blanket or rug of some sort with thick, coarse hair. Further exploration had yielded nothing significant until her fingers had found warm stones. Seconds later she'd snatched back her hand with a cry of pain. Though not warm enough to glow, hot coals from a recent fire had been lying on the other side of the stones. Her zeal for exploration diminished, she'd pulled herself up into a ball and sucked her burned fingertip until the stinging eased.

Suddenly something startled her out of the absolute peace that had sent her drifting toward sleep. The night seemed too still, as if nature held its breath. Then there came the faint sounds of rustling outside the tepee. Was an animal passing by? A city girl, she didn't know what sort of creatures might inhabit the wooded island, but that didn't stop her from speculating. Her mind instantly conjured up a dozen different fanged phantoms, all snarl and bite, each more fantastic than the last.

When the tepee was suddenly opened, every muscle of her body tensed with expectation. There, looming against a midnight sky speckled with stars, was the hulking outline of a man with flowing hair. An Indian!

A moment later darkness descended as the tepee was closed. The soft tread of feet told her that he had entered. Anticipation tingled along her spine as she lay perfectly still. He hadn't seen her, that was plain. What should she do? What would *he* do when he discovered that he wasn't alone? Stealthily, she ran her fingers up under the edge of her left cuff to feel for her knife, but it was not there. With a sinking feeling she remembered she had lost it at the grandstand.

With growing alarm she heard scratching, then saw the beginnings of a reddish glow. He was poking the fire. In the wavering glow she saw his dark shape squatting a few feet away. Afraid even to breathe, she stared helplessly at the bold profile of the man while a memory leaped to mind of the Indian with a dark, hard-eyed face who had said her hair would make a good trophy.

As though in answer to her unexpressed prayers, the light died away and she heard him mutter in disgust as darkness once more enveloped the tepee.

Escape uppermost in her thoughts, she reached out and began groping blindly for the edge of the hide where she had crawled in. She couldn't find it. Then all her courage drained away as she sensed his presence beside her.

Matthew stretched and yawned. He had meant to read for a while, but the night was so sweet and mild he couldn't even regret the loss of his fire. It was a night for sleeping and dreaming summer dreams. He squatted down and reached for his bedding.

The instant before his hand made contact, he knew that he wasn't alone. Two thoughts rose together in that instant: that the danger had been there all the time, and that he was becoming less sensitive to his surroundings with each passing day.

He lunged at the invader, his hand meeting and closing hard on an ankle, and he heard a sharp intake of breath in response. The ankle under his hand was trim and delicate—and clothed in a cotton stocking. There was a woman in his lodge!

His first thought was the memory of Red Shirt chiding him for refusing what was freely offered by the women of the cast. Had he, as a jest between friends, sent a woman to share Matthew's robes?

Then he remembered another, less heartening but still possible reason for the presence of a woman in his lodge. Once before a woman had offered herself to him. On that occasion, five years before, he was newly arrived in Boston. The white woman had been pretty and he had been gullible enough to agree when she asked for his help. Upon her suggestion, he had taken her to his room. Once they were alone, a man claiming to be her husband had suddenly appeared at the door, threatening to have them both arrested. After a series of pleadings by the woman, the man had been persuaded to accept all the money in Matthew's wallet, and they both had left together. Later he had learned from classmates that this "dodge," as they called it, was one of the oldest con games played on strangers.

Preoccupation with his own thoughts had made him vulnerable tonight, and the realization rankled. If this were a scam he'd make the woman wish she'd chosen a different dupe.

At his touch Fanny remained perfectly still. She'd been in danger before and knew surprise was her best advantage against someone half again her size. She felt his hand slide up her leg, past her knee, and onto the soft flesh of her thigh exposed above her garter. A moment later she was caught in an embrace as the man stretched out fully upon her. With a cry of outrage, she tried to shove him away, but her hands met the immovable wall of a solidly muscled chest. Another cry formed but never became sound because her mouth was engulfed in a silencing palm. Acting instinctively, she bit down. As he reared up and away from her with a wounded roar, she rolled away, sprang to her feet, and headed toward the opening through which he had entered. But she had forgotten about the campfire. The toe of her shoe caught on one of the stones, sending her sprawling full length into the dirt. A moment later she was caught by the waist from behind and lifted up off her feet.

"Get away from me, you ill-gotten, bloodthirsty savage!" she cried, kicking her dangling feet in a futile attempt to make contact with his legs. The next instant a hard hand was once more clapped over her mouth. This time he clamped her jaw closed with his fingers so that she couldn't repeat the bite.

In the silence Matthew strained for the sound of footfalls, a rustle, a whisper of cloth, any sound that would betray the presence of another person. But as he listened, he heard nothing out of the ordinary.

After nearly a minute, the hand about Fanny's waist slackened its grip so that her back slid down her captor's chest until her feet touched the ground and the hand muzzling her mouth eased its grip.

"Now you tell me," she heard him whisper against her ear. "Why you come here?" His hand moved from her mouth down to the slender column of her neck, which he lightly squeezed as he spoke again. "You lie, I cut throat!"

Fanny gulped back tears. The vivid portrayal of Indian attacks during the afternoon's performance and Phineas's desertion had left her feeling very vulnerable. "I ain't done nothing. I was only hiding, I swear it! I didn't think anyone lived here. I'll go quiet. Only, don't scalp me! Please!"

Amusement moved in Matthew's chest. Scalp her, indeed! "Tell me. Why you come here, little thief?"

Fanny compressed her lips as a shiver passed through her. Why did he call her a thief? Then she remembered running through the crowd as the man chased her. Many people had seen her and heard his accusations. Yet, how did the Indian recognize her when she couldn't see him at all in the darkness? Perhaps Indians were like cats, she thought fleetingly, and could see at night. "I ain't a thief," she said slowly. "It was all a lie. That man was after trying to murder me!"

"What man?"

"The one who called me a thief. I ain't took nothing from him!" she added indignantly.

Growing more confused by the moment, Matthew said in his normal voice, "I haven't the slightest idea what you're talking about."

The change in his manner of speaking was so sudden and complete that Fanny jerked her head around, trying to see him in the blackness, but it was impossible. Perhaps he wasn't an Indian at all but some sort of demon creature, the kind her da often told her stories about when she was a child. In alarm, she struck out at the man with all her might.

The blow caught Matthew unprepared, and she broke free a second time.

She gained the entrance this time, bursting through it into the night. But her victory was short-lived as he caught her hair from behind and dragged her to a halt.

The moon had risen, a crescent of cheesy curdles cradled in a brilliant rind of light. It wasn't much, but it was enough for her to see his face when he swung her about. The moonlight threw into harsh relief the wide cheekbones, the knife-blade thrust of his nose, and accented the pitchy depths of his dark eyes. This was the fierce warrior from the afternoon show, the one who'd killed Custer, the one who'd fought Buffalo Bill, the one from whom she'd stolen the bracelet!

In the recesses of her mind she heard the faint echo of blood-curdling war whoops as the Sioux rode into battle. Suddenly she was Custer and the man standing over her brandished a bloody tomahawk poised to lift her scalp. And, because she wasn't a brave soldier but a badly frightened young woman, she burst into tears.

In that same instant Matthew had stared down into a shadowed face with enormous eyes gleaming up at him and had been struck dumb by astonishment. What he saw wasn't a woman at all but the dirt-streaked face of a young girl.

As she began to cry, open-mouthed and unashamedly, his feeling of chagrin redoubled. He'd deliberately frightened her, had threatened her life. He felt foolish and confused and angry. What was she doing in his lodge?

"Why did you come here?" he demanded as he gave her a gentle shake to stop the flood of tears. "Who are you?"

"Don't hurt me!" she cried, lifting her arms in expectation of a blow.

Matthew dropped his hands from her arms, ashamed to the soles of his feet that he had so badly abused a youngster. "I won't hurt you. I promise. I'm sorry I frightened you."

Fanny gulped back a sob. "I wasn't frightened, not really." The words didn't carry much conviction, but they made her feel better. She glanced up at him and saw that he regarded her only with curiosity. He didn't recognize her! The thought shone brightly in the black sky of her predicament.

"How did you come here?" he again demanded.

Accustomed to telling lies when the truth seemed a doubtful proposition, she said, "I was kidnapped."

His expression gave no indication of whether or not he accepted this.

"You aren't after believing me?" she asked ingenuously. "Folks say Indians are always stealing womenfolk for their warriors and children to roast over the—" She broke off. Perhaps it was best not to give him any ideas. "Well, I wouldn't be knowing about such things, really."

"The Sioux do not kidnap women or children," he said in a flat voice.

"No, I don't suppose *you* would be the sort for that," she agreed quickly. "As I was saying, I was kidnapped right off the ferry, only I escaped from the motherless son of Satan who tried to take me!" She paused again to judge the effect her tale was having, but she still couldn't detect any response and so she reluctantly continued. "I was hiding from me kidnappers."

"First you said there was one son of Satan."

"One, two, I couldn't be telling for certain," Fanny responded indignantly. She must be more nervous than she thought to make so obvious a mistake. "Well, there I was, you see, lying all quiet like when you came in. I didn't know what to do. You might have been a kidnapper. Then you grabbed me and, well . . ."

Matthew winced at the memory of his actions. "I apologize for my bad judgment in the matter."

He dearly wished that it were daylight. It was like talking to a dream, standing in the moonlight listening to this girl. Then he remembered Red Shirt's warning that he never again offend one of the show's customers. "You must go," he said. "It is not seemly for a white girl to be here. Go home." As if that put an end to the matter, he turned and walked resolutely back to his lodge and disappeared inside.

Fanny stood a moment, wondering at her contrary luck. The worst luck had been that she'd chosen to hide in the tepee of one of her "customers." The good luck had been that he hadn't recognized her. She slipped off the silver cuff and put it in her pocket. She'd tested her luck once too often this day. The next mistake might be her last.

Now she was back where she had started, in need of shelter. In the distance the Indian village was illuminated by a dozen campfires. The lone tepee had been inviting, but the thought of facing dozens of strangers seemed the height of folly. There would be questions asked that she couldn't or wouldn't answer. And what if the man who'd tried to hurt her were still wandering about? No, she wouldn't chance going there. She was accustomed to getting along on her own, unless Phineas was with her. Poor Phineas. Where was he? Was he searching for her in the Bowery? Or was he, too, in hiding?

She swallowed the lump that rose to her throat. Tomorrow she'd find Phineas, but she mustn't think about that now. She glanced back at the lone tepee standing in the dark. There were no longer any sounds coming from inside it. Had the Indian gone to sleep? What was she going to do? She couldn't stand here until dawn, and she didn't relish the idea of sleeping in the woods.

A sudden rustle in the nearby oak grove made her leap like a startled deer. There were dangerous things in those woods, she was sure of it! She could hear them, almost see their frightening shapes against the sky.

"Better the devil you know!" she whispered and ran toward the tepee.

Matthew sat up as his lodge flap was lifted and he saw in surprise the young white girl step inside. "What is it now?" he asked.

"I—I want to stay here," Fanny said softly as she stepped away from the entrance. "I guess it should be safe enough. You ain't scalped me."

"Who are you?"

She didn't answer.

"How old are you?"

"Twelve," she lied because her own silence made her nervous.

"You're old enough to know that you cannot remain the night with a man who is not *Hakataku*," he replied.

"What's that?"

"It means a man who is your kin, your family, a guardian."

"I don't have a family, least not anymore," she answered. "Can't you be lighting the fire? I cannot see a single thing."

"Just as well," he muttered, for as usual he was naked beneath his buffalo robe. Something about her was familiar, and then he remembered what it was. "Your accent. You're Irish, aren't you?"

Fanny licked her lips. "What of it?"

Matthew smiled. Michael O'Leary had been his one and only friend for three years at Harvard. As silver-tongued a devil as ever the old sod had given birth to, was how Michael described himself. "Tell me the truth. Why have you come here?"

Fanny hesitated. "I need to stop the night."

Matthew's tone lost all friendliness. "You can't do that."

"You'd send me out to be kidnapped all over again." His silence prompted her to add, "Don't you believe me?"

"No."

Thinking quickly, Fanny changed her mind about pursuing the tale. "You're right." She wished she could see his face. She was accustomed to tailoring her stories to the responses they engendered in the listener. "I lied. Only 'cause I'm ashamed to be telling the truth. I got lost." She allowed her voice to wobble a little over the last word. "Me da told me to go directly to the ferry after the show, only I stayed too long. When I got to the dock the man said the ferry was gone. I didn't have money, and me da is going to be so mad, and . . . *oh*!" The rush of words drifted off into the beginning of a sob.

Matthew hung on grimly to his silence. He wasn't certain he believed this story, either. Hadn't she just said she had no family? Yet this tale made a certain kind of sense. After nearly every evening's performance, children were lost in the rush to catch the last ferry. The girl might be telling the truth. Why did he have this niggling sense of doubt? Maybe because she had lied in the beginning. Why would she do that? Perhaps the truth was that she'd spent her fare for the return trip on caramel corn and was afraid to admit it.

He debated dressing and taking her to the main settlement and handing her over to Buffalo Bill. Then he remembered how angry the show's producer had been earlier. Red Shirt had had to endure the man's wrath before confronting Matthew about the incident.

Showing up in the middle of the night with the story of a white child who'd wandered into his lodge didn't seem a prudent thing to do. Against his better judgment and because he couldn't think of an alternative, he said, "You may stay here." There'd be plenty of time in the morning to regret his decision.

In spite of reason, which said it was best to leave him alone, curiosity got the better of her. "You sure you're an Indian? You're after talking awfully fancy for one."

Exasperation colored his reply. "You've known many, I presume?"

"Well, I wouldn't be saying that, only I saw the Wild West Show today and that's something."

"That makes you practically an authority. Time for sleep now. No more talk."

Fanny wondered why he didn't offer her a blanket or some assistance in finding a place to lie down, though she supposed she shouldn't complain. After all, he was allowing her to remain. But as she groped about in the dark, she couldn't keep from resenting his lack of interest in her plight. After the performance she'd given, most people would have offered her a meal, at least a cup of water, and money for her return trip. Perhaps Indians were different from ordinary people.

She found a space on the floor that was covered by a blanket and gingerly stretched out on it. Yes, that must be it, she decided as she closed her eyes. Indians were different.

But sleep didn't come as quickly as she expected. What came into her thoughts was the memory of Phineas running away, leaving her in the clutches of a man who clearly meant her harm. "Just you wait till I find you, Phineas Todd," she muttered sleepily. "Just you wait!"

* * *

Fanny opened her eyes a slit at the first sound of movement. The black of night had faded until the interior of the tepee was gray with the promise of morning. But that wasn't what caught her interest. Her companion was awake. More than that, he was standing in the middle of the tepee... completely naked.

She shut her eyes quickly and then opened them again. Even through the thicket of her lashes there was no mistaking it. She'd never seen a naked man before, and though his skin was coppery rather than pale and the inky black fall of hair trailing over his shoulders seemed feminine, there was no doubting that he was male. And, by her estimation, very well formed.

As she watched, he bent and picked up a length of rawhide about the size of a scarf, passed it between his legs, and then looped a thong about his waist so that the material was held tightly about his loins while the ends hung down in front and behind. So that was how it was done. She had wondered how the Indians kept their skimpy clothing from falling off. Still, the garment left a remarkable length of hard-muscled thigh and leg exposed.

As he turned his head to look at her, she closed her eyes. She heard him moving about and she didn't want him to know that she, too, was awake. Finally she heard the flap being lifted and then lowered. She waited three heartbeats and then sat up.

For the first time she saw the inside of the dwelling in which she had passed the night, and the contents surprised her. Hanging from the poles that supported the covering were a variety of bags and objects she had never before seen. Yet she sensed that there was order in their display and thought given to their location. The fire in the middle of the tepee had begun to smolder, and she saw the stones flanking it which had tripped up her escape the night before. She glanced curiously from one item to the next until she came to a large number of leather-bound volumes in the far corner. More than a dozen books were neatly lined up on a board which was suspended between two poles to form a shelf. The Indian read books. That was amazing.

She sat pondering this new bit of information until she heard faint laughter in the distance. At once she was on her feet. This was her moment to escape. She had to get back to the city. She had to find Phineas.

She nearly missed them. They were laid out on a bit of leather in a single row, each gleaming dully in the light of sunrise. The three silver armbands were a temptation she wouldn't have thought twice about yielding to on any other occasion. But even as she reached for them, she changed her mind. He'd been kind to her, given her shelter. She wasn't so far removed from civilized behavior that she would steal from a friend.

Before she could think the matter over a second time, she lifted up one corner of the tepee at the back and crawled under. A moment later she disappeared into the half-light of the nearby woods.

CHAPTER
4

Fetid odors from the city's sewers and gutters pervaded the air as Fanny crouched on the rear platform of the trolley that ran to within a block of her home. A warm breeze stirred dust into the already stifling atmosphere, making her sneeze. "Snitching a hitch" was illegal, but like many of the city's street urchins, she often rode for free. She was accustomed to bending rules. By shedding copious tears, she had convinced a gullible ferryboat captain to fetch her back to the city, though she couldn't pay the fare.

The sight of the rows of dingy, dun-colored brick buildings lining the streets near the Bowery depressed her. She was nearly home, but the realization didn't lift her spirits. It was Sunday, a day of rest. The usual din of shoppers, trolleys, drays, cart vendors, horses, and cabs was missing. The few people aboard were on their way to church or just now returning home from their Saturday night's revelry.

When the trolley man rang the bell and slowed for the next stop, a sudden gust lifted her skirts as she slipped off the platform onto the street. The display attracted two tall boys in knickers and caps who stood smoking and leaning against a street post. As she approached the curb, they straightened up and blocked her path.

"Ain't seen you about lately, Fanny," said the taller of the two, his adolescent face a suet pie of freckles, pimples, and dirty smudges. He gave her an appraising look that lingered on the tight pull of her bodice. "Maybe you've been hiding yourself from me now that you're growing a bit."

"Here, give us a kiss," said the other as he grabbed her by the shoulders to haul her in against him.

Repelled by his wine-tinged breath, Fanny landed a quick, hard blow on his ear with a fist. "Let go, you great stinking lout!"

The boy staggered, misstepped, and careened head-first into the lamppost with a loud *thunk*. His roar of pain was answered by his friend's laughter. Fanny sidestepped the pair and hurried down the street. She didn't run, however, because she knew the older of the two boys, and it wouldn't do for him to think that she was afraid of him.

Charlie Lutz had been the neighborhood bully for as long as she could remember. Always big and strong for his age, he'd served his first "bit in the jug" at twelve for cutting off the ears of a younger boy who'd refused to steal for him. Now, at fifteen, he'd become a menace to the neighborhood girls. Fanny bristled remembering the lewd ogling he'd given her. He'd noted at once what

Phineas was reluctant to recognize. She was growing up.

No, Fanny amended, she *was* grown up. Not that the fact seemed to offer any advantages. It meant that she and Phineas would be forced to devise a new scam. Many prostitutes were also pickpockets. In fact, they preferred it. They'd pick up a man, encourage him to drink himself blind, then lift his purse and run. "Rolling the lush," it was called. Yet some men had very hard heads for liquor, and many a woman planning to steal had instead to earn her wages on her back.

Was prostitution in her future? Fanny mused for the thousandth time. It certainly had its attractions. The prettiest women she knew, all powder and perfume and silk bustles and roses on their bonnets, were "in the trade." Men admired them, bought them pretty clothes, took them to the theater, and paid for extravagant meals in the best hotels. Why didn't the idea appeal to her?

Fanny paused to stare into a shop window where a plum silk gown hung on a wooden mannequin. The dress was tight-waisted with a high collar edged in ecru lace. Pleated ecru fabric draped the hips in front, then formed bouffant drapery in the rear to accentuate the bustle. She'd seen women wearing similar gowns, their drapery swaying provocatively as they walked. Of late her eyes had followed them enviously. She'd never owned a pretty gown, never dressed as a woman. It was as if a part of her were being kept hidden, even from herself.

She tilted her head the better to catch her reflection in the glass. She wasn't pretty, she decided, but she had a slender waist and a natural flare of hips. In clothes like the dress in the window, she'd make a good showing.

Then she could have gentlemen friends buying her presents and flowers and fine meals. She made a face at her reflection, then continued down the street.

Slowly, though, her saucy mood drained away. Sometimes she hated being female. If she were a boy like Charlie Lutz, she could just continue her trade. But nature was inexorably forcing her to acknowledge that she was a woman—and that meant trouble.

She tried, in her own way, to be good. She never stole from the poor or the infirm or the very young or the old. But the world in which she lived didn't offer poor, unprotected women much hope of remaining good. Jobs were few and difficult to keep. As a waitress she would be constantly mauled and baited. Being a maid in a fancy house wasn't any better. As for sweatshop work, she'd rather be dead than shut up sixteen hours a day in a hot, noisy room without much light or air. No, the day she put up her hair and put down her hems, she'd have to deal daily with the likes of Charlie Lutz; and that was why she didn't fancy walking the streets.

Lost in thought, she entered the vestibule of the house where she rented a room.

"God love us! Where have you been? Tussling with the devil on Saturday night, were you?"

Fanny looked up to find Mrs. Mahoney, the landlady, blocking her path. No taller than Fanny but thin as the broomstick she clutched, Mrs. Mahoney exuded the nervous watchfulness of an alley cat. Not much escaped those feline blue eyes, least of all Fanny's comings and goings.

Those eyes were on Fanny now. "Well, Miss Fanny. It's time we had another little talk. Come into the parlor where I can have a proper word with you."

"I'm busy just now," Fanny replied and tried to edge past Mrs. Mahoney, but she blocked Fanny's path with her broomstick.

"It's the first of the month. Rent's due. Or are you thinking of leaving us?"

Reluctantly Fanny followed the woman into the tiny room just off the hall. It wasn't really a parlor but a single room that served as parlor, dining room, and kitchen.

Mrs. Mahoney propped her broom beside the door before turning to Fanny with folded arms. "You missed mass this morning. That's a mortal sin no young girl should be bearing. But, then again, maybe that's the least of your sinning this day. Just look at you!" and she pushed Fanny before the mirror hung above the fireplace. "You'd make a fine showing in the rogues' gallery at police headquarters."

Fanny allowed the barb to pass unchallenged. She glanced at the mirror, though she didn't need the reflection to tell her that she was rumpled and untidy. Her mouth tightened as she grudgingly tucked a limp strand of hair under her hat. She detested Mrs. Mahoney.

The landlady's mouth puckered in disapproval at Fanny's silence. "Where were you last night, if a body might ask?" Her tone implied that she had that right.

"I got lost," Fanny mumbled.

"Lost, is it? And what must your poor dead mother be suffering in purgatory—"

Fanny whipped about. "Don't you dare speak of my mother! Not ever, do you hear me! Not ever!"

Startled, Mrs. Mahoney took a step back. The girl had a temper, she knew, but it was so seldom on display that she had forgotten how daunting it could be. "Well, excuse me for living, I'm sure. Only, your Mister Phineas was beside himself when he arrived this morning and found you absent. I could no more than tell him the truth, that you never came home last night.''

Fanny's expression altered. ''Phineas was here?''

''Here and gone this past half hour.''

She saw Fanny's disappointment and knew that she'd found a vulnerable spot at last. ''You've been me tenant nearly four years, though I don't ordinarily approve of girls living alone. That's the devil's own work waiting to be done. If Mister Phineas weren't so punctual in paying your rent, I wouldn't have you here at all. Even so, I've got me reputation to think of now that you're coming of age.''

Fanny gave her a quick, calculating look. ''Is it the rent that you're about to raise again?''

Mrs. Mahoney bristled. ''I don't know but what I've been more than fair with you. Many a household wouldn't have taken you in. You don't work''—she paused to eye Fanny carefully again—''leastways not in any manner I've seen. As for the rent, I've often wondered why a man would keep a girl that's not his own kin. Just what is Mister Phineas to you? You've never said.''

''Didn't I?'' Fanny murmured vaguely, casting a look about. For years she had nimbly sidestepped Mrs. Mahoney's questions. It was a battle of wills she had yet to lose. She spied a pot bubbling on the stove and strolled over to it. ''That's onion stew! And me just fit to bust with hunger.''

''A body can't bust with hunger,'' Mrs. Mahoney reproved and took a spoon from Fanny as she was about to dip into the pot. "You're dirty as a mud lark. If it's a meal you want, you'd best go up and change."

Fanny shrugged. At least she knew now that Phineas had escaped their attacker. If he'd waited a little longer, he'd know that she wasn't in danger, either. As it was, he must think her still in trouble. Well, let him! He'd run away and left her. Let him worry himself to a frazzle.

"I don't suppose Phineas said when he'd be coming back," she remarked in a careless tone.

Mrs. Mahoney stopped stirring her stew, reminded of her indignation at Fanny's absence. "Half mad with fear, he was. Which is no surprise, considering. He near wore out your floorboards, pacing back and forth over my head. When he rushed out, his coattails were flapping. Barely had time to thrust this note into my hands." She pulled a folded piece of paper from her pocket and offered it.

Fanny snatched it. "Did you read it?"

"No business of mine," Mrs. Mahoney said indignantly. "Though how you expect to learn what it says if I don't read it to you, I'd like to know."

Fanny blushed berry red. "So what if I can't read? There's plenty besides you who can."

"You never said where you spent the night. I'll know the truth or be left to think the worst, and that means you must go."

For the second time blood rushed into Fanny's face. "If you must know, you old bat, Phineas and I went to the Wild West Show. Only we got separated."

"Where did you spend the night?"

Fanny smiled slyly. "With the Indians, of course. I

slept in one of them animal-hide tents with a big red savage who tried to scalp me!''

''Very well,'' Mrs. Mahoney said, affronted. ''If you won't tell me the truth, then you won't. Mister Phineas told me how you were lost at the fairgrounds, or you'd be out on the street in the blink of an eye.'' She paused to stare meaningly at Fanny's wrist. ''But he didn't say nothing about that.''

Mrs. Mahoney reached for Fanny's arm. ''Why, that's—that's silver, that is!''

''No, it ain't.'' Fanny snatched her arm back. ''It's only tin.'' She slipped the band off her arm and put it in her pocket. ''I won it. Tossing balls at milk bottles.''

''Tin, is it?'' Mrs. Mahoney could imagine several other ways the girl might have come by the bracelet. But Fanny's bedraggled appearance didn't coincide with her suspicions. What man would give the likes of Fanny Sweets something as precious as silver? Perhaps the bracelet was only a carnival trinket, after all. ''My final words to you: the next time you're absent the night, you'd best keep away for good. Do you hear me? Fanny!''

Escape uppermost in her mind, Fanny didn't reply. She was out the door and halfway up the stairway by the time Mrs. Mahoney's ''final words'' faded.

At the top of the rickety landing, she paused in the semidarkness, nearly overcome by the noxious odors of the basement water closets driven upward by the summer heat. But that wasn't why she mouthed a curse. Of all mornings to be caught by Mrs. Mahoney. Usually she was more careful.

Her fingers tightened on the note in her hand. Phineas knew she couldn't read. Why, then, had he left her a note? He might as easily have waited the full day to see if she would return. Why had he left in such a hurry? Had someone followed him here? The hair lifted on her neck as she climbed the next set of stairs. Who was after them? Was there more trouble brewing?

The moment she opened the door to her tiny attic room, she knew trouble had already found her. She marched straight past the patchwork bedding that had been tumbled from her cot and by her meager possessions that had been dumped from the orange crate that served as her chest. Her gaze was fastened on the loosened brick by the curtain to the right of the windowsill. Even as she pulled the brick from its place, she knew what she would find. She pulled the brick free with a sound that set her teeth on edge and then she plunged her hand into the breach and felt the emptiness she feared.

For a long moment she sat back on her heels, staring at the brick in her hand. Everything of value she owned had been tied in a gentleman's handkerchief and stuffed into that crack. Now it was gone. No one knew where she kept her savings. But Phineas had searched for them and taken them. Why, then, had he left her a note?

She glared down at the paper in her hand. She needed to know what he'd written, but she wouldn't give Mrs. Mahoney the satisfaction of asking for her help. She'd have to find someone else.

She rose slowly to her feet, aware only then that she was trembling. There was a strange, lightheaded sensation inside her, as if some part of her body had suddenly disappeared. Fury rushed in to fill the void even as she registered the first reaction. She'd been robbed! Phineas had robbed her!

Stuffing the note in her pocket, she turned and headed for the stairs.

Fanny dipped her fingers automatically into the holy water and made the sign of the cross as she entered St. Bartholomew's. The deep, dark cool of the nave enclosed her, turning the perspiration on her cheeks into chilly slicks. She genuflected, then slipped into a back pew and knelt, but prayers wouldn't form in her mind. Deep within her was an abiding anger against the invasion of her privacy. She'd been robbed. The rage settled like a dark, all-consuming blanket over her as she waited in the scented silence, where only flickering candles lit the interior.

Finally she saw a figure emerge from the sacristy, genuflect at the altar, and then turn to stroll down the main aisle. She rose and went to meet him halfway.

"Good afternoon, Father Moriarty."

The priest smiled. "Is that you, Fanny, underneath all that dirt?"

"Aye, Father," she answered, embarrassed that she'd forgotten to clean up. "I was in a bit of a hurry to see you, you see."

"Were you now? It must be a matter of great urgency that brings you unwashed into the Lord's presence. Is it, perhaps, that you've come to repent your absence from mass this morning?"

Fanny blushed. "Not exactly." She took the note from her pocket. "I need you to read this for me, Father."

The priest took the note and, after frowning over it a moment, walked toward the rear of the church with

Fanny following after him. Finally he paused in a stream of sunlight flowing in through a tracery window.

"It says, 'Never meant you harm. I'm leaving for good. You'll be safe now. Phineas.' The priest looked at her questioningly. "What does he mean, 'You'll be safe now'?"

More like he'll be safe from *me*, Fanny thought. She gave the priest a speculative glance. "Have you ever been robbed, Father?"

"Only of my good sense, a time or two," he replied with gentle laughter. "Why do you ask?"

"I've been robbed."

The priest laid a kindly hand on her shoulder. "It's a sad business, my child, but remember His riches are not of this world."

"No, but all mine were," she answered and repocketed the note. "Thank you, Father."

"Wait, child," the priest called as she started away. "You didn't say why Phineas should be concerned about your safety."

Fanny shrugged as she continued to back away. "Maybe he feared that I'd be robbed. It's a bad neighborhood. I must run along."

Fanny made her way through the boisterous sidewalk trade of Mulberry Street. Flushed with the high heat of summer, the residents of this notorious corner of the world had taken to the streets for relief.

Under awnings that offered little shade, overripe fruit of suspicious appearance lay side by side with barrels of unrecognizable wilted greens and burst tomatoes spewing seeds. At the curb, ash cans served as counters where women in bright head scarves haggled with their customers over the best price for loaves of stale bread. Every item for sale had been scavenged from the refuse of greengrocers and bakeries in the better neighborhoods.

Fanny held her breath in repugnance as she sped past a fishmonger's cart full of slimy, sunken-eyed fish that hadn't been in water in recent memory. In a nearby doorway long, ill-stuffed sausages hung above the entrance, to which a soiled white bow had been attached. Startled, Fanny took a step back. The white rag was the sign of measles within.

The Bend was known citywide as a malingerer's paradise, a disease-ridden fester with dozens of hidden alleys, where ragpickers and tramps lived toe by haunch with bandits and thugs. She'd only been here once before, and that was in Phineas's company. She wouldn't be here now if necessity hadn't prodded her to go in search of him. At first she'd been content to wait out Phineas's absence, feeling certain that he hadn't really left for good. Then Mrs. Mahoney had come that morning, pounding on her door for the third day in a row to demand the rent. The chilling realization that she would be out on the sidewalk by nightfall if her rent wasn't paid had pushed her to come in search of Phineas.

In preparation for her foray, she had borrowed from a neighbor a boy's coat and knickers, hidden her red-gold hair under a roomy cap, and rubbed dirt into her cheeks and brow to blend in with the denizens of the street. Still, she felt many a lingering eye on her as she passed by. She was a stranger and that alone made her suspect.

The time she and Phineas had come here, several men on the street had recognized him and called him by name. He wouldn't comment on the matter, but she had the distinct impression that the Bend was a familiar haunt of his. The right question put to the right person might reveal his whereabouts.

As Fanny scanned the crowd for a familiar face, she zeroed in, out of habit, on a likely "pigeon." He wasn't a resident of the street. He wore a fresh waistcoat and clean collar and cuffs. A long gold watch chain spanned the wide expanse of his belly. When she heard his lilting brogue, she recognized him for what he was.

Irish landlords were a common sight in this part of the city. She saw the bulge in his pants pocket and knew that he was collecting rents. Her fingers began to itch. It would be so easy. Nothing to it. A lark. Yet she didn't move. A slip in and out, she told herself. He'd never feel it. What was wrong? What held her back?

"Hey, *bambino*. You like a for to buy a pair of pretty stockings for you mama?"

Fanny jerked as a hand touched her elbow. An old woman with a red bandanna covering her graying hair gave her a toothless smile and lifted a pair of dirty stockings that had been mended in half a dozen places. Yet, as she held them out to Fanny, the woman's dark eyes cut quickly to the side in warning. Fanny followed her gaze. Standing nearby, their hands in their pants pockets, two young toughs in bowlers rocked back on their heels at the curb's edge.

Fanny felt the icy finger of danger touch her spine. The landlord's bullies were there to protect him and, if necessary, persuade a reluctant tenant to pay his rent. Her knees weakened. If she'd so much as taken a copper cent, she'd have been caught red-handed by that pair. She hadn't even thought to look around because . . . because she had always relied on Phineas to do that. They were a team. She never stole out of his sight and protection. Now she had nearly made a fatal error.

"You take pretty stockings?" the old woman pressed, dangling the items before Fanny's nose. "You're a clever boy, I can tella that. A clever boy shoulda always be kind to his elders."

Fanny shook her head briskly. "I've nae money."

The moment she spoke she regretted it. Her Irish brogue was as conspicuous on this street as Italian would be in the Bowery. When she glanced again at the toughs, she saw that they were staring intently at her. Though she looked away quickly, she had the impression that there was something vaguely familiar about the younger, slimmer of the pair. Small-eyed, with pushed-in features, he looked just like the tough who'd accosted her at the Wild West Show.

Fanny glanced at him again. Were they one and the same? She wasn't certain. As she began backing away, the younger of the two men still watched her, but nothing in his manner suggested that he considered her anything but a possible nuisance. As soon as the crowd closed in around her, she spun on her heel and ran pellmell down the street, her heart pumping as fast as her legs.

She heard the shout and knew it was meant for her. If she had merely sauntered away, they might have left her alone. One swift glance over her shoulder showed that the younger man was running after her. Fear for her life sent her careening into the first alley she came upon.

All at once she was in a different world, a twilight environment not much wider than the span of her arms. There were no windows in one of the walls forming the alley. The fire escapes from the windows of the other building nearly touched the opposite wall. What little light there was was filtered through laundry. Hanging from the iron gratings were damp rags of every size and description.

When she paused to catch her breath, she didn't hear footsteps behind her. Only the bravest or most desperate of souls would venture into an unfamiliar alley. Afraid to remain here, yet fearing to return the way she'd come, she groped her way farther along the gap in the dingy brick walls. Finally the alley widened. Here the stench of offal was mixed with the hot lathered aroma of soap suds. On the wooden steps leading from the rear of the tenement stood two young girls identically dressed in long skirts, aprons, and white bows at the neck. With dark eyes and black hair parted in the middle and pulled tightly back from their faces, they stood gravely with hands on hips, observing Fanny as she approached. At their feet stood two bags of rags which they had been washing.

Fanny smiled and wiped her brow with a hand. "Sure but it's a sweltering day, wouldn't you say, ladies?"

The older of the two, perhaps ten years old, scowled at Fanny but didn't speak.

Perhaps they didn't speak English, Fanny thought, or perhaps they didn't speak to strangers. Still, she needed help if it could be given. She lifted her arm to indicate the rest of the alley. "Would you know if there's a way out through there?"

The younger girl spoke to her companion, who hushed her with a hand. Then the older girl said with a thick accent, "Why you ask?"

"Well, there's a certain landlord I'd just as soon not

be walking into at the moment," Fanny replied with a wide smile of self-deprecation and indicated the way she'd come.

Fanny thought she saw the girl's eyes sparkle. "Rent day," she said.

"Aye. Ain't it always."

The girl nodded gravely and then pointed down the alley. "There is way out. Very small," and she brought her hands, palms flat, nearly together.

But enough, Fanny thought grimly as she threw the girls a cocky wave.

"Big enough" turned out to be a passage a mere twelve inches wide and twenty feet long. As she inched along with outspread arms, Fanny held her breath, thinking that she might panic and suffocate if she tried to inhale deeply and couldn't. No man could get through there, she told herself when she sagged against a lamp-post at the street's edge. She was safe for the moment.

Danger and trouble seemed to have become her constant companions these days. If Phineas was in the Bend, she wasn't likely to find him. If he wasn't, she would have to find her own method of paying the rent.

A shiver rippled through her despite the heat. She'd lost her nerve back there. Her sure touch was no good without a companion. Stealing enough to make the rent by nightfall seemed an impossibility. There was only one thing left to do—fence her last item.

She reached into her pocket and pulled out the broad silver band. In the sunlight the etching was vividly clear. She didn't understand the markings, but their beauty touched her as she ran a finger lightly over the motifs. She'd stolen it out of habit. Now, as she was about to give it up, she suddenly wondered why she hadn't taken the other wristbands.

The memory of the Indian's face, with its proud planes and broad angles, seemed to take shape in the gleam on the silver's surface. It was a face she wasn't likely ever to forget or see again. Her Indian—that was how she'd thought of him during the show. Her bracelet—she'd felt a strong affinity for the piece from the beginning. Now it was to be sacrificed. But the rent would come again. How would she pay it next time? Phineas had simply disappeared, just as her father had six years earlier.

Fanny pocketed the armband. "Fanny, my girl, there's going to be sad days ahead. Sad days."

"What do you mean, you'll be giving me only five dollars?" Fanny cried indignantly, and grabbed the armband out of Mother Tuck's hand. "It's worth ten times that!"

"Then get it from someone else."

Mother Tuck stared implacably at the young boy before her. He was nervous. A thin film of perspiration on his dirty face betrayed him. In spite of his cocky attitude, he'd likely stolen the item from a passerby, not really knowing its value. "Five dollars will fill your growler twenty times over, my boy. Think of that."

"I have," Fanny answered coldly. "I'll go elsewhere."

"I'm the best fence there is," the woman answered. "More cautious than most, more generous than some."

Fanny sniffed. "There's more than one 'family man' on the street."

"Maybe," Mother Tuck conceded with a shrug. "But none know the trade as I do, and none have the acquaintanceships I do. If a man's a professional, he's known to me.''

Fanny's eyes narrowed. ''Is that so? Then would you be knowing a man by the name of Phineas?''

The woman seemed not about to reply as she gripped the corners of the desk before her with big-knuckled hands. Finally she lifted her head. ''What of him?''

Fanny shrugged and pressed the toe of her heavy brogan against the desk, stalling her own answer for spite. ''I worked for him a time or two. Heard he left the city.''

''Where'd you hear that, child?''

The deceptive softening of Mother Tuck's voice alerted Fanny, and she stiffened, suddenly aware that the dark interior of the pawnshop might cloak the presence of unsuspected spectators. She waved the bracelet before the woman's nose. ''Will you be giving me twenty dollars or no?''

''Perhaps,'' she answered calmly. ''But not for that. For that I give five,'' and she dismissed the item with a wave of her hand. ''But for information''—her dark eyes were bright behind her white lashes—''for that, you might earn much more.''

Fanny forced herself to relax. ''I might be willing, the price being right.''

''That's more like it. Now, about this man Phineas. When did you last see him?''

Fanny smirked. ''I wasn't born yesterday. If you're willing to pay for word of Phineas, others might as well. Where's the money?''

Mother Tuck made an impatient sound and pulled three five-dollar bills from her pocket. ''This for the bracelet and a word about Phineas.''

"Saw him not a week ago, it was," Fanny answered. "He looked sort of queer, like he was scared."

"And?"

"And that's it. Now I'll be taking me money," and she reached down to snatch it from under the woman's hand.

"Here, now!" Mother Tuck rose from her feet. "Where's the bracelet?"

Fanny tossed her five dollars. "I've decided to keep it."

She was half surprised that no one tried to stop her as she left the pawnshop. But an occasional sharp look left or right as she walked home didn't reveal anyone following her.

The first inkling of impending danger Fanny had was a face. It loomed in her doorway, a faint pale oval in the night. It was an unthinking moment, a moment of total primitive instinct for survival. Even as she rolled from her cot onto the floor, the man launched himself at her, but he didn't have the advantage of familiarity with the room. He stubbed his toe on the corner of the half-opened door as she scrambled to her knees. As she darted past him, his hand fell on her shoulder, the nails digging sharply into her flesh. With a cry of fright she wrenched free and escaped through the doorway.

The steps creaked and snapped under her tread as she ran down them screaming, "Fire!" She screamed it again and again, for it was the one alert that would bring the tenement's sleeping residents to their doors.

The man was close on her heels, his tread heavier but no slower than her own. She flew, three steps at a time, down the black passage. Only at the bottom did she suddenly stop herself by grasping the rail cap and swinging herself about. The maneuver nearly tore her arm from its socket as she swung back under the stairwell where the garbage stood. A moment later the huffing, cursing man reached the ground floor and lurched out the doorway into the night.

Her heart roaring in her ears, Fanny waited as the tenants came howling down the stairway, hauling every belonging they could carry. Her cries of fire had been picked up and the house was suddenly swarming with frightened people. She heard Mrs. Mahoney's shouts drowning out the rest. In the pandemonium, Fanny slipped from the building, rounded the next stoop, and fled down the alley.

As she came to the end of the alley, she heard the trolley bell sound in the street ahead. Then, overhead came the rumble of the train. Calculating the distance, she raced out of the alleyway and up the wooden steps just as the train arrived in the station. She hung back until the last second, then thrust herself through the closing door.

As the train pulled out of the station, she thought she saw a shadow emerge from the alley, but perhaps it was a trick of light.

"Ticket, miss?"

Fanny started and then a big satisfied grin stole over her face. She pulled a crisp five-dollar bill from her pocket.

When the conductor had passed, she sank back onto her wooden seat and a sick, hollow feeling crept over her. Safe again. But for how long? Someone was after her. Someone wanted her. Who? Why? There were no answers. To find out the answers, she'd first have to be caught. No, she didn't want to know the answers, only to find safety.

CHAPTER
5

Matthew Morning Star adjusted the stiff wingtips of his starched collar as he stood at the rail waiting for the ferry from the city to dock at Staten Island. The unfamiliar itch of the cloth reminded him how long it had been since he had dressed as a gentleman. His long hair was even queued back with a thong, giving him the appearance from the front of a clipped head of hair. When he had joined the Wild West Show three months earlier, he had abandoned American dress in favor of the traditional garments of his people. Now, as perspiration gathered in the crevice between his neck and the collar, his appreciation of the practicality of native dress was renewed. Had he not had a bank appointment in the city that morning, he would be stripped to breechcloth and moccasins.

"Matthew!" came a shout from the shore as he gained the gangway.

Dressed in chaps and a well-lived-in hat, Lon Skerett

broke into a gap-toothed grin as Matthew came toward him. "That is you! Don't you look purty? Why, if I wasn't knowing you for an Indian, pure and simple, I might think you was one of them swarthy I-talian fellers just come over on the boat. Course, they ain't real Americans yet. Still, I figure looking new-fired American is better than not looking American a'tall."

Matthew fell into step with the man as they moved away from the dock. "Anyone ever tell you that you talk too much, Lon?"

"All the time," Lon answered congenially. "My dear mama, God rest her soul, used to say, 'Lon, you gonna use up all the words the good Lord give you afore you even figure out what they all mean.' Fooled her, though. I learnt a heap of new words as I grew. Figure I can talk a lifetime and still have a few words left over come Judgment Day."

"No doubt."

"So where's it you been?"

"To a bank."

"Bank? What's an Indian got to do with a bank?"

Amusement lit Matthew's gaze as he said solemnly, "Need wampum to buy many buffalo skins for new lodge."

"New tepee," Lon said incredulously. "Why, Buffalo Bill can supply you fellers with all the skins you need. Just go ask him. He— Hey! You're pulling my leg, ain't you?"

Matthew gave him a speculative glance. "You need one leg pulled to make it even with the other."

Lon laughed at the joke. One of his legs was shorter than the other, the result of a poorly healed injury suffered when a bronc fell on him years earlier. He walked with a limp, but the disability was of no consequence when he was in the saddle. A star rider and bronco buster, Lon knew he was any man's equal in the show.

He patted Matthew's shoulder. "Just you watch out for them city gals when you leave the fairgrounds. They ain't like your kind and mine. They take a liking to a feller, they forget everything their mamas ever told them about manners. Mind you watch your pocket as well. City gals got a pure love for the sound of a jingle in a man's pocket."

Matthew's expression lost its humor as he remembered his lost armband. "Your advice comes too late."

Lon moved his head up and down like the handle on a well pump. "That's cityfolk for you. If you're in the afternoon performance, you'd best hurry on over to the arena. They're rehearsing a new act and Buffalo Bill's got a burr under his saddle over it."

But Matthew was already moving away from the dock. The loss of his armband was still a sore spot.

Fanny nervously smoothed the bodice of her gown as she paced the interior of the Indian's tepee. The trip across by ferry had been uneventful. This time she'd even paid the fare.

She'd been in a panic the night before. But as dawn had climbed the eastern sky, she'd found new reserves of strength and resourcefulness coming to her aid. There'd been no fear in her when she broke into a tailor's shop and stole the dress in the window. She'd gone about the theft methodically, choosing a gown that was her size. The corset and stockings had been seized from one of many clotheslines that crisscrossed the alleys of her neighborhood.

The high-buttoned boots had been the most difficult item to obtain. She had waited until the vendors on Fourth Avenue set out their wares on the sidewalk, then snatched a likely looking pair. The risk of recognition had been great as she walked the familiar street, or so she thought until she saw her reflection in a shop window.

The corners of her mouth curved up as she recalled the moment when she'd spied the reflection of a slender young lady in a green-and-white striped serge gown. The tight-fitting bodice made her appear taller. The draped overskirt accentuated her hips. The top-knot she hurriedly arranged gave her elfin features a new maturity.

The hat perched at a saucy angle upon her head had come as a bonus. The wind had snatched it from some unfortunate young woman's head and sent it scudding around a corner just as Fanny reached the intersection. After quickly retracing her steps to avoid detection, she'd put it on. She looked every inch a lady. No one would recognize her as little Fanny Sweets.

The matter of where to hide was her next concern. She knew she mustn't return to Mrs. Mahoney's or even ask the help of anybody in the neighborhood. By now every sneak thief, stool pigeon, and petty crook would know that she was being hunted. There might even be a reward for news of her whereabouts. She needed to find a place where no one would think to look for her.

That's when the Wild West Show came to mind. What less likely place would anyone think to look for her than at the fairgrounds of this show? Now all that remained to be done was to persuade the show people to allow her to stay on the island for a few days, or until she could think of a better place to hide.

Not until she stepped off the ferry did she begin to doubt her strategy. She was hesitant to walk up to a stranger and ask for work. That's why she'd come here. The Indian whose home this was was the only person she knew on the island. He had been kind to her, in a gruff sort of way, allowing her to sleep in his tent. Yet perhaps she was counting on too much to think that he would help her a second time. He might not even recognize her, dressed as she was now. Even if he did, it didn't follow that he'd be willing to help her. He had looked dangerous in the moonlight. Who knew what sort of things he was capable of?

Back came the memory of his touch as he ran his hand up her leg, past the barrier of her garter, and stroked the sensitive skin of her thigh. A faint shiver tingled through her. She had heard the stories of Indian attacks where captured women were raped. The first time they had met, the Indian had thought she was a child. In her new clothes there was no mistaking that she was a grown woman.

She remembered Charlie Lutz and the way his gaze had crawled over her bosom and hips like some live thing. He'd seen through her childish clothing to the woman beneath. What if the Indian reacted like Charlie when he saw her? The very last thing she wanted was to fend off a lust-crazed Indian. She threw back the tent flap and stepped out.

Three cowboys who'd been passing by stopped in

their tracks at the sight of a young white woman emerging from an Indian tepee. Jeb, the oldest of the three, was the most shocked. He knew Morning Star as well as any of the men could say they did, and the very last thing he expected was to find a white woman sharing his lodge.

More likely sharing his robes, Jeb amended in his thoughts. He squinted to get a better look at the female. She was small—petite was the word that came readily to mind. But there was a thrust of young bosom and enough of a sway in her carriage to put a smile on his craggy face. She must be a prostitute. No other white woman would visit an Indian's tepee.

"Hey there, missy!" he called and waved a hand in her direction. If she was finished with Morning Star, he might as well try his luck.

Relieved to have found someone to speak to so quickly, Fanny walked over to the men and addressed the one who'd hailed her. "A good day to you, sir. Would you be knowing the whereabouts of Buffalo Bill Cody?"

The man, slim as a rail, broke into a grin that made rills and valleys of his sun-baked face. "Well, miss, I kin't say that I do. Howsomever, I'd be mighty happy to escort you over to the fairgrounds. It ain't safe for a purty young thing to be roaming around this far from civilization."

Fanny smiled. He'd called her a pretty young thing. "I thank you for your concern, but I can see to meself." She turned and started away but was brought up short by a hand grasping her elbow.

"Hold to, little lady," Jeb said as his grip tightened.

"What sort of business was it you had with that Indian, Morning Star?"

"Nothing that's any of your concern," Fanny snapped and jerked her elbow free. She didn't like the way he was smiling at her, after all. "Now if you don't mind..."

"But we do," chimed in another of the three men. He gave her a long look that made the hair lift on the back of her neck. Charlie Lutz in boots and Stetson, she thought fleetingly, and the thought intensified her annoyance. "How do we know you ain't one of them city gals come over to ply her trade?"

"I hear tell how some of them street women got a real itch to see a redskin up close," the third said with a snigger.

Fanny shot him a withering look. "You've a filthy mind, you have. Get out of my path!"

"Wait on," Jeb cautioned and took her by the arm a second time. "We kin settle this right now. Here comes Morning Star."

Fanny turned in the direction of the man's nod, but she didn't see anyone who looked like an Indian. Instead, she saw a tall gentleman in a city suit striding toward them. Yet the cowboy greeted the man with the words, "Morning, Morning Star. You're just in time to tell us all about the company you're keeping these days."

Fanny squinted at the man who walked up, but his features were hidden in the glare of the sun at his back. What she did see didn't look very Indianlike.

"What do you want?" Matthew's tone was wary.

Jeb winked and jerked his head in Fanny's direction. "We're just enjoying a friendly chat with your little *corazón*. You been holding out on us?"

"That's not him!" Fanny exclaimed as she tried to twist free.

"Just you simmer down, little lady," another of the men replied. "This here is Matthew Morning Star and this here is his tepee. Morning Star, do you know her or don't you?"

Matthew's gaze narrowed, but he didn't look at the woman.

"Ain't none of our business, o' course," Jeb said quickly as he saw the tension rising in the tall Indian. He'd seen Morning Star in a brawl with an Arapaho brave the week after he joined the cast and had earned a healthy respect for the Sioux's temper. "Only you know how Buffalo Bill is about such things. He hears you got a gal in your tepee and you're outa the show lickety-split."

This time Matthew gave the young woman a cursory glance. "I've never seen her before." In afterthought, he glanced at her again and the sight of the fiery red hair half hidden by her hat made him frown. He didn't recognize her, yet there was something familiar about that hair.

"Since you don't know her, you won't mind then if me and the boys keep her company a spell?" Jeb pressed.

"No." Matthew started past them, only to turn around, his black eyes glinting. "What were you doing near my lodge?"

"One of the yearlings got loose," the third man volunteered. "We was giving chase. That's when we saw this gal coming outa your tepee."

"Thought she might be a thief," Jed added, to give legitimacy to their meddling.

As the man's formidable gaze settled on her once

more, Fanny caught her breath sharply in recognition. It *was* Morning Star. The clothes and the queued back hair had fooled her for a moment, but the rich color of his skin and the jut of jaw from that square-angled face were unforgettable. Her stomach muscles contracted with the urge to run away, but she didn't move. She could see that he didn't recognize her. Best bluff her way through.

Yet, at that very moment, Matthew was feeling the tantalizing sensation of knowing something just beyond reason's grasp. The feeling intensified as he stared at her. Suddenly he thought he understood the familiarity. He'd been robbed once this summer by a white girl with red hair. Of course the thief had been a child, not an enticingly shaped young woman like the one before him. Reluctantly, he looked away. Why torture himself with temptation?

He turned to Jeb. "I don't know her. If you think she's a thief, turn her over to the authorities." He turned and walked toward his lodge.

Think fast, Fanny, me girl, she told herself. She hadn't taken anything this time, but that didn't mean she wouldn't be handed over to the police for trespassing. If that occurred, the police would find the silver armband in her pocket and that would mean jail for certain. No one would believe that she had considered returning it to its owner in hopes of gaining his help.

Sweat rose to glaze her skin at the thought of jail. Before she'd spent a full night in jail, whoever was looking for her would know she was there. The thieves' network was fast and all-knowing. There'd be no escape. She had to stop them from calling in the authorities.

"You can't think I'd come all this way to be stealing

anything?'' she began, only to see doubt reflected in their expressions. ''Now I ask you, what's an Indian got that I'd be after? I came to find work.''

''Work's easily come by in the city,'' Jeb said, for he was beginning to wonder what she was up to. If she wasn't Morning Star's fancy piece, who was she?

She gave him her most ingenuous smile. ''I was hoping to work here so I could see the show every day for free.''

''This ain't a circus, little gal. We don't take on just anybody. You got to be genuine western folk to work the Wild West Show.''

''I'm a genuine westerner,'' Fanny answered promptly, too accustomed to lying to see the outlandishness of the boast.

''Do tell,'' the second cowboy answered. ''Whereabouts in the West are you from?''

''Western Ireland, most like,'' the third cowboy offered with his characteristic snigger.

''A body can be born in one place and have lived in another,'' Fanny answered in a reproving tone. Because she had heard of only one city referred to as being in the Midwest and figured that the middle of the West was the best place to be from, she added, ''I lived a time in Chicago.''

To her surprise laughter answered the assertion.

''Chicago? Lordy, but ain't that a good 'un!''

''Being from Chicago's like being from this here New York City,'' Jeb said between snorts of laughter. ''Ain't a single genuine cowboy ever growed his spurs in a city.''

''Well, not Chicago, exactly,'' Fanny temporized. ''Near abouts Chicago, in the western part.'' By adopting the cowboy's jargon she hoped to recoup a little of her credibility. Westerners were harder to fool than city people, she decided.

Jeb gave her a considering look and then a slow smile spread his mouth. "Could be we could use another wrangler. You ride?" At Fanny's blank look, he added, "A horse. Kin you ride a horse?"

"Certainly," she answered, but a sudden memory of the Wild West Show and the hundreds of pounds of iron-shod, snorting, lathered horseflesh at full gallop made her heart begin to pound apprehensively.

"And shoot. Kin you shoot like Annie Oakley?"

Alert to a trap this time, Fanny shook her head. That name was familiar from her visit to the show. "Nobody can shoot like Miss Oakley," she answered.

"Got you there, Jeb."

Jeb wagged his head. "Now, you boys just hold your fire. If the little missy here wants a job, I say we try her out. Any you boys seen what they done with Twister?" His eyes pleated at the corners like drawn venetian blinds. "He's a mean cuss, but you, being a Chicago gal and all, kin tame him, kin't you?"

She wasn't afraid of much, but Fanny had an inkling that anything with the name of Twister, be it man or beast, wasn't going to be easily tamed. But at least agreeing to try would take their minds off other things, like calling the police. She lifted her chin. "Sur'n' I can!"

"I'll saddle him!" one of Jeb's companions offered and ran off ahead of them.

Matthew poked his head out his tepee just in time to see the young woman walking off in the direction of the corrals with the cowboys. He'd found nothing missing, but some indefinable feeling disturbed him as he watched the sunlight play on her extraordinary hair. Women of his culture didn't have hair like hers. Theirs was the dark brown of the beaver, or the midnight blue-black of a winter's evening, or the rarer russet umber of the great brown bear. None of them had hair like hers, hair that rivaled the pelt of the wily red fox.

The longer he stared, the more fascinated he became. When the group disappeared into the crowd near the corrals, he was left feeling a little foolish but unsatisfied. Who was she?

Sighing, he ducked back inside his lodge and began undressing. He'd nearly forgotten Lon's advice that he attend the afternoon practice. If he didn't hurry, he'd miss it.

When he had stripped off the starched shirt, he stopped to scratch his chest. He'd as soon strap a cactus on his back as put on another collar and tie. The hard leather shoes, trousers, and stockings followed the shirt into a pile on the lodge floor. Within two minutes he had donned a breechcloth and slipped his feet into the smooth, soft comfort of moccasins. The feel of the air on his skin pleased him. He rubbed his stomach, enjoying the texture of flat, hard muscle there. He had grown a little soft in the easterners' cities, but riding and running in the show had brought back his natural tough leanness.

He loosened the tie from his hair and shook his head. This was the greatest measure of his freedom from American education. As a student he'd been regularly shorn. But at the beginning of his final semester, he had begun letting his hair grow. He'd hidden the suspicious length in his collar until finals were complete. He would never forget the deans' look of astonishment as he strolled up the aisle to receive his diploma. His hair was free, flowing over his shoulders. He had even tied his personal hair ornament into his scalp lock. How proudly he had flaunted what ten years of the white man's education could not subdue. He was Matthew Morning Star, Harvard graduate—and Sioux warrior.

By the time Fanny reached the corral with her escorts, she felt a little more sure of herself. If she went along with the men, they might offer her work. A moment later she heard cheering at a nearby corral and looked over just in time to see a cowboy do a full somersault over the head of a horse and land in the dust.

"You wait right here while Carl saddles up old Twister." Jeb's grin deepened as he saw her face pale. She was scared, just as he hoped she'd be. It was only a jest, of course, but he wondered how far she'd take it. "Yes, sir, anybody can see that you're gonna do just fine."

Fanny smiled thinly. She had nothing much to fear, she told herself. They certainly wouldn't expect her to ride a horse like the one that had thrown its rider. Besides, she had sat astride a horse before. The animal belonged to Alfredo, the ash-can man. Occasionally he allowed the neighborhood children to ride the mare that pulled his cart. Sitting on her was like balancing on a broad tree limb swaying in a breeze. With a bit of practice, she might ride well enough to be hired for the show.

Her new confidence scattered when she saw the horse two men led into the corral. The animal was huge, bigger than any she'd ever seen. He was black as pitch.

Heavy muscles bulged and strained and trembled against the restraints holding him in check. A thick length of rope was wound about his neck and a second was threaded through the harness about his head, yet he seemed in charge of the two men holding him. Each time he moved forward, he dragged them with him. His neck was arched in rebellion against the ropes, and he lifted his head repeatedly, jerking the men nearly off their feet each time. His small eyes rolled in their sockets, flashes of white showing each time he reared. She'd heard tell of the "puca" in her native Ireland, of the demon which often took the form of a horse. Once he'd enticed a man or woman onto his back, he'd run away with his rider, and they'd never be heard from again.

"Whatever would you be wanting me to do with that great beast?" Fanny asked in dry-mouthed awe.

"Why, ride the ornery critter," Jeb answered. "Iffin you ride Twister, then there'll be no doubt you're a genuine westerner and deserving of a place in the show."

"And if I don't ride him?" she questioned faintly.

"Well, then, I figure you're gonna have to leave the island."

Fanny gave him a pleading look. "Couldn't I just stay on and watch for a few days?"

Jeb shook his head, almost regretfully it seemed to Fanny, but his words belied mercy. "You were found trespassing. Don't think that'd set well with the show folk. No, we might needs be calling the law."

Fanny blanched. Better she were dead, trampled beneath the iron hooves of this hellbound puca called Twister, than be sent back to the city to face unknown enemies. She hoped she wouldn't break too many bones. Pain and suffering didn't appeal to her in the least.

She gave a long sigh and nodded her head. "So then, I'll ride him and make an end to it."

Jeb didn't really believe her and made no move to stop her as she stepped over a lowered rung of the corral. It was only when she walked straight toward Twister that he was shocked into action.

"Hey, wait!" he cried and started across the barrier. Immediately his path was blocked by one of the cowboys sitting on the railing.

"Best not do that," the man said. "It'll spook Twister for sure. Call to her. Git her outa there pronto!"

The two men anchoring the horse shouted warnings at Fanny, but she didn't seem to hear them. She was staring up at Twister, a fixed look of determination on her face.

He's half again the size of Alfredo's cart horse, she thought, but he can be ridden, the cowboys say so. Perhaps it's just a matter of getting on, and then things get easier. Yet how am I to get that long way up onto his back?

As Twister reared before her, she had no inkling of danger, so fascinated was she by the sheer size and power of him. The deep-voiced shouts of the cowboys barely penetrated her thoughts as she reached out a tentative hand toward him.

"There now, macushla," she crooned softly as she switched instinctively to the soft, lilting Irish tongue. "What a great fine beast ye are. That impressed I am of ye."

At the sound of her voice, the horse ceased rearing but continued to paw the earth.

"Sure 'n' ye and I are going to be fine friends," she continued, growing bold enough to take a half step closer. "I know ye, ye see, for what ye are. Ye're what me da called a 'member of the gentry' and so must be addressed with proper respect."

The horse stopped pawing the earth, and its ears pricked forward as if it were curious to hear her words.

"If ye take a liking to me, I know ye'll nae harm me." She took another step and leaned forward to whisper, "I need a ride upon yer back, sir. For ye see, 'tis all that stands between me and the law!"

The sudden quiet of the corral made no impression on her as she focused on how to prove herself to the cowboys. She didn't dare look about. The horse was watching her, his red-rimmed dark eyes bulging slightly. How to get astride? Only then did she remember that she wore a gown with a bustle, which made it impossible for her to sit astride. Disconcerted by the realization, she turned back to explain her predicament to the men.

Everything happened at once. She heard shouts from the cowboys leaping from their perches on the corral fence, heard the horse's snort, his handlers' cries, and then she was suddenly shoved forward by a painful kick that caught her squarely between the shoulder blades. Pain radiated through her back like a knife blade, and then the breath was knocked out of her in a quick, painful gush when she hit the dirt. Tears filled her eyes, blinding her. Dirt clogged her mouth, gagging her as she gasped for air. She heard the cries urging her to her feet, but pain held her pinned to the ground as Twister's hooves repeatedly struck the dirt only inches from her face.

Matthew reached her first. He'd been passing the corral on his way to practice when he'd been brought up short by the sight of the redheaded woman talking to the most dangerous animal in the show. Few of the experienced riders dared climb on his back, and then only occasionally. But she'd stood there speaking in a foreign tongue, and what she said seemed to have the power of magic. Like a fox she was, charming the animal into quiet fascination. Why, then, had she released the animal from her spell and turned her back?

Like a demon from a nightmare, Twister had come alive and reared up. Matthew had added his shouts to the rest, but it was too late. Even as he cleared the corral railing, the woman had gone down under the animal's deadly hooves.

He bent and scooped her up from the dirt as the other men went to add their weight to the ropes holding Twister. In ten quick strides he reached the edge of the corral and climbed over. He couldn't tell how badly she was hurt, but he carried her to a shady spot before gently lowering her into the grass to examine her.

A trickle of blood coursed from one corner of her mouth and ran down over her dirty lips as she struggled for breath. He raised her, holding her upright as she gasped in air. He noted that a nasty scratch on one cheek was quickly darkening into an ugly purple shade. Finally her breathing eased and she leaned back weakly between his naked thighs. Her eyes were open, great sky-blue eyes, staring at him. For an instant he wondered if she was dying.

"Do I get the job?" she whispered so weakly he didn't understand her.

"Did you ever see the like!" Jeb cried as he reached Matthew's side. "That gal all right? *Shoo-ee*, I ain't never seen nothing like it!"

Matthew looked up at him in anger. "Are you the fool who put her up to that?"

Jeb took a step back. "Now, it weren't like that. She allowed as how she could ride, so me and the fellers figured to have some fun with her. Never thought she'd do a blame fool thing like get in the corral with Twister."

"Did you think that maybe she wouldn't know any better?"

Jeb reddened like a beet. "No, I didn't, now that you ask. Even city gals got some sense, ain't they?"

"She dead?" asked another of the cowboys who came rushing up.

"Course she ain't. Eyes open," Jeb said.

"Never seen the like!" cried another of the men.

"Purt near the damnedest thing I ever seen!" said yet another.

The once-empty grass had filled quickly as people came running from all directions, lured by the shouts and the sight of an injured woman. Cries of "What's happened, what's happened?" filled the air, to be answered by cries for quiet and hurriedly mumbled explanations.

Though she was nearly blinded by pain, Fanny was dimly aware that what she'd done had made her the center of attention. With one eye ever open to opportunity, she knew that she should capitalize on that fact, but she hurt too much to think how it might be accomplished. Except for the place where her shoulders met the firm support of a warm naked thigh, there wasn't a spot on her body where she didn't ache. "Water," she croaked.

"The gal needs a drink!" Jeb shouted toward the corral. "Bring the gal some whiskey!"

"No." Before anyone could object, Matthew scooped the woman up into his arms and turned to carry her off.

Racked with pain, Fanny gritted her teeth and buried her face into his hard-muscled chest. A moment later the dark relief of unconsciousness claimed her.

"Say, where you taking her?" Jeb called after him, but Matthew didn't answer.

He crossed into the nearby woods in strides smoothed to allow for the girl's bruises. He didn't look down into the face half hidden by red-gold strands of hair until he reached his lodge. She looked so small, so helpless. He had responded to that vulnerability without thought or consideration of the consequences. But now the consequences were pressing in on him. He had more than likely saved her life by snatching her out from under Twister's iron hooves. According to Sioux custom, she was now his responsibility until she was well. Judging by the sight of her, that would be some time. He couldn't be certain what Buffalo Bill would say when he learned what had occurred, but it was too late to change his mind. He only hoped he wouldn't regret his actions.

"It smells like horse manure!" Fanny objected as the Indian spread a dark, foul-smelling paste over her raw knees.

"It *is* horse manure," he answered grimly.

Despite her squawk of protest, he continued applying the liniment. "Be still, paleface. You have great courage in the face of devil horse. You need little courage to face evil smell.''

As was his habit when addressing visitors to the show, Matthew had resorted to his ''Indian'' stage voice. It set him apart. Right now he needed very much to remain aloof from the woman he treated. Otherwise he might do her greater harm. He regretted helping her, but it was too late. He was bound by his code to complete the task he had begun.

''Stop that!'' Fanny demanded when he started to lift the blanket covering her thighs. ''You've no right to touch me there!'' She bolted upright, only to gasp for breath as a sharp stabbing pain cut down between her shoulder blades.

Matthew caught her by the shoulders and carefully but firmly pressed her back down into the blanket. ''Paleface plenty stubborn. Maybe pain make her quiet.''

Behind the flow of tears, Fanny saw the fierce anger in his dark face, and her protest died, caught in the grip of another sharp pain. ''Breathe!'' she heard him order sharply as she continued to hold her breath against the pain. ''Breathe or you will faint again.''

She moaned, the fight gone out of her, and closed her eyes. She felt him rearranging the blanket covering her, but she hurt too much to care. Every muscle cried in reaction to her rash decision to sit up. She lay very still this time as his hard, warm hands began to gently apply the noxious mixture to her skin. In the instant before pain blurred her vision, she'd seen her bloody knees, and now the burning sensation of her scrapes was adding fire to the agony of her aching muscles.

When he moved from her legs to her arms, she peered at him through her lashes. He had exchanged his suit for that scandalously brief width of suede, the lush texture of which she felt against her skin as he lifted her arm into his lap to salve her scraped palm. Straight, shiny blue-black hair flowed across his shoulder and along his arm as he moved. It hadn't occurred to her that a man's hair might grow as long as a woman's. Or was it only Indian men whose hair grew so long? She wanted to ask but felt foolish in doing so. Besides, even speech made her ache.

As he leaned near to peer at the scrape on her cheek, his hair brushed her face and the heady aroma of pine needles teased her nostrils. His hair was scented! Yet, unlike the fragrance of violets or roses that a lady would wear, he smelled of wood and green forest and musky but not unpleasant odors.

"Paleface feel better?" Matthew questioned when he glanced up briefly and saw that she was watching him.

"Why are you doing this?" she asked between stiff lips.

"Do what?"

"Keeping me here?"

He didn't look up again. "You have many questions for one badly trampled. We talk later. Turn over."

"What are you going to do?" she asked nervously as he tried gently to urge her over.

"You have big bruise on back. Need much ointment."

She blushed and it made the abrasion on her cheek sting. "I gave you free handling of my arms and legs, but if you think I'll be allowing you to touch me—well, I ain't some fancy lady."

"No," he replied in a neutral voice. "You not fancy. You look plenty bad. No man like bruised face."

Her blush deepened. "I don't give a fig for what you think."

"Because I am not white man but Dakota?" he asked softly, but his expression had become even more forbidding.

"Because ... because you're a bully and a scalawag!" she answered, then moaned from the pain of the effort.

His black brows rose, but he kept his eyes averted. "What is scalawag?"

"A book-learnt spalpeen," she muttered.

"That's enlightening," he murmured. "Turn over."

She locked her fingers together on top of the blanket covering her. "Not if you were Saint Patrick himself doing the asking!"

"I already see everything," he said flatly, adding a nod of confirmation at her surprised start.

She slipped a hand beneath the blanket and found only her own soft skin. "You took my clothes. Och, but you're a horrid man!"

He sat back. "Palefaces all alike. Think the body is shameful. If that is so, why do we come into the world without a strip of cloth? Does the bird fashion clothes for itself? Does the wolf hunt only in the dark of night out of shame? You have woman's body. I have man's. Some difference. No shame, only stupidity."

Unimpressed, she said, "Give me back my clothes this instant."

"Clothes wet."

"Wet? Why?"

"They dirty. Need washing."

"You washed my clothes?"

He shrugged. "You even bleed on me."

Sure enough, bloody streaks marked the red-brown skin of his chest where she had rested her head. "I didn't ask you to carry me," she mumbled in faint embarrassment.

His scowl deepened. "I saved your life."

"I didn't ask you to."

"You right. Now I am sorry." He rose to his feet in one fluid movement and turned away. She looked very small wrapped up in his blanket, small and vulnerable and helpless. Yet he now knew that she was not what she seemed. He had found out the truth while undressing her.

She was the thief who had stolen his silver armband. She had been dressed like a young girl, but he should have recognized her. There were few women with hair the color of hers, even in a great city like this. And this was not the only time she'd been in his lodge. Though the night had hidden the features of the girl who'd spent the night with him, he'd heard her voice. The lilt was unmistakably the same. She must have relished his gullibility in offering her shelter for the night. Perhaps she had come to steal the remaining armbands. No, she had left them untouched when she disappeared the next morning. She had come to ridicule him, to count coup on him!

Anger and chagrin vied for control of his emotions as realization after realization came to him. The knowledge cut like a knife at his pride. He felt the desire to strangle her as she lay helplessly on the floor of his lodge. She had unmanned him and he wanted revenge.

Suddenly he turned back to her, looking her fully in the face for the first time. "I should not have interfered with the design of *Wakan Tanka*." He held out his wrist with the armband. "Maybe Twister sent to punish wicked thief!"

Fanny gasped. What could she say? "I came to give it back. That's why I was here. Honest."

His impassive gaze seemed like a physical weight on her, but he said nothing.

"What—what are you going to do?"

He was bound by Dakota law to care for her, but the anger in him rebelled at the thought. He was caught in a snare by a crazy woman, a *witkowin*.

"*Witkowin!*" he hissed at her and then, mouthing a spate of Dakota curses, he swung away and left his lodge.

CHAPTER
6

William Frederick Cody disliked spectacles, unless he himself created them. The news that had brought him to the Sioux village was of the most serious order. There had been an incident at the corral, a spectacle, if in fact he'd been told the truth, and it bordered on scandal.

The sight of the colorful camp usually engendered a sense of proprietary pride in him, but that feeling was absent this day as he entered the settlement of painted tepees. The dogs that dashed up to dance about his heels with joyous yips reminded him unpleasantly of reporters. How *they'd* yip and nip at his heels if word leaked out before he had a chance to squelch it. Scandal would envelop the show like a wildfire whipped up by prairie winds. The high-pitched squeals and laughter of the village children echoed in his head with the unsettling resonance of war whoops. One mention of a white woman carried off by an Indian brave, and those press

95

boys would be yelling for his blood, climbing over one another in order to claim his scalp as a trophy.

Absently, he brushed a long lock of his golden brown hair back from his face. He'd held on to his head of hair through many a campaign, and no citified, gouty, desk-bound greenhorn of a snoop was going to lift it in print.

He paused before Red Shirt's tent to adjust his beaded and fringed gauntlets. Ever a showman, even among his own retinue, he watched from the corner of his eye as the villagers gathered in interest. They knew he seldom came to their village. When he did, there was always something of great importance on his mind.

He purposely cut a dashing figure among the Indians. He wore his hat cocked at a jaunty angle, and his spotless buckskins were fringed, beaded, and quilled with workmanship worthy of a great chief. He had a soldier's bearing and an actor's easy flair for the dramatic. The Sioux especially appreciated dignity and were never impressed by a white man unless he was accompanied by the proper ceremony and dress.

When he was ready, Cody turned to the woman stirring the stew pot on the tripod before the chief's tent and said, "Tell Chief Red Shirt that I, Buffalo Bill, would speak with him on a matter of great importance."

The woman didn't answer him but stopped stirring immediately, lifted the tepee flap, and went inside. He smiled. A typical easterner would think she'd been rude, while he knew her actions were appropriate. The Sioux were a complex people but easy to get along with if one took time to learn their ways. For instance, he knew that they expressed respect by not looking directly at a person and that women were never permitted to speak to strangers. Because she hadn't ignored him, she would do as he asked.

A few moments later the flap was thrown open and Red Shirt appeared, dressed in a fine blue shirt with silver buckles, a vest, and a choker of dentalium shells. Even his scalp lock was dressed in feathers and beads.

"Buffalo Bill, I am honored yet surprised that you are here to visit me," Red Shirt greeted.

"It is always a pleasure to visit an old friend," Cody returned formally, but his mind was fast at work. The young chief was certainly aware of his exalted position among his people, for he didn't offer the handshake that would have been forthcoming had they met in the white section of the camp. "It grieves me that this visit cannot be one of renewing old bonds and sharing the peace pipe. Sadly, I am here to discuss a serious matter that involves one of your people."

Red Shirt nodded. Though he had no idea of the source of the trouble, he knew that it must be serious to bring *Pahaska* to their camp without warning. He indicated his tepee. "We will speak inside."

Once seated on the packed-earth floor of the interior, Cody spoke straight to the heart of the matter. "A serious accusation has been brought against one of your braves, Chief Red Shirt. Matthew Morning Star is said to have abducted a young white female from the corral this morning."

Red Shirt's usually impassive face registered amazement. "Matthew? Stole a white woman? I do not believe it."

"Jeb and Carl say otherwise." Cody paused to lift his hat from his head, for the tepee was warm though the dew cloths had been lifted to provide a breeze. "They say he carried her away after she suffered an accident at one of the corrals. I'm not convinced I got the full story from them. What do you know of this? Did Morning Star perhaps bring the woman to your medicine man?''

"I know nothing of any woman," Red Shirt replied, his expression no longer giving away his turbulent thoughts. "I have not seen Matthew since last evening's performance. He was to go into the city this morning."

"He's returned," Cody confirmed, "and carried off the woman. There're witnesses."

This time Red Shirt didn't speak his disbelief aloud. For *Pahaska* to have come to him, there must be some truth to the matter. But it didn't follow that Matthew had abducted a woman. Some other young brave, perhaps. He'd had his hands full with some of his warriors who missed home, their own stew pots, and their wives. To have one's woman as part of the show was a privilege reserved for the elders and the chiefs. But Matthew wasn't a rash young warrior. He'd lived long in the white man's world and knew the dangers of yielding to the temptation of a white woman.

Cody decided not to press the young chief for a reply because he'd been as surprised as Red Shirt was now when he'd heard the news. It was bad enough that his cowboys occasionally strayed into bad company. Street women found lonely cowboys, far from home and hearth, an easy target. But Morning Star, above all, should know better. He was an educated man, had lived among civilized people half his life, knew society's taboos. What he'd done was unpardonable—if he had done it.

Red Shirt looked across at the older brown-haired man and said quietly, "I do not believe Matthew Morning Star would dishonor himself in the manner you suggest. If there is a white woman with him, might she not be a friend? He has lived long among your people. Might not the woman be known to him?''

The idea gave Cody such a pleasant start that his grin bristled every hair in his goatee. ''Now, why didn't I think of that?'' The joy evaporated as quickly as it rose. ''Still, that doesn't make what he did proper. He shouldn't have run off with her. How's it look? Bad, that's how!''

He rose to his feet with a vigorous grace only slightly hampered by the generous consumption of alcohol that had been his favorite daily indulgence these last months. ''I'm going over to Morning Star's lodge to get answers myself.''

Red Shirt had risen also but was reluctant to allow *Pahaska* to confront his friend without warning. ''I will send for Matthew. It is proper that he should come to us.''

But Cody shook his head. ''I'm willing to meet a man fairly, but I mean to talk to that little gal myself. I'm a man of honor and won't allow shenanigans behind my back. We're a family show. A man must feel he can bring his wife and the young ones to the fairgrounds and not be exposing them to unwholesome goings-on.''

''Then, as leader of my people, I will go with you.''

Cody nodded. ''Lead the way, Chief.''

Matthew didn't rise from his cross-legged position before his lodge until Buffalo Bill and Red Shirt had crossed the open ground between the trees and himself. He'd known someone would come and so had added a leather shirt and leggings to his attire, for he knew white men didn't approve of nakedness. He'd been reading, the book braced in his lap. Now he closed the volume, inserting a finger to mark his place, and stood up. "Buffalo Bill. Chief Red Shirt," he greeted quietly.

"Morning Star," Red Shirt began without preamble, "*Pahaska* would speak to you of a matter of great urgency."

Matthew's dark gaze moved to meet the light brown eyes watching him levelly. "You have come for the white woman. She is here," and he indicated his tepee.

"You mean there is a white woman in your lodge?" Cody questioned in amazement.

Matthew nodded. "She was injured when Jeb and his friends played a trick on her. I brought her here to tend her injuries."

"Trick?" Cody echoed. "Nobody said anything to me about a trick."

"Some of the cowboys saddled Twister," Matthew said. "Jeb thought it would be a good joke on the woman to dare her to ride him."

Cody's mouth fell open. Even he refused to climb on the back of that heaving, plunging bundle of spit and devilment. "I don't believe it."

Matthew regarded him steadily. "The woman is brave but not wise. She entered the corral and bewitched the horse. But her charm was not strong enough. When Twister bolted and kicked her, they became cowards. I plucked her out from under Twister's hooves and brought her here."

Cody admired the way the tall young Sioux held his seasoned gaze. The Indian had learned much about the white man's ways. But he'd dealt with too many malingering soldiers and wily scouts to believe every straight stare. "Allowing that what you say is true, why wasn't I told? It's my responsibility to see to the proper care of any injured spectator.''

Matthew again indicated his lodge. ''Take her. I am sorry I interfered.''

The flat tone surprised Cody. This was not the manner of a lusty young buck. Obviously Morning Star had done no more than what he claimed. ''I'm not saying you shouldn't have stepped in, son. I'm saying I should've been notified. I'm sure you did your best.''

Matthew shrugged, neither in agreement nor denial.

''I suppose we should go in,'' Cody said with an appealing look at Red Shirt, but the young chief was simply staring at the ground. ''Well, um, I'll look in,'' he said in a more forceful tone than was necessary.

When Matthew stepped aside, Cody reached for the flap and slowly lifted it.

The sound of voices had awakened Fanny. Frantic, she had glanced about for a garment with which to cover herself and found one of the Indian's American shirts hanging on a peg not far away. Every muscle had ached in protest as she had levered herself upright to reach for it. Her face was slick with sweat and her complexion bleached by pain by the time she had struggled into it. She had only just pulled the blanket back up to her chin when the flap was lifted.

It was her deathly pale young face that Cody saw first. For an instant he thought she must be dying. Then he saw her mouth lift in a lovely smile. ''Buffalo Bill!'' he heard her exclaim softly in delight.

He swept his hat from his head. ''The very same, ma'am. I heard about your misfortune and have come to see how I might be of service to you.''

Fanny stared at him, awed by the fact that she was

looking at a man whose face was plastered on billboards and fences throughout the whole of New York. From his pointed beard to the golden-brown halo of shoulder-length hair, he seemed larger than life and twice as real. It must be something about the West, she decided, that made men's hair grow long. "I saw you scalp an Indian," she said at last.

"In the show? Well, yes, I do a bit of scalping, but only for fun." Cody blushed to the roots of his hair. "It's not real, you know. My Indians are the friendly sort." He glanced uncomfortably at the robes covering her, wondering how badly she was hurt and if she'd cause trouble over the fact. "What exactly happened, ma'am?"

Fanny's gaze shifted to Matthew as he ducked into the lodge. His dark face was inscrutable as ever, but she sensed a tenseness in him that had been absent before. Her elation plummeted. Had he brought Buffalo Bill to have her arrested for stealing his armband? Were the police waiting outside? Why didn't he say anything? "I was kicked by a horse," she said softly, her gaze never leaving Matthew.

"Yes, ma'am, I heard that, and sorry I am that it happened. A few of the boys are high on to mischief now and again. I try to keep them corraled most times, but high spirits go with high courage, ma'am, and I fear they didn't stop to think of the consequences."

"They nearly killed her," Matthew offered flatly from behind Cody.

Cody frowned but didn't turn around. "Now, ma'am, I have to ask you if there's anything else you wish to complain about." He bent over her. "You can be frank, I assure you. You're safe from all further harm."

All at once Fanny understood. It wasn't she who stood accused of misconduct but Morning Star. Whenever she was in trouble, she adopted the same stubborn stance he maintained now. "What exactly is it you're asking me, Mr. Cody?"

Cody straightened. "Have you been taken advantage of? That's what I'm asking. Don't be afraid to say so. If you've been offered any sort of insult, the law will be called in and justice will be done."

The mention of the law would have decided her course of action even if she'd been furious with the Indian. Nothing frightened her more than the police. Besides, it was the code of the street that not even an enemy deserved to be handed over to the coppers.

She looked over Cody's shoulder at Matthew. "Do me harm? Musha, this man saved me life, he did! Snatched me right out from under the iron hooves of that great roaring beast. Else I'd have been murdered to death in front of the crowd!"

Cody shuddered inside. A death, a spectator's death? He'd be ruined.

"You won't be blaming him for what the others done?"

Cody shook his head. "No, I believe we both owe Morning Star a debt of gratitude for looking out for you. There's just one other question, ma'am." He had an ace in the hole. No self-respecting westerner was ever without one. "Some of the boys say you claim to know Morning Star, that you came to the island today expressly to see him."

This time Fanny didn't look at Matthew. So far he hadn't betrayed her as a thief, but that didn't mean he wouldn't. "I—I did come looking for him, after a fashion. Only I didn't know his name, you see. Me uncle brought me to the show last week. And grand it was, Mr. Cody. I never saw the like! Every since, I've wanted to come back. I'm willing to work hard. I'll earn me keep and then some, only, please, let me stay with the show.''

This sudden change of topic took Cody by surprise. ''You mean you came here looking for work?''

''Aye, I did. The cowboys said if I rode that rare beast of a devil horse they'd find me work.'' She paused, all the expectant youth of her eighteen years in her eyes. ''You'll let me stay, won't you, now that I've proved meself?''

''Well, I don't know that that's possible,'' Cody began, only to be arrested by the resemblance of this young girl to his eldest daughter. He never could resist a pretty woman, and this was a helpless one to boot. ''We'll see. First we got to move you to the main village. Then we'll set about restoring you to your people. If you'll give me a name and address, I'll send for your kin immediately.''

''Don't have any kin,'' Fanny answered quickly.

Cody's brows lowered suspiciously. ''What about the uncle who brought you to the show?''

''Died . . . last week. After the show,'' she added lamely, then heaved a great moaning sigh. ''Oo-ooh!'' she crooned as she tried to sit up. ''I cannae move. The pain's too great a burden for me!''

''Easy there, miss. I'll send for a stretcher,'' Cody offered as he knelt beside her to help her lie back.

Fanny had closed her eyes, but now she opened them as she clutched Cody's coat sleeve. ''I'll be brave if you ask me to, Buffalo Bill, though me body aches something fierce! I'd be that ashamed of meself if I cried out with every step of the carriers.''

Cody looked up into Matthew's impassive face. ''Perhaps she shouldn't be moved just yet.'' The unhelpful fellow simply shrugged. Annoyed and embarrassed to be put in this awkward position, Cody patted the girl's shoulder before rising to his feet. ''Maybe we'll wait a day or two, until you're stronger, before moving you. I'm certain there's a woman in the village who can look after you until then.''

Fanny's gaze darted at Matthew and then away. ''I won't be a burden to anyone,'' she said sorrowfully. ''I won't have a decent man turned out of his house on my account. If need be, I'll crawl on me scraped hands and knees to another place,'' and she held up her abraded palms as evidence of what a sacrifice that would be.

Cody shook his head vigorously. ''You won't move an inch until I'm certain that you're fit. I'll send to the village for a woman to see to you.'' That said, he felt much better. This was action, which he preferred to discussion. ''Now you lie there, quiet as a mouse. Morning Star's a good man, a book-learned man. He's no savage. He has my complete trust.'' He bowed graciously and turned to leave.

Outside, he turned to Morning Star. ''Why, she's no more than a child. Jeb and the boys must be growing soft in the head to think you'd—well, never mind. She won't cause you much trouble, even if you keep her a few days.''

Matthew's expression altered. ''Keep her? Here? I can't keep her. She's a—a white woman.''

''She's a child,'' Cody countered. ''Why, she reminds me of my own sweet daughters. Of course, she must have a woman to look after her. I'll send Sarah Wiggins over. You can move into the Sioux village for a few days. Mustn't have rumors circulating.'' He patted Matthew familiarly on the back. ''You've done well, Morning Star. You saved her life and she's grateful to you. If the press gets wind of the matter, we'll let her talk to them. You could earn a citation, my boy!''

As Cody sauntered off toward his camp, Red Shirt and Matthew stood in silence.

Finally Red Shirt turned to his friend. ''What is she like, this white girl child whose life you have saved?''

''She's a thief and a liar,'' Matthew replied and pulled back his sleeve.

''You found your armband!'' Red Shirt said when he recognized the familiar object.

''She stole it.''

''She? How is that possible? You told me a child took it.''

''A girl child,'' Matthew reminded him. ''She was dressed as a child.'' His voice grew bitter. ''She's a thief.''

''If that is true, how did you get it back?''

''It was in the pocket of her gown. She said she was bringing it back to me.''

''Yet you do not believe her.''

''I do not.''

''This is very mysterious. You have saved the life of a thief who stole from you, and so you must bear the burden of caring for her. Do you not find it an odd thing, Matthew?''

''I find it damned uncomfortable,'' Matthew replied.

''Is she handsome?''

Matthew shook his head. "She is pale as goat's milk."

"A womanly form?" Red Shirt suggested encouragingly.

Again he shook his head, but he didn't trust his voice. She was formed as a woman should be. It had taken all the force of his will not to touch her beyond ordinary needs as she lay unconscious. That was the thing that goaded him most about her. He had found the armband before the sight of her nakedness provoked desire. He should despise her, and yet he had longed to—

"You will come to the village and share my lodge this night," Red Shirt offered.

"I would be honored," Matthew replied.

"It's not me fault the woman's a coward," Fanny said to no one in particular. Certainly she wasn't addressing herself to the heathen who sat in the lodge, his glossy dark head bent over a book. The glow from the kerosene lamp threw his shadow against the leather walls, where it loomed in a huge and gloomy silence to match its owner's mood.

Three days had passed since Sarah Wiggins had come to look after her. She'd been all solicitation, exclaiming in horrified tones about the bruises and cuts on Fanny's delicate skin. She had washed and dressed every sore inch and then dressed Fanny in a high-necked nightgown borrowed from no less than Mrs. Cody herself.

Not since she was a babe had Fanny been so cuddled and fussed over. With her hair washed, braided, and wound in a coronet about her head, Fanny felt like a princess. She sat propped up by a wicker backrest padded with a spongy cover of buffalo-hide hair. Surprisingly, the pain in her back was eased by sitting. If not for the brooding silence of her host, she could have called herself altogether happy. But that was not to be.

"I said, I didn't mean to run Mrs. Wiggins away." More deliberate silence. "How was I to know she's afraid of the wee folk? I was only after entertaining her with me tales."

Matthew shifted slightly, licked his forefinger, and turned the page of his book.

"A body might die for want of a kind word," she said testily. "Of course, I suppose heathen folk don't talk above the need, seeing that they don't speak a decent kind of tongue to begin with."

She had thought anything would be better than silence, but when his black eyes lifted from the book to stare just above her head, Fanny knew the very real sensation of awe. "I've told you I'm sorry for taking your bracelet. Will you not hear reason in the matter?"

"You are a thief." He said the words slowly, as if pronouncing a verdict.

"And you're a man with a hard heart," she answered right back. "Don't you see, I was bringing it back. Where did the cowboys say they found me? Here. Aye, in this very place. I'd come back to bring you your bracelet."

It amazed her that anyone alive could sit so still. "Oh, very well. Don't accept me apology. I don't know that it matters. You can think what you wish and stare great black holes in the place over me head for Mrs. Wiggins to patch up come the morning."

His head lowered. No tempering of his mood. No acceptance. No attempt to bridge the gulf.

"You've every right to be angry," she conceded with

a sigh. "I know what it is to lose something that means your whole life. I was robbed meself not above a week ago." She glanced at him. Nothing. "They took me life's savings, every clean cent of it."

"Stolen money?"

Fanny blinked. She'd not seen him move but heard the question clearly. "Aye. It's me profession, you see. I'm a thief, a good one. Phineas says he's never worked better than me, and he should know, being in the trade himself long before our acquaintance."

His head lifted again. This time there was puzzlement in the stare that didn't quite meet hers. "You're trained to be a thief?"

The incredulity in his tone made her smile. "It's a common thing. I'd rather lift a purse here and a lace hankie there than walk the street looking for a chance to lift me skirts. Don't Indian cities have thieves?"

"No."

No. How final he made the word sound. She smiled at him. "Oh, come now. Where there's aught to be had, there's them what will have it."

Matthew closed his book very carefully. "Among my people, thievery is not accepted. Only a madman steals what he might have if he worked for it or asked for it." He paused with a deliberate look that swept her slowly from chin to toe. "Sometimes a small child may take what is not hers. She is made to give it back and thus learns not to take again."

"I see," Fanny answered, coloring as though she'd just been caught in the act again. "May I ask a question?" Thunderous silence. "Ah, well, ask it I will. Why do you speak one way sometimes, and another at others?"

"I don't understand."

"Ah, yes, you do. All the day you spoke like this: 'White woman no good. Bad thing you take armband from me.' Now you're talking better than me."

Matthew shook his head. "You wrong. Maybe horse kick you in head. Make you hear funny."

"There you go again!" she cried. "And don't tell me I'm hearing things. Why, you're sitting there reading a book."

Matthew's black brows peaked. "Reading book no great thing. Any child can learn it." From the corner of his eye he thought he saw her complexion darken. "You no read?" he asked in surprise.

Fanny stared at him in bold challenge as she lifted her chin. "What of it? It's no great gain to me. I live in a proper house with brick walls and a bed. You can read, yet you live in a cowhide tent with no windows and no bed."

"Buffalo hide," Matthew corrected. "Buffalo great friend to Sioux. Provides him with shelter from the sky. Gives him clothes to keep out the cold. Fills his stew pot so that he may not starve."

"The buffalo ain't selling it," Fanny shot back. "You steal from the buffalo what you need, and commit a killing into the bargain." Her smile was smug. "I may steal to live, but I don't murder them I take from."

Matthew nearly smiled back at her misguided but clever logic. From the first he knew she had a quick wit. No doubt that made her a good thief. "The great buffalo god is asked to intercede on behalf of the Sioux before every hunt. We do not take more than we need and do not leave what we kill. All life is sacred. Man and animal and plant, everything that is in the sky and on the earth and in the waters belongs to the Great Mystery, *Wakan Tanka*. We borrow only so that we may live.''

''So do I!'' When he sighed and looked back at his book, she regretted her hasty defense. She knew the difference between thievery and his explanation of a hunt. What she didn't understand was this need in her to provoke him.

During the three days of his absence, she had missed him. Yet that made no sense. She hardly knew him. Perhaps it was because he had saved her life. The need to be protected was urgent in her these days. She glanced at him. He was tall and strong. She could use his strength, but she never again wanted to need someone, to depend on him for more than his usefulness to her. Phineas had completed the lesson her da—

No! Fanny wrenched her thoughts away from that subject. The Indian had done her kindness. She would find a way to return the favor if she could, but she wouldn't be maudlin about it. Just as she'd scared off Sarah Wiggins when her mothering became too much, she'd deal with the Indian in her own fashion.

Sarah Wiggins was a kind woman, but she chattered far too much for Fanny's peace of mind. Then there was the ongoing matter of her name, and who should be contacted as to Fanny's whereabouts. No one seemed to believe that she simply didn't have any family or friends; yet she dared not give them even a false name and address for fear that Buffalo Bill's inquiries would alert someone in the city to her presence on the island. At least in the Indian's presence she wasn't forced to lie. He didn't even speak unless she badgered him.

''I'm tired,'' she said as a yawn escaped her.

At first she didn't think he heard her. His head was bent so that his chin nearly touched his chest and his arms were crossed before his chest. She decided he had fallen asleep.

Only when she tried to move and a groan escaped her did he move. He rose and crossed the distance between them, kneeling beside her to draw the backrest away. Then, in quiet deliberation, he spread the wrinkles from the blanket beneath her. When he took her by the shoulders to support her as she lay back, Fanny set her teeth against the pain of spasmed muscles. She couldn't lie down.

"Hurt plenty bad?" he asked softly, but Fanny could only nod a little for shame that she would again give in to the desire to moan.

"Breathe deep," he commanded, his hands moving from her shoulders up to the slender column of her neck. "Again," he said as he came to his knees behind her. "Release it slowly."

At first his touch was so light she could scarcely feel it, but, slowly and gently, the pads of his fingers began to knead the slope of her neck from the base of her skull down to the intersection of her shoulders. Up and down his hands moved, spreading warmth and replacing pain with pleasure.

After a short while, she felt him reach around in front to fumble with the buttons at her neckline. He opened the first two and folded the high collar of her gown back away from her skin. Now his fingers moved into the hollows on either side of her neck, digging gently but firmly through the skin to reach sore sinew and swollen tendons and work them free of pain.

Fanny felt her body being softened and molded like

clay under his touch. When he reached forward and slipped free two more buttons, she didn't think to protest.

Very carefully he reached an arm around in front of her, his hand splayed across the space below her breasts, and he bent her forward over this support as he continued to massage her upper back with the heel of his other hand. The pain here was worse and she sucked in a quick breath in response to his touch.

"Too sore?" he questioned. At her nod his hand slipped back up to her neck. He pressed long, slow, heavy strokes over her shoulders, fanning others down over her shoulder blades but avoiding the throbbing bruise at the center of her back.

It was as though there were a sleeping draft in his touch, she mused drowsily. Every movement unhooked a pain, drew her farther from reality, pressed her closer to sweet rest. They were enemies. In words they'd found no accord. But the touch of his hands was another matter. In it she found nothing to reproach him for, and he, too, seemed content with her quiet acquiescence.

When Matthew felt no more resistance under her skin, he drew her back against him until she rested against his chest. He held her for a moment. "Better?"

"Aye," she whispered, half asleep already.

Carefully he lowered her onto the blanket. Her lashes fluttered upon her cheeks, but her eyes didn't open as he covered her with a second blanket.

Matthew resisted the spur of desire he experienced at the sight of a curve of breast exposed by the open neckline of her gown. She was his charge, his burden. He couldn't want her. He didn't even like her. Yet he was reluctant to cover the sight. Instead, he reached out to draw her gown closed, the backs of his fingers grazing the curve to learn that she was as soft as swan's down.

Only when he stood and moved away from her did he realize that he'd been holding his breath. Asleep, she seemed less real than reason demanded. He had touched her, held her, and not been completely immune to the woman he'd met first in the guise of a child. He glanced down at the silver armband. She was a liar and a cheat. Why had she come back to his lodge? What did she really want? He knew nothing, nothing at all about her, not even her name.

It is better that way, he told himself. He was here now only because Mrs. Wiggins had refused to spend another night in a lodge so far away from the rest of the camp. He hadn't learned exactly what the girl at his feet had said to frighten Mrs. Wiggins, but he knew this girl was an expert liar. She'd buffaloed Buffalo Bill from the first. Now, with her soft skin and persuasive ways, she was creeping into his thoughts and making him want things he couldn't have. Why had he come back tonight instead of allowing someone else to look after her? Was it only because he missed his home?

Matthew turned away from her. He hoped so—he really did.

Fanny awakened with the sensation of death. At least she thought it must be death. Someone was killing her, thrusting a knife blade of pain straight through her back, slicing into her lungs with an agony that set her heart galloping. She couldn't draw breath. The darkness was suffocating her!

Where was she? Her eyes were open, but the darkness was thick as tar. Only once before had she been in a place as dark. That had been the hold of the ship that carried her and her father to America. Then she had felt the rock of the sea beneath her, but now she felt only hard, unyielding earth.

A coffin! She had been buried! The bursting pain of her lungs was the last breath of depleted air!

The irrational thought took hold instantly. Pain, fear, delirium bled and blended into a red mask of hysteria. With a cry of terror, she thrust her hands upward against the imaginary lid and met a solid bulk. Terror confirmed, she screamed again, curling her nails into the wall. Surprisingly, it gave beneath her hands, becoming flesh.

Matthew sucked in a breath of pain as the girl's nails dug deep into his chest. Awakened by her moaning, he'd come to bend over her when she suddenly lunged at him. As she scratched and clawed at him in the darkness, he realized that she was dreaming or delirious or both.

In self-defense, he caught her wrists and held the clawing fingers away from his face, but she continued to thrash her head, kicking and bucking. Afraid that she would hurt herself, he swung a leg over her hips and lowered his weight across her thighs.

"Wake up!" he commanded sharply. "Wake up! You're dreaming!"

Fanny heard the voice as distant thunder, unintelligible but oddly reassuring. She wasn't buried. She was only struggling against something, someone. If only it weren't so dark she might remember what had come before this. Had she been on the street? Perhaps she'd been struck on the head and dragged into an alley to be raped.

"Don't hurt me!" she whispered, her breath coming in sharp drafts. "Don't hurt me! You can have . . . anything! Take me, but . . . don't hurt me! Please!"

Her pitiful cries told him that she was still caught in a nightmare's grip. Clasping both wrists in one hand, he gently touched her cheek with his other, but she whipped her head away. He caught her chin in his fingers and bent low to whisper in her ear, "Lie still. I won't hurt you."

Terrible, choked-back sobs came from deep within her. She trembled from head to foot. Though she no longer fought him, she was terrified and there seemed no way to reassure her in this darkness. He rose off her and, sliding his free arm under her hips, lifted her up into his arms.

The star-lit night seemed as bright as dawn after the smothering darkness of the lodge. The air was cool, spreading chilly drafts over his naked back and thighs, but Matthew welcomed the contrast. The air seemed to revive the girl as well. She whimpered, huddled in his arms, but she was no longer crying. He walked over to the nearest tree and knelt with her in his arms. But as he tried to set her on the grass, she suddenly sobbed and clutched at him, burying her face in the warm curve of his neck.

"Please, please don't ever be leaving me again," she whispered brokenly. "I dinna like the world without ye. Cruel it is, and uncaring for the likes of me."

Matthew sighed. She thought he was someone else. "Nothing's going to hurt you." He tried again to release her, but her arms tightened about his neck and then he felt warm droplets of tears on his cool skin.

Resigned for the moment, he sat down and drew her onto his lap. The grass was slick and the tree bark rough against his back; yet he didn't mind. Some nights when it was too warm to rest comfortably in his tepee, he slept in the open. Neither did he mind the girl's weight. She was small, scarcely reaching his chin when they stood side by side. The only discomfort he experienced was that of a man in close proximity to a soft and pliant woman. To put that thought out of his mind, he rested his head back on the tree trunk and gazed up at the stars.

She stirred restlessly against him, resettling her head upon his chest as if searching for the perfect spot. Her fingers flexed again and again along the tendons of his neck in a faint imitation of his own earlier massaging.

He drew in a breath, concentrating on the pinpoint brilliants in the sky. Yet the tantalizing play of fingers on his skin soon blurred his vision. With the increased sensitivity her touch brought, he became aware of every detail of their contact. He felt the sweep of her lashes brushing his chest each time she blinked. Was she asleep or merely dazed? The warmth of her hips pressed hard against his naked loins reminded him that celibacy was not a natural state for a healthy young man.

Without conscious thought, he began answering her touch with a soothing slide of his fingers along her cheek. It was meant as comfort, a sexless caress of consolation. It was a mistake. Her fingers trailed up to match his movements, stroking the contours of his face. Again he sighed. The blood was rushing from his face into his groin, filling and swelling the flesh there.

He closed his eyes, promising himself that nothing would happen, nothing could happen. He called to mind the ugly bluish-purple bruise spread across her back. He could not tumble her in the grass to lie upon that. Fingers stole across his cheek, found the shape of his lips, pressed gently, and drifted away. The hand at the back of his neck dove up into his hair and remained entangled there.

This time when he looked up, the sky was only a soft hazy violet with no features at all. Her hand moved to his chest, tracing the long planes of muscle as though she were brushing wrinkles from a sheet. The heat her movements engendered made his belly quiver. Why did she touch him so? Was she not only a liar and a thief, but a whore as well?

"Poor, poor soul," he heard her mouth softly. "I daren't love ye, nae any other." Her hand suddenly slipped from his chest and fell into her lap, where it was still. For several heartbeats he held his breath, and then he realized that she was slumped bonelessly against him. She was asleep.

What had she meant? Had he heard her correctly? Of whom had she spoken with such tenderness? These and a dozen other thoughts chased themselves around in his head until the sky pinkened with dawn. Only then did he rise and carry her back to shelter and privacy.

CHAPTER
7

Fanny awakened with the flushed feeling that often accompanied an indiscreet act. She felt shame creeping up her neck to tickle her just below the ears even before she opened her eyes. She couldn't remember what she'd done or why, but a vague sense of guilt made her reluctant to awaken completely. Then suddenly her eyes were open, and she was staring into the sleeping face of Matthew Morning Star only inches away.

He lay beside her on the tepee floor, his body angled protectively toward hers, though they didn't touch. Her astonished gaze took in the long black lashes against his cheeks, the clean, broad lines of his face unmarked by the beginnings of a beard, and the dark cast of his skin as deep as mahogany in the early morning light. Her gaze moved back to his wide, sensual mouth softened by sleep. She had never been kissed—if she didn't count the rough play in the streets as a child—but the possibility of a kiss loomed as a tantalizing prospect as she stared at his inviting mouth. Was that the source of the chagrined feeling creeping like an army of ants over her skin?

He's handsome, she thought with a tremble in her middle. Even though they weren't touching, she could feel the heat of his body register on her own chilly skin. He was like an oven, radiating a warmth that she longed to share. Flushing with trepidation, she lowered her eyes a discreet few inches and noticed red scratches on the firm skin of his chest. The five long marks had been made by human nails.

She sat up stiffly. The pain between her shoulder blades had lessened but not gone. In one brief glance she took in the rest of him. His belly was flat and hairless. Likewise his long thighs. Exposed by the tangle of blanket, they were corded in heavy muscle and smooth as tanned leather. Skimming her eyes back to his groin for an instant, she discovered the black bush of his pubic hair.

The sight made her cheeks burn, and she turned away from him. Why was he lying naked beside her? Had they—? No, she knew that wasn't possible. Yet she remembered the pleasure and ease his hands had brought to her bruised and aching body before she fell asleep.

The remembrance came slowly, like wading out of deep waters. She'd had a terrible dream, a nightmare about her enemies. She'd been clubbed and dragged into an alley, scratching and clawing!

Her glance swung back toward him again and chills danced up her spine. *She* had made those marks on his skin.

She stuck a finger in her mouth and began chewing the nail. Ever since Phineas disappeared, she'd made one mistake after another. She'd always acted with braggadocio and was self-sufficient with Phineas because she hadn't dared let him know how much their friendship meant to her. Why, within a month of their meeting, he'd forgotten exactly where and how he'd found her.

Yet she remembered, all too well. She'd been a frightened street Arab, living in alleyways, stealing fruit and vegetables from pushcart peddlers in order to survive from day to day. At night, hiding in alleys or dark places roamed by feral animals not all of the four-footed variety, she'd shivered and sobbed until sleep claimed her. Memories of those nights had fleshed out her nightmare.

Then she'd tried to pick Phineas's pocket and been caught. Instead of hailing the nearest policeman, he'd offered her his protection in exchange for work. Thinking back on those early days, she would have done anything for him, for his kindness. Yet in exchange for a clean bed, a roof over her head, and a full stomach, he'd simply asked her to steal. She'd learned quickly and gladly. Now that was all gone: Phineas, his protection, and her peace of mind. If only—!

No! Fanny snatched her finger from her mouth. Anger replaced the lost look in her eyes. She must think of a solution to her present troubles, and act quickly. Just when she'd found a moment's peace, she'd done something else to anger the man whose help she needed. What could she do to make it up to him?

All tenderness drained from her as she looked back at him. With a narrow gaze of the guttersnipe she'd once been, she surveyed the man sleeping trustingly beside her. What did she have that he might want? The obvious answer was the pleasure of her body. He looked like any other man; surely Indian men took pleasure in women.

She looked away. She didn't want to become a whore, but the idea of lying with this man wasn't repulsive to her. The realization surprised her and made her uneasy, as though in giving of herself she would give him a hold on her. No, she would wait a bit before offering herself to him. Though she'd never lain with a man, she'd seen and heard enough on the street to know the value of holding out the promise of her body while not delivering it. First she would appease lesser appetites. Something to eat! Men always liked the woman who could fill their bellies with nourishment.

As quietly as she could, she backed away from him, dragging one of the blankets with her. She ignored the twinges in her back. While the pain remained, it was subdued. She looked down, remembering the touch of his hands. He'd been so gentle that she hadn't wanted him to stop.

Some undefined sensation moved through her at the thought. It was a different kind of aching, a sweet pang not unlike what she'd felt as a girl when Phineas brought her an especially nice treat. She could hardly wait to eat the candy or cookie, but at the same time she'd wanted to suspend the moment, to savor every bite and yet have the gift remain untouched. She'd always given Phineas a big hug, which embarrassed him, though she could tell he liked it. What would the Indian do if she bent and hugged him now? Would he open those great dark eyes and look at her, really look at her? And if he did, would he touch her in turn, draw her close so that the heat she'd only felt distantly would pass directly from his feverish skin into her own?

An unknown tide, as thrilling as it was powerful, washed over her, drenching her in shame and guilty desire. Fanny raised her head and hugged the blanket close to her body. She was tingling all over. Desire? Was that what this feeling was? Had she come to desire—to lust for—a man?

Frightened by the possibility, she turned away, lifted the flap, and went out.

She found her dress hanging from a limb of a nearby tree, and though it was damp from the dew, she put it on. Her shoes were nowhere to be found and so she set off in the direction of the main camp without them.

Without a word, Matthew accepted the bowl of stew that Fanny offered him. He'd awakened to find her gone, but by the time he'd donned his breechcloth she'd returned with an iron pot of stew and a cheery smile of welcome. Except for the purple bruise on her chin and a swollen lower lip, she seemed to be healing very quickly. The terrors of the night might never have been.

He leaned over and sniffed the steam rising from the pot. It smelled edible. Carefully he eyed the bits of meat floating in the brown gravy. They looked edible, too.

"Well, then?" She stood over him expectantly. "Won't you be having a taste?"

Obediently he dipped the spoon in and took a mouthful. The flavor was surprisingly good. So good, in fact, that his eyes widened in amazement as he looked up from his cross-legged position.

"Good, is it?" she asked with a cocky smile. "Then eat your fill. There's plenty to be had."

He swallowed and said, "Where did you get it?"

"I came by it," she said evasively. "Don't you like it?"

"Yes." He took another mouthful. He hadn't had pemmican stew this tasty since he left the reservation. His head shot up again. "Did Mrs. Wiggins give it to you?"

Fanny shook her head. Then, because as usual, he wasn't looking directly at her, she said, "I came by it on me own."

"*My* own," Matthew corrected.

"That's what I said." She watched him chew in satisfaction. Her first action to please him was working. Only when he'd taken several more mouthfuls did she broach the matter of his scratches.

She dug a toe in the dirt. "I was a bit of trouble during the night, with me nightmare and all."

"*My* nightmare," Matthew said.

"Were you tormented, too?" she asked, misunderstanding his intent.

He smiled to himself. It was a matter of pride that he spoke English better than most white men, but he supposed he shouldn't be so critical. "What frightened you?"

"You wouldn't be after understanding it," she answered lightly. "Only I'm sorry I scraped your hide like I done."

Matthew dismissed her apology with a shrug. "I'll have worse before the matinee's over."

At the mention of the show she brightened. "Do you

suppose, since I did try to ride a horse and all, that Buffalo Bill will give me a job?''

"Perhaps he'll give you work as a cook," he answered. "If you can learn to make pemmican stew like this, there'll always be room for you in camp."

"What sort of stew did you say that was?"

"Pemmican. Didn't the woman who gave it to you tell you what it was?"

"Not exactly. I was in something of a hurry."

It wasn't the tone but the phrase that brought Matthew's head snapping up. "Why were you in a hurry?"

"It was early, you see, and hardly a soul about. So I thought to meself, Fanny, me girl, the Indian will be hungry when he wakes up. Best you take in hand what'll fill him best."

Matthew nearly choked. "You stole it!"

Her chin jutted out. "I borrowed it, in a manner of speaking."

He set the pot down before him in the grass. "When you do the talking, the 'manner of speaking' is always a lie."

"I did it to please you."

"You'd please me best by not stealing anything, ever again."

"I only wanted . . ."

"Wanted what?"

But Fanny shook her head stubbornly. She'd nearly said she only wanted to make him like her. How foolish that would have been. She must never give anyone that much power over her. "You're a hard man, Indian."

"Don't call me Indian!"

She glared at him. "You've given me none else to call you."

"My name's Morning Star."

Her lips twitched. "Morning Star? That's an odd name for a grown man."

"What is yours?"

She hesitated. She'd not even told Mrs. Wiggins her name. Yet she had to gain his confidence if she was to get into his good graces. "Fanny."

"Fanny what?"

"Just Fanny."

Matthew shook his head. "Well, Just Fanny, the first thing you're going to do before we go to see Buffalo Bill is return the stew you stole and apologize to your victim."

"I'll do no such thing!"

"You will."

Trembling with rage, Fanny turned her back on him. If he thought she'd humiliate herself by groveling before the foolish woman who'd left her pot unattended, he'd just have to think again.

"You don't appear to be a fool."

Fanny spun about. "Just what do you mean by that?"

He was gazing as usual a foot to the left of her. "I am Dakota. My people do not believe that a sane man would steal from his neighbors. Only fools and children are permitted that indiscretion."

"Ye gave this sermon yesterday," she remarked sourly.

"You're in need of a great deal of sermonizing, it would seem, Just Fanny."

The joke of her name annoyed her, but she refused to remark on it. "I steal to live, same as others, and I said that to you before, too."

"Yet you say you would work here, if given the chance."

"Aye, and I would."

"Why?"

Again her chin jutted out. "I like to work."

Matthew looked down at the stolen pot. "Or is it that you think by working here you'll be able to steal freely from visitors and show people alike?"

"That's a hard thing to say about me!"

"But just." He lifted the pot and held it out to her. "If you want me to believe that you can be trusted, take this back to its owner."

She folded her arms tightly across her bosom. "I'd as soon be struck dead!"

"Perhaps you will be, if Christian laws bind you. 'Thou shalt not steal.' Is that not one of your commandments?"

"How would a heathen be knowing anything about the matter?"

His expression darkened. "Very well. I give you back your freedom."

"Back me freedom? When was I ever without it?"

He didn't reply. He was weary of the conflict of cultures. He longed for home, for the Black Hills, the open spaces, the pure and simple life of his people.

Fanny watched him rise to his feet, struck again by his height. Yet that was forgotten as she saw his expression. He looked past her as though she had ceased to exist. She had lost every inch of ground she'd gained moments before.

"Oh, very well," she said angrily, and picked up the pot. "I'll say it but me heart won't be in it. There's no pleasing you, and that's the truth of it!"

Matthew didn't look toward her until she'd turned

away. Every muscle in her back was rigid as she stalked off. Though she must still be sore, he knew that most of the tension came from defiance. One of the braids of her coronet had come loose and hung in a shiny plait down her back. She was going toward the Indian camp, but he had no idea what she would do when she got there.

She infuriated him, and yet he was amazed. She was absolutely without a conscience. Wild and sly as the coyote, she had the recuperative powers of a cat. Only the night before he was certain that she'd be ill for the rest of the week. Yet she was up and dressed and into mischief before he had wiped the sleep from his eyes.

He didn't want responsibility for so unpredictable a creature. No white man would expect him to be bound by a code that was reserved for his people. Yet he was bound—not by her, but by his honor. He picked up the spoon she'd dropped and stared at it. Perhaps he should go after her, to make certain she caused no more trouble. No, he thought stubbornly. Any trouble she makes she brings on herself.

Fanny's thoughts were many and furious as she entered the Indian settlement. Unlike an hour earlier, the grassy lanes between the tepees were full of women and children. They paused as she neared them, their gazes silent but watchful as she passed. Look your fill, she thought defiantly. You'll be seeing a great deal more of Fanny Sweets before I'm done!

When she found the fire from which she'd stolen the iron pot, she walked up to the Indian woman standing beside it and dropped the pot into the grass at her feet. "I made a mistake in taking your pot," she said in a

loud but colorless tone. "You'll be wanting it back."
Not waiting for the woman's reply, she turned on her
heel and started out of the camp.

Before she took a third step, she was spun about by a
hand gripping her shoulder. The woman, her pecan-
brown features stretched in lines of anger, screamed at
her in words she didn't understand. Then she delivered
a stinging slap that drove Fanny back a step and filled
her eyes with tears.

Years of fighting to stay alive made her respond
instinctively. She doubled up her fists and delivered a
quick, hard jab straight at the woman's middle. The
older woman gasped in pain, stumbled back, and fell,
landing in the dust.

Roars of laughter from those nearby drove the Indian
woman to her feet with a cry of humiliation. Teeth
bared, her fingers curled into talons, she advanced on
Fanny.

"Aye, you try me!" Fanny taunted, her fists poised
and her knees bent as she'd been taught by Phineas.
Claiming to once have been the bare-knuckles, bantam-
weight champ of Galway, he'd taught her a few of the
finer points of boxing shortly after they'd become
partners. But she couldn't think of him at the moment.
Her full attention must be on her opponent.

As the enraged woman charged her, Fanny stepped
deftly out of her path while delivering a ringing blow to
the side of her head. Again the woman stumbled and
fell. This time the crowd of men, women, and children
formed a circle about her, taunting her and urging her to
her feet a second time.

Breathless and her face streaked with dirt, the woman
again stood up, but this time she didn't charge. Instead,

she bent and pulled a long skinning knife from her leggings.

Fanny drew a breath of surprise as the wicked blade emerged. She hadn't been afraid of a fair fight, but knives were a different matter. Though she'd always carried a small knife for protection, she'd never fought with one in hand-to-hand combat. With quick, darting glances, she looked about the circle of people. They had grown quiet, their enthusiasm for the fight diminished by the prospect of bloodshed, but she knew at once that they wouldn't interfere. She'd have to save herself.

Blushing a deep, angry red, she flexed her fists and nodded at the now-smiling woman. "Come on, then. Let's have at it, and the devil be served!"

With a terrible war cry, the woman lunged at her. Eyes fixed on the blade, Fanny tasted the brine of fear as the foot-long blade arched within an inch of her neck as she spun aside. The brackish fear seeped down through her as the woman turned and crouched low, her smile now a jeer as she sensed Fanny's uncertainty. She felt the stiffening rebellion of her bruised muscles, the quivering of her knees, and the emptiness of possible defeat. Do a good deed and repent, she thought in a flash. And, oh, how she repented it!

There came a shout beyond the throng of onlookers and the crowd split apart, but Fanny didn't look away from her assailant, for the woman took that instant to lunge again. With desperation born of futility, Fanny dropped to a knee and rammed both fists into the stomach of the advancing figure with all the force she could put into the act. The woman's screech ended in midbreath as she was stopped in her tracks. The knife dangled a moment in her loosened grip, then fell as she dropped like a sack of grain into the dust.

A moment later Fanny was grabbed from behind and hauled roughly to her feet. Afraid that she was being assaulted anew, she dug a sharp elbow into the belly of the attacker and swung about, careless of the pain caused to her by his grip, and aimed a foot at the crotch of the man holding her.

With a yelp of pain, the man doubled over and backed away.

She dove for the knife that lay in the grass and scooped it up. Half blinded by the tangle of red curls spilling into her eyes, she resumed her stance. She recognized Matthew as he came forward out of the crowd, but she didn't trust him. Wasn't it his fault she was in trouble now?

Matthew held up a hand as he cautiously advanced toward her. He'd come running at the first cry. He'd guessed before he reached the camp that he'd find Fanny at the center of the controversy, but he wasn't prepared for the sight he'd come upon. The Indian woman had lunged at Fanny with a knife just as he had reached the edge of the crowd. His heart had nearly stopped, even as he shoved his way through. One of the cowboys who'd come running had tried to haul Fanny out of harm's way but failed to hold on to her.

Matthew saw the whites of her wide, staring eyes and realized that she was still frightened. Though she trembled from head to foot, there was authority in her stance, as if she was accustomed to brawling. The notion surprised him. Yet that wasn't important now. He reached slowly toward her. "It's over," he said quietly.

"I didn't start it, but I'll finish it, if needs must!" she cried in answer.

He glanced over his shoulder to where the Indian woman was being held in check by two braves. Moving on, he met Red Shirt's gaze, and his chief lifted a brow in question. "Scatter the people," he said in reply. "The fight's over."

Chief Red Shirt held his friend's gaze a fraction longer before issuing a terse order in Sioux. The people moved back at once, some turning toward their tepees, albeit reluctantly.

Matthew looked again at the woman being held. The blood at the corner of her mouth and dirt marring her features marked her as the loser in the fight. "What began this?" he asked her.

The woman, her black eyes full of fury, spat words of anger in her own language.

"What is she saying?" Fanny challenged. "Whatever it is, it's a lie!"

One of the cowboys answered, "The squaw says for Morning Star to keep his whore away from her fire."

"Whore, is it!" Fanny started toward the Indian woman, raising the knife menacingly. "We'll see who'll be calling me a whore after— Awwh!"

Catching her off guard, Matthew grasped her wrist and, with a quick twist, extracted the knife. "Now," he said, letting her go, "you can finish what you started."

Fanny ached in every inch of her body, but she wasn't going to admit it. The expression she turned on him was wrathful, but her eyes were guarded. "I didn't start it. I brought the pot back, like you said. I gave it back and said it was a mistake. Only she wasn't after hearing that. She jumped me after I'd turned me back!"

Matthew sighed. She was trouble. He'd known that from the first. Yet perhaps she was telling the truth this time. It didn't matter. There was only one way to settle the matter with his people, and that was to prove her honesty.

Fanny stepped back as he suddenly held the knife up before her face, but he merely turned his wrist so that the blade was horizontal before her, the cutting edge turned away. As she looked across at him, he said, "Bite it."

Fanny gaped at him in amazement. "Bite that? Are you mad?"

He knew that they all watched her. If she refused, there was bound to be more trouble. "It is the Dakota way. To prove that you did not mean to steal the woman's food, you must bite the knife."

"And if I don't?" she challenged.

His expression was inscrutable. "A liar would be afraid to bite the knife."

Now she understood. "Ah, well, why not?" She leaned forward to do it, but he drew the blade back. "What now?"

"If you are a liar and swear this oath, then misfortune will befall you and the truth will out."

Fanny paled a little. So this was an oath, a pledge with a curse attached. She didn't need to be Dakota to understand the importance of that. "If I swear and promise not to take anything again, will I be left alone?"

He nodded.

This time he moved the blade toward her as she opened her mouth. From the corner of his eye he'd seen a man in a tall gray western hat striding toward them, but he allowed her to gingerly set her teeth against the blade before he withdrew it and turned to the new arrival.

"Buffalo Bill," he greeted, his face devoid of any expression.

"Morning Star. Chief Red Shirt," Buffalo Bill greeted. "What's this I hear about a fight among the squaws?"

"No fight," Matthew answered.

Cody glanced at Fanny, noting her flushed and sweaty face, streaming red hair, rough-dried dress, and dirty bare feet. Finally he looked again at Matthew, his gaze resting pointedly on the skinning knife he held. "You got any particular need for that knife?"

Matthew stuck it in his breechclout. "I was showing our guest one of the uses of a hunter's blade."

"Here? Now?" Cody's disbelieving glance swept Fanny again. "Miss, perhaps you'll be kind enough to tell me what's been going on."

Fanny lifted her chin, a spot of dirt on the tip of her nose making her appearance more pugnacious than ever. "I don't know nothing. I come for work, that's all."

Not a man to pursue a pointless matter, Cody stroked his chin whiskers while considering a new tactic. "Young lady, first thing this morning Mrs. Wiggins came to tell me how you scared her off after dark last night. Though you've been here four days, you still refuse to tell us your name. That being the case, I see no alternative but to send you back to the city."

"But you can't!" Fanny burst out. "Mrs. Wiggins is a craven coward, she is. Claims to have a dram of Irish blood in her! But wasn't she running away at the first tale of a banshee? I only said it *might* be a puca what inhabits that black-hearted beast you call Twister.''

"Is it Irish you are?" Cody questioned gravely, though his lips were twitching in mirth behind his mustache. From the moment he'd laid eyes on her he knew she could be nothing else. Her speech had confirmed the matter at once.

"What else, I'm asking you?" Fanny stuck a fist on each narrow hip.

Cody smiled. "I must tell you you've caused more ruckus than is proper for a civilized Irish lady."

Fanny nodded. "Aye, perhaps I have. But I'd be keeping off mischief's path if I were to have a proper job." She lifted wide blue eyes to him, all anger forgotten in the sunny gaze she bestowed on him. "I'd do any work for the chance to be part of your show, Mr. Cody. I'd be good as gold and twice as reliable."

Cody hesitated. He knew blarney when he heard it, but the young woman was earnest if nothing else. Besides, he'd seen the squaw with whom she'd obviously had a disagreement. Any girl who could best a Sioux was bound to be an asset to the show. "I'll think it over. First you must come with me to see Mrs. Wiggins and apologize." He saw her expression darken and added, "Of course, if you're not of a mind to, I'll pay your fare back to the city."

Fanny knew a bargain when she heard one. So what if she had to smile sweetly at Mrs. Wiggins while double-talking her way around an apology? She'd been as good as promised a job in the show. After a brief glance at Matthew, who stood as silent and expressionless as a tobacco-store Indian, she nodded. "Apologize, it is. I'm getting plenty of practice these days," she added in a mutter.

"Better Just Fanny practice with Buffalo Bill first," Matthew offered in his stilted show voice. "Mrs. Wiggins not carry knife but iron skillet."

"Fanny, is it?" Cody asked.

"Aye. Fanny will do," she answered.

"Well, then, Miss Fanny, come along." Cody offered her his arm just as she'd seen gentlemen on Fourth Avenue do. Greatly pleased, she rested her hand in the crook of his arm and lifted her damp hem clear of the grass as they walked off toward his tent.

"Trouble with Red Hair not over yet," Red Shirt offered in a whisper as he came to stand beside Matthew.

"You're wrong," Matthew answered. "She's now *Pahaska*'s problem, and he's welcome to her."

Red Shirt gave his friend a speculative glance as Matthew walked away. He didn't know what to make of the white woman but he'd seen Matthew's face when he spoke of her, and it gave away more than he knew. In spite of his anger and exasperation, he'd displayed genuine concern for the red-haired girl.

Though he wished Matthew the comfort that only a willing woman could offer, he doubted that the white woman was the best choice. He'd heard that they were as cool as the color of their skin and bony where they should be soft. Only the miraculous color of Red Hair's hair hinted at the possibility of a passion to match a Sioux woman's embrace. He smiled. Watching them would make the summer even more interesting than it had been thus far.

CHAPTER
8

"Now you're sure you can handle this?"

Fanny nodded vigorously. "Nerves of steel is what I have."

Buck Tarrington wasn't convinced. "I purely think we should wait until Buffalo Bill's done give his word on the matter."

"There's no time to ask him—you said so yourself," she reminded him. "Buffalo Bill's counting on you, and Oleta's in no condition to do the show. There's only me."

"But we ain't practiced. I mean, how do I know you'll stand quiet like until I finish? With Oleta and me it's like breathing together. She just about knows where them blades will stick before they leave my hand. What if you make a mistake?"

"I won't," Fanny assured him. "I'll be still as stone. You just do your part, I'll do mine." Without waiting for his acquiescence, she reached for the buckskin shirt and skirt he held in his hands. "I won't be a minute."

"Good," Buck replied. "That's about all we got, anyway."

Fanny dashed into the Tarrington tent and unbuttoned the gown she wore. A hand-me-down from Mrs. Wiggins, it was two sizes too big, faded, and caked with mud at the hem from her work at the fairgrounds. She was convinced that Mrs. Wiggins had had a hand in choosing the job. Cleaning up after the show animals was the lowliest, smelliest, foulest job about. No doubt Mrs. Wiggins hoped to run her off by assigning her to the job of shoveling the pathways so that city folk wouldn't soil their shoes.

But, thought Fanny as she wriggled out of the gown, I've been hanging on as tightly as a tick, I have!

For a week she'd shoveled horse dung, cow patties, and buffalo chips. Her association had been so thorough that she could now tell the difference between each animal's feces.

"After today, Fanny, me girl, you'll never shovel dung again!" she mused aloud.

She wasn't glad that Oleta Tarrington had broken her ankle while climbing down from the carousel at Coney Island. She wasn't pleased that the doctor had said Oleta would have to stay off her leg at least a week. She wasn't thrilled that she was now to be the target of a flurry of knives and tomahawks. What stretched her mouth into an indefatigable smile was the fact that she'd be, for a few days at least, a real part of the show. If it meant standing before a target while Buck aimed sharp objects within inches of her body, then so be it. Once Buffalo Bill saw how well she fit into the show proper, he'd find a better spot for her than behind a shovel and wheelbarrow.

Too excited to take her time, she stuck her fist into the blouse sleeve and heard the stitches at the armhole give. Muttering, she put her other arm in more carefully and then buttoned the blouse and arranged the bertha of lace. Next she pulled on the skirt. Oleta was taller and broader in the hip, but the woman's waist was wasp-thin and Fanny had to take a deep breath to fasten the skirt.

"You ready, Fanny?" Buck called just outside the tent.

"In a minute," she answered, smoothing down the nap of the suede skirt. She'd never worn anything like it. The wide bell stopped short of her ankles, exposing her high-topped shoes and white stockings. Ruefully she noticed the mud on her shoes, but it couldn't be helped.

"The band's playing our theme," Buck announced in a loud voice. "You coming?"

Fanny snatched up the fringed bolero jacket and donned it. As she hooked the front closed, she stepped out into the daylight. "How do I look?"

Buck screwed up his long face, pulling on his chin whiskers, and then a grin split his face. "You're a might stingy in the carriage, but what's up top looks about right."

Fanny tugged the tight-fitting jacket down. It was cut low in front to reveal the lace bertha, but the tightness pushed her bosom up and out. She glanced up at him. "Maybe I shouldn't wear it."

"Too late now!" he exclaimed as he grabbed her by the arm and dragged her after him as he headed for the steps at the back of the stage.

One moment she was backstage in the afternoon light. The next she was shoved through the curtain and stood blinking against the electric lights that surrounded the apron of the stage. The band was playing a lively tune as

Buck swept past her, half a dozen knives in each hand as he smiled and bowed and waved at the cheering crowd.

"Bow, gal!" she heard him encourage under his breath, but Fanny felt as if her legs were locked from ankle to hip. She hadn't thought of this, that she'd be stared at by thousands of eyes. And the noise. Always before, backstage or the one time she'd been a part of the audience, the noise of the crowd had seemed friendly and encouraging. But now the wavering roar that rushed up over the front of the stage seemed utterly hostile and threatening.

"Bow, Fanny, and take your place."

Fanny blinked, feeling the icy sweat gathering on her brow and upper lip. Her stomach turned over and began to sink like a ship in a storm. Stunned by the sheer magnitude of what she'd done, she couldn't take a step in any direction. The hand that grasped her upper arm didn't seem to have a body attached to it, for the range of her vision had narrowed to a pinpoint. Yet she was being steered toward the edge of the stage. Finally she was turned about and pushed back against the edge of a canvas-covered wall.

"Hold your arms away from your sides." Buck leaned near. "You all right, little gal?"

Fanny blinked again, and this time Buck's long-jowled face came into focus. "You all right?" he repeated.

"Of course I am," she muttered through lips so stiff she didn't know if she'd be able to draw another breath.

"Okay, then you take up your position and, God love us, don't you so much as blink 'til I'm done."

Fanny spread her arms out at shoulder height along the canvas back, as she'd watched Oleta do twice a day for a week, and waited.

The first hissing *twak!* of a knife a scant six inches from her right cheek made her yelp in alarm, but she didn't move. The second one followed the first, and then three more knives bit into the canvas in rapid succession as the crowd cheered its approval.

As Buck turned to acknowledge the audience, Fanny heard a faint chattering and wonderingly realized that the sound was made by her own teeth.

When he turned back to her, he held half a dozen tomahawks, all beaded and feathered. The sound of the first one whizzing past her ear made Fanny cry out in alarm as it split the wooden backing of the canvas. Sensing that there was something different about this performer and that her fear was real, a disquieted hush fell over the crowd.

But Buck was a trooper, and nothing less than her running off the stage would have kept him from completing his part of the show. Again and again the tomahawks flew, jarring the canvas backing and eliciting a squeal or gasp from Fanny. When the last one found its mark, between her slightly spread ankles, there wasn't a sound from the crowd.

For one horrified moment Buck stared blankly at Fanny. The stands were silent. Then she was flying toward him, her arms outspread. She wrapped him in a big embrace and planted a smacking kiss on his bushy cheek before turning to the audience and dropping into a full curtsy.

This bit of theatrics drew the crowd to its feet with applause and relief. So it was only a game after all, they reasoned. The girl hadn't really been frightened but only pretended to be. The relief doubled their applause and cheers. Only after a third bow were they allowed to leave the stage.

Fanny stumbled down the narrow steps on rubbery knees, her throat aching with the aftermath of fear and her stomach fluttering in queasy misalliance with her heart. At the bottom she stepped into the path of players arriving for their act.

Hard hands caught her by the shoulders to steady her and she looked up into the war-painted face of Matthew Morning Star. Without a thought other than that of pure joy at seeing a known face, she flung her arms about his waist and leaned her head against his bare chest as she closed her eyes. "I swear I didn't know how terrible it would be! I'll never, never set foot out there again!"

Though he'd not even spoken to her in a week, Matthew's response to the bodily contact was swift and undeniable. The feel of her cheek against his skin sent desire surging forth. He didn't push her away at once, yet he knew he must do something before they drew too many curious looks. He reached down and took her chin in his hand to lift her face up to meet his gaze. Her eyes were bright with tears and yet she was smiling. "What is wrong?"

"Fanny, gal, you done real fine, real fine," Buck said as he came up behind the pair and walloped Fanny on the back. "Afternoon, Morning Star. You see Fanny just now? Course she had me worried a mite at first, yelping with each throw. But she come through. Never moved a toe." He patted her heartily again, seemingly unaware that her arms were about Matthew's waist. "You just wait until the evening performance. We'll have them yelling for more. God to tell Oleta. See you later."

Embarrassed by his body's reaction to her embrace,

Matthew gently disentangled Fanny's arms from his waist and backed away a step, hoping that the break in contact would ease the need. "What has happened?"

Hiding her disappointment at his reaction, Fanny shrugged and brushed a tear from her eye with a finger. "I made a fool of meself just now." She looked back toward the stage, where a round of boisterous applause was greeting the introduction of Miss Annie Oakley. "I went out there. Took Buck's wife's place in his act."

"You did?" Matthew frowned as he searched his memory. "Buck's a knife-thrower." His brows shot upward. "You were his target?"

"It was nothing." She kept her face averted from him as new, vastly different emotions replaced the fright from the performance. How warm he had been, how densely rich the texture of his skin. He smelled faintly of earth and fire and horse, yet his wasn't an unpleasant scent. In the war paint were the odors of clay, pine resin, and berries. She could smell them all, even now that she'd turned away. Or perhaps it was because her cheek glowed with his perspiration. She wiped her face with a hand and her fingers came away sticky with a smear of color. "I've mussed your paint," she said as she looked back at the smudged line that spanned his chest.

Matthew looked down. The way she looked at him was not helping his discomfort. In fact, the smear of paint on her cheek was a potent reminder of her intimate embrace. "It doesn't matter," he said more sharply than was necessary. "There's time to repair the damage."

A spasm of regret crossed her face as Fanny continued to gaze at him. His jaw was set and his black eyes were forbiddingly opaque. "I'm sorry I ran into you.

And the paint, I—I'm sorry." Afraid he would guess her hurt, she turned and walked hurriedly away.

He watched her go, his eyes drawn to the enticing curve of her backside, which was revealed by the clinging suede skirt. He had first thought her skinny, yet he had seen proof that she was not. Why, then, did her costume, which hid so much, stir in him a feeling of familiarity and longing?

Then he remembered. It had often been one of the simple pleasures of life as he came into manhood to watch the women of his tribe in their suede dresses as they went about their daily lives in camp. Their clothing didn't fit tightly like white women's dress, which was molded over forms fashioned from whalebone and cloth. A white woman's body was caged and protected, hard to the touch. The thrust of bosom and sway of bustle was a sham hiding beneath an unconscionable amount of clothing. Sioux women wore dresses of the softest, finest skins of doe and calf. Their dresses clung and molded to the curves of a natural breast and unpadded thigh. Each time they moved, the free shape of flesh was clearly impressed upon the eyes and hearts of their men. Beautifully. Gracefully. Womanly.

Matthew turned away, abashed by his thoughts. Fanny was a white woman. He must remember that, and forget her.

By the time Fanny reached the Tarringtons' tent, her heart had calmed and her trembling was nearly gone. Even so, she paused to take a deep breath before going in. Buck was there with Oleta, and the smile she received from the pair made her glad she'd come directly here.

"Buck's just told me how good you were, dear,"

Oleta said, shifting her skirt to cover the cast on her leg. "I'm certainly relieved that he found so able an assistant."

"Och, I was terrible," Fanny admitted freely as she unbuttoned the jacket. "Buck could've stuck all them knives right in me and I wouldn't have known the difference. Only I didn't move like he told me, and that's why it worked."

"You done just fine," Buck answered. Giving his wife's shoulder a little squeeze, he added, "Only, of course, you ain't got the artistic flair of my Oleta. Still, we think you'll do till she's back on her feet."

Fanny paused in stripping off the jacket Oleta had loaned her. "You mean you want me to go out there again?"

Buck nodded. "This evening. And tomorrow and the day after. We can't afford not to do our show. We get paid by the act, you see. We'll pay you, though it ain't like you're experienced, so it won't be much."

Fanny looked from one to the other, and they each nodded, realizing that she didn't quite believe their offer. "But I—I was terrible. I nearly ruined the show."

"You had me worried," Buck admitted, "but after it was over, the way you came out there and give me a big kiss—"

"Kiss!" Oleta barked, her genial expression gone. "What's this about a kiss?"

"Well, it weren't rightly a kiss. More like a peck and a hug." Buck reddened from ears to brow. He turned a helpless look on his wife. "She's just a kid, and was scared as all getout, Oleta."

The look Oleta gave Fanny told her that the woman considered her anything but a helpless child. "I'm sorry about that, Mrs. Tarrington. I didn't think. I was just so glad it was over that I lost me head for a moment.''

"That's right," Buck agreed with a sheepish grin. "It didn't mean nothing. It was just like when she flew into Morning Star's arms backstage. She was just scared."

Oleta Tarrington looked Fanny straight in the eye. "I don't hold with young girls gallivanting about the grounds offering affection to any and all comers. You'll get yourself the sort of reputation you can't shake."

"I didn't mean anything," Fanny said, feeling a blush creep up her neck. "And I didn't exactly hug Morning Star. I bumped into him, that's all." Her gaze swung to her dirty gown lying on the floor where she had stepped out of it. "I'd best go change in Mrs. Wiggins's tent."

She picked up her gown and brushed away a little of the dust before looking at Oleta. "Should I keep the costume?"

Oleta compressed her lips into a thin line, her expression hard and uncompromising. She was tall and lean with a mass of dark brown hair that she wore swept back from her strong-featured face. In her time she'd been considered one of the eligible beauties of Cincinnati. Many women had competed for Buck Tarrington's attention, but she'd won him and kept his affections from straying since. No little red-haired gal was going to usurp her place in Buck's heart, or in the show. "I got a reputation to maintain with the show. You think you can take very good care of it?"

Fanny nodded.

"Then we must fix you up a bit. Come directly back here after you've done your chores. You need some help with that mass of red curls. If folks are gonna believe you're a cowgirl, you've got to look the part.''

"Oh, Mrs. Tarrington, you won't be sorry!" The smile that brightened Fanny's face eased a little of the tension from Oleta's face. Perhaps the girl meant no harm. Still, if her interest were fixed elsewhere—on that Indian, for example—Oleta would feel a lot better.

When Fanny had gone, Buck turned once again to his wife. "You know ain't nobody gonna replace you—in the show, I mean."

Oleta smiled tolerantly at her husband, the unspoken implication understood between them. "I know that. That's why I agreed to help the girl out. Tell me about this Indian Fanny's taken with. Ain't he the one who been to school?"

"Yep. Morning Star's his name. Not hard on the eyes, for a young buck. Still, I don't know as if a gal like Miss Fanny should be associating with his sort. He's a good enough fellow, but, well, many folk don't cotton to Indians and whites mixing."

Oleta Tarrington's lids lowered over her vibrant eyes. "Folks say the Indian blood in my veins is the reason why I'm famous for my long hair."

Ouch! Buck thought. "That's true enough. Only your grandpappy took up with an Indian squaw up on the Platte. We're in civilized surroundings. Don't know that an association between a city gal and a red man is gonna strike these folks as proper."

"I don't know that the girl is proper herself."

Buck blinked. "You mean you think . . . ?"

Oleta shrugged. "I ain't saying a word against her. But she's doing us a favor, and her behavior reflects on our reputation."

Buck stroked his chin thoughtfully. "She's no more'n a child," he murmured at last.

Oleta said nothing more. Why disabuse her husband of the notion that Fanny was merely a child? Wouldn't that be stoking the fire she meant to snuff? Still, she would be in the wings for each performance. There'd be no more kissing on stage or anywhere else.

Fanny smiled at her reflection in the tiny mirror hung on the center pole of the Tarringtons' tent. The western hat Oleta had found for her sat on her head jauntily while masses of fiery-red ringlets framed her shoulders. She rolled her hair into curls and tied them with rags to set every night, just as Oleta had taught her. Western women wore their hair loose, Oleta explained, and Fanny decided it must be true because Miss Annie Oakley wore her golden brown hair in long waves down her back. Oleta had even rouged her cheeks and lips a little, the better for them to be seen under the bright lights.

She turned back from the mirror, brushing her hands lovingly over the soft suede of her new outfit. Oleta had seen to it that she had one of her own. It wasn't as elaborate as Oleta's, and there was little beading on the sleeves of the jacket, but it sported buckskin fringe down each sleeve and along the side seams of the skirt. And she had moccasins to wear on her feet with leggings that came to midcalf. But her favorite part of the costume was the pair of Indian silver earrings Oleta had lent her.

After two weeks, she was no longer afraid of the crowd. In fact, she liked being the center of attention. Quite easily she had picked up the knack of pleasing an audience. By pantomiming, she had turned her natural fear of the knives into a joke between herself and the audience. Using great exaggeration, she drew laughter instead of concern.

"You wouldn't be believing your eyes if you could see me now, Phineas," she murmured.

The moment the words were out she wondered why she had said them. She hadn't given Phineas a thought in days. In fact, she'd nearly forgotten why she'd come to the island. The night she'd run down the alleyways in fear for her life seemed very far away. Now she lived with professional show people, shared their meals, watched them rehearse and perform. She didn't even mind so much that she shared sleeping quarters with Mrs. Wiggins. For the first time in her life, she felt as though she belonged.

Even before Phineas had disappeared, he'd begun pulling away from her. She realized now how secretive he'd been, how preoccupied, how unreliable. And when she'd gone seeking him, she'd nearly been killed for the effort. His note had said he was gone for good. She frowned. The note had also said she'd be safe once he was gone, but that hadn't been the case. She'd come close to losing her life to a murdering thief in the night. That was why she was here, and here she would stay.

"You're on next, Miss Fanny," a male voice called just outside the tent. "Buck says you'd best come running."

"I will," she answered as she adjusted her hat a final time. No time to think about Phineas now. She had a job to do.

A smile stole across her face as she left the tent and began walking through the crowded area behind the arena. Not a single soul in the Bowery would think to look under the brim of her ten-gallon hat for the child Fanny Sweets had once appeared to be. In her form-fitting bolero jacket and tight-waisted skirt, she looked every one of her eighteen years. She'd seen the cow-boys looking at her. One in particular, lounging now against the railing of a nearby corral, always tipped his hat. He did so now as she walked past. It felt funny to know a pair of male eyes followed her every movement. She wasn't interested in him or any of them. But it didn't hurt, she decided, to like being looked at.

Fifteen minutes later, when she stepped off the stage to the accompaniment of cheers and applause, her cheeks ached from smiling. Oleta had trained her to smile unceasingly throughout the act so that people would know she was having a good time, but Fanny had the feeling that she looked more like a dog with its fangs bared by the time the act was over.

"You coming to the hoedown?" Buck asked as she walked away from him.

"What's that?" she asked, turning back to him.

"It's a party, sort of. A dance."

She shook her head. "I don't dance."

"Don't gotta," Buck replied with his ever-ready grin. "Purty little gal like you only has to show up to give the fellas something to moon over."

Again Fanny shook her head. "Oleta says I must practice rope twirling if I'm to stay with the act once she's back on her feet. Them rope tricks is fair on the hardest thing I ever saw."

"Ain't nobody gonna be working tonight. The whole show's been invited. There's even a rib roast. Ain't many things in this world as good as slow-roasted beef and a slug of whiskey. Course, it's sarsparilla for little ladies like you. You gotta come. Oleta'd like for you to come.''

Fanny merely shrugged and started toward Mrs. Wiggins's tent to change. The truth was, though she tried to forget it on stage, the matter of Phineas and his whereabouts had stuck like a niggling itch in her thoughts, wearing down her high spirits. Where was he? Why had he left? Who was after him? Who wanted him so badly that they would threaten her life to find him? And when would she be free to go home?

She halted in her tracks. She wouldn't have a home when she returned to the city. Mrs. Mahoney would certainly have rented out her room to someone else. There had been rent owed even before she disappeared. A cold slice of reality slipped into her, appalling in its unforeseen implications. There was nowhere to go home to nor anyone to go to be with.

She wiped the perspiration caused by the stage lights from her cheeks as she walked slowly onward. There was no reason to go back to the city. Just like six years earlier when her da disappeared, she'd been left to start her life over.

Hurt bunched up under her heart, making it ache a little. The life of a street gypsy hadn't been pleasant. Phineas had found her at a critical moment. Now she was too old to expect anyone to find and care for her. She was grown. But she didn't feel grown. She felt small and humiliated and scared. Perhaps if Buck and Oleta knew that she'd been deserted more than once in her life, they, too, would turn away. Oh, they were friendly enough, but she was temporary in their lives. Once Oleta's broken leg healed, they wouldn't need her anymore. Except for Mrs. Wiggins, whom she still despised, there wasn't anyone else.

She dismissed the thought of Matthew Morning Star as quickly as it came. What possible interest would an Indian have in her? He'd made it plain that he disliked her. He seldom even spoke when they happened to meet, and he never smiled at her. It must be some flaw in her character that allowed people to fail her.

The aching under her heart spasmed and she drew a sharp breath against the pain. She wasn't going to cry. Mercy's grace, she wouldn't cry. She might be alone, but she was warm and dry and fed and earning her own way honestly. The feeling of honesty was new to her. She still didn't regard it as necessary, but she liked the self-pride that accompanied the payment of her wages. Three dollars, two full week's wages.

She looked back as the sound of voices drifted through the camp. The entire company was on the far side of the settlement, where a corral had been cleared for dancing. Lanterns had been hung in the trees and the Cowboy Band had been practicing extra hard all week. She had known there was to be a party, a celebration because the show was going strong in August, and, considering the gates, Buffalo Bill was thinking of moving the show indoors come the fall.

She smiled as she slipped inside the tent. There was no reason why she should think of leaving the show. Only a length of rope stood between her and doing just that. The secret of the tricks was all in the wrist, Oleta said.

Fanny spied the lasso that hung coiled on a nail inside the tent. When she had changed, she would spend the evening practicing the first of the tricks Oleta had taught her.

"Damn, damn, damn!" Fanny muttered under her breath as the stiff rope snaked down to close off the noose at the end. For half an hour she'd been trying to twirl the rope as Oleta had shown her. She laid out the rope on the ground and began spinning the loop at the end, but the loop got smaller and smaller until there was none at all.

She was perspiring freely, though the night was cool. Concentration was a laborious matter, she had discovered, so she had taken off her vest, rolled up her sleeves, and unbuttoned the first buttons of her fitted blouse so that her collar lay back, exposing her throat. She paused to push the masses of damp red curls back from her face and bind them quickly with a piece of ribbon to form a ponytail.

"All right, you ignorant bit of hemp!" she muttered as she bent to pick up the lasso. "I'm not giving up till I've done it once, so you might as well yield and give us both a night's rest!"

Once more she laid out the rope, holding the free end in her fingers just as Oleta had instructed. Slowly she began to spin the end about, lifting and spinning more quickly with each turn. To her consternation, the noose began to slip and then collapsed. In disgust she threw it from her with a muffled curse.

"Like trying to spin the eye of a needle, huh?"

Fanny looked up at the sound of a man's voice and recognized the cowboy from the corral who always lifted his hat when she passed by. He was grinning at her, the droopy edges of his bushy mustache framing and magnifying that grin, and the sight rankled. "You've no business spying on a body!"

"I was just looking, that's all. Can't fault a man for looking, kin you?"

She wasn't mollified by his self-deprecating tone.

He pushed his hat back from his brow, and she realized that he was younger than he seemed. There was a line in the middle of his forehead, separating his sunburned complexion from the fair skin shaded by his hat. He walked over and picked up the rope, letting out the noose as he spoke. "You ain't going about it right. You gotta coax a rope. Now you watch here." Like a magic trick, the rope was suddenly throwing a wide arc in the air, yet his wrist seemed scarcely to move.

"That's amazing!" she cried, though only an instant before she was determined to remain unmoved.

"You ain't seen nothing." The cowboy lifted the spinning rope into the air so that it spun above his head, and then he slowly lowered it until his head was inside the ring. Up and down he raised and lowered it about his head and shoulders like a circular yo-yo. All at once he snapped his wrist and the rope collapsed with a cracking sound. He turned and handed the free end to her. "Now you do it."

She crossed her arms under her bosom. "I can't."

He grinned again. "All you need is a little showing." He slackened the noose and then offered it. "Here, now. You take hold." Instead of handing it to her, his hand closed tightly over hers and he began to direct the motion of her wrist. "No, wait." He stepped up close behind her, his left hand grasping her waist. "Now you let me direct the rope," he said against her ear.

She was barely conscious of the hand directing the

rope, for the hand at her waist was tightening its grip to hold her even closer. But, amazingly enough, the noose was spinning. His palm was hard-callused against the back of her hand as he guided their movement. "There now, you see? Ain't nothing at all." He bent quickly and planted a kiss on her cheek.

Fanny whipped about. "Don't do that!"

"Weren't nothing but a friendly kiss. Least a fella deserves what's teaching you how to twirl a rope is a little thanks."

"I can be thanking you in me own way," she replied. "Thank you."

His eyes darted to the side and then he shrugged. "There's ways, and then there's ways. A man likes to think a purty gal's got more ways than words to thank him when he's done her a favor."

"You've done nothing so grand as that. Now be on your way before I think to be calling Buffalo Bill."

The man smirked. "You don't want that old man. I seen you looking at me when I been watching you. You like to come sashaying across them grounds, pert and purty as spring. A man's got to stop and thank his Maker for the sight." He stepped forward, his arms spreading in anticipation of a flight she wasn't yet aware she should be making. "I seen you looking, and I'm thinking there's got to be a way to git you to myself." This time when he stepped closer to her, she backed up a step. "Now, don't you go getting skittish on me. I heard how you done spent the night with an Injun. I got a sight more to offer than him."

There was no fear showing in her gaze, only a blazing anger and affront, and the knowledge emboldened him. "So it's gonna be like that, is it? What you want, little gal? I got five dollars in my pocket. You want a new pair of silk stockings?''

"I want you to go to hell," she said as his intentions became clear to her.

"I'm offering you your choice, for I mean to have mine with you," he said, closing the distance between them.

She waited until he was near enough and then she aimed a kick at his crotch.

His reflexes saved him from a boot in the groin, but he groaned a little as the hard kick landed high on his upper thigh. Still, he was a saddle-toughened, ropy-sinewed bulldozer who thought nothing of leaping onto the back of a steer and wrestling the two-hundred-pound creature to the ground. No tenacious female was likely to get the best of him.

Fanny turned immediately, skirts hiked, and dashed toward the distant noise of the hoedown, unaware that she had missed her mark until hard hands caught her from behind. With a cry of rage she twisted and jerked and kicked at her assailant, but her kicks were cushioned by his boots and his grip was like shackles. He simply lifted her off her feet and, like a hapless steer, brought her down with a thud onto the ground.

For one awful moment Fanny felt her skirts being lifted even as she struggled beneath him, and then she heard him cry out as he rolled off her. With a prayer of thanksgiving, she craned her head back to see what had happened.

Matthew stood over them. He didn't say anything, but the anger on his face struck in Fanny a more terrifying awe than the cowboy's rough handling. For an instant she fought for the breath to give an excuse for the act he'd come upon, but then she realized that he wasn't looking at her. He was watching the cowboy with the riveted black gaze of a predator.

The cowboy scuttled backward on his hands and heels away from Fanny. Matthew didn't move. His arms hung by his sides and his feet seemed rooted to the spot; yet she felt the tension of his anger upon her skin, and she shuddered in relief that it wasn't turned upon her.

When she glanced again, the cowboy was gaining his feet. "Evening, Morning Star." He flashed a chagrined smile as he dusted off his arms and legs. Then she saw that the placket of his trousers gaped open, the intent clear. She shivered again.

The cowboy's gaze flickered over Fanny, lingered a hungry second on the curvacious length of calf and thigh exposed by her hiked-up skirt, then came back to Matthew as he nervously wiped the drool from his mouth. "S'ppose you don't cotton to a man poaching on your territory."

Matthew moved toward him then, his hands still by his sides. Then, stunningly, one fist flashed up and he smashed the man's face. He struck him again, and then again, following his every backward step, every faltering retreat, delivering the punishment without intemperate rage but with the undeniable force of righteous wrath.

The cowboy was flat on his back before Fanny suddenly understood that Matthew might beat the cowboy to death.

She scrambled to her feet as Matthew dropped to a knee over the prone man. She seemed to feel the reflective shock in her own flesh of the brutal jab with which he struck the half-conscious man, and then she was upon him.

"No! No! You're murdering him! Stop! Stop!" She grabbed fistfuls of his black hair close to the temples and tugged until she knew there must be tears in his eyes. "Please! Please, Matthew!"

When he turned his head toward her, she released him and took a backward step. She'd seen this anger before. It was the savage rage that had been in him the first day she saw him perform. Then the impenetrable black stare softened. His hand reached to her shoulder and, though she flinched, she couldn't say the touch was anything but gentle.

"You go now," he said softly. "Others come. Big trouble for you. Go now."

"But I cannot—" Fanny began, only to see the darkening look resurface.

He shoved her. "Go! Go hide! Before they come! Go!"

She knew he was right. If she were found in the midst of another fray, no matter the circumstances, Buffalo Bill would fire her on the spot. She turned and ran into the woods, scarcely heeding the branches and bracken that pulled at her clothes. She didn't stop until she had reached the far side of the stand of trees and his lodge.

More than an hour later, seated before his fire, Fanny heard someone walking in the woods nearby. Finally the silhouette of a man emerged and came toward her. She knew it was Matthew long before she recognized his face. It was his height and catlike manner of walking that gave him away. His tread was so gentle it seemed it wouldn't disturb the dirt under his feet.

Then the firelight caught the hard angles of his cheek

and jaw, and she sucked in a quick breath and jumped to her feet. "You're hurt!"

He waved off her efforts, collapsing in a graceful fold beside her. "Cowboy have many friends." He touched his bleeding lip. "White girl much trouble."

Fanny bent her head. "I did nae start it. He tried to get in me drawers, but I didn't invite him."

Matthew gazed impassively at her. He was much nearer sympathizing with the cowboy's thinking than she realized. For her own safety she should know that. "Just Fanny should not walk about camp alone."

Fanny shrugged. "Oh, I don't know. I could've bested him if me aim had been better."

"Maybe that would be so," he dropped his stage voice, "if it weren't for one or two pertinent facts. One is something you can't alter. You spent many nights here in my lodge. It isn't surprising the men assume that you are my—ah . . ."

"Whore?" Fanny finished for him in outrage. "So that's it, is it? And me thinking they've made me one of them. All the while they think I'm here to spread meself for your pleasure. And you an Indian into the bargain."

His lids shuttered down. "Is that the insult, then— that you're presumed to be an Indian's whore?"

"And how would you like it?" she answered, unaware of the thrust of his question. "I've done a few wrong things in me time, but I'm not a whore."

"In *my* time," Matthew corrected.

"In your time what?" she demanded. Then her eyes grew round with wonder. "You ain't saying you been a—a, well, I don't exactly know what you'd be calling a man what services a woman for money."

This time it was Matthew who looked up. "What kind of female are you, to say such a thing?"

Fanny felt the tips of her ears burning, but she said, "I know a thing or two. There's women of a sort what will pay for a man's company."

"*Who* will," he amended.

"They will," Fanny replied.

"Women who will pay for a man's company," he repeated slowly between his teeth.

"That's what I said—women what will pay for it."

He groaned, his knuckles growing white with tension as he gripped his knees. "Talking to you is like speaking with the mad. Go away, Just Fanny. Go away and leave me alone."

Aware now that she had somehow offended him, she reached out and touched the bleeding cut above his eye. "That needs looking after."

"Leave it." He brushed her touch away, telling himself that it had nothing to do with the fact that it felt good or that her breath fanning his chest as she leaned near was sweet delight.

"You're a strange man, Indian," she said with a shake of her head. "I don't know that I'll ever understand you. But I'm in your debt again, and though you don't like it, I thank you."

Matthew knew he should acknowledge her thanks, but he couldn't and wouldn't even lift his head to look at her. Being with her was misery, torture, maddening. Why wouldn't she just go away?

CHAPTER
9

September 1886

"...don't know but that Mr. Cody should have thrown both them boys outa the show," Buck finished as Fanny entered the tent.

"Thrown who?" she questioned quickly.

Buck got up from his seat at his breakfast table. "Morning, Miss Fanny. Come on in and join us. I was just telling Oleta here about the fight last night. Course you wouldn't have heard nothing about it, being that you wasn't at the hoedown."

Fanny blushed. "I was practicing me rope tricks."

"I still say it was wrong to provide whiskey where an Indian could lay his hands on it," Oleta said to her husband. "It's only right they should both be fired."

Fanny's heart began a slow hammering. "Who's been fired?"

Waving Fanny into a seat, Buck said, "Now, Oleta, the boy swears he hadn't touched a drop, and I believe him." He turned now to Fanny. "Whiskey does purely funny things to Indian blood. Makes 'em madder'n a bull in locoweed. Was Morning Star drunk, he'd have killed and scalped young Ferris right before our eyes. I believe him when he said they had a disagreement over money. Ferris had took to borrowing from near everybody in camp these last weeks."

Oleta's dark brows lifted. "From you, Buck?"

His ever-ready grin turned sheepish. "I allow as how a man can find himself in need once in a while."

"You loaned Ferris gambling money?"

The tone of the question begged a denial, but Fanny could see that Buck was as honest as he was fair. "I staked him a time or two, when his luck was running poorly."

Oleta rose from the table, her bandaged leg less of an encumbrance after several weeks, and reached for her cane. "Hiram Nelson Tarrington, I'll be no wife to a man who gambles!" With that she walked out of the tent, leaning heavily on her cane.

"Why'd you do that when you knew what she'd say?" Fanny asked when Oleta was gone.

Buck shrugged. "The truth's easier to remember than a lie."

The answer astonished her. For as long as she could remember, lies were always easier than the truth. Honesty such as his would take some getting used to. Then she remembered. "Who was fighting last night?"

He grinned. "Morning Star and Ferris. Ferris lost."

Fanny looked about as though searching for something. "And did they say why they were fighting?"

"Money."

She turned back to him. "That's what Ferris said?"

"That's what they both said. Seems Ferris owed him money. After dusting him up a bit, Morning Star brought him right into the midst of the hoedown to tell Buffalo Bill about it. That's when he done fired Ferris."

"And Mo—the Indian?"

"Nope. Cody said Morning Star's losing his money was punishment enough. Seems Buffalo Bill likes him."

Fanny looked down at her hands in her lap. Her nails were biting into her palms. Matthew Morning Star had lied for her. What threat had he used to keep Ferris quiet about the real reason for their fight? It must have been a humdinger, as Buck would say. So the Indian could lie as well as she. It struck her as funny. She stood up grinning. "I must make a call before I forget."

"But you ain't even had your coffee," Buck protested.

"Mrs. Wiggins gave me some."

She found Matthew where she had left him the night before, or so it first seemed. He was still sitting cross-legged before his lodge, but he had changed his clothing. He wore a bright red shirt, and there was cork plaster above his right eye. He didn't speak as she neared, but his steady black gaze made her self-consciously aware of their last meeting.

She paused some five yards away. "Top of the morning to you."

He nodded but didn't speak.

Fanny looked about. "It's the makings of a rare fine day. Robins up early."

Again his slight nod.

She cocked her head to one side. "You're furious with me. And I'm not after blaming you for it. But you helped me, even if you did tell a lie to do it. Why?"

She thought she saw a softening in his gaze, but she

couldn't be certain for his expression remained impassive. "Just Fanny should be more careful in future."

She wrinkled up her nose. "I don't like that way you have of speaking when you're angry. You've a lovely voice and you've pretty words. When you want to, you can sound just like a priest or a politician."

There was no mistaking the smile that widened his mouth, and it was a fine, firm mouth, Fanny decided as she looked at him. Warmth spread through her to her fingertips and toes. She'd done that, made him smile.

"Just Fanny will sit down?"

"I think I will." Ever a mimic, she did as she'd watched him do a dozen times and dropped to the ground by bending her knees. Unfortunately her drop was faster than it was graceful and the ground jarred her teeth as she met it.

His smile lifted at the corners. "Just Fanny needs practice."

She smiled back at him. "I need practice at many things. But I'm a fast learner. That's what I was doing last night, practicing with me lasso."

"*My*—never mind." He held out the tin cup in his hand. "Would you like a taste?"

She leaned forward for a better look. "What is it?"

"Melted buffalo fat."

She recoiled and clamped a hand over her mouth. His laughter was as rich and deep and pleasant as his voice.

"You should see your face." He took a long sip and sighed in pleasure when he'd swallowed. He held out the cup again. "Good for digestion."

Fanny shook her head wildly and swallowed back the bile that rose in her throat.

"I thought you weren't afraid of anything?"

"I'm not," she answered behind her hand. "Only, it sounds purely awful."

"Have you never tasted anything that sounded 'purely awful?'"

She lowered her hand. "That I have. Haggis. The Scots eat it." She made a terrible face. "I'd as soon eat a boiled toad as touch it again."

He set the cup before him, and as he did so, Fanny found herself staring at the smooth strength of his hand and forearm. It was as though he were carved from wood that had been smoothed to a soft patina by loving hands.

"Why are you here, Just Fanny?"

Guiltily she looked up at him. "I came to say thanks."

"You did that last night."

"Then I came to say you needn't have lied for me."

"I didn't lie so much *for* you as *instead* of you."

His reply stung. "Did you think I wouldn't be telling the truth meself?"

He considered this a moment. "I thought you might try to tell something other than the truth because you would think the truth wouldn't be believed."

"And what was the truth, since you seem to think you know?"

He made a disclaiming gesture with his hand. "That one of your kind wished to press his interest upon you and that you were inconvenienced by his advances."

Fanny stared at him, her mouth slightly open. The wording was strange to her, but she gleaned enough to understand his meaning. "My kind? Are there no men of your kind who would force themselves on a girl?"

"There are."

"And what would your kind be doing with such a man?"

"Kill him."

His flat tone underscored the simple sentence. It was not said in the heat of passion but as a judge might hand down a decision: impartial, without rage or enmity. "So that's what you were about," she said slowly, wonderingly. She'd felt that vengeful tension in him, seen deadly intent in his gaze, and yet she hadn't quite believed her own eyes. Now, by his own admission, it was so.

"You'd have killed him?" When he didn't answer, she asked, "Have you killed a man before?"

"The ways of my people are simple but just. We cannot accept rogues within the tribe. They're banished or killed. That is the way of nature. It is the way of the Sioux."

He picked up his cup and drained it. It was fresh apple cider, but some impulse had made him reluctant to tell her so. She thought of him as a savage, a barbarian. He wouldn't disappoint her.

"Well, have you killed a man?" she pressed.

He nodded slowly, avoiding her eyes. But he knew what he'd see, how like the sky they were, bright and noonday blue one instant, clouded and stormy the next.

"I don't believe you."

He rose without a word and went into his tepee. A moment later he reappeared, carrying a tomahawk. Instinct made Fanny shrink back, though she didn't believe that he meant to harm her. He sat down beside her again, then offered her the weapon on his outstretched palms.

A little apprehensive, she took it, hearing the tinkle

of the glass beads and bits of metal decoration as it passed into her hands.

"Look." He pointed to the decorative tassels. "Among the quillwork and sacred symbols is the hair of my enemy."

Fanny stared at the plume of dusty brown hair that hung from the tomahawk. It couldn't be and yet it was. A hard shiver moved through her and the weapon fell from her hands. The sacred object never touched the ground, for he snatched it up.

She turned disbelieving eyes on him. "That's—that's evil!"

He brushed the tassel gently before laying the tomahawk in the crook of his arm. "The man had murdered many innocent women and children. I was thirteen summers, but large for my age. I begged my father to take me with him. I met my enemy fairly, as he did not meet those of my tribe he had slaughtered. The kill was my first . . . and last. The next summer missionaries came with the soldiers and I was sent east to learn to read and write the white man's way."

Nothing he said was spoken in anger or sorrow or regret, yet she wondered why it was not. She felt every one of those feelings as she listened to him. "I don't understand your ways, Indian."

Though he winced at her form of address, he said, "What would you know?"

"Is it honorable to do this, take a dead man's hair and keep it?"

"An enemy's scalp, yes. But there are other locks we treasure." To her surprise he took from his pocket a tiny leather pouch. This piece, too, was heavily beaded and fringed. Out of it he pulled a long, thin braid of hair and laid it on his palm. "This is the hair of my father. He is dead six summers past." For the first time she saw a softening and saddening of his exquisitely sculptured features. It made him more human than in any moment she had yet known him.

"Why do you wear your hair as long as a woman's?"

He spoke slowly, as if his thoughts had been far away. "In the past I cut my hair as the easterners do, in order to attend school. But to my people hair represents life. For us the human spirit is in and of this hair. Like life itself, it should be cared for, groomed, and allowed to grow in its natural path. To cut one's hair is to jeopardize one's spirit."

"Yet you did that."

"I did," he answered.

"Did you not fear for your life, then?"

"I shuddered each night before I fell asleep," he answered, so solemnly that she nearly didn't see the mirth hiding behind the forest of his straight black lashes.

"Then the taking of scalps, that's like capturing your enemy's spirit, holding it prisoner?"

Now he smiled. "I learned in the eastern university that scalping was not an Indian custom until after the coming of the white man who showed us how."

"That's a dirty lie!"

"Is it?" Surprised by her anger, he asked, "Is it only the savage who commits the unspeakable? Think, Just Fanny. Is that the truth in your life?"

She looked away. She knew he referred to the man who'd attacked her. He wasn't a savage . . . or was he? She looked up at him, confused. And then she saw the bracelet spanning his wrist where his cuff had ridden up. She was a thief. Did he consider that act part of the unspeakable things that some men do? Did that make her a savage, too?

"You find my people's customs not to your liking. Likewise, I find many of your people's customs unthinkable. There are reasons for what I do and say and think." He paused. "What guides your life, Just Fanny?"

A strange and haunting mixture of the savage and the intellectual held her captive. She was nothing more than the reflection in those dark, fathomlessly deep black eyes gazing upon her. She knew her breath quickened under his stare. Her heart's hammering was suddenly a conscious feeling. Was she being drawn in or was he leaning near her? She couldn't decide. Then, suddenly, softly, his lips were against hers.

There was nothing savage in his kiss, at least nothing of the crude and cruel. Recklessness, yes, and courage, and a will to bend all before it—those things she experienced in it and was not so frightened as humbled by it.

It was a seductive thing, his kiss. It made her reach out and hold his mouth to her own, to touch and taste and record what was so fleetingly offered. And deep inside she felt the woman in her begin to bud, a sudden burst of awareness, the first unfurling of passionate flowering.

His cheek was warm, clean, and firm. Daringly her thumb reached for the corner of his mouth and lightly stroked the edge of his lips. She heard the shuddering indrawn breath that parted his lips on hers and then the flick of his tongue.

She pulled away in surprise, and it gave Matthew the instant of sanity that had been lacking as long as her lips lay under his. He put a hand on her shoulder, not to draw her closer again as she seemed to expect, but to hold her at bay. He shook his head, his long black hair sliding forward over his shoulders.

"No." He said the word softly, as if he meant it only for himself. He did. He was trembling from the tension of fighting the passion within. He'd made a sacred, solemn pledge, and not even her desire—ah, yes, he'd felt it in that kiss—would lure him from his pledge.

"You must go now. It is as dangerous for you to be here with me as it was last night to be with that cowboy. Remember that when you would come here again."

He didn't wait for her to leave, sensing that the humiliation of being sent away would needlessly wound her. Instead, he rose quickly and walked rapidly away.

Fanny watched him go in disappointment. She wasn't insulted by his words or his actions. She'd heard something in them that perhaps he wouldn't have said had he realized how it would be received by her. He'd said he wanted her, found her attractive. Suddenly she knew that she felt the same, felt an attraction that had been there from the first day they'd met. She'd felt it in his kiss. The thoughts made her flush with embarrassment. He was an Indian. Should she feel as she did?

He's a man, whispered the voice of the new-budded woman inside her. Yes, he was. But did she like him as a woman likes a man? Certainly he wasn't the sort she might consider marrying. Would she have allowed him to hike up her skirts if he'd pressed her back against the earth just now?

Fanny laughed as she pressed fingers to her mouth. For more of his kisses, she might have. Yes, she might have.

* * *

Matthew let the day's glory fill his senses as he entered the stand of oaks. He threw back his head and closed his eyes, the better to drink in the sounds of rippling water, the melody of the birds, the chirp and click of insects. To lift himself out of himself, that was what he desired. To give ease to his desire, that was his aim. Many times he had done this, emptied all his vital energies into the moment of being.

For twelve golden, lovely summer weeks he had drawn on all that this country place had to offer him. As the days passed, he had learned to discount the hum of thousands of voices as he strode through the fairgrounds of the island at dusk. He had made peace with the myriad lights twinkling on the far shore. He knew how to trace the path of the stars. He was a Dreamer. He'd been born with the gift of visions.

Purity of spirit made him strong, but this morning he resented, just a little, the sacrifice. He'd never lain with a female, but the need denied so long would no longer be banished. He couldn't remember an hour in the last days when it didn't burn within him. The constant flickering warmth that sometimes flushed and filled his loins had been fanned to blazing by a single kiss. His attraction for Fanny was undeniable and yet more impossible than ever. Even as he had touched his lips to hers, he had known he was leaving. He was going home.

Twelve years ago visions had sent him running from the Black Hills when the chance was offered. Death waited there in the hills of his homeland—not his own death but the death of the way of life of all his people. He was helpless to change that. He'd known it from the instant of the first vision. Now it was time to go home again and face it, that he might know his destiny and his part in the visions over which he held no sway.

He would have gone home directly from school had he not received a message from Red Shirt telling him that he was coming to New York with the Wild West Show. And so he'd delayed his journey home, even joined the show for the companionship of an old friend. But now he must go home.

After nearly an hour of meditation, he lowered his head, his mind filled with the whistling winds of faraway places, of stark mountains, undulating hills, and broad prairies. They were painted in full glory on the canvas backdrop of the arena, but it wasn't the same. The real places called out to him. It was time he went home.

Yet as he walked back to his lodge, the whisper of his footsteps mocked him. *Foolish to give in to the moment. Foolish to be drawn by a sky-blue gaze. Foolish to tremble with desire. Foolish.*

"Looks like you got the hang of it."

Fanny turned about with a cocky grin on her face as she twirled the lasso up over her head. She'd been practicing every day for a week, and the effort was paying off. She didn't even mind anymore if visitors to the show paused to watch her. Of course she made a lot of mistakes, but when she got it right, the sound of their "ohs" and "ahs" was more precious than gold. This morning, however, she had only Buck for an audience. In the distance the repeated crack of rifle fire and the pungent aroma of powder in the air was evidence that

Annie Oakley and the other marksmen of the show were practicing, and they always drew the crowd.

With a quick flick of her wrist, she dropped the loop down over her shoulders and then snapped it back up over her head, ending the exercise with a flair by dropping into a deep curtsy. "Oleta says I'm as good as some who've practiced more than a year."

Buck nodded as she turned to begin the exercise again. Fanny had the talent for a lot of things. Anything she put her hand to seemed to work out one way or another. Why, even Oleta had commenced to praise Fanny when the girl was out of earshot. "Can't have her head swelling up," Oleta had said. As he watched Fanny turn in a graceful spin, he couldn't help noticing that, while her head wasn't swelled, her trim young body was filled out in all the right places.

He smiled, thinking that he wasn't the only one to notice the change in Fanny. Brick and Jim and Tom, to name a few, had taken to finding excuses to drop by his tent whenever Fanny was there. There was a new authority in her gaze, a maturing of her attention that drew men like flies to honey. Yet she didn't offer them what any sane man could call encouragement. He'd always believed that love made a body moony and calf-eyed, but Oleta, who claimed a sight more experience in the matter, had stated flatly that Fanny's new manner could only be the result of an infatuation. But with whom—that was the question.

"When will you talk with Mr. Cody about me joining the show proper?" Fanny asked when she'd successfully completed the rope trick a second time.

"Soon as he comes back to the show. He and his missus done gone home to North Platte for a spell."

"Why?"

"Some of the boys is leaving the show. They get a mite homesick about this time of year. Been away from family and friends since spring. Buffalo Bill don't blame 'em. He's gone home for the same reason, that and to recruit new folks for the show."

A chilling sense of foreboding crept over Fanny as she let her rope drop into the dust. "What about you and Oleta? Will you be going home, too?"

Buck shook his head. "We're staying. Got a new act to work up for the Madison Square Garden show. That fella in here last week, name of McKaye, he done put the idea in Buffalo Bill's head. Ain't nothing come of it yet, but Cody's been jawing it about. So me and Oleta know it's going to happen. You ever seen a man work a bullwhip? Well, you're in for a treat. Me and Oleta figure to amaze them city folks all over again."

"What about me?"

"Why, you're welcome to stay on with us, providing your people ain't agin it."

"Got no people," Fanny said impatiently. "I've told you a dozen times, there's just me."

He watched her closely as she answered. She said that every time the subject came up, but Oleta didn't believe her. No matter what the temptation, they'd not been able to persuade Fanny to accompany them to the city when they went there for the day. "She's hiding something, you mark my words," Oleta had said.

"No need to get riled up," Buck said now. "You're among friends, that's all I'm saying. See you later."

Fanny sighed and gathered up her rope as he departed. She'd been sharp with everyone lately. In fact, she'd been downright rude to more than one member of the cast.

"It's that stubborn Indian!" she muttered to herself. Matthew Morning Star had refused even to acknowledge her existence since the morning he'd offered her the noxious buffalo fat and then the sweet taste of his lips. He was avoiding her. She'd seen him ducking behind a tent or a tree when he spied her from the corner of his eye.

Why was he hiding? She wasn't ugly or too fat or too thin. She had proof of that in the eyes of the visitors and male members of the cast alike. What was wrong?

She entered the Tarrington tent with a deep frown marking her fiery-red brows.

"Poor practice?" Oleta suggested when she looked up from her knitting and saw Fanny's expression.

Fanny shrugged and plopped down in a chair. "I got the right of it, only . . ."

Oleta's sharp eyes searched the girl's expression, but she didn't comment on it. "Going to the dance tonight?"

Fanny shook her head.

"Shame on you, Fanny. You're a bright and clever girl. You could have your pick of the young men. And it's high time you were thinking of picking one."

Fanny rolled her eyes toward the ceiling.

"Now, don't you go gainsaying me in this. You say you've no mother to look after you, so it's my duty to take you in hand. How old are you?"

"Eigh—fourteen."

"Eighteen is more like it," Oleta said. "Nothing but bones when we took you in, but you've filled out real nice this last month. You're broad enough in the hips to carry a child and have bosom enough to feed it."

Fanny sat forward with a squawk, but Oleta didn't drop a stitch as she continued, "We're plain folks where I come from. We don't hold with the mealy-mouthed, shilly-shallying that passes for genteel conversation in these parts."

She laid her knitting in her lap, a wise and amused expression on her face. "When I was your age, I was married four years and with two babies to show for it."

"You married at fourteen?" Fanny held back the next reasonable question, but it was plain to guess from her curious expression.

"Where are my babies, you're wondering," Oleta said. "Taken by the cholera a year before we joined the show. Don't weep for them," she added as she saw the girl's face soften. "Me and Buck done that."

"I was thinking of you," Fanny replied. "Is that why you didn't have any more?"

Oleta smiled. "What makes you think we won't have any others?" She held up the knitting in her lap, and Fanny saw the beginnings of a tiny sweater. "Expect it'll be a mighty cool welcome into the world in these parts come March."

Fanny's eyes widened. "You're—does Buck know?"

"No, and I'd thank you not to tell him. He's all fired up about the prospect of working at the Garden. I wouldn't want him to withdraw from the show on account of so simple a matter as me being with child. I got my leg back near as good as new. Standing in front of a few knives won't tax me any. Long as the audience don't guess my condition, I'll stay with the show."

Fanny sank back in her chair to ponder this new information. She knew the facts of life, how babies were conceived, and had heard enough talk to decide that the business sounded both uncomfortable and messy. To think that Oleta and Buck . . . right here in this tent! Well, well.

"Do Indians marry?" Fanny blushed. Now why had she asked that? She sat up straighter, brushing down her skirt. "What I mean is, how do they become man and wife? Or do they?"

"They do. The ceremony's heathen, but I suspect the good Lord is glad enough to have even pagan words said over the bond. Leastways other folks know they belong together."

"Do they live as man and wife, like other folk?"

Oleta chuckled. "I suppose a man is a man and a woman is a woman, no matter what runs in their veins. They share the same rug, if that's what you mean."

Oleta was certainly blunt, Fanny thought, but she liked it. Questioning her was like poking a cornered cat. You never knew what would result. "Do you suppose Indians have feelings like us? I mean, do they fall in love? Like when a man looks at a woman and his eyes get all hot and his mouth goes slack like he's thinking he could gobble her up?"

Oleta kept her eyes on her knitting. "When a man looks at a woman like that, there's only two things to be done—hide the woman or grab the preacher. You got some man looking at you like that?"

Fanny grimaced. Matthew didn't even look at her, never mind hungrily. "I was only after wondering, that's all." She took a deep breath and glanced at Oleta's bent head. "I'm thinking it doesn't mean the same thing when an Indian kisses a woman as when a white man does."

Oleta lifted her head. "Indians don't kiss, deary.

They find the custom crude and distasteful. Why do you ask?''

Fanny knew she was blushing, but she didn't care. "Guess I must have mistaken something I saw."

Her curiosity piqued, Oleta again laid her knitting aside. "You saw one of the Indians kissing a white woman?"

Oleta's tone of voice alerted Fanny to the idea that this wasn't acceptable behavior. "I say I must have been mistaken." She stood up abruptly. "Got to ask Mrs. Wiggins something. See you later."

Crude and distasteful—those were the words Oleta had used to describe the Indian attitude toward kissing. Fanny felt her cheeks burn as she stalked out of the camp. No wonder Matthew was hiding from her. She'd thought perhaps he'd initiated the exchange. Now, from Oleta's words, she knew *she* must have kissed *him*.

Crude and distasteful. Fanny cringed. She wanted to crawl into a hole and hide. She glanced right and left, the error growing all out of proportion in her mind. She would die, drop dead right on the spot if they met. There wasn't a thing she'd done right from the moment she'd stolen the Indian's bracelet. She had offended him, angered him, hurt him, annoyed him, and now revolted him.

She wandered over to the maple grove. The tips of the leaves were already touched with flame, though the days were still as fully warm as those of late August. She pressed her hands to her still stinging cheeks. What a fool she was. She felt hot all over, hot and too tightly bound, and close to tears. Deep in the grove, the air was cooler and she took several breaths to draw the coolness inside herself until the stinging abated.

When she opened her eyes again, she saw an empty fringed hammock swaying lazily between two strong saplings. One of the show people had strung it. The oak grove was full of them. How inviting it looked. She went over to it and sat down. After a moment's hesitation, she swung her legs up into it and lay back. The shifting of her weight set it in motion, and she smiled as she gazed up into the canopy of trees overhead. The dappled greens and reds and golds seemed to sway instead of her. She felt cool and hidden, safe. Maybe she'd lie here forever, or at least until show time.

The first thing she noticed when she opened her eyes was that the color of the leaves had changed. No longer were they semitransparent with light. They were opaque, green and umber replacing the veiny greens and reds of before. Her world had ceased to sway comfortingly. In the distance she heard rifle fire. The matinee!

She sat upright and nearly fell out as the hammock tilted wildly with the shift. As she grabbed the sides to steady herself, she caught a glimpse of feathers over the edge of the hammock. Indian feathers. An Indian in full regalia stood not ten yards from where she'd been sleeping. Her heart sank. Not just any Indian. There was no mistaking his height. Matthew Morning Star was here in the maple grove. She heard the whisper of the fallen leaves as he came toward her, and for one wild moment she nearly bolted. What was the use? He'd run away quickly enough when he found out who sat in the hammock. With weary resignation she rose and turned to meet him.

Matthew stopped short when she rose from the hammock. Half the cast had been looking for her. When she didn't appear in time for Buck's act, his had been the first heart to sink. Though he avoided her when she was aware of him, he'd taken a certain perverse pleasure in watching her when she was unaware of his presence. Like driving thorns into one's own flesh, he took a certain satisfaction in the self-torment.

Fanny eyed him warily, yet she was glad to see him. He wore his hair parted to one side on this occasion, half wrapped in painted buckskin as it fell forward across his shoulder. Under his vest of dentalium, he wore a blue shirt, the sleeves of which were banded above the elbow and at the cuff by his silver bracelets. She didn't know what to say or even if she should say anything.

He moved as if to turn away, and she realized that he wasn't going to speak to her. Indignation burned through her chagrin in an instant. She stepped forward, hands braced on her hips. "Good day to you, Morning Star, or is it that you'll not be wishing me any kind of day at all?"

Matthew's expression softened at her challenge, but he didn't look directly at her. "Hello, Just Fanny. Buck and the rest of the cast are looking for you. You missed the matinee."

"I fell asleep," she answered, her anger dimming. She'd missed the show. That meant Buck wouldn't be paid for the performance. "I should go and tell them I fell asleep."

Matthew shifted his gaze. This was the last time he would look at her and he wanted to remember every detail. How her hair vied with the color of the fall maples for brilliance in the afternoon light. Once he had thought it ugly. Now it seemed to him as soul-searing as a prairie sunset. She was small, dainty like the women of his tribe. Only her fairness disturbed him, for it was a measure of their differences.

Fanny saw him look at her but she couldn't guess his thoughts, couldn't imagine why he'd want to gaze upon someone who'd offended his sense of decency. And then she thought she knew. He waited for an apology. "I'm sorry I insulted you." She met his gaze squarely, refusing to give in to her embarrassment. "About the kiss, I mean."

Matthew didn't reply. Her words were the very last thing he had expected to hear from her. Why had she apologized? It was he who had kissed her. Should he tell her that the memory of her kiss stayed with him, a torment, a thorn in his flesh, a constant vivid reminder that he was a man destined never to know women, and that he nearly hated her for the reminder of what he could not have?

Fanny shook her head impatiently. She'd done what she could to span the difference and he hadn't accepted it. She'd had plenty of hard knocks in her life. She'd accept this one more, but it hurt.

As she started toward the arena, he stepped in front of her. "I will say good-bye to you here. I am leaving."

She looked up. "Leaving? Where are you going?"

"Home. To what your people call the Dakota Territory."

Fanny didn't know where the Dakota Territory was, but it sounded like a long way off, by the way he said it. "But you'll be coming back, like Buffalo Bill?"

He shook his head.

"Why are you going?" she demanded, forgetting that she wasn't going to care anymore.

"My people need me. Or perhaps I need them more."

Her gaze narrowed. "There's someone waiting for you?"

He nodded.

It was a woman! It must be! Without another thought Fanny detested the woman with a clear, searing hatred that was absolute and complete. "Well, now," she said as casually as she could manage, "you should bring her back with you. Mr. Nelson's got his Indian woman with him. And many of the chiefs do, as well." She looked up in hot anger. "Or don't you think she'd fit in the show?"

"There's no woman," he said quietly. "There can't be."

"Can't? But wh—?" Fanny clamped a hand over her mouth, but it was too late. Before she could scotch the impulse, her glance slipped down to where his buckskin leggings clung to his hips. There was no mistaking that he was endowed with the necessary male part. In fact, before her astonished gaze, that part of him stirred and began to swell beneath the cloth covering it.

Matthew resisted the impulse to cover himself, for it was far too late to deny his reaction. A dull heat infused his neck and he knew that he was blushing.

"I am a Dreamer," he said in a husky voice. "That I may know the wisdom of my visions, I deny myself the company of women."

Fanny's mouth fell open. "Like a priest, you mean! Jesus, Joseph, and Mary! I kissed a priest!"

He was grateful for the laughter that shook him. It broke the tension in a way little else could have.

"Why didn't you tell me before?" she asked indignantly. "Faith, I'm no priest-breaker."

He liked her, no doubt about it. Her thinking left him

amazed, her morals deplored him, but he didn't feel isolated when she was with him. He slipped one of the silver bands from his wrist and held it out to her. "So that we may part friends."

She glanced down at it, then shook her head. "It wouldn't be right, seeing as how I once stole it. It's important to you."

"Then accept it as a measure of the change between us, Just Fanny. Among my people, to give away the best of what one has is to bring great honor upon oneself. If you refuse, I'll think that you don't consider me worthy of your regard."

Fanny reached for the gift, hesitating as her fingers closed over it. "I didn't know you were a priest. What I've been thinking... well." She cocked her head to one side. "Do Indian priests hear confessions?"

Matthew shook his head. "I'm not a priest, or shaman. I am what is called a Dreamer."

"But you cannot marry?"

"I do not choose to."

She took the bracelet. "Why not?"

He couldn't explain it to her, just as he'd never tried to explain it to Red Shirt. "It must be so."

"And you'll not come back?"

"I must not," he said. Then, because he would never see her again, he reached out and touched her hair. The bright curls encircled his fingers, clinging even as he withdrew his hand.

Fanny picked up a curl of her own hair. "Would you like a bit? For one of them sacred pouches?"

"*Those* sacred pouches," he corrected.

"Yes, well, I'm offering you a gift, like you gave me. Would you be accepting it?" She smiled at him.

"Or would you be leaving me to think I'm not worthy of the honor?"

He smiled back. "Strong magic in hair like sunset. Maybe work for me."

He pulled a knife from his leggings and cut a lock of her hair. Then he tucked it into the pouch that hung from his waistband. "Good-bye, Just Fanny."

"Fanny Sweets," she said. "Me—my name's Fanny Sweets."

He nodded, then turned and walked away.

"You ain't a priest," she whispered to herself. And, if that were so, then he wasn't bound by any rules but those of his own making. She smiled. Rules were made to be broken. That's what Phineas always said.

Phineas. Fanny looked down at the bracelet she held. "Where in Hades are you, Phineas?"

Once again a man was walking out of her life, but this time he hadn't disappeared without explanation. She knew he was leaving.

For a moment she contemplated what she was losing by Matthew's departure. She had a job that paid real wages. She had found friends in Buck and Oleta. She was safe and content. Yet something was missing. She needed something, someone of her own.

But she had her pride. She'd think about it. Surely she'd see Matthew again before he left. And when she saw him, she'd think about asking him to stay. And if he wouldn't... Well, she had her pride.

CHAPTER
<u>10</u>

Fanny worried the lace of her blouse as she waited in line for a cab on the dockside on Twenty-third Street. She'd eaten a whole box of popcorn on the trip by ferry from Staten Island, but the hollow feeling in her stomach persisted. It had been more than a month since she'd last set foot in the city. Many things had changed. Then she had been returning home. Now she was leaving what had promised to be a new future for reasons she couldn't even put into words.

That thought had dogged every moment of the ferry crossing. Only once, as they rounded Bedloes Island and she'd caught sight of the huge, half-finished drapery of the Statue of Liberty, had she forgotten about her troubles for a while. When she and Phineas had made the trip nearly two months earlier, all that had been there was the massive base on which the statue was to be erected. She'd made the second crossing on a foggy morning when nothing but the sounds of work in progress had reached her. Now the lower half of a female figure was formed with girders reaching out of it toward the sky.

The sight was arresting, awe-inspiring. Buck and Oleta had been to see the torch that was to be held in the statue's right hand when it was on display in Madison Square. Oleta had said that people would be able to climb up inside the statue as one did in a building. Buck said they would all go and do just that when it was finished. With a pang of sorrow Fanny realized she wouldn't be there to go with them. If Matthew refused to see her, she would—

"Where're you going, miss?" a cabbie called down from his perch as he halted before her.

Fanny stepped up and clutched her bundle closer. Where was she going? "The Fifth Avenue Hotel."

The cabbie gave her a speculative look. She was dressed in her stage costume, a fringed suede skirt and bolero jacket with ruffled blouse and a high collar that tickled her chin. With a matching soft suede cowboy hat topping her cascading curls, she was scarcely the sort of fare he'd pick up for Fifth Avenue.

"You one of them Wild West Show people?" he asked at last.

Fanny smiled, imitating Buck's twangy drawl as she said, "I surely am!"

"You Annie Oakley, by any chance?"

His expectant expression made her answer, "Yes, sir!"

His face broke into a big grin as he leaped from his perch to open the door of his cab. "My family and I've seen your show four times. Absolutely amazing, that's what you are. It's a pleasure to meet you, Miss Oakley. You just climb on in.''

"Did I hear you say this is Annie Oakley?'' questioned the man standing nearest her.

The cabbie nodded. "That's right, and she's my fare!''

The man turned to her and stuck out his hand. "I just want to congratulate you, Miss Oakley, on your fine marksmanship. I've seen your performance. A bang-up act!''

Fanny shook his hand, and no sooner had she done that than three more were stuck out for her to shake as the whisper of Annie Oakley's name raced through the dockside crowd and people came running to meet the famous person. Smiling, she shook a few more hands, but it quickly became obvious as the crowd jostled her in an effort to get near that her little lie was growing out of all proportion to her intent.

Faintly alarmed, she turned and entered the cab. Following her lead, the cabbie hoisted himself into his seat and snapped the reins. As the hansom lurched away from the curb, she saw a blur of faces waving and calling out to her. She smiled, waved, and then settled back into a corner of the cab. It had never occurred to her that the show people might be celebrities outside the fairgrounds. The feeling was nice but sort of scary.

Hard on the heels of that thought came the question of how those people would have reacted had she given her own name. After all, Frank Richmond, the show's announcer, called out her name each time he introduced Buck's act. Was she even a little famous? She would never know. She had left the show.

There'd been an emergency—that's what she'd told

Oleta and Buck. Buck had believed her, offering to go along with her in case she might need help, but Oleta hadn't accepted her excuse for a second. The woman had pinned her with a knowing look, yet said nothing.

Only when she'd gathered up her few belongings did Oleta speak. "It's Matthew Morning Star, isn't it? You don't have to say anything. I know a body's got to do what a body's got to do." In a rare gesture of affection, Oleta had placed her hand on Fanny's and given it a gentle squeeze. "Only, my dear, don't pin any hopes on him."

"I'm accustomed to disappointment," she'd answered.

Oleta had smiled wistfully. "No woman ever grows accustomed to disappointment in love."

"I ain't in love!"

"Well, then, Fanny dear, just know that you can come back to me and Buck anytime."

The hollow place in Fanny's middle didn't seem quite so deep as she recalled Oleta's words. She could go back to the show if she couldn't find Matthew, or if he didn't . . . didn't what?

She'd nearly told Oleta where she was going and why, until she realized that she didn't quite know herself. What she did know was that she needed answers, answers that would fill the frighteningly hollow place that had opened up inside her when she learned that he'd left the island without a word to her. He'd said he was leaving, but she'd thought he would say one last good-bye.

She'd felt robbed when she learned that he had taken the ferry during her afternoon performance. He'd stolen away like a thief when her back was turned. Her hands flexed into fists. She felt hurt and humiliated and the familiar terror of abandonment.

If she hadn't overheard one of the cowboys telling the ferryman where to send the last of Matthew's belongings, she wouldn't even know where to look for him. The Dakota Territory, she'd learned from Buck, was hundreds and hundreds of miles to the west, farther away even than Chicago. That's where Matthew had said he was going. But luckily he'd gone no farther away than the Fifth Avenue Hotel.

Suddenly she felt warm tears sliding down her cheeks. "If this is love, then it's a crock!" she muttered and rubbed away the tears. She wasn't going to cry now. She'd made her decision. She'd find him and make him do—oh, something! To distract herself, she leaned forward to look out at the city.

In just a few short weeks, she had forgotten how loud and noisy and dusty the city was. The green grass and cool woods of Staten Island had wiped from her mind the stark brashness of the city, where four-story buildings stretched for block after block. The traffic was snarled at every intersection. Cabbies hurled abuse at one another while the more brave of the pedestrians threaded paths between the rows of carriages, riders, cabs, and drays. By the time the cab pulled up in front of the Fifth Avenue Hotel, she was raw and cross, and more than ready for a quarrel with Matthew Morning Star.

She hadn't known what to expect, but she was taken aback by the sight of the magnificent six-story building of white marble with a columned portico. Matthew was staying here? It didn't seem possible. Why, by the smart, elegant looks of the patrons entering the place, it must cost a fortune to rent a room.

For a moment she didn't move. She couldn't go in there. She'd never been in so fine a place in all her life.

"Miss Oakley," the cabbie called when he'd jumped down to open the door. "You did say the Fifth Avenue Hotel. This is it."

Fanny accepted the hand he extended to help her step down and then, belatedly, remembered that she should pay him. But as she began digging in her bundle, he shook his head. "That won't be necessary, Miss Oakley. It's a privilege to have driven you. An absolute privilege."

She smiled tentatively at the doorman in livery who stepped forward to open the door, but his face remained impassive. If he was impressed by her attire, he certainly kept that fact to himself, she thought irritably.

Once inside the lobby she was again swamped with the impression of being out of her class. Everywhere she looked there was marble and gilt and velvet and gold tassels. And the people! They were beautifully groomed and dressed in clothing more lovely than any she'd ever seen. Perhaps she'd misunderstood. Perhaps Matthew had gone to a different hotel on Fifth Avenue. Perhaps he wasn't . . .

She saw him from the corner of her eye, through the archway of the saloon at one end of the lobby. He was lounging against the end of the long curving bar, one booted foot poised on the shiny brass railing. There was a drink in his hand, but he was deep in conversation with a smaller man, whom he bent forward to listen to.

Her gaze covetously followed his movements as he turned away from his partner and lifted his glass. He was dressed as a gentleman, in suit and tie, but his deeply bronzed profile was unmistakable. His hair was tied back, accentuating his broad brow, hawkish nose, and square chin. The odd little pang below her heart that caught her off guard each time she saw him throbbed gently as she started toward him. She didn't know what to say or how to say it. What would he think when he saw her? Would he be angry or pleased? Or would he simply ignore her? No, he wouldn't do that. She wouldn't allow him to, even if she created the biggest scene this grand old hotel had ever seen.

"Sorry, miss, you can't go in there," said a man in black tailcoat and striped trousers as he stepped out from behind the main desk. "That's the gentlemen's lounge. If you care for a refreshment, you will find a confectionary shop right through there." He indicated an archway at the opposite end of the lobby.

"I want to speak to someone, that's all," she said and started around him, but he backed up a step, maintaining his position between the lounge and her.

"We can't allow that, miss. It's the rules. If you'd care to write the gentleman in question a note, I'd be happy to deliver it to him."

Write a note? She couldn't even print her own name. "No," she said slowly, trying to see past his shoulder but failing to do so. "That won't be necessary. I'll just be sitting"—she glanced about and found a velvet settee between two hothouse palms—"I'll just be waiting over there."

He subjected her to a quick but thorough glance that brought the color to her cheeks before saying, "Very well, miss. You are a guest, of course?"

Fanny's eyes narrowed at his supercilious tone. "Am

I after needing to be a guest to be sitting on your settee?"

"Not at all. However, we don't encourage random visitors."

"There's nothing random about me being here," she replied, though she wasn't quite sure what "random" meant.

"Very well."

He turned away and she knew she'd been dismissed. All her life she'd been snubbed by her betters, but this time she felt it acutely. She nearly went after him to tell him that she was the famous Annie Oakley, just to see what he would do. Then reason reasserted itself. At the dock she'd used the name to tease the cabbie. The fact that he believed her wasn't intentional. But Matthew wouldn't be at all happy if she deliberately duped a man.

She sat down on the settee, perching on the edge like the ladies in bustles nearby were doing. In disappointment she realized that she couldn't see the entry to the saloon from this angle. After a few minutes of fidgeting, she could stand the suspense no longer and looked about for a more strategically located spot.

She spied a peculiar seat at the center of the lobby. It was circular in design, and in the center of it an enormous fern grew in a brass pot. She went over and sat down. A frond brushed the crown of her hat as she turned to look toward the saloon. In alarm she saw that Matthew was no longer standing in the archway.

She stood up and started toward the room, only to be checked by the movement of the man behind the desk. He was still watching her. Reluctantly she went back and sat again. She was certain that Matthew hadn't walked past her, but she couldn't be certain that this was the only entrance.

Rising yet again, she went over to the man behind the desk. "Is there another way out of the saloon, besides this one, I mean?"

The hotel manager's eyes narrowed. "Yes, there is."

She smiled at him. "I don't suppose you'd be allowing me to just step a toe in that room, just to see if the gentleman I'm waiting for is still in there?"

"That's impossible." He paused, then said, "May I inquire for which of our guests you are waiting?"

"Ma—Mr. Morning Star."

"The Indian?" he asked in surprise.

She smiled. So Matthew was staying here. "That's right. We're in the Wild West Show together. He's expecting me."

"He is?"

The scarcely disguised condescension was there again, but Fanny ignored it. "Now if you'd be so kind as to let me—"

"I'm afraid I've explained how that's impossible. However, if you give me your name I will tell the gentleman that you're waiting."

Fanny took a backward step. If Matthew learned she was here before she saw him, he might run away, or at least try to dodge her. "Thank you, no. I'll be waiting."

She turned away and cast one more longing look at the archway before breaking into a smile. Matthew was standing at the end of the bar again, and a dish of food had been set before him. She nearly called out to him but knew that would only embarrass him. Too often she'd made mistakes when dealing with him. She would wait quietly and with dignity until he came out. With a smug glance at the man behind the desk, she went back to sit down.

Resuming her seat, she put her belongings on the floor at her feet, then crossed her arms and ankles. Several times over the next hour he moved out of her sight, but he always came back. Yet he never looked toward the lobby.

"It's almost as though he knows I'm here and doesn't want to see me," Fanny muttered to herself at one point. The muttering drew the attention of two gentlemen crossing the lobby, and they tipped their hats to her as they passed.

At least there's some friendly folk about, she thought as she smiled back at them. Every lady whose eye she tried to catch simply ignored her. When a young man sat down beside her and opened his paper, she nearly spoke to him but decided against it. He was dressed in a checkered suit and bowler, and with his waxed mustache and shiny boots he looked as arrogant as an aristocrat.

Finally she could stand the waiting no longer. If she couldn't go to Matthew herself, she'd send someone, but not that puffed-up pigeon behind the desk. She turned to the man next to her. "Pardon me, sir, but I was after wondering if you'd do me a great kindness."

He closed his paper at once and turned to her so quickly Fanny drew back a little. When he smiled she saw that he had one gold tooth. "Well, well, what have we here?" he said in a silky voice.

"Nothing that would be interesting to yourself!" She turned away. He wasn't at all what she'd thought. With that gold tooth and oily smile he looked like a pimp. After a moment she looked back over her shoulder. He was still leering at her from behind the barrier of the newspaper he had reopened.

"You've no business in here," he whispered, though she didn't see his lips move. "If you're going to work the uptown trade, you'll need to dress better than that. I could help you. Are you interested?"

He was a pimp! Fanny picked up her belongings, rose, and hurried toward the hallway where she'd seen ladies going and coming while she sat. Sure enough, there was a ladies' lounge around the corner.

She went inside and sat on one of the little gilt chairs before a mirror. Imagine that, she thought. A pimp, here in this grand fine hotel. She looked at her flushed face and began to chuckle. She'd forgotten to remove her stage makeup. No wonder he'd thought she was in the trade.

She took out a handkerchief and quickly removed most of the kohl and rouge before getting up and going out. After all, she didn't want to miss Matthew.

When she returned to the lobby, she smiled at the man behind the desk, but he was busy. The lobby was filled with guests returning from the day's activities. She glanced at the circular seat and saw with relief that the odious man was no longer there. Finally she looked toward the saloon. Matthew wasn't there.

After a surreptitious glance at the desk to make certain the man was as busy as she'd hoped, she walked hurriedly to the entrance of the saloon and looked in. Matthew wasn't among the customers at the bar. In fact, he wasn't anywhere to be seen.

She whipped about and spied him across the lobby just as the elevator opened and he stepped in. With a faint cry of alarm, she hurried across the lobby, but the elevator was clanking and whizzing its way upward before she reached the iron grating.

In mute frustration she watched it rise. He'd been so close. Now he was farther away than ever. When the elevator stopped on the third floor to discharge its passenger, she sighed in relief. At least she knew what floor he was on. Now all she had to do was find the room.

Matthew held himself stiffly as he negotiated the hallway. He seldom drank. He really didn't even like the taste of whiskey. That was not the reason he had spent the afternoon in the hotel tavern. He'd gone in there to forget, and whiskey had a way of helping him do that. Why, at this very moment he couldn't remember which room was his.

A smile spread over his face. In fact, it seemed to him that his whole face became a smile. He felt it in every shifting muscle spanning his skull. Even the back of his head was tight with smiling. His ears lifted with the effort. His cheeks were broadened by the exercise. Yes, whiskey helped a man forget. No wonder the white man drank so often and so much. There was a great deal he no doubt wished to forget.

"Like treaties and land boundaries," Matthew murmured. No, no, he mustn't think things like that. They made him sad, and he'd been sad when he went into the saloon. He wanted to be at ease, to forget and smile because it felt good.

Fanny felt good, too.

Matthew paused in the hallway and shook his head. Where had that thought come from? He wasn't thinking about the past. He wasn't thinking about the future just yet, either. He wasn't going to think about anything right now. He would just feel.

As he took another step, he felt like a man under water. Oh, he could breathe, but the air felt thick and resistant as he moved slowly down the hall. He felt, well, reluctant to go against the current. Perhaps he would just float back down the way he'd come, unresisting, just feeling ... feeling. ...

He was surprised to find himself standing before a door with a key in the lock. He didn't remember how he knew the number or that he'd taken the key from his pocket. The white man's firewater had its uses. Forgetfulness was quite pleasant.

The door opened easily and he repocketed the key as he stepped into the dimness. He saw the bed, but he was too tired to walk all the way to it. In the dimness the sheets gleamed like snow in a distant high valley. It was lovely, but it was so far away. The green prairie of the carpet was much closer and nearly as pleasant in his eyes. He'd rest awhile on the prairie before climbing into the high valley. After all, sleep was the best forgetfulness of all.

The scratchy texture of the carpet under his cheek reminded him of his first buffalo rug. His older sister had made a terrible mess of it. Even after days of soaking and twisting, the hide had remained as scratchy as porcupine quills. She'd been horrified and given it to him more to keep him quiet about the debacle than to keep him warm. He'd kept his peace, though he'd often threatened to bring out the robe as an example of her work whenever a prospective suitor called. She was married now, living with her husband's tribe, and they had two children. As he drifted off to sleep he wondered if they, too, slept on scratchy robes.

He heard her voice from a long way off. She was calling softly to him. Fanny's sweet voice. Not even an afternoon of whiskey had drowned it out. He stirred restlessly. Maybe when he had put a thousand miles between them she would be silenced.

Fanny stopped at the next door along the hallway and called Matthew's name. It was a risky business. The first door had been opened by a pinched-faced woman who threatened to call the house detective when she saw her outlandish costume.

"Wrong door," Fanny had said quickly and hurried down the hall.

Now she moved on, pausing outside another door, and listened for sounds of people within. At the far end of the hall she heard the elevator stop. There was absolutely no sound coming from beyond the door before her, so she rapped lightly on it and whispered, "Matthew? Are you in there, Matthew?" No reply. She was nearly at the end of the hall. There were only two doors left, and the one opposite was standing ajar.

She went over to it and stood very still, listening. After a moment she heard the sounds of deep sleep coming from inside. She raised her hand and rapped very gently. The door swung open a little at her touch. Alarmed, she reached for it to draw it closed.

"That's far enough, my girl!"

Fanny whipped about to find the man in the checkered suit from the lobby standing there. "Is this your room?"

He smiled and reached into his pocket to withdraw

handcuffs. "It is not, and neither is it yours. Doing a bit of independent work, were you? Or were you just about to steal whatever you could put a hand on?"

Fanny stared at the handcuffs in shock. "I was only— Who are you?"

"The hotel detective," he said as he reached for her wrist. "You're under arrest, my girl!"

"For what?" she cried as she stumbled back against the door to get out of his reach.

He grinned at her, not at all concerned that she'd get away. The room behind her was the only place she could go. "Breaking and entering. Felonious solicitation belowstairs. You've racked up quite a tidy sum of charges in one short afternoon."

"I've done none of that!" She took another step, but the door halted her. "I'm looking for somebody. His name's Matthew Morning Star. He's a guest at this hotel."

"Is he? And did he pay you to come up and meet him here, or were you to get your money afterward?"

"You've a filthy mind," she said indignantly.

"It's part of the business. Now come along like a good girl. You know the score. If you're smart you'll be back on the street by dark." His friendly expression turned ugly. "Only, don't come back here. I don't like putting pretty girls in jail, but I won't have chippies cluttering up the lobby where decent folk are welcome."

"Don't touch me!" She jerked away as he reached for her a second time. The door gave way under the force of her body and she lost her balance and toppled backward into the room.

Matthew awakened to the sensation of having been buried under an avalanche. At least that's what he supposed it was, for he'd been dreaming of high mountains and icy streams and snow so deep and clean it took a man's breath away.

An instant later the instinct of a young brave raised on the wild prairies took over as he sensed a body pressing him down. He rolled over and at the same time pulled the body under him. He heard a young woman's scream and a man's cry and wondered who was with him. Even as he shook his head to free himself of the fog whirling through it, he felt arms slide around his neck and then the tender pressure of lips on his cheek. His eyes flew open and the fog cleared. He'd captured someone, all right. The sky-blue eyes of Just Fanny were staring up at him.

"Matthew!" Fanny breathed, less surprised to have toppled over him than he was to find her looking up at him.

"Get up from there!" the hotel detective cried, alarmed that his "collar" had disturbed a hotel guest.

Fanny looked up at him over Matthew's shoulder and said, "This is the man I was looking for. This is Matthew Morning Star."

The detective smiled, his gold tooth glinting. "So it's that way, is it? Then I'm sorry to tell you, sir, that you'll have to let the little lady go. She's been arrested. Better luck next time, sir, but you can't bring your fancy ladies into this hotel."

Though he heard the stranger's remarks, Matthew's attention was riveted elsewhere. He was sprawled across Fanny, and while she didn't seem to mind, he was acutely aware that her skirt had ridden up and that his loins were pressed tightly against her naked thigh. The very thought caused the reaction he wanted least and he saw her eyes widen when she, too, felt the change. He rolled off her and in one fluid movement gained his feet. Only when he was swaying to the pounding in his head did he decide that perhaps he should have moved more slowly.

Fanny sat up and whipped her skirt down while glaring at the detective, who had enjoyed the display. "You can go now. I found the man I was looking for."

"You don't seem to hear too well, girlie. We don't allow whores in this hotel." His gaze cut to the swarthy-faced man leaning against the door. "Even if they got an invitation."

Fanny gained her feet quickly. "I'm no whore!"

Matthew reached out and clamped a silencing hand over her mouth. Whatever it was she was saying about whores shouldn't be said in front of strangers. He turned to the strange man glowering at Fanny. "Please excuse me. I—I fell asleep, it seems. What is the problem?"

The man nodded at Fanny. "This girl claims you sent for her. Says she knows you."

"We are acquainted," Matthew answered, keeping his hand over Fanny's mouth. "We work the Wild West Show together."

"Wild West Show? You mean Buffalo Bill's show?"

Matthew nodded, but then wished he hadn't because the room was already turning slowly on a tilted axis.

"Well, now, that's a different matter, I suppose." The detective subjected Fanny to a squinty-eyed look. "How can I be certain you're telling me the truth?"

Fanny reached up and pulled Matthew's hand away from her mouth by the thumb. "Have you not eyes, man? Why else would I be dressed like this?"

"That is something to think about," he conceded. "You look just like—" His eyes opened wide. "You wouldn't by any chance be Miss Annie Oakley?"

Fanny was already forming the word "yes" when Matthew said, "Of course she's not!"

"I'm Matthew's wife," Fanny added quickly, changing tactics. She didn't dare look up at Matthew as she hurried on. "That is, I will be in the morning." She smiled sweetly at the detective. "We've run away, you see, because me da isn't half glad that I'm marrying an Indian." She reached for Matthew's hand, and while he didn't shake off her grip, his hand lay lifeless in hers.

"Why didn't you say so at once?" the detective asked suspiciously.

"I couldn't chance that me da would come looking for us."

Matthew sighed. He knew he'd missed something, something that he should remember. But right now, all he could think about was that Fanny was standing beside him, that she'd pressed her lips to his cheek and slid her arms about his neck, and that she now held his hand. None of it made any sense. Perhaps he was dreaming. That might be the best thing.

"Well, you can't stay in this room with him. Not till you're married. It's the law."

"I'll be right down," Fanny said, gripping Matthew's hand hard in hopes he'd get the hint to say something, anything. Nothing. "Surely you're a man with a heart and wouldn't have me leave me betrothed's side only the very moment I've found him?"

"It's against regulations," the detective temporized.

"Oh, thank you," Fanny answered, as though he'd agreed, and she quickly moved forward to place a kiss a scant inch above his cheek before withdrawing to stand within Matthew's shadow.

"Thirty minutes," the detective said with a glance at the tall Indian. That was enough time for trouble, of course, but by the brewery smell of the redskin he doubted that much would happen. "You see me when you come down. I've me job to think of."

Fanny didn't even look up at Matthew until the detective was halfway down the hall. When she did, it gave her a start. He was standing squarely on his feet, but his eyes were shut and definite sounds of slumber were issuing softly from between his lips.

"Poor old soul," she said softly as she turned to him. He mumbled as she put her arms about him. "Come along and get in bed. Whew! You must have drunk half the saloon, to smell as you do." Guiding him with an arm about his waist, she steered him toward the bed and then gave him a little shove that sent him sprawling across it catty-corner.

It took her several hard pulls to remove the first boot. The second was easier, and then she stripped him. When she was done, she stepped back and surveyed her work. He lay facedown, his dark skin gleaming like polished bronze in the gaslight. It was a bracing, disturbing sight. Her body flushed in response as she filled her vision with his long, muscle-shaped calves and thighs, the tight curves of his buttocks, the tantalizing indentation of his spine where it joined his hips, and the wide flare of his back.

She felt a tensing in her breasts and her loins as she bent to pull the leather strip from his hair and spread it out on the sheet. She'd touched him so seldom that each experience sent delicious shivers along her fingertips.

She brushed the back of her fingers along the clean line of his cheek to the jawline. He was warm, so warm he seemed more alive than she.

Matthew moved under the caressing touch. He was dreaming and he knew it, and that made him free of the guilt. He lifted his head slightly, in search of the source of the pleasure. Fanny's face swam into view, and that made him smile. He suspected that the dream was of her, for so many others had been these last days. It was safe to dream of her. No man controlled his dreams. They were of things to be, things unexplained, magic and longing and desire.

He wanted to speak to her, but the words weren't coming. Instead, he caught her wrist to pull her close. As she bent over him, he smiled and raised his head a little more. "Kiss me," he whispered. "Just once more. Please."

Astonishment didn't keep Fanny from doing as he bid. She bent low to place her lips lightly against his, and the gentleness of the touch was magnified a thousand times in her heart.

He smiled, murmuring against her mouth Sioux words of endearment, for it didn't break his vow to love her in his dreams. His mouth moved urgently under hers, seeking a warmer embrace, and then the need was answered as he felt her hand move under his cheek to support his head as she again brought her mouth down on his. Desire sprang up inside him, scalding his mind and his heart. There was power in her kiss, in his desire for her. He needed to know it. Yet he felt a slow slipping away of everything, even as he fought it. His head was too heavy to hold up, and in sad regret he felt himself spiraling downward, away from her and away from this new knowledge of himself.

He'd kissed her! Fanny stood up and touched her lips with her fingertips. She couldn't be mistaken this time. He'd asked for the kiss. Oleta was wrong! Indians did like kissing, or maybe only some did. She laid her hand on his shoulder. Matthew Morning Star, her Indian, her man, was one of those.

A strong sense of proprietary pride came over her as she sat on the edge of the bed beside him. He was so beautiful, not like the artificial beauty created by man but the clean, pure beauty of a natural thing. She bent her head and rubbed her face in his hair. Yes. As she remembered, it smelled of pine. She reached out to stroke his hair. What sort of place was this Dakota Territory, that it drew him back? Why did he need so desperately to go home, to be with his own kind?

Her hand paused in midstroke. Matthew had said there was no woman waiting for him, but she couldn't be certain that was true. What were the women like? Were they as beautiful as he? She'd never really paid much attention to the Indian women in the show. Most of them were Arapaho, Oleta had told her, not of Matthew's nation. The one Sioux woman she'd met had wanted to stick a knife in her.

She smiled. She'd want to stick a knife in any woman he looked at. But for now, she must be patient. He hadn't turned her away when he saw her. He hadn't told her to leave. He hadn't said much of anything, she thought wryly. He was drunk. Maybe that was why he had kissed her. She wouldn't know anything for certain until he awakened.

She rose and bent to pick up his clothing. As she

lifted the jacket, a bundle fell out of the pocket. She picked it up and looked at it. She didn't need to read to recognize it as a train ticket.

Biting her lip, she turned to look back at him. He wanted to go home. She sensed that she shouldn't stop him from going. That didn't mean she couldn't follow him.

She slipped the ticket into her pocket and hurriedly scooped up the rest of his things and placed them on a chair. She had no idea how long he would sleep, but she hoped it was long enough for her to go down and ask the detective how to buy an identical ticket and then return his before he realized she'd seen it. She had nearly four weeks' wages in her pocket. Wherever the Dakota Territory was, surely that was enough to get her there.

"O-o-ooh!"

There were a thousand buffalo stampeding through his head. Their hooves had kicked up a thirst to rival that of the dusty plains of late summer. And tom-toms—someone was beating out a warring tattoo that drove the herd harder and faster.

Matthew sat up in bed with both hands clutching his head. If only he could lift it off his shoulders, he'd willingly do it, to be free of the pounding, rumbling pain.

"Ugggh!"

His lids felt glued to his eyeballs as he struggled to open them. Finally they lifted, and even his lashes seemed to ache as they parted. The room was bright with sunlight. He squeezed his lids shut again, but the stabbing intensity of the light had already reached his eyes and soared behind his closed lids as blinding white pain.

"Aaaah!"

Whiskey—there'd been whiskey the afternoon before. Lots of it. He'd used it to drown out his thoughts of Fanny, and he had succeeded, until he began to dream. It was natural and right for a man to gratify his passion for a woman. He'd been taught that very young. He was a man now, and that passion was a burden nearly beyond his bearing. He had to get home, and soon, before his oath was broken.

A low moan escaped him. He had a train to catch. Only then, when he had returned to face the *hanbelachia*, would he know whether or not he had fulfilled his destiny.

He opened his eyes again. The dream had been so strong. She'd been here beside him, stroked his hair, kissed his mouth. The whiskey hadn't succeeded, after all. She still walked beside him.

He dressed quickly and left the room. As he walked across the hotel lobby, a stranger approached him, a man in a checkered suit and bowler hat, and stuck out his hand.

"Hear you're going to Omaha and then the Dakota Territory. Sorry about last night's events. You've a fine girl there. Wish you both great happiness."

The hair lifted on Matthew's neck. Ignoring the man's extended hand, he quickly walked away. The man had spoken to him of his future, and of his dreams. Was the spirit world now speaking to him through the mouths of white men, or was he simply going mad?

CHAPTER
11

"Howdy, little lady." The smiling stranger had paused in the aisle beside her and lifted his hat from his head. His arm was extended toward her, the small brown bag in his hand swaying rhythmically with the movement of the train. "Would you care for a peppermint?"

Fanny shook her head, though her mouth watered at the thought. "No, thank you."

The man hesitated. He was young and handsome, in a sandy-haired, ruddy-featured sort of way, and he knew that went a long way in pleasing the ladies. Why, he often boasted in male company, he could sell a spinster lady anything after sitting a quarter of an hour in her parlor. She'd tell him how he reminded her of this nephew or that old flame, and pretty soon he'd be walking out the door with a full order. For three days he'd been trying to catch this young lady's eye, and he didn't like the idea of failure.

After tucking his hat under his arm, he reached in

and took a candy out of the bag and popped it in his mouth. "Mighty tasty," he said, smacking his lips. "Cuts right through the soot that traveling packs in the throat." He jiggled the bag again.

"No, thank you," Fanny repeated and turned her head to stare out at the grassy plains flowing past the train window.

"Suit yourself," the young man said sourly. "Only, you know where to find me if you change your mind. I've got plenty."

Fanny gazed unseeingly at the vista. The window had become so caked with soot that she could more easily see her own reflection than what lay beyond the glass. She was hungry and thirsty, very thirsty. She swallowed and licked her lips. She wanted that candy. She wanted a full meal and a soft bed. But most of all, she wanted to get off this train. Where was the Dakota Territory?

At the start she hadn't considered how long a trip this would be. After two days and three nights, she was beginning to suspect that it must be equal to the length of a voyage from Ireland to New York, the only other journey she had ever taken. There the similarities ended. The ship had at least afforded her with space to move about in, a bed which her father had fashioned by hanging a shawl in the beams to make a hammock, and regular meals.

The train was another matter. The aisles were narrow and all the way from the Pennsylvania railroad station in Jersey City to Pittsburgh, they had been blocked by bags and baggage of every sort. If the train hadn't stopped for water at regular intervals, she wouldn't have been able to budge from her seat for the first day and a half.

After they'd dispatched passengers at Pittsburgh, a new crowd had surged on. Now there were families aboard: husbands, wives, and children carrying the entire belongings of their lives with them on their westward journeys. Added to the fretful babies and arguing children were the boisterous voices and laughter of plaid-suited drummers who were headed west with the latest eastern merchandise. At every stop one or two more got on. They smoked huge black cigars, drank whiskey from shiny silver flasks, and played cards until it was too dark to see. The man in the plaid suit who'd offered her candy was one of them. She remembered him because he had gotten on in Cleveland, the place where her money had run out. And while he looked nice enough, she knew a flimflam man when she saw one. The Bowery was full of them.

There were no beds, except for those in the sleeping coach, which were only available to first-class passengers. After the first night, she suspected that the rusty red plush seats were secret torture devices. Her back ached and she had a permanent crook in her neck from sleeping with her head propped against the window.

Overriding all other considerations was the torment of the train ride itself. Whenever the windows were open, the wind blew in cinders from the engine that burned her eyes, and smoke that made her cough. A fine powder of ash covered everything. She envied the ladies she occasionally glimpsed leaving and entering the first-class cars. They wore voluminous traveling coats with hoods that covered even their hats to keep the dust from ruining their clothing.

Fanny swallowed again, trying not to think about her grumbling stomach. Eighty dollars! A first-class ticket from Jersey City to the place called Omaha was eighty dollars. Matthew's ticket was for a first-class fare, yet she'd only had seven dollars in her pocket. Still, she'd learned a thing or two about selling the public from her weeks with the Wild West Show. Before leaving New York she had sold all her belongings on a busy street corner. She'd sold her possessions: her suede skirt and jacket, her Stetson, her autographed picture of Buffalo Bill, even the lace handkerchief that Buck and Oleta had given her.

Her things had brought top prices because she'd told stories to go with every item. After all, she'd been a member of the show. By the time she was done, she'd added thirty-seven dollars to her purse. As it turned out, the day-coach fare to Omaha was only forty dollars. She'd boarded the train in Jersey City with one dollar in her pocket.

Absently, she rubbed the silver bracelet she wore. She hadn't considered selling it and would have walked to Omaha before selling it. No, she admitted frankly, she'd have broken her vow not to steal before selling Matthew's gift. It was the thing that kept her going. He was on board this train. She'd glimpsed him several times a day when he got out to stretch his legs. She watched closely at every stop because she didn't want him to sneak up on her accidentally, and because the sight of him gave her more pleasure than she could have thought possible only a month ago.

When they got to Omaha, she'd have to reveal herself. She was broke and could go no farther without his help. But until then, she would remain a secret.

Once aboard she'd learned that she could have ridden third class for a little more than half the amount of the day-coach fare. Intrigued, she'd gone back to look at the third-class coach at the next stop. One look at the car fitted with rows of wooden benches and filled with every sort of rough type of individual imaginable had changed her mind about trading her ticket in.

Then, while she stood there, the third-class coach was unhooked from the train. In answer to her question she was told that these coaches were most often hauled by freight trains and that the passengers would have to wait until one came through. Had she joined the third-class coach, she would have been separated from Matthew; and, since she didn't know precisely where he was going when he got to Omaha, she couldn't afford to be separated from him. After spending her last dime for a cup of milk and a roll from a ''news butcher'' working the passenger stop, she'd gotten back in the day-coach car.

Though the train stopped at regular intervals at what the conductors called way stations, she would have had to go without had her seat companion of a day before not been a woman of ample provisions.

Ample provisions seemed to describe everything about the woman. She had been deep-bosomed and broad-hipped, with a wide face and an equally generous nature. She'd plopped down next to Fanny the morning before, declaring, ''You're about the only body on this train who's narrow enough to share a seat with me. The conductor always wants to charge me twice.''

Her laughter had been ample and freely given. She'd called herself a short-haul passenger, saying she was going only a half day's distance. Then she'd lifted her hat box and produced a bounty that caught the nose of every person in the car. ''Have a piece of strudel, dearie. It's my specialty. Milton's Barbershop and Bakery of Richmond, Missouri. We're known far and wide."

Fanny had accepted the pastry gratefully and hadn't demurred when the woman pressed an apple turnover and a bit of cheese on her later in the day as she left the train. She'd devoured it all before the train left the station. But now she regretted her gluttony, for she was twice as hungry as the day before.

The young drummer in the seat across the aisle still glanced at her from time to time. He seemed to take the opportunity to pop another peppermint into his mouth whenever envy couldn't keep her from glancing at him.

"You've more pride than to allow your friendship to be bought for a bit of sugar!" she muttered and crossed her arms tightly across her stomach.

Minutes later she was still concentrating so hard on not thinking about food that she didn't realize the conductor had paused beside her until he cleared his throat very loudly.

"Getting along all right?" he asked. At her nod he added, "Thought you should know you'll be changing trains at the next stop. We've reached Kansas City."

Fanny sat up. "Change trains? But I bought a ticket to Omaha."

The conductor nodded. "That you did, and so you must change trains in Kansas City. It'll be the Union Pacific that takes you into Omaha. Will you need help with your baggage?"

"No, I can manage," Fanny answered quickly. When the conductor moved on, she sank back against the red plush seat in misery. There was no baggage, only the gown, hat, and shoes she'd boarded the train in three days ago.

"I wouldn't mind escorting you to your train, seeing as how we're both going in the same direction."

Fanny looked across the aisle at the young man smiling earnestly at her. She was a little afraid of getting lost, but that didn't mean she should accept his help. "That won't—" What if she missed the train? "That would be kind of you. Thank you."

His expression brightened so suddenly that Fanny turned away to keep from laughing in his face. What did he think he'd won in gaining her agreement? Certainly nothing worth that degree of happiness. Her expression sobered. What if he planned to spirit her away somewhere, or deliberately led her to the wrong train? She wasn't a helpless female, though he wouldn't know that, and had dealt with hucksters of every cut.

Even as she looked up to take back her acceptance, he turned away, apparently satisfied not to press their acquaintance. Reassured by his manner she turned to look at the city coming into view.

Matthew walked through the Kansas City station with one thought on his mind—that he'd been rash in leaving Staten Island without saying a proper good-bye to Fanny. Yet he'd seen in her eyes that afternoon in the maple grove a reflection of his own desire and knew that he'd failed to keep his feelings secret from her.

Guilt pricked him. He shouldn't have revealed his attraction. If she'd begun to develop tender feelings, then the fault was his. He'd saved her life; of course she would regard him with kindness. It was nothing more than that. It couldn't be.

He had no certain future. He wouldn't return to the show, though Buffalo Bill had offered him a spot in the winter show to be staged at Madison Square Garden.

Cody had said that this show would be bigger and more extravagant than ever before and that Matthew could have a leading role. But that was playacting, a children's game, just as his feelings for Fanny were an indulgence he couldn't afford. He'd learned that lesson the hard way after a night of drinking. Dreams of Fanny had never been stronger.

He winced. He would never drink again.

After pausing to buy a paper from the newsboy, he opened it and his heart skipped a beat. There, splashed across the front page in big black letters, was the triumphant news of the surrender of the most famous Apache warrior of the decade, Geronimo.

Matthew lifted his eyes from the bold print, the room before him momentarily disappearing. Geronimo had given up the battle! How were his people to survive without him? How were any of the many proud nations who'd once walked this very ground survive the relentless onslaught?

The answer, he had once thought, lay in learning everything he could about the white man. That was why he had gone east. Once he understood white men, he'd thought, he'd discover the method by which to deal with them, and then bring that method home to his people. But the most important thing he'd learned was the one thing he feared most: the white man's greed was unstoppable because it was a way of life for him.

The white man's history had told him that the Europeans had conquered their neighbors and been conquered in return for hundreds of years. And when they discovered worlds outside of their previous knowledge, they had set out in ships to conquer those worlds. They had never left in peace a land that they had discovered. Not one. Until they settled all of this land they called America, they wouldn't rest.

He closed the paper and let it drop from his hand. He didn't want to know the details of Geronimo's surrender. He and the chief were not of the same nation, yet they shared a common enemy. That the enemy would prevail he already knew. This was the reason why he was going home: to carry to his people the message of the inevitability of their surrendering their way of life. This message was as old as the European world. Some would fight: that was inevitable also. He didn't know what he would do—stay and wait for the death rattle or leave and watch to see the names of his loved ones listed in a paper one day—if they survived.

He walked slowly through the crowded station, unaware of the curious stares he drew. This was a western city, but people here seldom saw Indians, and certainly not an Indian in a well-tailored suit who carried himself as proudly and unafraid as if he walked his own land.

He was about to board the train to Omaha when he looked up the track and saw a young woman with red hair walking arm in arm with a gentleman. Fanny! He nearly said the name aloud, and the thought alarmed him. It wasn't Fanny; it couldn't be. He was a thousand miles from New York, and that was where she was. Just because the woman had hair very nearly the shade of Fanny's and walked with a graceful but youthful jog like Fanny's, and even wore— That gown! He'd washed that gown with his own hands!

He was running toward the couple, appalled, ashamed of himself, yet determined to know the truth.

Fanny decided that the young drummer, who'd introduced himself as Daniel Cade, was quite harmless after all. He had been most solicitous of her welfare, refusing to allow her to pay for her meal in the coffeehouse where they had waited for their train to be called. This time she took the precaution of not eating all of the beefsteak and potatoes served with her fried eggs. She'd wrapped the leftovers in her napkin and stuck them in her purse. But now that the young man had served his purpose, she didn't know quite how to get rid of him.

"You never did say what it is that takes you to Omaha," Daniel said as he guided her by the elbow through the crowded platform. "You aren't a teacher, by any chance?"

"Me? A teacher?" Fanny's laughter made him blush. "Would you be hoping to sell me a book or two?"

"No, ma'am, I wouldn't impose upon our new friendship in any manner. I just thought, as long as you're heading into my territory and being that Omaha is one of my regular stops, I thought I might, well . . ."

"I don't recall saying that me final destination was Omaha," she said. "Do you tell all the ladies—?"

The words still forming on her lips, Fanny was suddenly swung about by a firm grip on her shoulder. Even before her eyes focused, she knew who it was. Through feelings of dread and elation, she looked up into the face of Matthew Morning Star.

She saw utter astonishment in his black eyes as he recognized her. Joy, anger, hurt, and disbelief followed quickly. For an instant the conflagration of emotions quickened the all-too-often expressionless lines of his starkly handsome face, and the blistering intensity of it seared Fanny's soul. He cared!

"Take your hand off her, you filthy redskin!" The drummer reached out and wrenched Matthew's hand from Fanny's shoulder. "Who do you think you are, to touch a white woman?"

The man's words had the effect of water on a blaze. All emotion left Matthew's expression. Only his black eyes smoldered, the smoky aftereffects dulling their depths as he held Fanny's gaze. "My mistake." Though he could easily have broken the hand of the man gripping his wrist, he shook off the hold and turned to walk rapidly away.

"Morning Star! Matthew!" Fanny took a step toward him, only to have the drummer catch her elbow.

"You know that redskin?" he asked in amazement.

Fanny impatiently freed herself. "Of course I do. We're—we're old friends. I'll be back."

The tracks were so filled with people that she had to push her way against the stream. Matthew's glossy black head, rising above the crowd, was her beacon. At first she thought he wasn't going to board the train, but at the end of the last car he suddenly veered toward the steps and climbed in.

She was breathless when she reached the car, her heart pounding wildly. She hadn't meant for him to come upon her like that, unprepared and unsure of what she would say to him. Her knees were shaking so badly she could hardly climb up the steps, and so she took the conductor's proffered hand.

"Have your ticket ready, miss?" the conductor inquired.

Fanny didn't reply but quickly entered the car.

The first thing she noticed was the elegance of the car. The walls were paneled, the windows freshly washed and sporting velvet shades with gold tassels. The floor was carpeted and the seats were deeply cushioned and tufted. Then she spied Matthew seated with his back to her, and she forgot to be surprised and envious of the luxury in which he had traveled these last days. Dry-mouthed and sweaty-palmed, she approached him.

Matthew felt her presence before she reached him, but he didn't move. In the last seconds he'd had a chance to think many things, and all of them led to one conclusion: she'd followed him.

"Matthew?"

He didn't respond to her touch upon his shoulder, and her hand moved quickly away.

"Well? Aren't you going to say anything?"

Steeling himself against the vision, he lifted his head to look at her.

Fanny tried to smile but her face was frozen. He didn't look friendly. In fact, he looked mad enough to murder her on the spot. "I—I suppose you're after wondering what I'm doing here."

A muscle ticked at the left side of his long mouth, but that inscrutable "Indian face" was back in place.

"You've a right to know."

No answer.

Annoyance flickered through her fright. "There's no call for you to be so rude, unkind, and generally unhelpful."

"Your ticket, miss."

She looked up to find the conductor in the aisle. "Yes, well, I've got it." She pulled it from her pocket and gave it to him.

"I'm afraid you're in the wrong car, miss. Second class is farther along. You'll have to change."

"I will, only I've just found an old friend and we're having a chat."

The conductor glanced in surprise at the person she'd

been addressing. An Indian! Still, it was none of his business. "Sorry, miss. If you wish to talk, the person will need to follow you back to your car for that purpose. First class is reserved for those passengers only."

Fanny looked at Matthew. To her consternation, he picked up a book and began to read it. She reached out to touch his shoulder again but thought better of it. "I'm in second class. Going to Omaha. Then the Dakota Territory." She turned stiffly and walked the length of the car.

There were tears streaming down her face by the time she reached her own coach. She'd been humiliated once again. He'd cut her, absolutely shunned her! She'd wanted to slap him, to claw his handsome face, to kick and scream until he admitted that he knew her. But he'd said not one word. No rebuke, no anger, no . . . joy at seeing her.

"Why, miss. Fanny! You're crying!" Daniel Cade said, popping up from his seat at the sight of her.

"Of course I am! Any fool can see that!" She snatched the handkerchief he dutifully offered and mopped her face, uncaring that she was the object of dozens of curious stares from the other passengers.

"Did that savage accost you again?" His ruddy face brightened to crimson. "If he did you can be certain that I'll—"

"Be beaten to a bloody pulp for the effort," she finished for him. "He's not hurt me, not in the way you mean." She took a deep calming breath and sat down, allowing him to do so.

"Would you care to have a cup of something, coffee or tea, perhaps?"

"I'd like to kick the living daylights out of a certain stubborn party," she muttered low.

The violent speech took Daniel aback. The only women of his acquaintance who talked rough were prostitutes and saloon hall dancers. His gaze narrowed as he looked her over. Was that what she was? "You said before that you knew that redskin. Is that true?"

"Aye," she said, preoccupied by her own dark thoughts. "We worked together. In the Wild West Show."

"Not Buffalo Bill's Wild West Show?"

She looked at him in annoyance. "Aye. What's so strange about that?"

"Nothing," he said quickly. "Only you don't, well, look the sort."

"What sort?"

"Well, western, you know."

"Ah, well, it's a long story."

"We've quite a while before we reach Omaha."

Fanny leaned back against the uncomfortable seat that smelled faintly of tobacco and sour unwashed bodies. She didn't want to talk, least of all to Daniel Cade. She ached all over. She was tired, disappointed, and so sad she wanted to get down on all fours and howl her misery. "Tell me about Omaha," she said, closing her eyes.

Matthew had gained a new perspective by the time morning rolled around. It was just after his breakfast of antelope steak, eggs, hot rolls, jam, and coffee that his mind settled. He'd been watching, as now, the long uninterrupted vista of prairie grass as the train sped through the midwestern plains. There was nothing to break the eye here. Mile after incredible mile, there was only the rippling sea of waist-high grasses, dappled by shadows where the wind undulated the golden stalks.

He frowned when a single sod house, the work of a white man, broke the imagery. He saw more homesteads on this journey than there had been the last time he'd traveled home. Wherever they were, the prairie grass was gone, hacked down to make room for domestic grain and foodstuffs. Each loss of prairie land could be measured by the loss of grazing land for the buffalo and other game on which his people survived. The farmers always paused in their work as the train went by, sometimes waving, sometimes just watching, but never indifferent to the train's passage.

Fanny would have to go back.

The rails rang in accompaniment to the thought, even as it formed in his head. Fanny go back, Fanny go back, Fanny go back. The rhythm was irresistible. The logic infallible.

He would wait until the train reached Omaha before confronting her. He'd spent a near sleepless night wondering if she'd come back to the first-class car. He'd hoped—no, he'd been afraid—that she'd come back and that he'd have to look again at the misery and hurt he'd inflicted. He couldn't bear the misery in her pretty face. Well, perhaps she wasn't pretty, not like the handsome women of his tribe with their aquiline noses, doe-soft dark gazes, and willowy walks. Fanny was pleasant to gaze upon, like a playful puppy or a frisky pony. He doubted she would appreciate the comparison, but for him it was appropriate.

Fanny sat staring glumly at the countryside. The farther west she went, the more desolate and depressing the land became. Well, it matched her mood. She'd spent a fitful night in argument with herself. What had she expected, that he would welcome her with open arms? He would have stayed in New York or at least come to see her one more time if that had been the case.

She refocused on the treeless plains. They'd passed a few settlements—towns, the conductor called them— but to her eyes they were only a collection of unpainted wooden sheds and box-shaped buildings, uncared for, forlorn, and isolated. She couldn't imagine that any human being would willingly live there. Now she was about to be stranded in such a place. Omaha was her last stop.

Pride's done this to you, she reminded herself. She'd been so certain that Matthew felt something for her.

"There was something, all right," she murmured inaudibly. Passing lust, plain and simple.

Now he couldn't be bothered with her, or, perhaps, he was so thoroughly mortified that she'd followed him that he didn't know what to think or say. He'd said something about a vow that he couldn't break; that's why he was going home.

"Blarney," she muttered. Pure blarney to save a girl's pride, and she'd misinterpreted it to mean that, if he could, he'd have stayed with her.

Still, she'd give a pretty penny to know what it really was that lured him back here. Grass and dirt for as far as the eye could see; that's what was out there. When the sun rose higher, the glare would blind her. She'd thrown over a perfectly decent job for a selfish, rude, stubborn Indian and land that looked as if it had suffered a biblical scourge. Maybe she'd stick around and see this place for herself. Just maybe she'd even follow him farther. Just maybe she was right and he was wrong, and he did care about her. Just maybe.

"In for a penny, in for a pound," she murmured.

The city of Omaha was surprisingly green after miles of prairie. There were rows of clapboard houses with fresh white paint and colorful rose gardens and picket fences and trees. By the time the train rolled to a stop at the station in the center of town, Fanny's spirits had lifted considerably.

"I do wish you'd tell me where you'll be staying, so that I may call on you to see that you've settled in proper," Daniel Cade said as he stepped down beside her onto the platform.

"I told you, I don't know. I may not even remain in Omaha."

She wasn't even looking at him. Cade reluctantly followed her gaze to see the tall Indian step down from the first-class coach. "Miss Fanny, just a friendly word of warning. I know you consider that redskin your friend, but you should know that Indians aren't to be trusted. They don't take to civilized behavior like us. One minute they're fine, the next they're apt to be after your scalp. You knew him in the show, where he was watched by Buffalo Bill, whom the Sioux respect. But you aren't in a show anymore. He's in his own element out here, and the call of the wild is strong in him, you take my word for it. I'd be mighty relieved if you were to forgo his future acquaintance altogether."

Fanny turned a cool expression on him. "Those being your feelings, I'd be mighty relieved if you were to forgo *my* future acquaintance altogether."

Fanny stepped quickly away from him, concerned

that Matthew would try to avoid her. Yet he had stopped after stepping down and was surveying the crowd. When he saw her, he didn't look away but turned his full and steady gaze on her as she approached.

The first thing Matthew noticed was how tired and bedraggled she looked, rather like a small, starving kitten. "When did you eat last?" That wasn't what he meant to say, but her appearance shocked him into voicing the concern.

"Not since lunch yesterday," she answered guardedly.

"And before that?"

She shrugged, blushing. "Not for a while."

"You have no more money."

So that was it. He wanted to know how much farther she'd be able to dog his tracks. She returned his flat stare. "I can look after meself, if that's what you're wondering."

"Would you care to have breakfast with me? I've not eaten yet," he lied.

"Why would you want to do that?"

Matthew's gaze softened. She was still a scrapper, he'd give her that. "We need to talk. We can do so here on the street with half the population gawking at us, or we can go somewhere quiet."

He was right, she noted. People passing them were craning their necks to get a better look at the tall, dark Indian and the small redhead who spoke with him.

"Where are your bags?"

Her chin rounded stubbornly. "Ain't got any."

"You don't—?" He swallowed his surprise and picked up his leather case. "Come on. The coffee shops fill up quickly when the train comes in."

Fanny took the arm he offered her, faintly surprised

that he did so, considering he'd never done so before. She could feel the warmth of his skin through the cloth of his coat and the hard muscles beneath, and she self-consciously closed her fingers tightly over his arm. She might never touch him again, might never see him again.

She followed him across the street and up the block, wondering why they didn't stop at the first pretty little confectionary shop they passed, its windows full of lace curtains and homemade pies. They walked on past several other places that looked as suitable until the wooden sidewalk began to narrow and the buildings became less well cared for. Finally he paused outside a boarding house whose facade was in need of new paint. "Just a moment."

Leaving his bag by her feet, he went up on the porch to the door and knocked. A moment later a middle-aged woman in an apron came to the door. She couldn't hear what Matthew said to her, but the woman bent around Matthew to look at her and then nodded. Matthew opened his wallet and paid her, then came back down to the sidewalk.

"We can have breakfast here."

"Morning. I'm Mrs. Lund," the woman greeted with a smile as Fanny entered the house. "Would you like me to take your bags up?"

Fanny shook her head, but Matthew said, "We left most of the baggage with the stationmaster, since we'll be leaving in the morning. There's just this one," and he handed her his bag.

"You just go on in the dining room. You're too late for breakfast and a mite early for lunch, but I'll see what I can do." She smiled at Fanny. "We don't get many visitors anymore. Glad to have you. I won't be a minute.''

''She'd get more visitors if she took a paintbrush to the place,'' Fanny observed as Matthew led her into the dining room. ''This room is quite nice.''

''She can't afford to paint the place,'' he said tersely.

The tone made Fanny turn to him. ''Why not?''

He looked at her with the neutral expression she recognized now as defensive. ''This was once one of the best boardinghouses in town. Then Mr. Lund started entertaining some guests that the town disapproved of.''

It took her a moment to understand. ''Indians, do you mean? And that's why people stopped coming here— because Indians sleep here?''

''Yes.''

''Is that why we didn't stop before? To eat, I mean.''

He nodded. ''You still don't understand, do you?''

''That some people treat you like you were scum? Oh, I know about that, right enough. Wasn't I raised half me life in Ireland? The landlord sending his agent by with ever larger rents when the land was dying and the people were dying because of it, and them caring about neither but the rent!''

The passion in her voice surprised him. ''But you were never turned off your land,'' he said.

''Weren't we just!'' she returned. ''Me da was near murdered by the soldiers who came to clear us off our land. Our landlord had decided to turn the farm into pastureland. Didn't need tenants. Near killed me. . . .''

She broke off abruptly as Mrs. Lund appeared with a tray. ''Here's coffee and two large slices of apple pie. First apples of the season.''

"That smells wonderful!" Fanny said as she went over to the table to sit down.

She smiled. "Mr. Lund and I were young once." Her expression clouded as she lightly rested a hand on Fanny's arm. "I wouldn't distress you for the world, my dear, but I must warn you, you may not be received in the best manner by the townfolks, should you decide to go out with Matthew. Things are different here than in the east." She glanced at Matthew as he sat down opposite Fanny. "Perhaps you've been told. I just want you to know that you're welcome here."

There was something she'd missed, Fanny decided, but she didn't want to talk to Matthew in front of a stranger and so she was silent. She picked up her fork and tasted the pie. "It's delicious."

"Could you perhaps find us a slice of bacon?" Matthew asked. "My—Fanny is particularly fond of bacon."

Mrs. Lund smiled again. "Is it that way?" She patted Fanny's hand. "You poor dear, traveling at this time. Now you just eat up. I'll bring you a nice fresh glass of milk to go with the bacon."

Matthew looked down to keep Fanny from seeing the laughter in his eyes.

"What was that about?" Fanny demanded when the woman had gone.

"I don't know what you mean."

Fanny put her fork down. "What did you tell her about us?"

He shrugged. "The only thing that would get you a bed for the night—that we're married."

"That we're— why?"

"Because Mrs. Lund isn't entirely lost to the proprieties. She wouldn't have had us otherwise."

"And the milk is because she thinks..." Fanny's thoughts raced ahead of her speech, and she blushed a deep red.

He said nothing.

They ate the rest of the meal in silence.

When Mrs. Lund had poured him a third cup of coffee and departed with the dirty dishes, Matthew leaned forward across the table but didn't reach for Fanny's hand, as impulse urged him to do. "We must talk. The train for Sioux City leaves before dawn. I want you to wait for one that will return you to Kansas City so you can return to New York. I will pay your way back."

Fanny didn't say anything. She didn't even look up from the patterns she was marking on the tablecloth with the end of her teaspoon. She knew what he would say. Why argue?

"You must know you can't go on. Where I'm going there are no trains or stagecoaches. No white people."

She didn't argue. How could she?

"You'd hate it. The summers are too hot and the winters are colder than anything you could imagine."

She nodded.

"Why did you follow me?"

Fanny looked at him, all that was in her heart revealed in her eyes but not a word to express it on her tongue.

Matthew found her gaze the most difficult thing he had ever faced. He shouldn't have asked. Yet there was a feeling of triumph inside him. The feeling was pride when he knew it should have been shame. She loved him. She'd said it as clearly as if she'd spoken the words at the top of her voice. And he, coward that he was, wouldn't offer her the truth in return because he feared too much the consequences.

Months ago, in early summer, Red Shirt had told him that one day he would face his most dangerous enemy and that that enemy might be himself. He was fighting now, in a death-grip struggle between his deepest beliefs and his strongest feelings. Loyalty to his people came first. It had to. They had so little and would soon have much less. To break a vow would be to spit on them and all their ancestors before them.

"My people are no different from yours when it comes to outsiders. They wouldn't accept you. You'd be shunned and scorned."

Fanny put up a hand to silence him. "You don't have to try to frighten me away." She stood up, not really seeing anything for those damnable tears were in her eyes again. "I'll do what you want. I wouldn't even take your money, only I've none of me own. But I promise to repay you. I'll give it to Buffalo Bill. He'll know how to get it to you." She paused. There were tears in her throat. Was she crying inside? She unbuttoned her cuff and took off the bracelet he'd given her. "You should have this back."

Matthew looked down at it lying on the table. "It was my gift to you."

She shook her head, not looking at him. "It was more than that. And I want me hair back. You're to have no more responsibility for me."

Matthew felt as if she'd struck out at him with a knife. "No."

She lifted her head, looking a little beyond him as

he'd done to her so often in the past. "Then you're a liar, Matthew Morning Star. You're a liar and a cheat!" She turned and walked blindly out of the room.

"I know, Just Fanny," he sighed when she was gone. "I know I am."

Fanny was deep in sleep when she heard the bedroom door open. After crying herself dry that morning, she'd washed up and then gone out to walk the city streets. She didn't mind that she was perfectly alone. She didn't even care when she got lost and had to suffer the censorious stare of the first lady she'd asked for directions back to the Lunds' boardinghouse. The walk set up her appetite for dinner, and she was even able to carry on a reasonable conversation with the other boarders at the table. Mrs. Lund had supplied Matthew's excuse for being absent, but she didn't even remember what it was.

The creaking of the floorboards brought her to complete wakefulness as she sat up in bed. "Who's there?"

"Matthew."

Fanny's throat went dry. "What do you want?"

He didn't answer.

The floorboards shifted against one another, and then she felt his leg bump the bed. Only then did she remember that she was naked beneath the covers. Her gown and undergarments had been washed and hung to dry in the laundry below.

She heard him moving about, the thud of first one, then the other of his boots, and then the whisper of cloth as he removed his clothing. When he bumped the bed again, he was much nearer to where she sat clutching the covers. She felt him searching and then lift the bedding. She didn't move, didn't dare speak.

The shock of a hot thigh sliding into bed beside hers made her gasp, and it was echoed by one of his. "You're naked!"

It sounded like an accusation. "So are you," she answered in a choked-back voice.

She felt his hesitation; the bed quivered with it. She didn't move away from him. The sheets were cold where she hadn't yet lain. And then he slid the rest of the way in.

Matthew put an arm about her shoulders as she sat upright in the bed. "I won't touch you."

"You already are touching me," she whispered faintly. As his arm started to move, she grabbed his hand to hold it about her. "No. It's all right. It's a chilly night."

"Yes. Cold." Was it cold? Matthew wondered. He'd never been more on fire in his life.

Fanny lay back in the bed. Because his arm was about her, the action pulled him down beside her. She felt the weight of his leg next to hers and the jut of his hipbone against the flesh of her thigh. He was so warm. His breath was warm upon her cheek. His arm was like a furnace where it wrapped her shoulders. As he shifted to fit more comfortably onto the bed, his chest grazed her right breast, scalding her with its heat. She heard his sucked-in breath and knew that she was not the only one aflame with the sensations of their bodies touching. She felt his free arm move and then his palm found the plane of her stomach and settled there.

Matthew felt the quivers of her belly and his man-hood sprang to turgid life. So then, this was the ultimate test. Could he sleep with her and yet not touch her? And if he couldn't, how would he face her and himself in the morning?

The test had come to him as he walked the prairie at the edge of town after dark. He had been seeking wisdom. Of the four virtues of his people—bravery, generosity, fortitude, and wisdom—wisdom was the most intangible and elusive. In order to achieve wisdom a sacrifice was often made. There'd been no *Hunka,* no buffalo-singing, no ghost-owning, no White Buffalo ceremonies to help him this night, and so he had chosen this test of fortitude to exorcise his guilt over his desire for her. If he failed he would submit himself as a coward to his people. But if he succeeded, then perhaps there could be a future for them.

Fortitude, Matthew cautioned himself as she softened against him, turning her head to lie in the hollow of his shoulder. Her hair brushed his face with the clean scent of violets.

Courage, he counseled himself as her hand reached up to caress his cheek.

Stoicism, he moaned through gritted teeth as she curled closer to him, her hip inadvertently brushing the tip of his manhood, extracting exquisite pain.

His hand moved to the indentation of her waist and held her slightly away as he shifted. One more touch and he would shame himself and ruin the bedding.

"Are you comfortable?" Fanny asked, feeling him move about restlessly.

"Yes." It sounded as if he were choking.

"I can move over a bit," she suggested.

"No."

Fanny sighed. It was marvelous to lie with him. If

only he had kissed her she would have been perfectly happy. At least she thought that was what was missing, for her body hummed with taut strumming that the touch of his body both encouraged and assuaged. She had already made up her mind. If he paid for her ticket, she would exchange it for one with which she could follow him. She wasn't a fool, after all. That wasn't a tent pole propping up the sheets.

CHAPTER
12

Fanny walked beside Matthew to the station. They had spoken to each other only once since rising, and that was when he awakened her. She felt like a new person, or perhaps her old self in a new skin. Her dress was freshly pressed and didn't look too bad, for all that it had endured in the last week. She might have been happy if she weren't leaving Matthew.

She stood patiently while he purchased the tickets, and then he turned back and handed her one of them without saying anything.

"What time does my train leave?" she asked, trying not to think about the night before or the fact that he was sending her away.

He looked embarrassed. "I forgot you can't— It's a ticket for Sioux City." He hesitated as if there was more he meant to say but couldn't find the words for. "The Dakota Territory," he said finally.

Fanny stared at him. He'd told her the day before that

she wasn't to follow him anymore, that she was to go back to New York, and she'd agreed. "Why?"

He looked intensely uncomfortable. "You've come this far. . . ." His gaze moved beyond her. "Perhaps I misunderstood."

She didn't pretend to follow his line of thinking. After last night, she didn't understand him at all. But her feelings, all those strange, mixed up emotions inside her were at present engaged in a unified expression of joy. He wanted her to come with him!

She didn't know what strange ritual she'd satisfied the night before by sleeping in his arms, but she'd sensed that it was some sort of test. Whatever it was, she didn't care. He was acting out of some law of his own making, and she was happy enough to be a part of it.

"Do you want to go back?"

She shook her head. "No, the Dakota Territory will do just fine."

He didn't smile, but he took her arm and steered her toward the train, halting before the second-class coach. "We ride here. I'm sorry."

She looked up. "I don't mind. It's where I've been riding all along."

He looked down but not directly at her. "One day you will ride first class. I promise."

She nodded, and when the conductor came up and took their tickets, she said, "I'll find us a place," and climbed aboard.

The moment she entered the car she knew that this train wasn't like the ones she'd ridden thus far. There were the same plush seats, gas lanterns overhead, and brass spittoons in strategic places, but its passengers

were a different breed from those before. Many of the
men were cowhands, but they weren't clean and neatly
dressed like the Wild West Show cowboys. They were
stained brown by the sun, whipcord thin, and sported
long droopy mustaches and battered hats. Others were
clearly frontier men in buckskins who openingly carried
knives and rifles. They brought with them the feel of
the frontier, its wild, untamed nature and its smell.

Fanny covered her nose with her hand as she reached
one particularly noisome man. He was sprawled across
two seats with one spurred boot hung over the armrest
into the aisle. An oily hat shaded his eyes and she
thought he slept. But as she passed him he suddenly sat
up, pushed his hat back on his head, and threw his
second leg up on the armrest, trapping her in the aisle
between his boots.

"Son o' a bitch!" he roared. "If I ain't caught me a
tasty morsel."

Fanny turned on him a look that was as inviting as a
bared knife blade. "Let me pass."

"Go on!" said the man across the aisle. "Get yourself a handful of woman!"

Her captor leaned forward, grinning, his teeth stained
black by tobacco. "Where were you goin', little gal,
afore you met me?"

He was drunk. That was good, Fanny thought as her
gaze swung widely in search of a weapon. She found it
hanging from a peg behind the man accosting her, just
as he reached out and grabbed her by the waist. As she
bent toward him, she saw Matthew coming up the aisle,
his neutral expression traded for one of fury. She
grabbed the iron skillet as the man buried his face in her
bodice and cracked him smartly on the back of the

head. The ringing blow felled him like an ax blow, and he slumped back in his seat, releasing her.

A cheer went up among the men in the coach as she hung the skillet back on the peg. Matthew was standing beside her, his dark face burnished by anger. She put a hand on his arm but didn't look at him. "Oh, there you are, husband. I think I've found our seats down this way."

"Husband?" she heard the heckler across the aisle echo in astonishment. "That little gal's married an Injun!"

"Some child's goin' git his scalp lifted," another man said with a long whistle of amazement.

Fanny ignored them as she found an empty seat and slid over next to the window. Only then did she look up at Matthew. "What's that basket for?"

Matthew handed it to her. "Lunch and dinner."

Fanny bent over it and lifted an edge of the napkin. "It smells like fried chicken and apple pie."

"That's what it is," he answered, still towering over her. She saw his gaze move back up the aisle as the man she'd beaned with a skillet roared profanities as he regained consciousness. One of the men near him touched his arm and then nodded in Matthew's direction.

The man shook his head to clear it, then looked straight at Matthew. "She's with a damned Injun?" he shouted as though that were an added insult.

Matthew stood in the aisle, meeting the man's stare, but the blow on the frontierman's head seemed to have daunted his interest in fighting, and he turned away, holding his aching head and spewing more curses.

When Matthew sat down beside her, Fanny let out

her breath in relief. "You will wait for me in the future," he said in his flat tone.

"Because of the likes of him?" Her brows lifted. "I've handled his kind all me life."

He gave her a sidelong glance. "Most eastern ladies would have fainted had a man like that touched them."

Fanny grinned. "Nobody ever thinks of me as a lady."

"I do." He folded his arms and sat back, not looking at her, but she saw the corner of his wide mouth lift and heard him murmur, "A lady who's handy with an iron skillet!"

For the next day and a half, the train took on and discharged every stripe of humankind that inhabited the West. Indians in robes and feathers, gamblers in ruffles and gold-nugget stud pins, fancy women in silks and paint, farmers in serge shirts and denim pants, drummers, cowboys, miners, trappers, and more made up the train's day-coach passengers. Huge clouds of smoke enveloped the car from time to time as the men smoked and drank and generally filled the air with coarse voices, loud laughter, and profanity.

The few women and children who boarded the train found their way to Fanny's end of the coach, where they sat stiffly and disapprovingly until they reached their destinations.

Progress was much slower on this journey as the engineer stopped repeatedly to pick up and deliver passengers into what seemed to Fanny the infinite reaches of the prairie. Finally, on the second morning, when she awakened she saw the outline of a town on the far horizon.

As she yawned, the dust cake on her face crackled.

No amount of brushing, dusting, or shaking could remove it for long. The next thing she realized was that she was shivering. It had turned sharply colder during the night and the blanket Matthew had rented for her was small comfort. She turned to look at him, wishing they were back in Omaha at Mrs. Lund's under the covers with nothing between them. Matthew opened his eyes at that moment and she knew by the sudden dilation of his pupils that he must have read her thoughts. For an instant he smiled at her, but then was sober-faced again.

Fanny sighed and looked back out the window. Something was happening. The longer they rode together, the more remote he became. It was as if he were withdrawing into himself. It wasn't that he was indifferent to her or uncaring of her needs. He wasn't. He would even go to stand guard before the buttoned curtains that hid the toilets on board because the cowboys thought nothing of peeking in to see who was there.

But he was holding himself away from her. He either read or slept or sat for long periods staring at nothing. He was thinking of the future, their future, she hoped. And there was nothing she could do to reassure him because she didn't even know what they faced. So she sat for hours, trying very hard simply to be happy because he was beside her. Patience was a virtue often rewarded, she reminded herself, and she expected a big reward. She was glad when they pulled into Sioux City before noon. At least she could walk about now without the incessant clatter of the railroad tracks in her mind. Matthew said they would be changing trains again but that he had some errands to take care of. He took her to a dry-goods store where he bought her a pair of heavy boots, a buckskin coat, and a suede skirt with two flannel petticoats. She had changed into these things in the backroom, and when she came out, he had bought provisions for the rest of their journey. As they left, the owner of the store waved good-bye to them from his porch, saying, ''You have a good trip now, Mrs. Morning Star.''

Fanny looked at Matthew, but he had withdrawn again. *Mrs. Morning Star.* He was telling everyone that they were married. Was it only for her protection or was he laying the foundation of their future? She didn't know and he didn't seem in the mood to be questioned.

This time when they boarded the train, no one looked at them. Which was just as well, Fanny decided. She had braided her hair into two thick red plaits and wore the buckskin coat with fringe. If not for her pale face and the color of her hair, she decided that she might have been mistaken for an Indian.

Certainly there was no doubt about Matthew. He had changed into his leggings and breechcloth and wore a flannel shirt under his buckskin shirt. His hair was free now and flowed majestically over his shoulders, and she found herself thinking that he looked more at home here on the prairie than he had in the Wild West Show.

The car they rode in now was little more than a cattle stall. The walls were bare wood and the benches that lined those walls weren't wide enough for Matthew to sit on comfortably, so he had to brace himself with his feet against the floor. As the day wore on into nightfall, the wind picked up, whistling through the cracks in the siding and carrying a fresh coat of dust to powder the passengers.

She had nodded off, her head pillowed against

Matthew's arm, when the train suddenly slowed, brakes squealing as the passengers were thrown from their seats by the lurch.

Matthew caught her about the waist as she pitched forward and held her steady until the train stopped. She wasn't frightened, but she rested her head in the curve of his neck and shoulder a moment, glad for any excuse to touch him. When she felt him stiffen against the intimacy, she quickly backed off, more angry than hurt.

He held on to her by the arm. "There must be trouble. There's no water tower," and he pointed outside.

Fanny bent and peered out, but she couldn't see anything in the blackness. Even as she straightened up, the conductor came through with a party of two soldiers, rifles at the ready.

"Sorry folks, but the track's been damaged up ahead. Looks like we're stuck here for the night. Come the morning we'll have it repaired and be on our way."

"What sort of damage?" asked one of the men who occupied the car.

The conductor hesitated, but the soldiers weren't so reluctant. "Look's like some of them Sioux from up on the reservation done busted up the rails."

All eyes turned at once to Matthew, who sat very still.

"Do you know for a fact it was Sioux?" Fanny asked.

The soldier shook his head. "No, ma'am, I don't, but we've had trouble before with them straying off the reservation and getting into mischief."

"Perhaps if your government would stop changing the boundaries of the reservation, my people would be better able to stay within them," Matthew said and stood up. "How far are we from the nearest Sioux encampment?"

"About a day and a half by foot, due north along the Missouri," the other soldier replied. "That where you're headed?"

Matthew nodded.

"You got papers showing why you were allowed off the reservation in the first place?"

Fanny turned to the soldier. She saw the slightest shake of Matthew's head, but she was too angry to heed it. "Have you a paper giving you the right to come in here brandishing a rifle and questioning passengers? Or do you suppose my husband jumped on the train after breaking up the tracks so he could enjoy being stranded with the rest of us?"

Her scorn was lost on the soldiers, one of whom turned to the conductor. "When did the Indian come on board?"

"Back in Sioux City," the conductor said. "Ain't been no trouble. Just him and the wife, quiet as mice."

The soldier turned to Fanny with surprise in his eyes. "You that Indian's squaw?"

Matthew beat her to the answer this time, stepping between her and the men. "She's my wife."

"Well, ain't that interesting," he said while his partner gawked at Fanny.

Matthew turned and picked up his gear. "We'll be getting off here. Wife."

Fanny picked up her belongings, which she'd tied into a bundle, and followed him off the train.

"It ain't a night for a woman to be on the trail," the conductor said when they were all standing on the slope of the track. His gaze moved between Matthew and Fanny. "You could wait until morning."

"I'll look after her," Matthew answered. "You look after the train." With that he turned and started down the embankment.

Fanny hurried after him, wondering if he was making the right decision. The wind hadn't died down at dusk, as it most often did. It whipped at her skirt and tugged at her hat. Yet there was no time to ask questions. He was covering ground at an amazing pace, and it took all her concentration just to keep close behind him. Outside the dim circle of light cast by the train, the night was black, so black that she soon heard more than saw him moving ahead of her. At first she was afraid that she might stumble and fall because she couldn't see what was before her, but she finally realized that all there was was short prairie grass and that she could manage without vision.

The sky was black, without a single star, and the wind howled past her ears like some wild thing in the throes of pain. For the next half hour, she walked on with shoulders hunched against the wind and her eyes searching uselessly for features on the ground. Once she cast a look back over her shoulder and saw the train like a tiny thread of light in the fabric of the nighttime prairie. The sight chilled her, but she hurriedly pressed on. She took deep, slow breaths, matching her pace as best she could to Matthew's long strides, but she knew that he was outdistancing her because she no longer felt him near her, or was it only that the wind was growing more fierce by the second?

Finally, after more than an hour, she halted as she felt the ground begin to rise gradually with each footstep.

She couldn't see where she was going and didn't know what lay before her. When she looked back, she saw with a shock that the train had disappeared from view. Her heart began to hammer in her chest. What could Matthew have been thinking of, to simply walk away into the night like this? Did he know where he was going? Had he stopped to think that she might not be able to keep up with him? She turned quickly around and knew in that instant that he had disappeared.

She clapped her bundle to her chest, thinking, He'll turn around at any second and see that I'm not behind him. He'll turn about and come looking for me. I should just wait, just stand here and wait. I mustn't cry or be scared. There's nothing out here in the blackness to hurt me. I've been looking at the prairie for days, and I know there's absolutely nothing out here. Nothing at all.

She shivered as the wind cut through the suede and flannel. Her hands were tingling with the cold, her fingers numbed. Her toes inside her boots ached. Her cheeks burned with the blast. The wind tore tears from her eyes. She wanted to turn back, to search for the thin filament of light that marked the security of the train, but she was afraid that if she weren't facing the vast, empty prairie into which he'd vanished that he wouldn't be able to find her.

As the minutes passed, she began to grow angry. How dare he leave her like this! He was selfish, inconsiderate, stubborn! He was sulking; that must be it. He was angry because the soldiers had insulted him. But that was no reason to stalk off into the night like some uncivilized savage!

A new thought struck her. Maybe he'd forgotten all

about her. He'd been so preoccupied. Ever since Omaha, he'd been withdrawn and silent. Perhaps, just perhaps, he'd been regretting it ever since they'd boarded the train. Maybe he had hoped she would refuse to go with him. Perhaps he had thought she'd grow tired of the journey long before they reached his people and would beg to go home. Perhaps he had just simply walked off and left her because he didn't know what else to do. Maybe he wasn't coming back, because he didn't want to.

Terror poured its poison through her. She'd been abandoned! That no-good, dirty-dealing, scalp-lifting savage redskin had abandoned her! Oleta had warned her! She'd said not to trust too much in him. And she knew better! Hadn't Phineas abandoned her after stealing everything she had? And before that, her—! No, she was thinking of Matthew Morning Star. He'd used her, exactly how she wasn't certain, but she felt used and abused and, oh, so very frightened!

Fanny turned around and took a step and then halted. Hadn't she turned around once before, to look for the train? If so, then she was now facing the wrong direction. But what if she hadn't turned back? No, she'd turned back to wait for Matthew—who wasn't coming back—hadn't she? Which direction? If she chose wrong, then she'd be going even farther away from the train instead of toward it.

Panic seized her, destroying the last shreds of her confidence. She took a step forward. No, that couldn't be right. She spun about and ran three paces before a gust of wind struck her in the face with a sandy blast. She coughed and turned away, the grit itching her eyes and crunching in her teeth as she grimaced.

Her coughing ended on a sob. She shivered so hard she couldn't imagine ever stopping. Another hard sob racked her and she covered her face with the bundle in her hands to protect herself from the wind and the threat of tears. But they wouldn't be stopped. Sobbing, she fell to her knees when her legs wouldn't support her any longer. She bent over to protect herself and to squeeze the sobs into submission, but the hurt wouldn't be silenced. She was moaning, the low "ooh—ooh—ooh—ooh," going on so long that she thought her lungs would burst with the agony.

She didn't know he was there at first. First the wind suddenly seemed to skirt a path around her. And then she felt hands taking hold of her shoulders and lifting her.

She was angry, so angry she wanted to kill him! That wild anger made her strike him even as he tried to draw her close. "Damn redskin! Dirty savage! Brute! Cheat! Liar! Damn you! Damn you! Damn you!"

Matthew caught her tightly to his chest. His heart was beating a wild tattoo. He had lost her! He had thought he might never find her in this midnight wilderness. Such a stupid thing to do! How frightened she was! How frightened he had been. He was dry-mouthed with it. His skin was icy with the sweat of it. His heart felt as if it might burst open with the strain of it.

She was screaming at him, crying profanities that the winds tore from her lips even as they emerged. He bent low and covered her mouth with his, not to still the vehemence but to prove to himself that it was really she in his arms.

Fanny stilled under his kiss, but she refused to be lulled by it. Terror held sway in her thoughts, every muscle, every nerve in her body held tensely against the moment when he would release her. He had left her. Only guilt had brought him back, no more.

As soon as his lips lifted from hers, she jerked away, breaking free of his embrace. She ran faster than she had ever run in her life. She didn't care where she was going; she just had to get away from him before it was too late!

Matthew couldn't see where she went, but he heard her. He followed her silently. It was useless to cry out in the wind. When she stumbled, as he knew she would, he was there before she could rise, gentle hands holding her.

"I hate you!"

He gathered her closer, gently, tenderly, soothingly as a mother with a child, not listening to her words but feeling the trembling fright that caused them. "I'm sorry."

Fanny shuddered against him, feeling his warmth. She was so cold. It wasn't fair that he should be so warm. Didn't the wind touch him? Didn't it chill his blood? Wasn't he like other folk? No. He was an Indian and this was his land.

Suddenly she was clutching his shirtfront and crying. "Don't leave me! Please don't leave me! I'll do whatever you say! Please! I'm sorry! Don't leave me! Please!"

These words wounded him as her anger hadn't, for they were the words of a broken spirit, a mindless, frightened creature, and he was the cause.

He picked her up in his arms and started across the prairie. He had reached the riverbank, his destination all along, before realizing that she'd fallen behind. He'd been ashamed before her to have his freedom questioned by an army private. He'd been too angry to remember that she wasn't accustomed to the prairie, that she wouldn't hear the river's deep-throated roar below the howl of the wind and know that was where a man went for shelter from the wind. There were always trees near the river, and trees provided protection and firewood.

He had expected her to be close behind when he began backtracking. It was only as he realized how far he'd come that it dawned on him that she might have gone off on a tangent, not knowing that she was no longer following him. That had started the fear quickening through him. He had found her so quickly because she hadn't left the trail. But she had been lost and frightened.

Fanny was barely conscious of the time it took them to reach the riverbank. She didn't even know where they were going and didn't care. Matthew had come back for her. When the wind suddenly keened high, she shut her eyes and tightened her arms about his neck, too tired to think.

Matthew found a ledge under the embankment near the river by feeling about with his feet. Then he put Fanny down in the grass and began digging out a deeper cave with his hands. When he reached for her again in the darkness, she gripped his arm tightly. She crawled into his lap and threw her arms about his neck. He felt the deep tremors coursing through her and held her until they abated.

Finally he shifted her and pressed her back into the shallow cave he had carved out. Then he turned, with his back to her, and wedged himself in against her. He relaxed as her arm came around his waist from the back to hold him close. She was hurt and frightened and angry, but she wasn't rejecting him.

* * *

Fanny awakened with the sensation of warmth pervading every fiber of her being. The last thing she remembered before falling asleep was the numbing cold. Now she was enveloped in a wonderful warmth that was like being wrapped in fur from head to toe.

She stretched, only to find her body tightly fitted against someone's back. She opened her eyes to darkness, but she knew it was Matthew who lay against her, his heavy body weighted with sleep. The contentment she felt was more complete and all-consuming than any she'd ever known. It made her yield again to the pull of sleep.

It was not quite dawn yet, but the absolute blackness of the night was giving way to the sooty sky of near-light when she awakened again. It was the stillness that awoke her, she decided, for the wind had finally died down to an occasional short gust. In the dimness she saw part of Matthew's profile, and memories of the other night they had lain together stirred within her.

Her arm was still about his waist and she splayed her fingers across the flat expanse of his stomach covered by his buckskin shirt. The action didn't satisfy her. She missed the touch of his skin. Reaching down with her hand, she found the edge of his shirt and gently tugged it upward until she could run her hand underneath it. This time she met the barrier of his flannel shirt. Finding a button, she slipped it free of its hole. She then did it with a second. At last she found the smooth, hot skin of his stomach as she pushed her hand through the opening. He didn't move, but she sensed his awakening by the gradual tension that came into his body.

She knew then what she'd not been certain of at the

Lunds'. She wanted him to make love to her. Shamelessly, desperately, brazenly, she wanted him to touch her, to press his naked body to hers and make known the secret of his loving.

He was turning to her, shifting around until he faced her in the shallow space. She could see his face now. It was solemn, but there was a hot need in his eyes that she knew was echoed in her own. His face was so close that his breath teased her lips and she parted them in anticipation that he would kiss her. Yet he held back, though his right arm came up to draw her closer. "Please," she whispered.

She could feel him trembling. She was trembling, too. And then his mouth was on hers and she closed her eyes and gave up to the rapture of his kiss. Without a thought of modesty or dignity or hesitation, she pressed her hips to his, wanting, needing to feel his response as she had that night in Omaha. He answered her with a wild and rough urgency that left no doubt of his arousal.

His hands were moving over her, opening her jacket and then her blouse. She hadn't worn a corset underneath, for the earlier days of traveling had left her ribs bruised from it. His hand found her breast and her skin burned with the touch.

She was murmuring now, incoherent words that simply urged him to touch, yes, and to touch there, and to squeeze, oh, so gently—that she would die of the pleasure, if he didn't. Her skirts were being lifted, and she shifted to help him. There was only sweet, sweet joy in his touching, and this beautiful desire for their bodies to be melded.

As his black head moved from her lips to kiss the

pulse at the base of her throat, and then that hot, hot mouth moved lower still upon her naked skin to kiss her breasts, she began to sob softly with pleasure. He found the waistband of her drawers. With a single jerk he broke the buttons that held them closed and drew them down to her knees. His hand was moving up her thigh, his lightly callused palm abrading her skin with tiny shocks of pleasure. His fingers shaped the curve of her hip, slid under to cup and squeeze a buttock, and then moved to the apex of her thighs.

Fanny gasped as he touched her there, and he lifted his head from her breast, his face taut with passion. Suddenly he rolled out from under the ledge, carrying her with him out onto the riverbank. Then he was atop her, hot and heavy, as he roughly thrust a knee between hers.

Surprised by the violent action, an involuntary protest came to Fanny's lips. He didn't seem to hear her as his head moved back to her breast. This time he suckled her with strong, hard tugs until she again felt pain. She tried to lift her head, to squirm away, to tell him to be gentle, but he was forcing his other knee between hers, spreading her against her newfound fear of him. As he engulfed her mouth again in a hot thrust of his tongue, she struck at him with her fists. He was hurting her, the pleasure of his touch gone as he bucked his hips against hers in a mindless search for entry.

Fanny grabbed handfuls of his hair and pulled hard, but he was oblivious to the pain. He was wild, using her as would some wild creature in a frenzy of lust. Tears came to her eyes. They were no longer one but two: the conqueror and the victim.

Matthew heard a woman crying as if from a great

distance. There was mad, blood-red passion surging through him. It was a live thing, writhing and throbbing, that would tear him apart if he didn't find a release from it. But the crying, who was crying? He shifted his hips, found with the accuracy of instinct the point of entry... and hesitated. Fanny's eyes were looking up at him, their morning-sky depths clouded by pain and fear.

He threw back his head and groaned low in his throat. Then he flung himself off her, landing flat on his back on the grass beside her. His heart was racing like an antelope crossing the prairie. His loins ached with excruciating pain. Just a thought, just the idea of submission and his body would finish for itself what he'd begun.

Fanny turned her head to watch him. His eyes shut, his back slightly arched, he grimaced like a wounded man. Then ever so slowly his breathing eased, the inflexible muscles loosened, and he slumped back against the earth, the battle won but lines of weary defeat etching his face. He turned to look at her and she stopped breathing. He didn't speak and she couldn't.

For a long moment they stared at one another in wonder and confusion and apprehension. What had happened, so nearly happened? How had what they had both wanted in the beginning changed to become the hungry selfish greed of one for the other? As the minutes played back through their minds, their expressions altered subtly until each knew what the other remembered and found first pleasure in and then guilt.

Then, like two chastised children, they looked away and rose with their backs turned to rearrange their loosened clothing.

Fanny found tears rising in her eyes again as she fumbled with the buttons of her blouse. I shouldn't have stopped him. I didn't mean to. Only, he was hurting me. I shouldn't have stopped him. I didn't want him to stop. Only, I didn't want the hurting. I wanted the kissing. The heat. He'll hate me now. I shouldn't have stopped him.

Matthew tugged his breechcloth straight over his tender and still swollen manhood. I shouldn't have touched her. I only wanted to kiss her. But she was touching me, coaxing me. I shouldn't have touched her. But she wanted my kisses and my hands on her breasts. She ripened under my touch. I shouldn't have touched her. I didn't know a woman could be so soft, so warm and damp. She hates me now. I shouldn't have touched her.

Fanny turned back first, really only a half-turn as she slanted her shoulders to look at him. He stood watching the river a few yards away. His hands were on his hips and he seemed to be thinking deeply. When he turned he didn't look at her but walked up the riverback to the place where he'd left his supplies the night before. She watched him kneel and reach into the bag to withdraw a length of rope. When he rose he turned to her and she looked away. But she knew he was coming toward her, and she didn't know what to say or do.

He stopped before her, but she kept her eyes on the ground, his moccasins and leggings the only part of him in her view.

"Lift your skirts."

Fanny lifted her head instead. "What?"

"Lift your skirts."

He said it without looking at her, his gaze trained somewhere beyond her head.

She stared at him for a long moment, wondering what he intended to do. But he wasn't about to speak again; she could tell that from the way he stood, stiff but patient. Because she knew she would never know the reason for it until she did so, she lifted her skirts.

He knelt down and saw her drawers still hanging about her knees. Without a word he pulled his knife from his leggings and cut the tangled cloth from her legs. He heard her gasp, but he didn't look up. He reached up under her skirt and tied the length of rope about her waist, then made a knot in front, passed the rope between her legs, and wound the ends about her thighs, tying them above each knee.

Grim-faced, he stood up. "That will do."

"Do what?" she demanded, her earlier shame forgotten.

"It is the custom of my people that a maiden wear a chastity belt until she is betrothed. To keep her virtue safe."

"I know what it's for," she answered irritably. "But I don't need it."

"I do."

He turned and started to walk away.

She took a few steps after him but stopped. "This is damned uncomfortable!"

"For both of us," he answered and continued walking.

It was late in the afternoon when Matthew finally stopped, his chin slightly raised as he gazed off into the distance. When he turned back to Fanny, who was coming up slowly behind him, she saw the first gentle look on his face all day.

"Do you smell it?"

"Smell what?" she grumbled.

"Campfires. Over there."

Fanny gazed at the long stretch of prairie trailing out before his lifted arm. "Can't see or smell a thing."

"White woman not have keen nose or eyes."

She was too tired to take umbrage at his gibe. They had been walking since dawn, pausing only once about midday to eat stale biscuit and jerked beef. Her feet hurt and she was sure her thighs were rubbed raw by the coarse hemp tied about them. Why was she being punished for something that was his fault—well, half his fault?

"We will reach the camp by nightfall. Then there will be hot stew and shelter."

She was too miserable to speak the sharp retort that came to mind. It had rained in the early afternoon, and the leather clothes she wore were soggy about the edges and her hair was plastered to her skull where her hat had not covered it. His sudden cheeriness seemed to her the height of callousness. As he picked up his pace, she deliberately hung back, strolling along as if she had the rest of her life to reach wherever it was they were headed.

"Past glory, I'm after thinking," she muttered.

She hated everything about his home: its vast empty gray sky, the vast empty gray-green prairie, the wide, endless muddy-gray Missouri River nearby. Everything. She was determined to take the first train back east. Love be damned! It was all too much trouble.

His prediction that they'd reach the Indian camp by nightfall was accurate. She couldn't kill the leap of joy she felt when she finally spotted the illumination of the campfires at the edge of the horizon.

She was surprised when he suddenly stopped within half a mile of the destination and began sorting through his bags once more. He first used a comb to smooth out his long mane and then offered it to her, but she refused. She knew that nothing less than a good shampoo would untangle her mass of curly red hair. Yet she did follow him to the riverbank, where he scooped out water for them to wash their faces and hands. In mute curiosity she watched him wind a feather-and-bead piece of jewelry, to which he had added her hair, into a lock of hair near his crown. Then he pulled a clean shirt from his belongings and changed into it. After that he slipped on his upper armbands of silver and another on his right wrist. Only then did he seem to remember that she was with him, and he offered the fourth bracelet to her.

"You will wear my gift—as your protection."

"Protection against what?" she asked, not reaching for it.

"Stubborn white woman," he muttered and grabbed her wrist to slip it on. "Leave it!" he said when he saw that she was about to take it off.

She glared at him. "Oh, all right. Why shouldn't I wear something else I don't want?"

No movement betrayed his acknowledgment of her mention of the chastity belt. The events of the morning were gone from his mind. He had won a victory at a great price, but won it he had, and victories were only to be related over the campfire at night when one counted coup.

"White woman should wear dress."

She gritted her teeth. "Red man makes white woman crazy!"

Amusement flickered in his dark gaze. "White woman makes red man . . . hot."

She looked away. No more of that. She'd sworn off love hours ago. She snatched up her bundle. "Turn your head if you expect me to put on me dress."

"*My* dress."

"*My* dress, you arrogant bastard!"

She knew they made a strange pair as they walked into the village, the well-dressed young Sioux and the bedraggled white woman who trailed after him. Her teeth were chattering from the cold, for the wind had risen again. The barks and yips of the dogs who ran out to greet them unnerved her more than she would have suspected. Then the villagers themselves came pouring out. They didn't speak, but Fanny felt their curious stares though they wouldn't meet her eyes.

Matthew went straight to the center of the camp, and she followed. Finally he halted before a large, elaborately painted lodge, the designs of which were clearly visible because the campfire inside made the leather walls glow like a lampshade. One of the women who stood nearby hurried into the lodge, and a few moments later a man emerged.

He was much shorter than Matthew but had the same bold-featured face, which age had leathered but not ruined. He wore a bonnet of feathers and a beautifully beaded buckskin shirt. She knew from her weeks with the Wild West Show that these were the trappings of a chief. With a little trepidation she noticed all the hair threaded through the seams. He spoke to Matthew in the Sioux language, and there was nothing in either man's expression as Matthew replied to tell what was happening. Friends or strangers? She couldn't tell.

Finally the long discourse ended and Matthew half turned to her, not looking directly at her. "You are welcome to the village of my ancestors. My grandfather in particular greets you. You are to go with these women."

As he turned away, Fanny took a step toward him. "When will I see you again?" He didn't answer or even break his stride before disappearing inside the chief's lodge.

Left without any recourse, she followed the woman standing beside her to a tepee at the far back edge of the village. The woman entered first and lit the fire and then departed without a word or glance. Too tired to care, Fanny took off her hat and damp jacket, wrapped herself up in one of the woolen cavalry blankets folded in a neat pile, lay down on one of the pallets, and fell instantly into a deep, dreamless sleep.

CHAPTER
13

Dakota Territory, Autumn 1886.

Fanny gazed forlornly at the snowflakes swirling about her. It was late October, yet the blast of frigid air yanking at her doeskin dress and moccasins felt like the icy-toothed wind of late January. She had just finished delivering the last bucket of water from the river, nearly a mile away, and her back ached from the leather harness she used to carry the pails. Because she was untutored in the Indian way of doing things, she'd been forced to do the most menial tasks of fetching, carrying, and collecting buffalo chips for the fires in order to earn her keep. She didn't mind the work. She'd even had to smile over collecting the buffalo feces, for she'd had more than a nodding acquaintance with them those first days at the Wild West Show.

It was the loneliness that brought the familiar ache to the back of her throat. Days went by without her catching even a glimpse of Matthew. When she did, he never gave any indication that he knew her. Once she'd stood near him at a campfire assembly while the men conversed in words she didn't understand and the women ignored her, as usual. She had tried repeatedly to catch his eye. Only embarrassment had kept her from calling out his name, that and the certain though inexplicable knowledge that to do so would damage him in the eyes of his people.

His people. Fanny let the harness slip from her shoulders, then sat down before her expiring fire. After three weeks she was no more adept at building a lasting fire than she was at communicating with Matthew's people. She couldn't call them unfriendly so much as unresponsive. The women never traded smiles with her, no matter how much she tried to find ways of sharing the simplest joy with them.

As for the men, she didn't dare look at them. She sensed in their passive faces a curiosity and animal lust that she couldn't afford to attract. The one time Matthew had come to her tepee, he'd been accompanied by several women and his grandfather. The men had entered without a word, and then one of the women had unceremoniously lifted Fanny's skirts to bare her to the waist. Even as she cried out indignantly, two other women had grabbed her arms while the woman who'd lifted her skirt thrust a hand between her thighs to explore her in a mortifying fashion.

Fanny had struck her with a foot, but the woman had not retaliated. In fact, she jerked Fanny's skirts down and smacked her affectionately on the thigh before turning to address the chief. The chief had nodded, and then they all left without a word or a look or any kind of explanation. Oh, she'd figured out the purpose of their actions. She'd been confirmed a virgin. That was important to Matthew, she thought bitterly. He had made a vow, sworn an oath. Any woman who traveled with him had to be a virgin.

Two big fat tears ran down Fanny's cheeks and fell on her bosom. She didn't want to be a virgin. She didn't want to be here. She wanted to go home. All the love that had brought her out west had evaporated with the weariness, loneliness, and neglect.

She had thought that all she needed was patience, but now she knew that patience wasn't nearly enough. It was time she left. The only question was how.

Matthew helped to place the last robe over the willow frame of the dome-shaped wigwam. In the center of the lodge an *iniowaspe* had been dug to hold the heated stones that would be needed for the purification rite. A blanket of sage, which the women had gathered, was spread around the floor of the wigwam. The entrance faced east. The earth that had been removed in digging the *iniowaspe* had been mounded up two paces beyond the entrance and before the fire where stones were being heated. The mound was known as *hanbelachia*, or "vision hill." It represented the real place to which he would be traveling soon in order to search for his final vision, the vision that would determine his future. Between the *iniowaspe* and the *hanbelachia* ran a cleared way called the "smoothed trail." This, then, was the path he would follow.

He was glad that his grandfather, Stolen Arrows, himself a Dreamer, was to accompany him on this the first stage of his journey. He had felt very much a stranger during the first days home. So many things had changed. So many new faces and the absence of so many old ones had made him homesick for a time that was long gone. But his grandfather seemed to understand, asking nothing of him, listening to whatever he had to say, keeping infinite patience while his grandson stumbled over the words he hadn't spoken for so long. Then gradually Matthew found himself thinking in Sioux again, thinking as a Sioux again, and the homesickness had faded. He was home. This was home, for the present.

When Stolen Arrows appeared, the shaman, Shifting Stars, had just finished tying red flannel streamers with bundles of tobacco to the ceiling of the lodge. Nothing was said as other young men, also seeking visions, joined them. Each knew his part. Silently they removed their clothing while the helper gathered up the things and placed them in a pile to one side. Each one was given a spray of sage with which to cover his privates, and then they entered the wigwam while the helper waited outside.

Everyone but Shifting Stars seated himself near the *iniowaspe*. When satisfied with their readiness, Shifting Stars went to the lodge entrance and asked for the sacred pipe which the helper passed through. With great ceremony Shifting Stars handed the pipe to Matthew. The significance of the honor being given to a newcomer was not missed by the other two men. He was chosen to receive the benefit of any signs that might appear as a result of this rite. The shaman was old and of great power, and they didn't protest. Then, with a forked stick, the shaman lifted the first of four stones to be put into the pit. As he placed each one inside, Matthew touched the pipe stem to each stone. When they were in place, Matthew passed the pipe to Shifting Stars, who now seated himself.

Shifting Stars held up the pipe, saying, ''All my relatives—living and deceased.'' Then he passed the pipe back to Matthew, that he might smoke it. This Matthew did and passed it on. Four times the pipe was passed around the group in silence, the smoke calming, clearing the mind, making peace for the journey ahead.

When the pipe was empty, Stolen Arrows rose to give it back to the helper, that it might be refilled. When he was reseated, Matthew reached for the sheep-horn spoon and dipped it into the pouch of water at his side. As he flicked the water onto the stones, great clouds of steam rose to fill the wigwam. Four times he did this until he felt his skin stinging from the intense heat. He closed his eyes against the heat as the shaman began to sing a song. He matched his breathing to the rhythm of the song, repeating the words silently, losing himself in the smothering vapor, seeking to cleanse his mind of everything that had crowded in on him these last months. There was only the heat, the music, and the need for a vision.

Four times the ritual was repeated. Four times new stones were brought in; four times the sacred pipe was smoked; four times the shaman sang. By the fourth time the smarting steam enveloped the wigwam, and Matthew felt as though great stinging insects had pricked his nipples, a spot in the small of his back, and the tip of his penis. He chewed bits of sage and, spitting the mass into his hand, smeared the burned places with it as his grandfather had told him he might do. Yet he seemed to be on fire everywhere, and the painful burns increased with every second.

Finally he heard one of the other men shout, "All my relatives!" and the shaman's answering cry, "Open up!" and the flap was thrown open for the steam to escape.

They rose together, one of the men rushing out before the rest, and went out in the snowy night. The shaman paused and bent over the *hanbelachia* to look for tiny hoofprints of the Dreamer's supernatural helper.

When he straightened up, he was laughing. "Morning Star, you bring strange game from the supernatural world. There is a woman's moccasin print here."

Matthew blushed in anger, thinking that he was being teased on so important an occasion, but his grandfather was bent over the marks, and when he looked up there was no laughter in his face. "This is true, Morning Star. A woman rules your dream world. Dangerous *Wakan*, indeed. Now we must finish the rite."

The men turned and ran toward the distant riverbank, heedless of the light snow that had begun to fall.

Because he felt the need to be alone, Matthew quickly outdistanced the rest. A woman *Wakan*. What did it mean? That was a rare symbol, sought only by a man who wished to marry. He hadn't asked for that. He had asked for a glimpse of his future. When he reached the riverbank, he threw himself headlong into the water, crying out in amazed relief as the chilly water doused the fever of his superheated skin.

"It is not enough."

Stolen Arrows regarded his grandson with tolerant affection. "Would you wrestle from the supernatural that which you desire? Are you not humble before *Wakan*?"

"It is not that, Grandfather," Matthew replied. "I feel I do not yet deserve the full attention of the *Wakan*. Perhaps some other ceremony would better serve me."

"What do you suggest, Morning Star?"

"Is it not said that the *Wakan* respect a man who is willing to endure physical sacrifice?"

"It is not the season for *o-kee-pa*."

His expression didn't change, but Matthew gave a silent prayer of thanks that this was so. The self-mutilation and torture rites of tradition weren't often practiced now, and he had no desire to skewer his flesh with pegs and drag a buffalo skull around until the pegs were torn free. "May I not undergo *hanbelachia*?"

Stolen Arrows nodded. "Why, my son, do you not accept that it is your fate to wed?"

"I will accept it if I am certain that there is not something more to be understood in the dreaming."

"Very well. But will you abide by the results this time?"

Matthew nodded.

Four days without food, naked to the elements, lying in a hole in the ground, Matthew waited for the darkness to come over him again. The lacerations from the bits of skin that had been cut from his upper arms and chest as offerings no longer pained him, yet they hadn't been enough. For three days he'd stood as the sun followed its path across the sky, crying out until he was voiceless. Then in darkness he'd waited as the owls swooped low on the prairie and the wind shriveled his skin, but the voices of the supernatural world were silent. Only after midnight would he retire to the protec-

tion of the pit. But he did not sleep. He lay and waited
for the sun to rise and the ritual to start again.

Now he knew that he had failed. He had failed during
the night and had come to himself in shame. As he
lay here listening, the wind was howling furiously,
frighteningly. For ten years he'd believed that he was on
a journey of great importance. Now he knew that it had
been the illusion of a young boy who wanted honors
that were beyond his power to own.

He didn't hear her voice at first. The wind keened
even higher than the sweet speech it carried. But gradually
the voice separated itself from the wind, and as it did
so, the wind seemed to give way before it, growing
calmer.

*Look, Morning Star. Come and look at your village.
See what you would see.*

He scrambled out of the pit into the blackness of
night. Though the village was miles away, out of sight,
he suddenly saw it clearly on the horizon. Even as he
saw it, it seemed to move closer until he was looking
into every lodge of the village. Finally he saw her,
Fanny, with the power that allowed him to see into her
lodge. She was gathering together her belongings. And
she was weeping.

*I have come a long way to find you, son of the Seven
Council Fires,* the kindly female voice whispered in the
wind. *I send my child to you, yet you reject all that I
offer you.*

Matthew watched Fanny as she scattered her fire and
turned to leave the lodge.

I have a woman's heart, not that of a warrior.

He wondered why the voice sounded older than the

woman he followed with his eyes. Then he understood, and he wept.

You have sought wisdom, son of the Dakota Sioux. You have read your enemy's history, but it is only words. You must seek farther to find true wisdom. You must look into your own heart. Are you strong enough?

Matthew watched as Fanny left the village, moving south along the riverbank, and he knew that she was going home.

I will not call to you again, son of Nado-weisiw-eg. You must find me.

The wind rose with a fury and lifted the vision of the village and carried it out of sight over the edge of the horizon.

Matthew lifted his head to the night sky. "I know you, *Whope*, the Beautiful One, defender of chaste ones! And your ally, *Yummi*, the Whirlwind! I know and will obey!"

Fanny took only what she thought she could carry. She had exchanged her soft-soled moccasins for the heavy boots Matthew had bought her. She wore her flannel petticoats under her Indian doeskin dress and a buffalo robe over her buckskin jacket. She had tied the leather leggings high up on her thighs, removing the chastity belt to do so. That she had left, laid out in ritual fashion between her bed and the fire.

It was growing colder. Snow had begun to fall again. She might well die before she reached the railroad tracks. She and Matthew had walked for a day and a half before finding the village. A day and a half seemed a long time when her toes already ached from the cold and her cheeks burned from the punishment of the wind. At least the incessant wind was at her back, pushing her along.

She wondered who would find her in the snow if she should die. Would it be the Sioux or the soldiers, or a coyote? The last thought increased her pace. She didn't want her bones gnawed by a wild creature. Let her lie and die in the snow in peace. Or, if she realized that she was dying, she would throw herself in the river.

The river ran swift and purring on her right. South— she was moving south. If only she made it to first light, she felt she would survive. If only she was far enough away that no one would consider her worth looking for. First peace and then endurance. One foot in front of the other. Left, right, left, right.

She was stumbling on numb feet as dawn lit the eastern sky. There would be a sun today, she told herself as she went down heavily on one knee. When the sun came out, the snow would melt away and she would be halfway to her destination. She pulled herself to her feet and lurched forward again. River on the right. Wind at her back. She was going south. Not long now. Maybe sooner than she knew.

The train had been going farther when she and Matthew left it. Why, the tracks might be just out of view in the prairie grass. She might look up any moment now and see a plume of smoke and then the black engine puffing along. She could nearly hear it, the rhythmic chugging. Only it seemed to come from behind her. She halted, confused. Behind her? Yes, the ground vibrated with the rhythm. She'd made a mistake. The train was coming along behind her. Her heart seemed to lift in her chest. It was so close. So close!

She spun about, welcoming salvation.

Matthew reined in his mount a few yards short of her, uncertain of his welcome. At first she didn't seem to know who he was. Then she dropped her bundles and began to cry, open-mouthed, like a small child, as she had the night he had found her hiding in his lodge. And he knew she didn't want to go back, didn't want him any longer. He didn't, couldn't blame her.

She felt like ice in his embrace as he picked her up and carried her back to his horse. The tears were dampening his neck where she buried her head against him. How often he had hurt her, how often he had been wrong and blamed her for his mistake. How much he had to make up to her, if she would let him. She would break her heart with the crying, and he didn't know how to stop it.

He bent his head, seeking some wordless solace for her pain, and found her cheek under his lips. It was like ice, and he instinctively licked it to warm it. She shook her head slightly, but she didn't pull away as he continued to lick and blow his breath upon her skin. Her sobs stopped as she stilled under his tender nuzzling. He rubbed her cheek with his, licked the curve of her lips when he found it, and then moved to bring the soft, cool shape of her mouth under his.

Her lips warmed quickly to the hot breath he expelled on them. They were chapped by the wind, and he licked the crispness until they were soft. She felt so good to him, better than any joy, sweeter than any cherished sorrow, more precious than any single thing he'd ever known. How could he have been so blind as to think of this as wrong? It was natural, as natural as life. It was life. From this pleasure came birth and the future, new beginnings and a continuation.

"I don't love you anymore."

Matthew smiled, his lips spreading upon hers. "I know."

"I won't do it," she sighed under his mouth. "I cut meself loose."

Matthew lifted his head to the lightening sky. He'd found the chastity belt. The height of folly.

He lifted her up sidesaddle onto his horse and then hoisted himself up astride behind her. He opened her robe and brought her close against him to share his heat. He felt her arm go around his waist as he turned his mount back north, toward home.

Fanny laughed with the girls who were helping her prepare for the wedding ceremony, though from what Matthew had told her, this wasn't a religious ceremony at all. He'd promised her an American wedding of her choosing the next time they were in a town, and she'd readily agreed.

They were fitting a long-sleeved elkskin dress over her. It was a loan, made of the finest, softly bleached skin. It felt like velvet and draped and clung to her body like heavy silk. The shoulders were decorated with red and blue seed beads, and three rows of beadwork formed curved bands at the bottom just before the fringe began. Cowrie shells trimmed the bodice, and a deer tail had been attached at the neckline. Matching leggings had been wrapped from ankle to knee, held in place by fur strings. Her moccasins were fur-lined and worked with beads and quills.

One woman applied red paint to her cheeks while another inspected her newly plucked brows. That had not been the only unpleasant part of this toilet, Fanny reflected ruefully. She had had her ears pierced in order to wear the silver earrings Matthew had sent her as a wedding present. But there had been other wonderful preparations, like having her body rubbed with oils of sweet grass and fir.

They arranged her bright hair with much touching and playful tugs, as though they couldn't believe it was real. After careful washing and rubbing with perfumed oils, her hair had been parted in the middle and made glossy with cactus pitch while the part had been painted red. It hung loose now to catch the light. Then they added a choker of dentalium and a painted belt and finally a soft robe lined in fur.

Finally they made her stand in the center of the lodge while they discussed and pulled and fiddled with her until Fanny thought she would scream.

The jingle of a bridle outside the lodge door sent the women scurrying to the entrance, and then they held back the flap for her to exit.

She went out into the daylight to find the entire village waiting for her, but not Matthew. Bewildered, she looked about.

"Daughter of the white man," Stolen Arrows said in English as he came to stand before her, replete in his warbonnet and painted shirt fringed in the hair locks of his people. "You are the choice of my grandson in marriage. Do not bring disgrace to his lodge."

As a marriage blessing it was decidedly lacking in enthusiasm, Fanny decided as her knees began to shake beneath her beautiful dress.

Now two men came forward, one who she recognized by his dress to be the shaman. They lifted her up onto the back of the horse whose bridle she had heard jingling. Then, taking hold of the reins, the men led her through the village as the people fell into an irregular line behind her. She felt silly and awkward on the back of the horse, but she didn't know what else to do but smile and search for Matthew's face in the gathering. He wasn't there.

They led her out of the village to a stand of trees near the riverbank, and she noticed a new tepee had been set up where none had been before. When they halted before the lodge, a man emerged.

Fanny smiled, her heart quickening its pace. Matthew. He was handsomely groomed in new buckskins with quillwork and beading and painted symbols. Jealously she wondered what woman had made the clothes for him. Someone who hoped to catch his eye, no doubt.

Then Stolen Arrows had stepped forward and was addressing his grandson. *"Wiyan he cinacaqupi!"*

When he finished, Matthew stepped forward and lifted her off the horse. Fanny knew she was blushing, but she doubted he knew it. He hadn't looked directly at her but turned and walked back to the tepee.

A sharp jab in the back by one of the women told her that she was supposed to follow him. And she did, stepping inside the lodge without a single idea of what she should do next. But she didn't need to, she discovered by the time she stood alone with him in the tepee. Matthew was looking directly at her, and what she saw in his eyes told her everything she wanted to know.

As they stood regarding one another, they heard the laughter and chatter of the people moving back toward the village.

Fanny frowned. "Is that all, then?"

Matthew nodded, his eyes filled with the beauty of his bride.

"But what about the ceremony, the words?"

"Did you not hear my grandfather speak?"

"He didn't say much."

"It was enough. *Wiyan he cinacaqupi* are the words of the ceremony."

"That few? What does it mean?"

Matthew's mouth twitched. "A loose translation would be 'You want the girl, so I give her to you.'"

Fanny blushed. "Just like that? Like a sack of meal?"

"I'd have had to pay for a sack of meal."

Fanny shrugged and looked away. This wasn't quite what she'd expected. She looked back. "What about the feast?"

"They're having it without us. Unless you wish to join them?"

She shook her head, looking about. There were two beds laid out side by side. A bright fire with a pot hanging from a tripod burned at the center of the lodge. The smell of the stew was quite inviting. There were buffalo robes neatly folded in one corner. Bouquets of dried flowers hung in bunches from the lodge poles. Neat. Clean. Quiet.

"Do you like our new home?"

"Our—it's ours?"

"You are my wife now. My lodge is your lodge."

"I see." Fanny began to gnaw her lip, suddenly unsure of herself and everything she'd agreed to.

Matthew understood her feelings perfectly. They were his own. "Are you hungry?"

"No—yes." Why not? They needed to do something. She found the army-issue tin plates and served him first. Then they sat cross-legged and watched each other over the fire. She noticed that he ate quickly, hungrily, but she couldn't find the interest to lift the spoon to her mouth. If the wedding ceremony was to be so short, it should have taken place at night, she thought miserably as she pushed a piece of meat around her dish.

"You are beautiful."

She looked up to see him smiling at her. "You're not after looking so bad yourself ... for a redskin." She looked down. "There's something I've be meaning to say to you. About the night we left the train and I was lost. I called you terrible names. I can't think why I said them. I'm sorry."

"Forgiven."

She shook her head and looked up at him. "You don't understand. I think I meant them. I called you a savage and a dirty redskin, like that trapper did on the train from Omaha, and I felt at the moment like I meant it."

"You were angry and scared."

"That's no excuse."

"You were angry with me. You wanted to hurt me. It was personal, not a general slur."

"Still, I could have said anything but what I did."

"You've a good heart, Just Fanny. That's why I love you."

She tried to smile but she couldn't. He'd never said those words to her before.

As she watched, he put down his plate and rose, coming to her side, where he knelt before her. "I love you," he repeated.

She nodded, silenced by the truth of his vow.

Lifting both hands, he gently framed her face. "Do you love me, just a little?"

"You know I do."

He smiled. "I know. You've shown me in so many ways for so long that I'm afraid you'll stop."

She cupped his hands in hers. "I don't think I know how."

He bent and kissed her with the gentlest touch he knew how to offer.

Fanny shut her eyes against the beauty of it. This time there would be no turning back, no guilt and sorrow, no reluctance or shame, no pain and frustration, only what they wished to offer of themselves.

As he drew back from her, her fingers tightened on his hands to hold his mouth to hers as it blossomed under his, offering him all of its pleasure. The kisses changed, grew more urgent, demanding, as his mouth slanted across hers in an effort to have more of her, and she met his eagerness. They clung together, trading kiss after kiss until her lips were swollen with passion.

Finally she drew back a little, laughing breathlessly. "And to think Mrs. Tarrington says Indians don't like kissing."

"White women know little about Indian," he answered in his stage voice. "This Indian like everything about Just Fanny."

She put a hand on his chest, just over his heart. "Me too. I ain't never been kissed till you. I don't know that we've got the right of it, but I don't care. I like it just fine. Kiss me again."

There was a new tension in his kisses now, a quickening demand that made her stomach quiver and her loins soften. His hands moved from her face to her shoulders, drawing her to her knees before him, and then they moved lower to guide her hips against his. He guided her movements, finding that the slightest change in pressure increased his desire and brought little gasps of pleasure from her.

She was naked beneath the thin, clinging dress, and he rubbed the leather over her skin as though his hands were touching her, molding her, finding all the contours of her back and then the proud curve of her hips. He caressed her buttocks and lifted her slightly to meet his gentle thrusts so that she would know how badly he needed her. She began to move of her own accord, playfully meeting his thrusts with a wiggle of her hips that left them both gasping and sighing.

He reached up to mold the dress to the shape of her breasts, and she threw back her head, arching her upper body toward him. "Oh," she cried softly as his fingers closed over the nipples outlined through the leather. And, "Oh," again as he released them. He reached down and shimmied her dress up past her waist, and then the warm weight of her buttocks was in his hands even as she moved invitingly against him.

He kissed her again because he needed desperately to taste her, and Fanny clung to him, her lips moist, her hands clutched in his hair.

Fanny felt as if she could weep, so strong was the need inside her. He was holding her so beautifully, kissing her so wonderfully, and yet it wasn't nearly enough. She turned away from his kiss, and then she was lifting the edge of his shirt, pulling it over his head.

The first thing she noticed were the thin red lines of newly healing scars on his chest. She touched one tentatively. "What happened?"

"Sacrifice," he said huskily, not wanting to discuss it now.

She looked up at him. "For me?"

He smiled ruefully. "In a manner of speaking."

The look on her face made him sorry he'd spoken, but then her lips were pressing his skin over a scar, and then another and another. He closed his eyes, glad to have suffered so little if it brought him the pleasure of—she licked him! Carefully she licked every scar as if by the touch she could mend it. And they felt mended.

Fanny smiled as she tasted his skin. He felt so good, the tactile sensation sending shivers soaring through her from her lips to her groin. There the palpitating need gathered strength with each passing second.

Matthew reached for her dress again, drawing it up past her shoulders, and she ducked her head to allow him to pull it off.

He had lain with her, pressed her naked length to his, but he'd never seen her, and the sight stilled his hands. She was pale, surprisingly so, but well formed, with jutting breasts that bore nipples like new-budded strawberries. Her belly was flat, and then a thatch to match her hair marked the beginning of her thighs.

Fanny stood his scrutiny as best she could, her hands by her sides, though she fought the urge to cover herself. She was his wife. It was his right to see her. His wife. She grinned at him. "Satisfied?"

"Aye," he answered, mimicking her.

"Then, isn't it me—my turn? To see what I've bargained for m—myself."

He grinned back and stood up. He wore only leggings and a breechcloth and moccasins. The moccasins went first and then the leggings quickly followed. As his hand went to the thong that held his breechcloth, he hesitated.

Fanny stood up. "Let me," she said and reached for the knotted string.

She was not exactly surprised by what she saw, but her eyes went quickly up to his face and he blushed deeply. "It is possible," he said quietly.

"I hope—I suspect it must be," she answered faintly.

He reached out to draw her close, each conscious of the unfamiliar touch, of the new sensations, of the yet-to-be-solved moment of joining. He kissed her again, trying not to think beyond the present, the beauty of now. Soon she was again eagerly returning those kisses and he wrapped his arms around her again, gently increasing the pressure of his embrace until her full length was tightly joined to his.

When they moved slightly apart this time, he didn't allow her to break contact completely. He didn't want to think beyond the present. He stepped backward with her in his arms, drawing her to the bedding he had laid out, and then he pulled her down with him as he knelt. He held her close, kissing her as though each kiss would last forever.

Fanny submitted to the command of his hands when he pushed her onto her back on the bedding. His hands never left her; they were stroking her so lightly that she began to move under them, trying to increase the pressure. The pressure increased, on her shoulders, her breasts, her thighs. His lips were soft on her mouth, then softer still, and then harder, more urgent, and she nearly cried out in thanksgiving.

She reached up to stroke his shoulders, to hold on to the solid reality that was slipping away and then careened back as his dark head bent lower as she felt his mouth enclose her breast. She cradled his head in her arms, whispering her need and her pleasure and her happiness that he was the one doing this to her and that she needed it, needed him, and would forever.

Matthew heard her shy whisperings through the haze of a passion so great he couldn't answer. He thought only of pleasing her, of increasing her joy, all the time directed by her answering cries which further emboldened him. When he moved to press a knee between hers, he found the path already open. He moved between them, his hand parting her just a little more, and then he was arching against her, searching for the place that was made for him, welcomed him.

Fanny buried her forehead in his arm as she felt the pressure of his search, and then her body gave and sweetly parted. Then there was resistance again.

Matthew smoothed her hair from her face, wanting to reassure her but as ignorant as she of the next moments. Yet his body was urging him powerfully to thrust and thrust again, to move inside her, to know the full extent of belonging to her. He bent his head in the hollow of her neck and thrust. He heard her moan, but he couldn't stop. He gritted his teeth, thrusting again, and then once more. Then he was sliding deep, so deep into the wet warmth of his wife.

Fanny thought she would burst with the fullness of him. It didn't seem natural to be so filled. When he moved she gasped with the enormity of the sensations quaking through her. He would sunder her and she couldn't, didn't know how to stop the powerful waves of pleasure-pain sweeping over her with each tiny movement. Every breath brought her ever more sensitive body to another peak.

Matthew moved slowly, but he didn't try to stop himself. This was the great mystery, and it was even more cataclysmic than he'd ever dreamed. Fanny was sobbing under him, and somewhere deep inside he felt her weeping. Then she was gasping and thrusting her hips up to meet his. He heard her inarticulate cry. He was on his knees, thrusting with all the joy of his need until he, too, cried out as his seed burst with release.

For a long moment there was only silence as their bodies reverberated with the aftershocks of spent passion.

After a moment Fanny felt him begin to stroke her, soothing her with words that sounded regretful and tenderly solicitous. And she wondered why. So this was the great glory, the pride of kings and paupers alike. How could a women sell it so cheaply on the street? It was worth more than jewels, more than silks, more than palaces and kings. To know this moment, to feel as she did was such glory!

Her hand came up and stroked his cheek. "*Macushla*," she crooned softly. "I love you more dearly than me own life."

His cheek moved on hers. "I didn't mean to hurt you."

Fanny chuckled. "If that was pain, then I'll be having a whole measure of the punishment delivered to me every day for the rest of me life."

"*My* life," he answered.

"Your life. My life. It's our life now."

He lifted his head, uncertain that she was truly laughing. "Didn't I hurt you?"

"I've known worse. Having m—my ears pierced, for

instance. Now that's a pain I wouldn't like to have repeated."

He stared at her, grateful yet confused. "You're *witkowin*."

"A madwoman, am I? Well, I'm your madwoman now, don't you be forgetting it." She felt him, still inside her, stir. "Weren't we supposed to wait until nightfall, as is the custom?"

"Whose custom?"

"Why, civilized custom."

Matthew laughed. "I'm a savage, remember?"

"Aye," Fanny said, her eyes darkening with passion. "Aye, I remember. Now show me the way of it again, my fine savage husband."

CHAPTER
14

February 1887

"Your neighbors complain. The sighs and moans keep them awake. And laughter. There is too much laughter."

Matthew smiled. "Yes, Grandfather."

"Four months." Stolen Arrows ticked them off on his fingers. "Still, you are like young foxes in heat."

"Yes, Grandfather."

"The single men are envious. They say she has hair the color of the fox's tail and that they can smell in it her constant readiness for you."

Matthew's face sobered. "Who says that?"

"It is unseemly. To be too much with a woman endangers a man's strength."

"Do I look withered, Grandfather?"

"No." Stolen Arrows regarded his favorite grandson with tolerant affection. "But you set a bad example for the others. Perhaps you should take a second wife."

"There would be more than laughter and sighs within my lodge should I even suggest that." Matthew shook his head. "I do not need another wife, only this one, and often."

Neither man was embarrassed to joke about sexual matters. It was the custom. But Matthew knew that Fanny would be mortified if she learned what the young men of the village said and was thankful again that her lessons in Sioux were proceeding very slowly.

Stolen Arrows looked about his grandson's lodge in disapproval. "You have no new items in your home. Where are your wife's achievements?"

"She is not Sioux and cannot be expected to learn in a few short months all that a girl of our tribe is taught from birth."

Stolen Arrows grunted. "There would be more time if you left her alone."

"The nights are long," Matthew answered. "It is the days that are short. That will change. It will be spring soon."

Stolen Arrows nodded, his leathery face growing solemn once more. "And you will be leaving us, grandson."

It was a statement, but Matthew couldn't keep from questioning it. "Have you seen this in your dreams?"

Stolen Arrows replied with a question of his own. "Are you satisfied that the events of your Vision Quest have come to pass?"

Many times during the long, frigid winter months Matthew had discussed with his grandfather and the other *wiscasas* his Dream while undergoing *hanbelachia*. It was the custom, and it gave him a feeling of being connected to the tribe when there were so many ways in which he was no longer bound.

"I have dreamed the Dream twice since the Moon of Frost in the Tepee," he said finally. "A woman, not my wife, calls to me. It is *Whope*. She has another task for me other than marriage, but I do not know what it is."

"*Whope* asks you to seek her. To do so you must go in search of her. She speaks to you in the white man's tongue. It is not Sioux business she sends you on."

"But why should *Whope* be concerned for people who do not even know of her existence?"

Stolen Arrows sat very still for a long time. "Does the rain not fall on the prairie because you are not there to see it? Does the river cease to flow because you do not know it is there? The Great Mystery exists though people may forget. Dreams are a personal matter, grandson. From birth you were destined to leave us. For ten summers you passed your life among the white man. You wear the seasons of those years in your eyes. I welcomed you home, but you are not Sioux any longer. You are a Traveler."

The words chilled Matthew. He wanted to protest them, but Stolen Arrows had *Wakan* beyond his knowing, and the truth would not be altered by denial. "You are asking me to go."

"Never, grandson. I would not send a child of mine away. But the time will shortly come when you will ask permission to leave and, as before, I will not stay you."

"Well?" Fanny asked impatiently when Stolen Arrows had departed and she was once more allowed inside her own lodge. "What did your grandfather want?"

Matthew reached out to pull her down into his lap.

When she was comfortable, he said, "Grandfather says we are not to make love any longer."

Fanny jerked within his embrace. "Why not?"

He said very solemnly, "Because my wife's cries of pleasure keep the camp awake half the night."

Fanny stared at him in disbelief, but there was something about the complaint that rang true. A stinging blush climbed her neck as she remembered that All Blossoms had been trying to tell her something about lovemaking only the day before, but she didn't know enough words yet to understand. "Did he really say— well, you know?"

Matthew nodded. "I am the talk of the single men's campfire."

"Why?"

He smiled. He wasn't about to tell her the ribald joke circulating about her. "They fear that my member will shrivel from the frequent labor to which I put it, and then you will be without a lodge pole for your tepee."

She struck him playfully in the chest. "You're boasting, you are!"

He kissed her and then turned her so that she fell onto her back and he stretched out atop her.

"Remember Grandfather," Fanny warned half-seriously.

Matthew grinned at her. "It is midday. No one sleeps now. But if you would be extra careful, then don't make a sound, my love."

In the past months they had learned together what pleased each of them. The long winter nights offered many hours to be alone, since neither of them had family with whom to share their campfire. But they were still flush with the newness of this expression of love. They went at one another a little wildly, kissing and caressing and nipping until their breath came quickly and their skins were slick with their exertions and neither could resist the urge to join.

Matthew entered her carefully, knowing that sometimes his enthusiasm would end too quickly what they wanted most. When he had mastered the first moment, he sighed and opened his eyes. She lay with her face averted from his, her fiery hair splayed out about her like a flood of sunset color. A deep flush mantled her shoulders and the tops of her breasts, and he knew that she was ready, more than ready. And it was a miracle, as always, to him.

He moved slowly on her, arching high into her in a move that always made her gasp with pleasure. But this time she only gritted her teeth and squeezed her eyes shut. He withdrew, paused, and then thrust again. The nails of her hands bit hard into his upper arms and he felt her shudder, but she made no sound.

Matthew closed his eyes and retreated once more. This time she will sing for me, he thought. He teased her with tiny movements that threatened but did not fill her. Her head was thrashing from side to side, tears slid out from under her golden-red lashes, her breath was labored, and he knew she was beyond control. He slid in fiercely this time, with the certainty of her delivery.

Fanny was weeping silently with frustration. Suddenly she could stand it no longer and she was fighting him, striking him with both hands and squirming and bucking under him, desperate for her freedom.

"Please stop! Please!" she whispered frantically.

Astonished, Matthew raised himself up, but he didn't release her; he wouldn't have for the world. "What is wrong, Fanny?"

She shook her head. "I—I can't—do it!"

"Do what?" He stroked her damp cheek. "Am I not pleasing you?"

"Yes! Only you must stop! I'll shame you with me cries!"

Matthew's laughter shook them both. "Poor, poor love. Did you think I was serious? It was a joke, Fanny. Only a jest."

She cuffed him on the chin. "You cheat! I won't ever be believing your words again."

"I didn't lie. The complaints may be true. If so, then we must wear ourselves out during the daylight hours when the sounds will be lost in the noise of the camp." He grinned at her. "Then, at night we will be too tired to cry out more than a little with the pleasure we feel." He moved strongly on her.

She gripped him as he set the rhythm for them, but this time she didn't close her eyes. She wanted to see his dark, black-eyed face above her, to see in the tense lines how his pleasure grew. This man alone made her feel that the sky was within reach and that the stars were trapped in his gaze and that, if she chose, she could take all of him into herself until the *he* and *she* of their existence would be blurred beyond recognition. Then she was carrying out her joy unashamedly and hearing his flattering echo as shudders carried them over the edge of reason.

Later, when the stars had returned to the sky, which was once more high above their heads, Fanny climbed up onto Matthew's prone body and propped her elbows on his chest. "You should be ashamed of yourself."

He nodded weakly, not opening his eyes.

"You're a terrible example for the single men of your tribe."

One dark eye opened.

"Look at you, lying about like any sort of spalpeen when you should be hunting or counciling or smoking the pipe."

"Is that all?"

"Of course not. Look who you've married. I can't cook. I can't keep a proper lodge. I don't know how to prepare a hide or where to find the roots and herbs for medicines. I am useless to you."

"This is true. I should think of taking another wife."

Fanny's lids lowered. "I won't divorce you, even if your tribe allows it. I'm your wife until you're dead!"

He didn't miss her point of reference. "I wasn't thinking of being rid of you." He cupped a buttock. "You've your uses. I was talking of adding a second wife to my lodge."

"That's sinful! And against the law."

He opened his other eye. "Polygamy isn't against Sioux law. A man may have as many wives as he can care for. Besides, I am only thinking of you. You point out that you're sorely lacking in the wifely virtues, save one. Another woman would ease the burden, show you how things are done, and—"

"Get you murdered in your robes," she finished sweetly.

"No second wife?"

"No wife but me."

"It is the month of the Sore Eyes Moon," he said, suddenly serious. "Next comes the Moon When the Grains Come Up. The river will begin to thaw and the snow cease. I am thinking that it will be the time to go back east.''

Fanny's mouth fell open. Never once since their marriage had he said anything about returning east. ''Why?''

He shrugged. ''Wouldn't you like to see your friends again?''

''I have no friends. You know that.''

He began thoughtfully to arrange her ringlets along her back. ''You have told me about Phineas. I don't like that he made you a thief, but I am grateful to him for bringing you to the Wild West Show so that we met.''

''You didn't seem thankful at the time.''

He pulled one curl sharply. ''You were a thief then. Now that you are my wife, I am certain you have reformed. So, wouldn't you like to know what has become of Phineas?''

Fanny laid her head down on his chest. During the months of the Hairless Calf, Frost in the Tepee, and Tree Popping Moon, she had told him nearly everything about her life. There was little she held back, except about her years before she came to America. ''I hope Phineas is dead.''

The flat statement worried Matthew. It spoke of hurt feelings and unresolved anger. ''You will never know unless you go and see for yourself.''

She lifted her head. ''Is that really why Grandfather came to see you? Does he know that you want to go back east?''

''He knew before I did.''

She frowned. ''He has had a dream?''

He nodded.

So that was it. While she hadn't come to understand

completely the Vision Quest that ruled the lives of Sioux men and women, there was in her Irish background an innate sympathy for things of the other world, of powers stronger than mortal knowing, of events that superseded mere magic and superstition. "Where will we go? What will we do?"

"I don't know." He'd heard from visitors to the camp that the Wild West Show had been a great success at Madison Square Garden but that it was disbanded at Christmastime, and no one knew when or if it would revive.

She reached for a buffalo robe and drew it up to cover them because the chill of February was creeping in under the dew cloth. "I will go with you."

He tenderly traced one red-gold brow. "Yes, you will. Always."

The great commotion in the camp reached Fanny's ears slowly, and she pulled her robe up over her head to block out the faint sounds. The day before Fanny and All Blossoms had had to dig in the snow for fuel for their late winter fires while snow swirled and dipped in carefree circles about their heads. They had strapped rawhide to their hands for protection, but her fingers had cracked and bled from the cold. Matthew had been worried that she would lose her fingertips to frostbite, but the color had come back after a few hours and he had put her to bed early after wrapping her hands in bandages and filling her full of the vile herbal tea the shaman had concocted for her.

The dogs were wild with joy, their piercing yips invading the thickness of her robe, but she refused to give in to the beginnings of curiosity. Matthew had risen long ago. Let him come and tell her what was happening.

Matthew stood by his grandfather's side as the procession made its way into camp. They had been spotted by a lookout hours earlier, and a messenger had ridden out to meet them. The names that had come back with the scout had brought joy to Matthew's heart, and surprise. Red Shirt was among the party, as well as Cut Meat and Rocky Bear, who were also former cast members of the Wild West Show. He knew from prairie gossip that they had returned to the Dakotas. But the last member of the party was a totally unexpected guest in the territory, Buffalo Bill Cody himself. He looked the same, long curly hair and pointed beard. Only his usually theatrical clothing had been traded for more practical trail-riding gear.

Greetings were exchanged with ritual politeness between *Pahaska* and the Dakota chiefs, and all the while Matthew stood impatiently waiting to learn the reason for the visit. Buffalo Bill was more than a showman. It could well be that some new government policy had brought him west again. Were there rumors of new unease? Had some new treaty been written to break the last one? Were Stolen Arrows' people to be herded yet again? Matthew caught Red Shirt's eye, but his friend merely indicated by the slightest movement that he was glad to see him. Matthew relaxed. This was a good-neighbor visit.

Something of the same must have communicated itself to the people of the tribe, for they were soon scattering to make preparations for a celebration as soon as Buffalo Bill disappeared into Stolen Arrows' lodge for the smoking-of-the-pipe ceremony. Provisions were dreadfully low at this, the end of the winter, but thanks to the bearded white one, there were three slaughtered carcasses ready to be roasted.

Only when the elders were settled in the lodge were Matthew and Red Shirt free to greet one another less formally.

"It is good to see you, old friend," Matthew said as they shook hands.

"It is good. I wondered if you had really spent the winter here as you planned."

"Come to my lodge. I have many things to tell you and much more to ask." Matthew indicated that Red Shirt should precede him. "One thing first," he added as he fell into step beside him. "Is it serious business that brings Buffalo Bill to the camp?"

"Not the kind you mean," Red Shirt answered. "*Pahaska* has a new plan for his next show. He is determined to travel across the Big Water, to bring his show to a place called England."

"England? Why England?"

"There is a great old woman there, very wise, much *wicasa*. She is the chief of her tribe, *Pahaska* says. She is having big celebration, big feast day, and she wants to see a Wild West Show."

Matthew halted in his tracks. "The Queen of England has requested a royal visit from the Wild West Show?" He whistled. "That is a great honor for Buffalo Bill, my friend."

Red Shirt shrugged. "Great honor for white man. Great danger for Sioux."

Matthew nodded slowly. There was an ancient legend that said that any Indian who crossed the Big Water would sicken and die. "Still, some have done it, I've heard."

Red Shirt nodded. "So have I." He looked at his friend. "But have you talked to any of them?"

The implication was clear. "Will you go?"

Red Shirt shrugged. "I have come to discuss it with you. You have lived and studied much with the white man. Does he truly have a canoe that can carry men safely across the Big Water?"

"Many times over," he answered. "You saw them in the harbor in New York City. If they can come here, it is reasonable to think that we can go there."

Red Shirt grunted and Matthew answered in kind. Brave words for a man who was not thinking of taking the risk.

When they halted before his lodge, Matthew suddenly blushed. "I have something to tell you, Red Shirt. I have married."

His friend grinned at him. "You have given up your celibate life!"

"How did you know?"

Red Shirt grinned. "Not only men like to brag of their conquests. It was well-known in the show's encampment that a certain Arapaho woman boasted that she would pass under every brave in the cast. You were her only failure. Since I have seen that you are not deformed, it could only be that you refused to accept her."

"It does not follow—"

"That you were keeping yourself from women deliberately? I saw how you looked at the red-haired one. Your breechcloth betrayed a man in heat." He looked at his friend curiously. "What happened to her?"

Matthew lifted the flap of his lodge. "She is my wife."

"Now I'm saying I'll pay each brave twenty-five dollars a month and his wife fifteen if she'll participate in Buffalo Bill's Wild West." Cody smiled proudly. "I want America represented by her finest native sons, the Dakota Sioux. If I must, I will go reluctantly to the Cheyenne and the Pawnee, whom you respect, but I'd purely like to have the Sioux nation presented to the greatest monarch this world's ever known! A right nice lady, too, I'm told."

Stolen Arrows leaned forward to consult in whispers with the other chiefs while Matthew and Red Shirt stood respectfully in the rear of the chief's lodge, awaiting a decision.

Finally Stolen Arrows straightened. "*Pahaska* offers our people a great honor. We would go to see this white woman chief that she may know us as a proud and brave people. I would go myself but I am old. It is for the young to make this treacherous journey." He looked at Matthew. "I offer my grandson, Morning Star, in my place and any that would go with him."

Cody smiled and nodded. "Well spoken, Chief Stolen Arrows. I would be proud to have your grandson with me. He has distinguished himself before in my Wild West, as has his wife." Cody grinned in spite of himself. The last thing on earth he'd expected was to find that Irish lass Fanny in a Sioux camp, looking every inch an Indian in her doeskin dress and leggings and braided hair. Married to Matthew Morning Star. Who'd have thought it?

"My train is leaving St. Louis in early March. Every

brave and squaw and papoose who wants to come should be there by the first of the month.''

Wrapped in her fur-lined robe, Fanny stood with the other women in the misting rain to learn of the chief's decision. Part of her wanted to remain in the village, but a greater part, a part she hadn't allowed any leeway in her thoughts, hoped that she and Matthew would one day return to civilization. At least Cody's coming had accomplished one thing. She and everyone in camp had eaten their fill for the first time in weeks. The leftover roasts had been carved up and given proportionally to each lodge. There would be meat for days.

When Matthew appeared, he didn't look her way. Husbands and wives weren't supposed to speak in public, but she saw that he was smiling and that Buffalo Bill was shaking his hand. Finally Cody turned to scan the crowd, and when he spied her, he spoke briefly to Matthew, then came toward her.

He extended his hand to her. ''Why, Mrs. Morning Star, if it ain't a delightful surprise to find you here.''

Fanny blushed. ''And you, too, Mr. Cody.''

''That's Colonel Cody now,'' he corrected with a wink. ''Governor Thayer of the great state of Nebraska, my home state, that is, has seen fit to bestow upon me the title of colonel.''

''That's wonderful, Colonel Cody. You must be very proud.''

He nodded. ''It looks right nice on the handbills, too. Reckon it won't hurt my reputation with the queen, either. Are you coming with your husband?''

''Matthew has agreed to go with you to England?''

Colonel Cody nodded. ''Stolen Arrows is sending

him as his representative. Oleta and Buck will be tickled pink if you come, too.''

Fanny grinned. ''They're going? But that's wonderful. It'll be a reunion.''

''That it will. Do you still remember your rope tricks? Good. I've got a place for you in the lineup. After all, you may be the wife of a Sioux, but you certainly won't fit in in the Indian village, if you know what I mean.''

She did know. She didn't even fit in in real life.

Later when she and Matthew lay snuggled together for the night, she said, ''What will we do after the show season's over?''

''We'll see.''

Matthew sighed. He didn't know if there would be a future for him after they crossed the Big Water, but he couldn't tell her that. She accepted so much of what he believed without any sign of disdain or ridicule. But she was not Sioux. She didn't know of the old legends. She had crossed the ocean and had lived to thrive. Yet, if she knew the story of the wasting sickness, she might not want him to go, and Stolen Arrows had had another dream that told him his grandson's destiny lay far far away. He was a warrior, he was well-educated, but he had also come to realize that knowledge counted for little when the rhythm of ancient drums beat out a tattoo to which a man's heart had responded long before he had left his mother's womb. He would go, but he didn't know if he would survive.

New York City, March 1887

Fanny couldn't believe the luxury in which she and Matthew had traveled east on the Wild West train, twenty-six cars painted gold and white with the huge letters BUFFALO BILL'S WILD WEST emblazoned on the sides. In nearly every town where they stopped, Colonel Cody had been given a dignitary's welcome, sometimes with a brass band and streamers and the whole town turning out to cheer him along. Even in smaller places, people had gathered to wave at the one-of-a-kind train sweeping past their little hamlets and communities.

Personal accommodations were such that the ladies had traveled in cars separately from the men. The seats turned into bunks for the night, much too narrow to allow for couples, in any case. So it was a great relief to Fanny when they finally arrived in New York City and the Fifth Avenue Hotel.

"I didn't realize how much I'd grown accustomed to having you by my side," Matthew said as he hugged her tight.

She smiled up at him as they stood just inside the hotel-room door. "We could be getting that much closer," and she glanced meaningfully at the bed nearby.

Without releasing her, he began walking her toward the bed. "You have the loveliest thoughts, wife. That must be why I married you."

"I'll show you why you married me in a minute," she answered with a laugh.

He turned her onto her back on the bed, not even undressing her but lifting her skirts to drag down her drawers. "I don't approve of the way white women dress," he said as he fought the buttons that held them closed. "A man should have easy access to his wife."

Fanny squirmed deliciously as he knelt between her parted thighs and pulled at the laces of her corset. "I rather like it. Gives a woman time to decide if it's loving she wants or only a kiss."

His dark face rose over the bulk of her thrown-back petticoats. "Has my wife made her decision?"

She propped herself up on her elbows and smiled at him. "Will you be all day about it, or have you forgotten how to use your skinning knife."

Matthew hesitated. He wore buckskin and leggings because he was now a part of the show, even off the stage, but Fanny was dressed in the best that St. Louis could offer a lady of means. He had watched in pride as she outfitted herself down to her underwear. "You like these clothes."

"Then help me to rise and I'll be taking each and every piece off and hanging it up with the respect it deserves." She heard the slip of steel through the fine lawn drawers almost before she finished speaking.

An hour later, after a nap had revived them, they dressed to go down to dinner. She was still smiling when the elevator descended to the lobby. It had been much too long since they made love. She had been like a wild thing in his arms, laughing, weeping, clutching him with her warm, eager thighs, grasping his hips and then his buttocks, digging in her fingers in her want and need of him.

She was thinking of their amazement at themselves and then their smug satisfaction when they were satiated. She wasn't looking at anyone in particular. When the cage of the elevator slid open, the remarkably happy face she presented to the world came from an inward consideration.

He was nothing more than a dark shadow at the periphery of her vision, a silhouette with a familiar shape. If he hadn't paused, hadn't stopped in his tracks, he would never have drawn her disinterested gaze.

Even as her eyes swung toward the vaguely familiar figure at the edge of her sight, he began moving again, tearing across the lobby in a trot and going out the door even as her eyes honed into focus.

"What is it?" Matthew asked as she paused, impatient now to satisfy his hunger for food.

"That man? Did you see him?"

"Who?"

Fanny shook her head. She had to be mistaken. Months had passed since she'd lived among city dwellers, and they now all looked alike, just as the Sioux had when she first arrived on the reservation. That was it. No reason to press her mind for details. She was simply mistaken because she'd been thinking about him earlier in the day. That couldn't have been Phineas Todd.

Then she forgot all about the shadow of her past because Buck and Oleta were coming through the lobby, and Oleta's expectant state couldn't be missed.

"Oleta! Buck!" Fanny flew into the older woman's arms, more happy to see them than she would have thought.

Oleta patted Fanny's cheek as her eyes brightened with moisture. "If it isn't our errant Fanny. And just look at you! You've grown a bit taller, I'd swear. And a married woman, they tell me." She looked up at Matthew, who hung back a little. "So you didn't break her heart after all. I must say you've behaved better than I might have expected, considering." She patted Fanny's flat stomach. "At least you weren't breeding before the fact."

"Oleta!"

"Well, there's many that do; that's all I'm saying. You're a clever girl, Fanny. I like clever girls."

Buck cleared his throat and stuck his hand out to Matthew. "Congratulations, Morning Star. Always did think you were a fine feller. And, well, if Fanny's took you for a husband, that shines with me, too."

Matthew shook hands and then the four went in to dinner.

Fanny paced her hotel room. She should tell Matthew about it. She should wait until he came back. But she couldn't explain to him why she was going nor to herself why she didn't want Matthew to know where she was going. She was simply going to go, and that was that.

She looked at the note in her hand. It was addressed to Fanny Sweets and had been slipped under the door not ten minutes after Matthew left to go down to the docks to assist with the boarding of the animals on the *State of Nebraska*, the ship that would take the whole cast to England. She had recognized her name on the envelope but had had to go down to the concierge to have the note read. By now she had memorized the message.

Fanny. Come to Riker's Drugstore 23rd and Sixth Avenue at noon. P. T.

P. T. Phineas Todd. It had to be. It was he she'd seen in the lobby two nights ago. And he'd seen her, seen her more clearly than she'd seen him. He even knew which room she occupied. If that was so, why hadn't he simply knocked on the door? But she knew 'he reason. Most likely, he was still in hiding.

She folded the note and tucked it into her purse.

* * *

She had dressed very carefully in a magenta and black plaid gown, black velvet jacket, and matching black velvet bonnet with ribbons that tied under her chin. She didn't want Phineas to think that she'd fared badly without him. In fact, she wanted him to see how she'd thrived. Yet, as she entered the drugstore, her heart was pounding and her palms felt slick inside her leather gloves. She was stepping back in time only a few months, yet it seemed like another lifetime ago.

It was her first visit to so elegant an establishment, and she couldn't help noticing that the fountain bar was prettily decorated in figured marble and onyx and that along the opposite wall ran dark cabinetry crowded with bottles and jars of the druggist's trade. The shop was filled with customers, and as she scanned the crowd she began to think she would never recognize Phineas. Then she saw him standing at the far end of the fountain bar, and she knew she would never have mistaken him for anyone else. He stepped apart from the customers pressing close to the bar, but he didn't signal her.

So, thought Fanny, he's giving me a chance to snub him, as he deserves. But her curiosity ran too high for her to simply walk away. She walked toward him.

When she came within two yards, he suddenly took a step forward, his worried expression relaxing into lines of joy.

"Fanny? Fanny! It is you!"

He took another step and reached out a hand toward her. "I thought it was you." His gaze swept avidly over her. "You look different. All grown up. And grand. You look grand, Fanny!"

"Hello, Phineas," she said smoothly and took the hand he'd extended. "How have you been?"

A spasm of doubt flickered in his features. Then he was smiling again. "Oh, well enough, well enough. But you, you look like you've done very well for yourself, indeed!"

Fanny released his hand. "I have. I'm married."

His face brightened, but there was an element of bewilderment in his eyes. "You don't say? Married. My little Fanny."

"Not yours any longer. You left me behind, if you're after being honest about it."

He licked his lips as his gaze fell before hers. "Well, now, there's things to be said about that, Fanny. But first have yourself a soda. Any sort you'd like. My treat."

"Very well," she said politely, but she could feel the tension rising. She wasn't going to behave very well shortly, and she knew it. Anger, the old street urchin's touchy resentment, was roiling inside her even as she turned to the counter.

Behind the marble bar aproned clerks were serving customers sodas in tall glasses with whipped cream and cherries. She ordered a chocolate soda, tapping her foot impatiently while the clerk scooped up ice cream and then filled her glass with carbonated water from a spigot mounted on the bar. Phineas didn't order anything, but he paid for hers and then led her to the back of the shop, where a few wrought-iron tables and chairs had been set up for customers.

"Well?" he said a little too heartily when she had tasted her soda.

"It's good," she replied, but she didn't touch it again.

"Just like old times. I knew it would be. Watching you with your treat, just like before. My little Fanny and me. We always were the best, weren't we?"

"When you were after having things your way," she temporized. Old fart! she thought. "You don't look well, Phineas. Your hair's thinned a bit more and there's a spot on your tie."

He touched his cravat self-consciously. "I—I've fallen on hard times lately."

"Since me money ran out?" she suggested between clenched teeth. At least he had the grace to blush, she noted.

He licked his lips again. "About that, Fanny. I didn't go there to steal from you. You know I wouldn't have hurt you for the world. I went there to see if you were all right. But when you weren't there and you didn't come, I thought—"

"That I was dead and that you might as well help yourself as well as the next." She shot to her feet. "You great stinking liar and cheat! You didn't even wait to see if I was in trouble!"

The sound of her voice carried and the customers near the back lifted their heads as conversation died.

"Fanny, please. I want to explain," he said as he rose. "Just sit and listen. You don't have to say a word. Just listen, Fanny. It's important."

Embarrassed in spite of her anger, she sat down. She was a lady now—well, at least a married woman. She had an image to preserve. "So then, speak your piece, Phineas."

He smoothed his mustache, his brow puckered in

thought. "You'll remember the day I took you to the Wild West Show? You'll remember that before that I thought we might have been followed? You remember how I left you in the stands and told you how you shouldn't move until I returned?"

"Tell me something I can't remember."

"It's hard, Fanny. I can't tell you everything. But I will say this. I'm in trouble from old connections, things that happened long before we met. It has nothing to do with you."

"Then why did some son of Satan try to murder me not long after you disappeared?"

He turned ashen. "I didn't know."

"Of course you didn't, you coward!" She took a deep breath, for her voice was rising again. "You don't know anything of what's happened to me these last months," she whispered hotly, "because you never came back to find out! Well, I'll save you the trouble of asking now. After I was near murdered in me own bed, I took to the streets. The only favor you done me that last day was to take me to the Wild West Show. That's where I went to hide."

She smiled triumphantly at his amazed expression. "You didn't think of that, did you? Neither did them connections of yours. I'm a member of the cast now. Me husband is, too. He's chief of the Sioux!" Forgive me this lie, Matthew, she thought fleetingly. "So you see, you don't need to feel guilt on account of what you done to me, which was evil enough. I don't need you now. I've turned honest. *I'm* off tomorrow to see the Queen of England!"

"Fanny!"

"You don't believe me? Read the papers. It's all

there, about how Buffalo Bill's taking the whole show to England for the queen's birthday.''

''The Jubilee?'' Phineas went livid.

''Well, then you know.'' She stood up again. ''So don't bother your poor head over me, Phineas Todd. I should never have trusted you, never lo—never mind!'' She turned and hurried away.

She'd nearly said, never loved him. She didn't love him. She didn't! He'd lied to her, cheated her, used her, and then left her! He was no one to love, no friend, as bad as her da!

CHAPTER
15

Fanny could hear the snorts and bellows of the buffalo in the forward hatch as she paced the deck of the steamship *State of Nebraska*. She was restless, ready to leave.

There had been a big procession to the dock that morning, the Cowboy Band playing "The Girl I Left Behind" as the cast members paraded in full regalia along the dock and up the gangway to the ship. Some of the performers were recognized on sight by the vast crowd who'd come to wish them bon voyage. Shouts of "Buffalo Bill!" and "Miss Oakley!" were the most frequent. But there were others greeting such performers as Mustang Jack; Buck Taylor, the bronco buster; Miss Lillian Smith, Annie Oakley's fifteen-year-old competition in marksmanship; and Miss Emma Lake, trick horsewoman and daughter of Wild Bill Hickok. In all, there were 197 members of the cast, not including 180 horses, assorted buffalo, ponies, elk, antelope, mules, steers, and dogs. There were also wagons, scenery, harnesses, saddles, and the Salisbury Stagecoach on board. For the next ten days or so they would be at sea, crossing distances that were still amazing even to the modern mind.

As the ship's whistle sounded over the harbor, signaling departure, the crowds on shore cheered and waved, and Fanny couldn't resist going to the railing to wave back. But she was still angry with her husband.

Matthew had been acting very strangely ever since they'd awakened. He'd been inattentive, and for the first time since they'd married, he'd not responded to her desire to make love when they'd awakened. He'd rolled out of bed, murmuring about the need to find the water closet, and then returned and hurriedly dressed, complaining about being hungry. Yet he'd eaten little at breakfast. He'd sat there staring at his coffee as if there were some message to be read in the bottom of the cup, and so she'd said to him.

Now he was below with Red Shirt and Cut Meat and Poor Dog, who were gathered in their quarters to discuss something of "great importance" about which he'd say nothing more. "A queer business," Fanny grumbled as she watched the land receding. Well, she wasn't about to go below and sit in that tiny box the captain generously called a cabin to wait for Matthew. Let him come and find her, if he remembered.

The day was overcast, threatening rain, and she was glad she had retrieved her fur-lined robe from her cabin before coming up on deck. As soon as they were out of sight of the harbor, it began to rain and the sea turned choppy. Determined not to be tempted into going below before Matthew came in search of her, she went to the railing and gripped it to watch as the last sight of land dipped below the horizon.

Soon, however, she found herself nearly alone. It seemed that the inclement weather was quickly dimming the cast's enthusiasm for the journey. Even Buffalo Bill, resplendent in thigh-high black boots and fringed gauntlets, excused himself and went below. Fanny smirked, feeling smug as one by one the passengers went below. She'd seen worse seas on her voyage to America. The salty spray was a familiar taste on her lips. The up-and-down motion reminded her that, unlike the prairie, the thousand-mile stretch of water before her promised a less monotonous ride.

She bent her head into the wind and hunched her shoulders. Not even if she were soaked to the skin would she surrender and go below. If Matthew cared, he'd come and find her. And if he didn't do it quickly, it would be a long, long time before he entered her harbor again.

The sea swells continued to increase in size as the afternoon wore on. Finally, hunger gnawing at her, Fanny went into the dining room of the ship for lunch. There was a noisy group there before her, and Oleta and Buck waved her over to sit with them.

"They're serving oyster stew!" Buck exclaimed excitedly as he rose to pull out a chair for her. "Reckon they ain't the same as prairie oysters, but they'll do."

Fanny wrinkled her nose at the thought of prairie oysters, having passed up her only chance, on the reservation, to partake of what was considered to be a delicacy among westerners. She didn't mind hauling buffalo chips, but she drew the line at eating buffalo testicles.

Buck looked about expectantly. "Where's Morning Star?"

"Below. With the Sioux."

The tone of her voice didn't encourage questions, and though she saw Buck and Oleta exchange glances, neither said anything.

Fanny consumed her stew in silence as the talk at the table turned to professional questions. Only Oleta seemed not to like the oysters and roasted ears of corn. She even passed on the nice rare slices of beef and ate only a little of the creamed potatoes.

"You're feeling poorly," Fanny said when she finally shook off her own misery enough to take a good look at her.

"It's the ship," Oleta said breathlessly, as if she was trying to keep from belching. "This motion." She whipped a napkin up to her mouth and rose to her feet. "I feel . . ."

Fanny came to her feet. "Seasick, that's what you feel. Come on, Oleta, I'll be taking you below. You need to put your feet up, that's all." She turned to Buck. "If Matthew comes looking for me, tell him I was after jumping overboard!"

Once below, however, Oleta didn't feel better. In fact, she was sick once in the passageway and then again just inside her cabin door. By the time Fanny had cleaned up and gotten the pregnant Oleta flat on her back with just a sip of tea on her stomach, an hour had passed. Oleta dozed a bit, but then the ship lurched suddenly, as if it had fallen off the edge of the world, and she came awake with a loud groan that portended another bout of sickness. When Buck came below, it was past dark, and in the light of the cabin he appeared green-tinged.

"Ain't feeling so good," he said with a burp. "Must

have been them *ersters*. I can feel 'em swimming about, right here," and he pressed his belt buckle.

Fanny grabbed the fire bucket just in time and thrust it at him. Moments later she was in the passageway, gasping for fresh air. It appeared that the Tarringtons would look after each other.

She didn't even think about Matthew as she went down the passageway to her cabin. She was tired now, and the ship was rocking as if it were in the grip of some violent giant. Up the deck seemed to rise like an elevator, and then down quickly with a shuddering slam that made her grab the brass railing to keep from falling. She heard a chorus of moans along the hallway and knew that Oleta and Buck weren't alone in their distress. But she'd always had a hard head and a cast-iron stomach, and, except for the momentary feeling of disorientation when the ship suddenly rose and fell, she was fine.

She was surprised that the light wasn't on in her cabin until she took a breath upon opening the door. She reached for the gas lamp and turned it on. There, sprawled across their bunk, was Matthew, as pale as death.

His lids opened, but his eyes rolled about in their sockets. "Sick! So sick!"

He'd been ill near the door and she sidestepped the mess to reach him. "Seasickness, is it?" She bent and brushed the hair back from his face. "Oleta and Buck's got it bad, too. I'll look after you, don't you worry."

It took her awhile to undress him, for the slightest movement made him groan with misery. At first she thought he might be playacting to gain her sympathy, but after he was sick all over her shoes, she decided that he wouldn't have deliberately carried things that far.

For the rest of the night she sat with his head in her lap, crooning old Irish shanty tunes, stroking his face, then holding his head while he was sick. He was ashamed of his sickness. At first he tried to make her leave and then he tried to swallow back the heavings. It only made it worse when he succumbed. Finally he gave up to the absolute misery of his condition and allowed her to clean him up without turning his face to the wall in shame.

By dawn Fanny looked as wretched as he felt, but at least he had fallen asleep. Feeling guilty, she brushed her hair, changed her gown, and then quickly went up to the dining room in hope that she would find food and fresh air. What she found was a near-empty dining hall. Only Annie Oakley greeted her jovially, and they sat together during breakfast to compare notes on who was sick and how badly.

The sea was rougher by midday, and the captain informed the few passengers remaining on deck that they were in a full-scale storm which they would just have to plow through. Mindful of her health and her friend's pitiful state, Fanny carted tea and toast up and down the passageways all morning long, often leaving the trays outside doorways. Buck was a little better in the morning, but by noon it was Oleta who dragged herself to the door when Fanny called. She waved off the idea of tea and asked Fanny to come back at dinnertime.

Each time she checked on Matthew, he tried to make her believe that he was feeling better. But by midafternoon, he was becoming ill every twenty minutes, like clockwork, and she abandoned her other tasks to be with him. Even when there was nothing in his stomach, he continued the dry heavings until she began to fear that he was really seriously ill. The ship's physician came and looked him over and pronounced his condition to be seasickness. He ordered Matthew to take a tablespoon of burnt brandy every hour, having heard of the cure from an Australian seaman a few months earlier and finding it not an unpleasant remedy.

Fanny went up to get the spoon and brandy and came back to find Matthew struggling into his best buckskins.

"And what do you think you're doing?"

He turned about like a guilty child caught in the act. "I'm dressing. I want to be with my people."

Her face turned crimson with anger. "Feeling better and so you think to abandon me, is that it?"

He frowned. "No. But I know they are all sick."

"How do you know that?"

"Red Shirt came here." He swallowed, and to her amazement she saw that he was near tears. "I should never have encouraged them to come on this voyage." He took a deep breath, steeling himself against whatever strong emotion moved in him. "They are about to begin the funeral dirge. I must be with them."

"Funeral dirge?" Fanny went cold inside. "Who died?"

He shook his head. "No one yet, but Cut Meat is very ill. He may be the first."

Fanny laughed. Though she didn't mean to seem callous, his look of fury made her blush. "I'm sorry, but no one dies of seasickness."

"No white man," he countered. "The Sioux will die. We have taunted the *Wakan Tanka*. Now we will pay."

Fanny felt her face freeze, caught between two conflicting urges. He couldn't be serious . . . and yet she knew he was. "Matthew, almost everyone gets seasick.

Buffalo Bill is ill. So are Oleta and Buck and all the rest. It will pass."

He said nothing, and she could see him shielding her from what he was thinking because his face suddenly went blank. "I must go."

"When will you be back?"

He shook his head.

"I'll go, too."

"No!"

She lifted her chin and crossed her arms. "Very well."

Matthew looked at her, a long, hungry look that tried to fix for all times in his mind the image of her. She was all he regretted leaving behind in this world. He should have spared her this. He reached to her, touched a lock of her hair. "I love you."

The chill around her heart thawed a little. "I know. But you infuriate me; you do that!"

He smiled weakly; then the ship dipped and he groaned, reaching for the bulkhead to steady himself.

"Before you go, you'll be having a taste of this," Fanny said crisply and turned to the tiny shelf that served as a table. She poured a tablespoon of brandy into a dish and set it afire with a match, just as the doctor had instructed. When the flame died she handed the dish to Matthew. "Drink it all."

He looked at the liquid suspiciously, then quickly gulped it. "I'm going!" he said abruptly and pushed past her through the door.

Fanny sat down on the edge of the bunk, worried and angry and helpless and tired. "Stubborn Indian!"

* * *

The whole ship was disturbed by it—the wailing, the incessant beat of the tom-toms, and long, sad, monotonous songs of the Indians below deck.

"It's enough to give a feller a turn," grumbled one seasick cowboy who'd ventured up on deck to get away from the noise.

All night and half the day the funeral dirge had gone on unceasingly while the ship floundered in the high seas of a North Atlantic storm. At dawn Fanny had gone to the Indian quarters, but she'd been turned back by two Arapaho braves acting as guards for the sacred ceremony. Sick at heart, if not at the stomach, she had crept up to the dining room at first light and drunk all the coffee she could hold. Matthew hadn't returned during the night.

"You figure any of 'em died yet?" the greenish-looking cowboy asked, sitting down beside Fanny because she was the only other cast member about.

Fanny shook her head wearily, not really wanting any company save Matthew's. "They won't die, not from seasickness."

"It ain't seasickness that's got 'em worried," the cowboy answered. "They're scared on account of their religious beliefs. There's a legend that says any Injun who crosses the ocean will sicken and die."

Her head snapped up. "What did you say?"

"The Injuns figure they're going to die. Don't you hear that funeral music? They're just sitting in a huddle in the hold with the buffalo, waiting for death."

Fanny could picture it vividly, for she'd witnessed one funeral in the Dakota Territory. Matthew, in his best dress, had left her to die!

She stood up. "Excuse me. I've a man to see."

"If it's an Injun, you tell 'em for me to quit that danged miserable singin'! I feel gut-shot as it is."

Fanny could scarcely keep her feet as she made her way along the foaming deck to the forward hold, where the Indians were. Once she lost her footing and was saved by the strong arms of a sailor who happened to be passing. When she finally reached the safety of the gangway, she was half drowned. Too angry to be intimidated, she accosted the two braves standing guard.

"I'm going in!" she cried loudly. "That or me husband, Matthew Morning Star, will be coming out of there this minute!"

Not too surprisingly, there was a brief interval of scuffling before Matthew appeared in the doorway. "There you are, you . . . you!" Overcome with relief, she turned and stomped back up the gangway, not daring to wonder if he would follow her.

The journey back along the deck seemed twice as far and twice as hard, but she had the knowledge of Matthew's continued existence to bolster her. To frighten her and leave her without any explanation, letting her believe that he was dying . . . !

She slammed the door of her tiny cabin before throwing herself on the bunk and giving up to tears.

She didn't look up when the door opened a quarter of an hour later.

"Fanny?"

"Go away!"

"Are you all right?"

No answer.

Matthew touched her shoulder in the semidarkness. "Fanny. We must talk."

She lifted her head. "Oh, now we can talk because

it's your choice, is it? Go away! Go back to the people you chose over your wife!"

Matthew eased himself onto the edge of the bed, wishing that he didn't have to make sense while his stomach swayed inside his chest like a pendulum in a clock. He touched her shoulder again, but she tried to shrug him off. "Fanny, listen to me. I have something important to say to you."

She rolled onto her hip. "I know what you're after saying, and I don't want to hear it."

"I'm dying, Fanny."

She had a handy retort ready, but it fled as she actually heard him say the words. She sat up and touched his cheek. It was slick with salt spray. She moved her hand to his lips and shivered as his breath threaded through her fingers. "Don't say that, Matthew, not ever again."

He reached to hold her hand to his face. "I wanted to tell you, but I hoped that it was only superstition. Now I know that I was wrong."

"How thin you are!" Fanny exclaimed and reached past him to turn on the light to confirm what she dimly perceived. "You aren't eating!"

"It's the wasting sickness," he answered. "It is what was foretold. An Indian may not cross the oceans."

Fanny bit her lip. It was incredible that this man, so much more worldly-wise and competent than she in many ways, should believe something that the merest child wouldn't accept as truth.

"Matthew, was I ever after lying to you? No, never mind that. Have I lied to you lately?" She looked about, spied his knife in his leggings, and reached to pull it from its scabbard. "How do you do it?"

He stared at her. "Do what?"

"Swear on the knife blade. What's the words, because I'm going to swear that you won't die on this voyage. It's superstition, Matthew, and I'm going to prove it. May me tongue fall out if I'm lying!"

"That's a fairly good oath," he said mildly.

"Very well." She bit down on the blade, holding it between her teeth like a pirate as she said, "I swear to you that you won't die, and may me tongue—"

"*My* tongue."

"*My* tongue, damn your education, fall out if I'm lying."

The gesture touched him deeply. That, for his sake, she could believe in an oath sworn on a knife blade and yet hold herself in judgment against a legend that was old when her people were still running naked in their woodlands made him feel both humble and a fool. He took the blade gently from between her teeth and kissed her. "I love you, Just Fanny."

She looked at him as if she could read his reaction in his eyes. "Do you believe the oath is truly sworn?"

"I do."

"Then why didn't you tell me before that you thought you were dying?"

"I was ashamed. I could see the disbelief so strong in your eyes. You would have thought me a fool. I am a fool."

"You are my own dearly loved husband, and I'd fight the devil himself in hell to protect you. Did you think I'd let you die without a fight? You don't know me very well, Matthew Morning Star. I'd protect you with me last breath."

"I believe you."

"Then you must believe that you'll all get well?"

"If you want it, I will."

"I want it. I need a lodge pole for my tepee in London."

He smiled at her, grateful to have chosen so wise a woman.

London, May 1887

Fanny sat in her front row seat at London's Lyceum Theatre yawning. She knew it wasn't polite, but she could scarcely keep her eyes open. The performance of *Faust* was wonderful. At least Matthew, who enjoyed such things as serious drama, told her that it was quite wonderful. As for herself, she had much preferred the visit to the Tower of London and the West End comedy they'd seen the night before. Still, she wasn't complaining. It was a nice change to be sitting in silk and satin.

For the six weeks since their arrival at the campsite in Earl's Court, Kensington, she'd been daily working the crowds who'd begun streaming through the campgrounds from the first day. Acting as a sort of tour guide, she led gawking Londoners about the muddy camp, showing them Annie Oakley's gun display, herds of shaggy, still sea-legged buffalo, and the Indian tepee village. Often she wore Sioux dress, but occasionally she changed into western wear for an impromptu demonstration of her ever-increasing dexterity with a lariat.

They were still weeks shy of their official opening, as the last touches were still being put on the thirty-thousand-seat grandstands that had been built especially for the occasion. But Colonel Cody, as everyone now called him, was not about to let the English forget that he was among them and soon to open his doors—and their pockets. Fanny smiled to herself. That was why she was here with Matthew, Red Shirt, and half a dozen other Indian notables from the show. Their appearance here made it a news event, and that meant another mention in the papers. Not that they needed it. As far as she could tell, London was practically papered with advertisements for the show. Everywhere she looked, on walls, fences, buildings, lampposts, billboards, the wild West was picturesquely displayed in colorful signs.

When the performance was over, they were rushed by reporters as they exited the theater.

Everyone was crying out questions, and Fanny felt the men about her stiffen in response to the ordeal. Red Shirt in particular looked haggard, and Fanny's heart went out to him. His young wife was expecting their first child, and the voyage had been as difficult for her as for Oleta, who'd delivered an eight-pound boy the day they docked at Greenwich. Red Shirt's wife was safely ensconced back at the camp, but his duties as head representative of the Sioux nation frequently kept him away from her.

"What's a redskin think of live theater?" one boorish man cried out, sticking his pencil and pad under Matthew's nose.

Fanny held her breath, for Matthew looked thunderously angry at finding his path blocked, but then his eyes changed as she heard him say in excellent imitation of a cultured English accent, "Really, old boy, I don't know that you've the manners of a man who deserves an answer."

The startled man took a step back. Laughing in his face, Matthew steered Fanny around him and into a waiting hansom cab.

"That's enough!" Matthew said as they drove off. "We're going back to the campgrounds in the morning and stay there until this madness calms."

Fanny snuggled up against him. "I rather like being all dressed up and going about where everyone can see that you're m—my husband."

He looked down at her, his gaze narrowing as it always did when it fell on the décolletage of her gown. "I don't like men looking at you. In that gown you look like you're being served up as dessert!"

"Kiss me!"

"I don't know that I should. You should obey your husband. You set a bad example for other Sioux wives."

"Kiss me!"

"Woman who does not obey is no good to any man."

"Then don't kiss me."

And, of course, he kissed her, as she knew he would.

One of the drawbacks of London, Fanny decided as she scraped mud from her boots with a stick, was that it seemed to rain every day, whether it was needed or not. She was muddy up to the ankles. She knew now why western women wore their skirts above their ankles. Anyone who had to negotiate dirt roads on a daily basis needed to keep her gown clear of the muck. Nothing stopped the gawkers, however. The fairgrounds were full as usual.

She wasn't surprised when two men in bowler hats approached her behind the tent, where she'd gone to clean the boots. She was accustomed to being asked directions. She threw the stick away and straightened up with a smile.

"Are ye Fanny Sweets?"

The question surprised her because she was billed as "Fanny Morning Star, Sioux Princess" in the handbills circulating through the city. "And who's asking, I'd like to know?"

"It's her," said the other man. "That ain't Cockney she's rolling off her tongue."

They were Irish. There was no doubting her ears as they weren't doubting theirs. "Who are you?" she asked, backing away.

The first man took a step toward her, his hands thrust in his pockets. "We're friends of yers, in a manner of speaking, that is. Ye'll be remembering yer old friend Phineas Todd, now, won't ye?"

"Aye," she answered cautiously.

"We're friends of his," the second man supplied, moving to one side of her. "We've come to take ye to see him."

"Phineas is in New York," she answered, wishing she'd kept in hand the stick she'd used to clean her boots.

"No, he's in London, and that's me word on it."

"Well, I don't care if he is. We ain't friendly anymore." She took another backward step, wondering if her screams would be heard above the general noise.

"Tut, tut, ain't that a shame, James? And Phineas himself in a rare state to have ye by his side again."

"Don't touch me!" she cried as the man called James grabbed her arm.

"We don't mean to frighten ye, do we, James?" his partner said. "We only mean for ye to come along with us, nice and quiet, to see a friend."

She turned to flee, but she knew that it was too late.

She screamed twice before they overpowered and gagged her. She hadn't noticed the cart parked behind the tent until now, and it was toward that that they dragged her. Amazingly, not one person was here to see them, she thought in irrational anger against the sightseers who daily turned her life into a public circus. Where were they when she really needed a curious eye prying into her private business?

Once up in the cart the first man drew a pistol and pressed it to her ribs just below her left breast. "I've nae reason to kill ye. Don't give me one."

She slumped back against the wooden seat as the second man snapped the reins.

She didn't know where they were going, and after they left the fairgrounds, the man holding the gun made her lie facedown in the cart and then covered her head so that she wouldn't be able to recall landmarks. She traveled this way for over an hour. When the cart came to a stop, she was no longer afraid; she was angry. Phineas was behind this, blast him to hell. What sort of matters was he mixed up in that he would do this to her?

When she was ordered to get up, she saw that she was inside a warehouse. Phineas stood beside the cart, but he looked far different from what she expected. He was jacketless and his shirt was wrinkled, but what startled her was the fact that his hands were tied.

"Are you all right, Fanny?" Phineas asked as he took a step toward the cart.

"I've been better."

"I'm sorry," he said, his voice breaking on the final syllable.

"Get down," the man with the gun ordered, and she

obeyed. He pointed at a stack of barrels piled in one corner. "Go over there and sit till ye're told to do else."

She looked at Phineas. "I'd have forgiven a lot, but not now."

He looked away, defeated.

For the next hour she sat alone, as it grew dark and the two men chatted in Gaelic with Phineas sitting uneasily between them. Finally she heard a rider approach, and the men rose to open the door.

A man entered and came straight toward her. He was tall with bulky shoulders and contrastingly narrow hips that gave him the impression of being whittled away. He was dressed as a seaman, but his first words to her betrayed the fact that he was an educated man. "Miss Sweets," he said with drawing-room politeness. "Or should I call you by your real name, Miss Sweeney?"

Though the name startled her, she didn't answer directly. "Me name's Fanny. Mrs. Morning Star to you."

"Yes, we've heard you'd married. Quite convenient for our purposes, as you shall see." He looked around. "Have they not offered you tea? James? Tea for the lady. She's an honored guest."

"Hogtied and dragged here against me wishes, is the truth of it!" she challenged.

He looked at her, his long, lipless mouth curving in a manner she suspected he thought was charming. "Why, Miss Sweeney, you've a temper to match your hair." He whipped off his seaman's cap to reveal a head of graying red curls. "So have I. Remember that. Do sit. James will be awhile at his brewing.

"Now," he continued when she'd sat, "I think you

should know straightaway that this isn't a matter of personal threat to you. You're one of us and have been from birth. I knew your da, Pat Sweeney, and he knew me. We were lads together, always into mischief.''

Fanny's gaze swung to Phineas, who sat silently, as though not a part of this.

"We'll get to Phineas in due time," the man assured her. "Tell me what you remember of your da and his life before he left Ireland."

She shrugged, "There's little enough to tell. We were farmers. Then we weren't."

"And?"

"And that's that."

He smiled again. "You're a clever girl, Fanny. I like cleverness, in it's place. Tell me what you know about the Fenians."

Her gaze again darted to Phineas.

"You gave yourself away that time, my girl," her questioner said. So you knew about the group?"

"That's not surprising. The whole country knew."

"But you knew more than most because your da was one of them."

"That's a dirty lie!" she cried, rising to her feet.

"Easy, girl, you're among friends here."

She crossed her arms tightly. "Me da's dead, has been these last seven years. Anything I could tell you would be older than that and of no use to you."

"You could remember names of men still alive."

"That I could not. Didn't know any."

"I find that hard to believe."

"You can think what you like. It won't change the truth."

"James! Blast the man. Where's that tea?"

Fanny sat back down, her mind working furiously. What did these men want? Why did they ask her about her father? How was Phineas connected? What did they want?

"Are you still a loyal daughter of Ireland, Fanny?"

The question brought her head up. "Of course I am."

"Then you remember why your da fought the English, what he hoped to win?"

"Freedom," she answered cautiously.

"Aye, freedom. It has a fine, grand sound. Rolls right off the tongue, doesn't it, Fanny?"

"Me da said it was hopeless. That's why he left."

"Your da turned traitor to save his skin; that's why he left!"

He moved so quickly Fanny had no inkling until he was upon her. He had grabbed her jacket front and hauled her to her feet. She twisted to free herself, but he caught a handful of her hair near the temple and pulled until she was forced still by the pain. He thrust his face in hers, his light eyes round with anger. "Your da turned in me best friend, and his. He turned in four in all. I saw them hanged while your da was sailing away. That's the truth of your da, girl. He was a traitor!"

"Dirty lies!" Fanny hissed at him.

Suddenly she was freed as the man swung around. "Tell her, Phineas. Tell her everything."

Phineas stood up, his gaze on Fanny. "I couldn't ever tell you. I didn't want you to know."

"No!" Fanny raised her hands to her ears. "Don't lie to me! I don't want to hear it!"

"Tell her why you found her and kept her all those

years, Phineas!'' the man cried. ''Tell her how it was because you were sorry for her after you tracked down her da. Tell her how it was you who found him for us, how we paid your passage to New York, how you turned him in to the local branch, how he confessed before he died. Tell her! Tell her!''

Fanny was weeping, rage and shame tearing her apart. She had known, had known all along but refused to believe it. For seven years she'd kept the secret, even from herself. When her father had disappeared a few months after they reached New York, she'd thought at first that he'd simply gone into hiding again, that he would return. It was months before she'd faced the truth. And then she'd hidden that truth deep in her heart and never looked back.

She flinched from the touch on her shoulder, but the hand stayed. ''Fanny, my little Fanny,'' Phineas said softly. ''I went back to look for you. Searched months until I found you. I've loved you as my own. It's all I could do to make it up to you. You were innocent then and you are now. These men know that.''

Fanny looked up at him, hatred blazing in her eyes. ''Then why am I here?''

''To prove your innocence, and your loyalty,'' said the redheaded man.

''How?''

''You're going to help us assassinate the royal bitch who sits on the English throne, Queen Victoria!''

CHAPTER
16

Matthew looked at his wife. "You promised Buck and Oleta. She's not as strong as she'd hoped to be, and with the baby to look after, Buck doesn't want her to perform."

"I don't care!" Fanny rose from one of the many long tables set up in the tent where the cast ate their meals. "I've changed me mind. I'm not after having me body made a target for tomahawks and knives!"

Matthew watched her stalk away, frown lines deepening between his black brows. She had been acting strangely for three days, ever since she'd disappeared for hours and then returned to camp without an explanation. He hadn't pressed her. They were both trying to adjust to yet another way of life. If she felt as he did, then they wouldn't be staying long in England. Even the thought of the return voyage didn't keep him from the desire to return to his homeland. Yet her withdrawal from him chafed.

He had tried to tell himself that she was simply

paying him back for all the weeks he had secluded himself with his people on the reservation while she lived alone and lonely. She was a very literal person, who, like a child, remembered all hurts and all favors. Perhaps she didn't realize herself what she was doing. Yet he didn't quite believe that was the reason she looked unhappy all the time, rejecting him during the day and then clinging to him during the night as if monsters in the dark might carry her away.

"You talk to her yet?"

Matthew looked up to see Buck standing over him. "I did. She's not feeling well. Give her a few more days to think it over."

"Ain't got but one more," Buck answered mournfully. "Colonel Cody's calling a meeting in an hour to announce that the queen has set a date for the command performance and it's the day after tomorrow. If Fanny can't help with my act, I'll be cut from the program."

Matthew didn't answer.

After the announcement was made, Matthew caught up with Fanny again, and the look in her eyes made him pull her aside. "What's wrong, and don't tell me it's the weather."

Fanny rounded on him stormily. "Then I won't tell you it's the weather. It's you, you stubborn, interfering, prying . . . Indian! Go away. Leave me alone! I don't want you by me anymore!"

Matthew went cold inside as she marched away. She had been trembling, her tone angrier than any he could remember since the night she'd gotten lost on the prairie. Even then it was not anger but fear that had driven her to say vicious things and . . .

He followed her, but at a distance.

* * *

Fanny found the place which matched the address she'd been given before she was released by her captors. It was upriver from London, near Greenwich, a tavern on the docks in a noisy, rough area. She'd taken a cab and offered the driver a bonus if he'd wait for her. Clutching her bundle tightly, she entered.

The rough chorus of liquor-soaked voices reminded her of the taverns along the Bowery. The accents were different, but the boozy ambience was the same. She'd dressed in regular street clothes and covered her hair with a scarf because she didn't want to be recognized or connected with the Wild West Show. She went straight to the bartender and said, "I'm looking for a man by the name of Rory MacAvoy."

The bartender nodded. "That's be the toff at the top of the stairs. Renting the room for a month, 'e is." He bent over the bar and peered at her. "You're not one of me regular girls."

"Say, not yet," she answered saucily and turned away before he could study her further. Mother of mercy, did all men think that women who weren't their mothers were in the trade? She climbed the stairs quickly, before her nerve gave out, and knocked.

He came to the door at once and opened it, pistol in hand. "Why, Miss Sweeney! A pleasure it is to see you."

Fanny stepped inside, looking quickly about to see who else was there, but the man seemed to be alone.

"You're wondering how your friend Phineas is keeping, I suppose," Rory said when he'd closed the door.

"He's well enough, if a bit anxious for his release. And you've come to see to that, haven't you?"

"I don't understand you. You say Phineas was one of you, yet you hold the threat of murdering him over my head."

"Phineas is one of us, but like your da, he'd begun to rethink the oath he'd sworn. No man can turn back once he's sworn. He sees the reason of that now, as will you."

"Why do you want me? I've no interest in the qu—!"

He had raised his pistol. "You're overfree with your names, Miss Sweeney, in a place with ears for walls. I know who you mean, and what I'll answer is that you're sworn to us. Your da swore for his family in his oath, and because we can use you, we will."

"No man can swear an oath for another."

"He can if it means their lives. Isn't that why you're here, to keep Phineas and your heathen husband alive? But I'm keeping you from telling the news you've brought." He poked her bundle with the gun barrel. "I can sniff the gist of it. Tell me the date."

"The qu— the lady is coming on the day after tomorrow."

Rory grinned. "As soon as that."

"You don't need the costumes to murder her. You could be in the crowd."

He nodded. "That was the original plan. But the change gives the plan grand dimensions. As a part of the cast, we'll be free to walk right up and blast away at the audience. They'll think it's part of the show. When she's shot, we'll escape in the confusion."

"The show will be held responsible for the murder!"

"Oh, no fear of that. We'll announce our victory to the world right enough. As soon as we're back in Ireland and can lead the insurrection, the world will learn the name of Rory MacAvoy, and history will inscribe it long after I'm dead."

"It can't work. You'll be seized."

"You'll see that we won't be, or your loving husband will have the chance to watch you hang by your pretty little neck beside the rest of us."

"I ain't afraid of dying," she replied.

"But you're afraid of something. Maybe we'll add your husband's name to our confession. Think of that, Miss Sweeney."

She stared at him, afraid to admit the melting fear oozing through her. "You'll be caught."

"We'll see. Now, what have you brought us? Ah, I do think I'll like wearing this hat. I've always had a fancy to see the American West."

Fanny swore under her breath when she stepped out of the tavern and discovered that the cabbie no longer waited for her. She hadn't been inside half an hour. It had begun to rain again and there wasn't a hansom in sight. In fact, the street was nearly deserted as people sought shelter from the drizzle. Pulling her scarf closer to protect her face, she started down the street.

She was helping to plot to murder the Queen of England; the enormity of the idea stunned her. It was inconceivable, yet it was true. And she was helpless to prevent her part in it. If she ran away, they'd kill Phineas. She'd no doubt of it. She'd seen his face at the warehouse. There was nothing false in his palpable terror. Maybe he was dead already, now that he'd brought her to them.

"Damn you for a coward!" she whispered as her footsteps sounded loudly up the cobblestone street. The sick dread that had dogged her these last days gnawed at her. There was no way out, unless she killed Rory MacAvoy.

She'd thought it out, had nearly stolen a pistol from Annie Oakley's collection while she was stealing clothes. They'd made her do that, too, take what wasn't hers after she'd promised Matthew that she'd never steal again. He would despise her when he learned what she'd done. To plot a murder with cold-blooded assassins—she would hang, if she didn't kill Rory MacAvoy first.

She knew nothing about guns. That's why she hadn't taken one today. But the day of the command performance, she would take a rifle and shoot Rory MacAvoy, in the back if necessary. That thought was all that kept her going. And if Phineas—no! She couldn't think about him. He was responsible for her da's murder. No! She wouldn't think about him, either. He'd been a traitor!

Her half-formed scream was cut off before it escaped by a hand over her mouth. She was grabbed about the waist and lifted up off her feet. He'd come up behind her and was carrying her backward. Finally she was hoisted up into a carriage behind her assailant.

"Got a live one, have ye, guv'nor?" asked the cabbie who stood holding the door.

"Yes," came the short reply.

As the door was slammed in her face, Fanny twisted around to confront her attacker. "Matthew!"

Icy rage distorted his handsome face, and she wondered not for the first time how many men he had killed.

"Tell me who you went to see. And don't lie! Who is he?"

"Murder Queen Victoria?" Matthew stared at his wife across the tiny table of the London tearoom.

Fanny nodded. "I know. It sounds mad. But in a mad kind of way, it might work. They wanted costumes so that they can join in one of the spectacles, like the stagecoach holdup. No one would be thinking to protect the queen from the gunfire going on before her. In the smoke and pandemonium, a whole army might escape."

Matthew sighed. An hour earlier he hadn't known what to think. When she'd entered the tavern, he'd gone in after her, only to be told that she was upstairs with a "customer." So he'd sat in a corner and drunk—though he knew it was stupid to drink—while waiting for her. The men, mostly sailors, thought he was an East Indian off a ship from Calcutta, and he'd nodded and kept silent.

When she came down, after much too long a time in which he'd thought and drunk more than he should have, he was mad with worry and hurt and rage. Now he knew the truth. He knew her family's history, Phineas's role in her life, and the bizarre turn of events that were unfolding.

"If I don't help them, they'll kill Phineas," she said aloud to confirm her own thoughts.

"We'll go to Colonel Cody."

"If they learn that I've told anyone, they'll kill Phineas. They will. They murdered my da."

And they'd threatened his own life; Matthew could see it in her eyes. "How did they know about us?"

She lowered her head. "I told Phineas. I saw him in New York two days before we sailed."

"Why didn't you tell me?"

"I didn't think it mattered."

"And he told his friends."

"They aren't his friends. They were after him to pull him back into the group. Once a man's sworn his life to the Fenians, he's never free till he's dead. They're madmen, anarchists. It's the queen's Golden Jubilee, and they're after thinking it's the perfect opportunity to strike a blow for their cause. They were plotting to assassinate her some other way until Phineas told them that he'd seen me. I don't know why he told them. Maybe he thought they'd leave me alone if they knew I was married and completely out of their paths."

"Until they learned that the Wild West Show had a command performance to play for the queen." Matthew reached for her hand. "You couldn't have known."

Fanny blinked back tears. "Did you really think I was, well, going to be with another man?"

His black eyes gleamed with emotion. "Never ask a man if he believes that his wife could be unfaithful. He believes it even when he thinks he doesn't. It's his nature."

"I wouldn't betray you. Never!"

"I know. And I don't. And we'll leave it."

She nodded. "What are we going to do, Matthew?"

He smiled at her. "It's been a long time since I went on the warpath. I will counsel with Red Shirt."

"But, Matth—!"

"Shut up, Just Fanny. Just this once."

* * *

The campgrounds at Earl's Court were a flurry of activity. The queen and her entourage were due to arrive by royal coach in less than a hour. The newly completed grandstands had been hung with bunting and draped with English and American flags. The royal box had been carpeted and garlanded with flowers. Ferns graced the front of the box and drapery had been hung to keep the wind from blowing the dust that would be raised by horses and cattle onto the royal personages.

Colonel Cody addressed his cast from the back of his favorite horse, Old Charley. He was resplendent in snow-white, heavily fringed buckskins, gleaming Hessian boots, and his favorite sombrero. "You know the honor that's being given us this day. We're here representing that fine and glorious nation of ours, the United States of America. Give of your best in pride and humility. We have an hour to entertain Her Majesty. Make it the best hour the Wild West has yet known!"

With a rousing cheer the company split up, each to get set for his or her part, but Fanny hung back, her eyes trained on the road from the city. She hadn't seen Rory MacAvoy, yet she knew that he must be somewhere nearby. When she saw the first of the royal carriages wending their way toward the campgrounds and heard the Cowboy Band strike up the opening bars of "Rule, Brittania," her heart plummeted. Matthew had hoped to overpower the assassins before the show began, but now that wouldn't be possible.

The grounds filled quickly as the carriages rolled up. Though the performance was a closed one, the queen's entourage was quite large, including many dignitaries and officers of the court, as well as royal friends, family members, and other representatives.

Reluctantly Fanny took her place behind the lofty new canvas screen at the rear of the arena, which depicted the badlands of the Dakota Territory. The show had been trimmed to an hour, at the queen's request, so Buck's act had been cut. She was to portray a pioneer woman kidnapped by Indians while Colonel Cody and the cowboys rode to her rescue. Curiosity overcoming even her nervousness, Fanny stuck her head around the canvas to peek at the queen. At the far end of the arena, the lady looked like a tiny doll in black drapery. And then the show began.

The opening procession moved out from behind the canvas, Colonel Cody at its head, an American flag in his hand. After him came the Indians in full regalia, Matthew among them. He smiled at her in passing, not in the least nervous, she noted with envy, and kicked his horse into a gallop as war whoops erupted from the throats of the Sioux party. One by one the other groups followed until nearly the full cast filled the arena. Finally she heard the announcer.

"Her Majesty, Queen Victoria, ladies and gentlemen, Colonel Buffalo Bill Cody proudly presents America's national entertainment, the one and only, genuine and authentic, unique and original Wild West Show!"

The next three-quarters of an hour passed rapidly as, one after another, the acts were performed. Buffalo Bill demonstrated his skill with a rifle by breaking glass balls. Annie Oakley galloped into the arena, snatched up a pistol while still mounted, and performed various feats of shooting skill, including breaking targets while sighting backward with the aid of a mirror. There was a buffalo stampede and demonstrations of Indian dance and song. Finally it was time for the rescue of the pioneer family.

Fanny was bathed in sweat as she went forward into the arena to take her place inside the log cabin that had been hauled to center stage for the scene. She hadn't seen Rory or Phineas or either of the two men who'd kidnapped her. Perhaps they weren't coming after all, she thought. Perhaps they'd changed their minds, or been delayed and would miss their opportunity. Or perhaps they'd only hidden themselves better than she'd hoped.

She entered the cabin and, with shaking hands, picked up the rifle that had been placed there for her as a prop. She was to pretend to be working outside her cabin when a raiding party appeared. Then, snatching up her rifle, she was to try to hold them off. Only when they'd broken in and taken her prisoner would Colonel Cody and a party of cowboys ride to her rescue and save the day. Then came the finale. The Cowboy Band struck up a waltz tune, her signal to go outside and begin the performance. She picked up the laundry basket in her free hand and pushed the door open with her toe.

Polite applause greeted her entrance onto the arena floor, but she didn't acknowledge it. She propped the rifle against the cabin, stopped to rock the cradle with a doll inside, and then went to begin hanging clothes on the line strung for the purpose. Count to ten slowly, Colonel Cody had told her. It gives the audience a chance to react to the Indians' approach before you do. She counted slowly, hardly able to wait for the sight of Matthew, who led the raiding party.

Sure enough, the audience began to rustle in their seats, impatient for the pioneer woman to look up and see what they did. When she suddenly went stiff, a hand lifted to her ear to listen, the audience fell silent.

Then she turned and saw against the far background of the badlands seven war-painted warriors on horseback.

Fanny was so nervous that her cry of fright sounded quite authentic, and the audience responded in kind, urging her to hurry and hide. She turned and raced toward the crib, and the Indians' whoops drowned out the crowd as they came galloping toward her. She reached the cabin, babe in one hand and rifle in the other, and slammed the door shut. With the butt of the rifle she broke a window and stuck the rifle barrel through it. Though the rifle was filled with blanks, the recoil surprised her, for she'd only shot it off once before in practice. Still, she fired repeatedly as the war party circled the cabin, firing back at her, waving tomahawks, and making threatening cries.

The cabin was turned so that the audience had a good view of the Indian who reined in at the back of the cabin, dismounted, and crept up to the back window. Caught up in the playacting, the audience cried out warnings now, but Fanny kept firing away through the front window until she was caught from behind and the rifle taken from her.

She turned in Matthew's arms. "I haven't seen them."

He kissed her swiftly. "Good. Come on. And make the struggle look real. You look much too satisfied in my arms."

He opened the cabin door with a flair, then pushed her outside, holding her by the hair. While the audience cried its dismay, Fanny made the most of her acting, struggling and clawing and kicking Matthew in the shins. When he looked at her in surprise, the audience cheered her on. Then he grabbed her about the waist, slung her facedown across his war pony, and gave an earsplitting war whoop.

That was the signal for Colonel Cody and his men. They came charging out from behind the canvas backdrop, firing as they came. The Indians, shocked by the sudden attack, began to scatter, some going back toward the badlands backdrop, others riding straight toward the queen, as if they would try to escape through the grandstands.

Slung across the saddle, Fanny saw the cowboys coming first, and then she saw Rory MacAvoy among them, wearing the hat she'd given him. Shimmying backward off the pony, she spun about as Matthew was about to leap on his horse. "They're here! In the white hat with the red feather!"

He didn't answer. He pushed her aside and leapt astride his horse with a hand signal to Red Shirt, who was beside him. They turned in unison as the man in the red feathered hat rode past, straight toward the royal box.

Matthew let out another war whoop that reverberated throughout the arena as he kicked his pony into full gallop. The man ahead of him had lifted a gun from his pocket, but he wasn't riding fast, and Matthew realized that he wasn't accustomed to being on horseback. Smiling, he gripped his pony between his knees and, tossing his rifle aside, reached for the tomahawk that hung from his waist.

He came up behind as the man lifted his arm to fire into the grandstands. The force of Matthew's body as he launched himself onto the other man sent them both over the side of his horse and they fell into the dirt. Matthew rolled gracefully with the fall, to come to his feet as the dust raised by the other galloping riders enveloped them. The man gained his feet slowly, and Matthew noticed that his gun was missing.

The man lifted his hand and said, "That's enough!"

Matthew felt his lips drawing back from his teeth in a grimace that held no hint of amusement. "No. Not enough. I Sioux warrior, Morning Star. Fanny my wife. You threaten her. You die!"

He saw the man's fear and saw him reach inside his coat. But Matthew charged him, tomahawk raised. He heard the report and felt a mild burning sensation, but then he was on the man, had him by the throat with his free hand, and was ready to bring the tomahawk down through his skull when Red Shirt grabbed his wrist.

"Enough, my friend."

Matthew looked down at the choking man clawing his arm and turned his blade to knock him senseless with a dull blow to the side of the head. Then he dropped to his knee beside the unconscious man and took the trophy he'd earned.

Red Shirt shook his head as the show's roustabouts came out with stretchers to carry off the "dead." "Bad business follow this," he said.

Matthew stood looking at the lock of hair. "It doesn't matter. We're going home."

"What the blazes was that out there?" Colonel Cody roared as he reined in behind the canvas, where the cast had assembled for the grand finale. He looked down at Matthew. "Did I hear tell right? You tried to take a scalp out there, right in front of the queen?"

Fanny stepped forward. "It's my fault, Colonel Cody."

Cody sighed. "Now, why didn't I think of that? What

have you got to say, Miss Fanny? And make it snappy; the queen is waiting.''

"Assassination!" he cried at the end of her short speech. "Why the devil wasn't I told?"

"There was no time," Matthew answered. "I stopped the man. The police have been sent for. Buck and the boys have him tied up in the mess tent until they get here."

For the first time Fanny saw that Buffalo Bill was sweating. "To think the queen might have..." He shook his head in bewilderment. Then he looked at Fanny. "Miss Fanny, I don't know how or why you're at the bottom of every dustup this company has, but I'm sorry to have to tell you that I don't rightly see how I can carry you on after this."

Fanny's face paled, but Matthew put his arm around her. "That suits us fine, Colonel. We're going home anyway."

Fanny looked at him. "We are?"

"Good!" Cody said. "Now, any of you folks like to meet Queen Victoria? She's asked to meet you."

Fanny turned to Matthew. "Why are we going home?"

He steered her away from the rest of the players, who were filing out to be presented to the queen. "Because Colonel Cody's right. You get into trouble too often for my peace of mind. I need for you to be where I can more easily keep an eye on you."

"Where, for instance? Matthew! You're bleeding!"

He looked down at the mark on his upper arm. "A bullet graze, that's all."

Fanny put a hand to her mouth to keep her lips from trembling. "You could have—"

"I'm not that easy to kill. Sioux warriors have magic, you know."

She shook her head. "I can't get the right of you. One minute you're reasonable, logical; the next you're a half-mad savage taking other people's scalps."

"It was only a small piece," he answered. "Just his forelock, but I think he'll remember me."

Fanny slapped at him. "You're *witkowin*!"

"I'm a man. Your man. And your protector."

"Aye," she said, leaning against him. "I wonder what will become of Phineas and the others?"

"Do you care?"

She nodded against his shoulders. "I shouldn't, but I do. He may have helped murder me father, but he did look out for me for a time."

Matthew gathered her close. "Perhaps you're already even, then."

"What are we going to do?"

He smiled as she curled naturally against him. "First we are going to go somewhere where we can be alone and make a great deal of happy noise that will disturb the neighbors. Then we're going to find a ship. After that, I'm not certain. But, Just Fanny, I think it's time you learned to read and write."

Dakota Territory, September 1887

"No! It's an aah-ch! Any spalpeen knows that!" Fanny drew a big *H* on the board with chalk. "Now what's next? Come on. Don't be shy. I just learned them me—myself. Eye, that's what." And she drew a capital *I* beside the *H*. "All right. This is an easy one. It's the same as the name of that pesky bird we're after murdering for eating all the gooseberries."

"Jay!" cried a young girl in the front row.

"Jay it is! Clever girl." And she drew a *J* on the board. "Okay, lads, are you going to be letting the lasses count coup on you? What's next?"

"Well, I don't know," said the minister as he withdrew his head from the classroom door. "Her methods aren't quite what I'd hoped."

Matthew pulled the classroom door shut with a smile. "Her methods may be unusual, but she's getting results."

"Still, the government is very particular about the schooling it funds," the man temporized. "This doesn't really qualify as a reservation school because, you understand, it's not on the reservation."

Matthew escorted the man toward the front door of his home. "That's the point exactly, sir. We are hoping to become a boarding school away from the reservation so that the young people of my tribe may have a chance to see this world for themselves and yet remain among people with whom they are familiar."

"I see the good sense in that, Mr. Morning Star, and you may be certain that I shall point that out to the Bureau of Indian Affairs." He smiled tightly. "As well as your wife's unorthodox methods. Good day."

An hour later Matthew was bent over one of the many letters of correspondence he'd begun in order to set in motion the vision that had come to him on the voyage back from England four months earlier. He'd more connections than he'd first thought. His years at Harvard were beginning to pay off with their first small endowment coming from a source made available by the college. But he'd known from the first that they would always be in need of money and that every victory would be short-lived.

"Well, what did he say?" Fanny stuck her head

around the corner of the study door when her class was done for the day.

Matthew lifted his head and smiled. "He said you've a most unorthodox teaching method."

She stepped inside the room. "Does that mean yes or no?"

"It means, my love, that we must wait and see."

Fanny's smile dissolved. "I failed."

He reached out for her and she came toward him slowly. "You're a natural teacher. It's just that most classroom teachers don't call their students spalpeens and talk of murdering birds during the ABCs."

"Ach, well, that was to get them to think," she said as she sat in his lap. "It's terrible hard to think of all them squiggles as being sounds and words unless you can make them pictures in your mind."

"Exactly. I'm very proud of you."

She rested her head against his. "I wish I were a better teacher. I'm so ignorant. I can hardly keep ahead of the brighter ones. Pretty soon I'll be in the seats and they'll be teaching me."

Matthew kissed her cheek, his hands naturally roaming her soft body. "I wouldn't worry about it. In fact, I think we might just double your lessons to insure that that won't happen."

"What do you have in mind?" she asked, but he was unbuttoning her bodice. "Matthew, it's four o'clock in the afternoon!"

"So what?" he murmured as he bent to nuzzle her breasts through her chemise.

"I've got me reputation to think of."

"*My* reputation."

"I really don't care much about *your* reputation,"

she answered with a giggle. "Only, schoolteachers are supposed to be the souls of virtue, I'm after thinking. Matthew!" she squealed as he unlaced her corset.

"I'll admit I never had a schoolmarm quite like you," he said as he stood and pressed her back against the desk. "But then, I didn't have much of an imagination at thirteen." He reached down to lift her skirts and grinned when he discovered that she'd already removed her drawers. "Otherwise I wouldn't have chosen chastity as a test of fortitude." He loosened his trousers.

"Oh, I don't know," Fanny mused as she leaned back on his desk. "I rather like having you all to me—myself. It's like having a whole pie to eat."

Matthew bent over her, lifting her up and then echoing her sigh as he found her more than receptive response to his embrace. "Lucky for me, you've a big appetite, Just Fanny."

She sighed as he began moving against her and draped her arms over his shoulders to draw him even closer. "Well, now that we've got a house, and a school, and five boarders, I suppose we should settle down to become solid citizens of the community."

Matthew took a deep breath, still amazed after all these months that she felt so good. "You'll never be rich."

"No," she whispered in his ear and then licked it.

"You'll never be wholly respectable. After all, you're married to an Injun."

"Hm," she sighed as she reached for his lips with hers. "But we'll be happy," she murmured against his mouth. "And that's enough for anybody, I'm thinking."

And then she ceased to think at all because he was moving so sweetly inside her, and she couldn't imagine another place worth being in the whole wide world.